life with such a huge shadow cast

it becomes clear that someone else knows her secret
and is hunting her down, time is running out for
Elizabeth to keep her family safe.

In the bestselling tradition of Clare Mackintosh and
Jenny Blackhurst, Cynthia Clark has written a heart-
stopping story about the choices we make and how
far we'd go to protect our families. Even if it means
deceiving the people we love most…

To J

Hello, I'm Elizabeth and I'm a killer.

I've dreamed about saying those words. I've always thought that it would be a relief to finally say them out loud, to stop suppressing the one secret that haunts me every single night. Every single day. Every single second of my existence.

You see, secrets have a way of repressing your being, making you feel stifled, as if you're not yourself any more. And the longer you keep a secret, the more it crushes your soul, making you want to scream, scratch at your skin, tear your hair out. It's the desperation of being alone, of knowing that nobody else can be told, that you can't share your secret with anyone, allow them to help you carry the burden. Because, after all, who would understand? You know that instead they would just see you as a monster. I know that's what people would think about me if I ever dared to tell them.

Because it doesn't matter why I did what I did. The bottom line is that I took a life. That was someone's child, someone's neighbour, someone's friend.

I've thought about being able to tell at least one person what I've done. Test the waters and hope that they would understand. I've come close on a couple of occasions. But in the end, fear has always taken over and I've backtracked, my resolve to share my deepest, darkest confession shaken to the core. I'm too scared *that the life I've built for myself will be shattered. I'm terrified of having to face the consequences of my actions, carried out in the heat of the moment.*

No, I cannot tell anyone. I need to remain the sole custodian of the truth. My scary reality. Nobody can know that I'm Elizabeth and I'm a killer.

Chapter 1

2014

I'm clearing the remnants of this morning's breakfast from the kitchen when my work phone rings, stopping me in my tracks. I see my assistant's name flashing on the screen.

"Hi Jennifer, what's up?"

"There's this girl." Her voice is coming in rapid pants. "She's going to be slaughtered by the prosecution unless you take over her case."

Cradling my phone between my ear and shoulder, I rinse Coco Pops from a cereal bowl. There's no time to waste; I'm already running late. "Ok, I'm listening."

"I got in early to file the Preston paperwork. I was waiting for the clerk to come in and heard Sarah, from the public defender's office, talking about this case."

Jennifer pauses for breath.

"So, what is it about?" I urge.

"There's this girl, Chloe. She's fifteen and is being charged with attempted murder."

"What did she do?" Moving my phone to the other ear, I carry on clearing the kitchen, mentally urging her to give me the whole story rather than scraps of information.

"She ran over this guy and fled the scene." Her voice is tinged with excitement.

"Hold on, how come she was driving? You said she's only fifteen?"

"Yes, she is. She got into his car and reversed over him."

"How did she get the keys? Did she steal them?"

"I'm not sure…" Jennifer's voice trails off.

"Ok, we can find out later. Is he injured?"

"Oh yes." She is suddenly animated. "He's still in hospital. Both of his legs are broken, he has a couple of fractured ribs, a punctured lung, and severe internal haemorrhage. Doctors aren't sure if he'll ever walk again."

"Ouch," I wince; shuddering as I try to freeze out images of the unknown man's wounded body.

"Sarah suggested running the case by you, to see if you have time to take it on," Jennifer continues.

Taking a deep breath, I mentally run through my current workload. "I don't know. You know how busy I am right now."

"Yes, but you're always looking to help young women, girls who don't have anywhere else to turn.

And you haven't taken a pro-bono case in a few months."

Jennifer's right. Cases where the accused has a tough story, where others would have run a mile, always get to me and make me work my hardest.

"Are you still there?"

"Yes, yes," I quickly answer, jolted back to reality. "I don't know. It's a hit-and-run. Is it worth the effort?"

"Well, it's not like the usual cases you tend to take on. But just because she's not the victim of abuse doesn't mean that she doesn't deserve a solid defence."

"And you know how busy the public defenders are," she presses. "Sarah is juggling eighteen other cases. She has no time to provide a proper defence. This girl is doomed."

Something about Jennifer's description of the case doesn't tally. There's a small voice inside me warning against wasting time, telling me to move on. "Can't her parents find a good barrister?"

"I don't know, but if she's been referred to a public defendant, that's probably her only choice. Just guessing."

Despite my reservations, I'm intrigued. "Can you ask Sarah for the case file?"

"I got you a copy already. It'll be on your desk when you get in." A smile creeps onto my face.

Jennifer's extraordinary organisational skills allow me to focus on what really matters – defending clients.

Jennifer hangs up and I continue clearing the kitchen. This morning has been hectic as usual as I got my two children ready for their day, prepared their lunch, and made sure that they finished breakfast. As normal my husband ran out first, leaving me to deal with the mess of our harried morning routine. "Gotta go," he'd said. "Want to beat traffic."

"You say that every day and you still always get stuck," I responded, shaking my head as I looked at all the clutter.

"Today's the day. I can feel it," he said, kissing me on the cheek before rushing out. His optimism is admirable but it would be nice if he helped me clean up for a change. I still cannot understand why he insists on driving to work instead of taking the Tube. It would certainly save him some time, not to mention the aggravation of being stuck in traffic. But then again, I too refuse to be like the vast majority of other Londoners and take public transport. Driving provides me with time to think, the ability to jump in my car and get away whenever I need to. And I hate being in close proximity to so many other people, squashed against the side of the carriage during rush hour.

The dishwasher makes a rumbling sound as the cycle starts. As I turn around to leave, the bright Peppa Pig cup grabs my attention. Stretching to pick up my daughter's cup from the other end of the kitchen island, I grasp the pink mouthpiece. As I do, the top comes off, spilling cranberry juice all over the white counter.

A strangled scream escapes before I can stop it and I quickly close my eyes as my whole body shakes. Putting the cup's lid down, I brace both arms against the counter to steady myself. I hate the colour red. Loathe it so much I go through extremes to try and avoid seeing it. For many years I avoided all red food. There were no strawberries, or beetroot, or tomatoes in my diet. And meat had to be cooked through, steaks singed to their core until every drop of blood had been dried out. That's the only way I would eat it. My husband knows that my aversion towards anything red is related to my fear of blood, but I have allowed him, and anyone else who becomes aware of my hatred for red, to believe that it is a symptom of seeing a dog killed after being run over by a car just outside school when I was a teenager. Little do they know that it was another bloody incident, only a couple of years later, which cemented my hatred for anything that reminds me of blood.

Chapter 2

15 Years Earlier

It had started as a normal day. I woke up late and ran to class in my pyjamas. Well, nobody needed to know they were my pyjamas. Only my black flannel trousers could be seen, tucked into my Dr Martens. I'd thrown a woollen jersey over my tank top and pulled my red hair into a bun as I ran from my room in halls towards the lecture theatre, my bag jumping up and down on my shoulders.

I made it to the lecture room just in time, out of breath, and chiding myself for sleeping through the alarm again. It was becoming a habit and I no longer had Mum to make sure I was awake. I was all alone in my small room.

Wednesdays were my easy days. I only had three lessons in the morning. But that didn't mean I could go back to sleep. Instead, I'd have to bike to Chesterton where I'd spend the rest of the afternoon and evening stocking shelves at the supermarket. When I got into Cambridge, my first choice of university, my parents had been clear – they'd pay my tuition fees but I had to get a job and help with the bills. And if I wanted to go to law school, I needed to save every penny I could.

To be fair my job was not strenuous. Yes, it meant going up ladders and carrying down boxes, but at least it was mindless work. I could listen to music or escape into an imaginary world as I stuck price stickers on products and lined them up on the shelves. The manager had asked me whether I wanted a job on the checkouts, but while I'd agreed to get the training, I wasn't pushing to change my shifts. I wanted to be able to work in relative silence, without being bothered by people, able to lose myself in my dreams, imagine that one day I would be a successful barrister, making enough money so I didn't have to struggle like my parents.

So, I was not exactly happy when I got to the supermarket to find out that one of the checkout girls had called in sick and they needed me to fill in. I was tired and grumpy and really didn't feel like talking to anyone. But I couldn't risk losing my job, so I just nodded and took my place at the checkout, smiling weakly at shoppers and answering their questions with one word replies. I've never been good at making conversation with strangers. I could never understand why people bothered to chat about the weather, or traffic, with someone whose name they didn't even know. It's probably what made it difficult for me to forge strong friendships. I was always the loner who preferred to spend hours in the library rather than on the playground. I hoped that my short answers would put shoppers off trying to make conversation, that they'd get the message and stop pestering me. But it was just wishful thinking and by the time I left the supermarket at 8 p.m., I felt mentally drained from being forced to make small talk for hours on end as the conveyor belt chugged on and the till beeped.

Walking out in the brisk April air, I zipped up my jacket and put on my gloves. The winter was over but there was still a chill in the air. Tucking my jeans into my boots to avoid them catching on my bike chain, I started the fifteen minute ride back to college. I was so eager to get back to my room and have a shower before climbing into bed that I decided to take a shortcut through Midsummer Common, ride along the paths that meandered through the greenery, and not have to worry about oncoming traffic, allowing my brain to relax.

It was a pleasant ride. I could smell the wildflowers that were in full bloom instead of fuel and pollution. I could see the stars glistening in the sky instead of the blinding headlamps of cars. Even the distant sound of trains sounded mystical rather than a menace. Perhaps it's because I was distracted by my surroundings that I didn't become aware of the pickup truck creeping slowly behind me until it was too late. It hit the back of my bike, sending it off course and me flying into the field.

For a second I was in shock, trying to gather my thoughts and make sure that I hadn't suffered any big injuries. Taking stock of every part of my body, I realised I was ok, just a little stiff from the fall. As I was scrambling up, I saw a man running towards me. "I'm so sorry." His voice was etched with concern. "Are you hurt?" He stretched out his hand to help me up.

"Are you ok?" he asked again and I nodded. "Yes," I added, in case he couldn't see me in the growing darkness.

"I didn't see you. I keep the lights off to see the stars. I must have been looking at the sky when I hit you," he explained. Nodding my understanding, I walked towards my bike aware that he was following me. I picked it up and cursed under my breath. The front wheel was bent making it unusable. I'd have to walk to college and it would take forever.

"Oh no, I'm so sorry," he said. "Obviously, I'll pay for the damage." My sigh of relief was audible. The bike was only a few months old and I could scarcely afford a new wheel, and fix whatever other damages I couldn't see right now.

"Look, you can't ride this now. Why don't I drive you home and we can discuss getting your bike fixed?" he asked.

In retrospect I know I should have known better than accept a ride from a stranger. But it was late and I didn't feel like carrying the bike all the way back on foot. And the guy seemed nice enough. He was probably a few years older than me, with green eyes that sparkled in the moonlight and a soft smile. Maybe it was because he was so easy on the eyes that I threw caution to the wind and after seeing him put my bike in the back of the truck, I climbed into the passenger seat. The last thing I remember was turning to put on my seatbelt.

*

I don't know how much time had passed when I finally woke up. The smell of chloroform was still burning my nostrils. At least I assumed it was chloroform. I'd never smelled it before so I couldn't be certain. Opening my eyes, I looked around. I was lying on a thin foam mattress on the floor of a dark room. The only light came from a tiny bulb hanging from the ceiling. There were no windows, only a large wooden door.

He was sitting on a chair, a beer bottle between his legs, his head resting on his chest, obviously asleep.

My limbs felt heavy but my mind whirred as I tried to think of a way out of this situation. My heart raced as fear was replaced by a burning need to save myself. I'd have time to be scared later, to blame myself for my stupid decision to get in a car with a stranger, for going through the Common in the first place. I started to get up and realised that my legs were bare. The momentary confusion was replaced by panic, as it dawned that he had removed my shoes, jeans, and even underwear. Tears pricked at my eyes as I wondered whether I'd been raped and I held my breath for a moment to see if I could feel any pain. I couldn't and the relief at the realisation was instantaneous. But I needed to find a way out.

Twisting my neck, I looked around the room and spotted my jeans and shoes at the foot of the mattress. I didn't have time to put them on, but I didn't want to run home half naked or barefoot. Careful not to make any noise, I slithered towards the edge of the mattress and got to my feet, grabbing my jeans and shoes and holding them against my body. I remained bent over, not wanting to wake him up with any sudden movements and walked slowly to the door, holding my breath and hoping that the floorboards wouldn't creak. I could hear his snoring; heavy breaths that gave way to low grunts. At least he was still asleep.

When I got to the door I straightened, placed my still-gloved hand on the knob, and turned. My heart sank when the heavy wooden door didn't shift. I willed myself to stay calm even though I could feel the panic bubbling inside my chest. A large metal bolt was drawn across the door and with shaking hands I reached out to unlock it. It slid open easily and miraculously without making a sound. Cool air blew in. The door led outside. I'd be able to get out and run to safety. Run until I got home or to a police station.

The sound of glass shattering pierced through the silence. The door was slammed closed and I saw his hand in front of me, dark hairs springing from his uncovered arm. Before I could think, he grabbed me with his other hand and turned me around. "Where do you think you're going?" he asked, his face contorted into an ugly scowl. The green eyes that had seemed so beautiful before were now blazing dangerously at me. I wanted to plead with him to let me go, not to hurt me. But it seemed that I couldn't form the words. "We have some unfinished business," he said, pulling me away from the door and pushing me into the room with such force that I fell onto my back.

"I thought you were never going to wake up," he said with a sneer. "I've been waiting very patiently so that we can have some fun." I could only imagine what his idea of fun was, and even if I hadn't yet guessed he made it clear by unbuckling his belt. I frantically looked around, trying to locate anything I could use to defend myself. But even my boots had fallen when he threw me into the room. Not that the rubber soles would have been much help against him.

"Please, let me go," I finally said, aware that pleading was the only thing I could do. But even as the words left my mouth I knew that they wouldn't do much good. I could see in his face how intent he was to finish what he had started. He laughed in response, a cruel-sounding snort, as he took a step closer. I shrunk back, trying to move as far away as possible, forgetting the embarrassment of being half naked in front of a man. All I wanted was to get away. To close my eyes and wake up from this nightmare.

But it wasn't a dream. This was reality.

He laughed again as he took a step in my direction, towering over me. He grabbed me by the hood of my jacket and pulled me towards the mattress, before he kneeled down next to me. I kicked my legs, trying to hit him but he was out of my reach. He laughed at my failed efforts and then his expression changed into one of anger and he slapped me hard across the face. I instinctively covered my smarting cheek with my hand, but he pried it away. "Are you going to behave?" he asked.

He reached out for the zip of my jacket and yanked it down. It was an old jacket and the zip tended to catch, leading to a few seconds of fumbling to get it released. But this time it slid down without a problem. "Remove it," he ordered. When I hesitated he hit me again, this time on the other cheek, making my head turn with the force of the blow. "Remove your jacket," he repeated, and this time I did as he asked, ashamed to be following his orders despite not having a choice. "Good girl," he said when I'd put the jacket next to me. His demeanour changed when I obeyed him. He brought his hand to my smarting cheek and stroked the burning flesh gently for a few seconds.

He sat back on his heels. "Unbutton your shirt," he said next. When I didn't immediately do as he asked, a mask of anger descended over his face. "I said unbutton your shirt," he snapped.

With trembling fingers I fumbled with the top button of my flannel shirt. I was shaking so badly that it took me forever to undo it, the leather gloves not helping but I was in too much shock to remove them. "Hurry up," he barked at me, his green eyes flashing with anger. I managed to open two more buttons but the next I couldn't get undone. I met his eyes pleadingly. It was a mistake. His hand flew to my face, grabbing my jaw and squeezing tightly until I gasped in pain. "Do as I tell you," he said. Then, fed up waiting, he ripped the shirt open, sending the tiny mother-of-pearl buttons flying across the room.

"Remove it," he ordered. And I shrugged out of my shirt, knowing that I had no choice if I had any chance of leaving this place alive.

He snatched the shirt from my hands before I could put it down. He grabbed at my chest, tearing off my lace sports bra, leaving me completely naked and exposed. I crossed my arms over my chest, trying to cover my breasts, aware of the ridiculousness of the gesture even before I heard his sinister laughter. "Let's have some fun," he said, forcing me back onto the mattress and leaning over me. I tried to push him back, but he grabbed my wrists and pinned them over my head, holding them there with one hand while he pulled down his fly with the other. I kicked him but again he laughed before his hand struck my cheek. I knew at that moment that there was no avoiding what was coming and I closed my eyes for a second, trying to distance myself from what was about to happen.

I felt his heavy breathing in my face and then the searing pain as he tried to thrust into me. I screamed and he laughed. "This is my lucky day," he said as he burst through the resistance of my virginity. Fat tears formed in my eyes and rolled down the sides of my head. I kept my eyes closed, willing it to be over. I tried to think of something else and stop myself from hearing his grunts as he continued to thrust into me in what seemed to be a never-ending nightmare.

Finally, after what felt like hours, he stilled for a second and then pulled out of me, getting back up to his knees. "See," he said, finally releasing my wrists. "That wasn't too bad." He scrambled to his feet before continuing: "Next time will be even better." Panic unfurled inside my body like a spreading fire as my hopes that he'd let me go now that he'd got his fill were destroyed.

Ashamed of my nakedness, I sat up, bringing my knees to my chin to cover as much of my body as I could. He walked to the end of the room and threw a crumpled ball of paper towels at me. "Clean yourself up," he said. I picked up the towels and wiped the sticky blood from between my legs. "A little virgin," he chuckled. "Who'd have known!"

He turned round and picked up his jacket, which was hanging over the back of the chair, and rummaged in the pockets. My breathing grew heavier as I wondered what he was looking for, what was in store for me, and I almost heaved a sigh of relief when he took out his mobile phone. Turning back to face me, he dialled a number.

"Hey, Terry," he said gruffly. This was my chance. "Help," I screamed, crying out as loudly as I could. But instead of rushing to shut me up or hang up, the man just laughed. "Yeah, that's her," he told the person on the other end of the line. "We got a feisty one here. A little virgin."

He walked towards me, covering the short distance in three long strides. His eyes never left my face as he bent down to pick up my jacket. Nestling his phone between his ear and chin, he rummaged through the pockets until he found my wallet. He opened it and started rifling through the compartments, until he fished something out.

"Let's see," he said bringing my library card closer to his face. "Elizabeth Phillips," he read out. "She's as fiery as her red hair. I'm going to take my time with this one. I'll call back when I'm done and you can come over." Then he hung up, flinging my card and wallet onto the ground, placing the phone on the chair and walking towards the mattress.

He stood in front of me and stared, an inhuman leer that took in all my shame and submission without pity. I don't know how much time passed. Neither of us said anything for a while, but thoughts were rushing through my head. Someone else knew I was there. This other person must know what he was doing to me. Why were they coming here? Would they take me away or were they going to continue what he had already started? Or do even worse? I had to find a way to leave before I was completely outnumbered. I mustered the courage to speak, to try and argue with him to let me go. "Please, I have lectures in the morning," I begged.

He snorted with laughter, and moved towards me. I knew then that I shouldn't have said anything. All it did was turn him on again. I knew what was going to happen and I knew there was no way out. Still, the slap to my cheek took me by surprise. "That will teach you to stay quiet," he said. "You're my slut now."

While I was still reeling from the pain to my cheek, he pushed me back onto the mattress, forcing my legs open and kneeling between them. "I didn't think I'd be ready again so soon," he said. "You're the best I've ever had." That's when I realised that this was even worse than I thought. This was not his first time kidnapping and raping someone. This man was a pro. From the chloroform to the windowless room, he must have planned this well. I wondered how many others there'd been and where they were now. How long did he keep them captive and did they finally manage to escape?

I wondered whether he'd kill me. I thought of my parents getting a knock at the door and police telling them that they'd found the body of their only daughter. The thought of the pain this would cause them was more than I could handle. I punched him as hard as I could on the side of his head, but he just grabbed my arm and slammed it on the ground. I shrieked in pain as my hand landed on something pointy. As soon as he let my arm go, I felt around for whatever had pricked my gloved hand and my fingers closed around a shard of glass. I felt its jagged sides and pointed edge, remembering the beer bottle he dropped earlier. This was my only chance to escape. I grabbed the glass tightly in my hand, not caring about it cutting into my skin, and as he prepared to thrust into me one more time, I used all my strength and struck him in the side of the neck. I pulled the glass out and thrust again, this time hitting him just below his protruding Adam's apple as he turned his head to see what was happening. I pulled the glass out again and was readying myself for a third strike when he fell on top of me, the blood gushing out of his wounds. He didn't scream, but made a bubbling sound. I used the last strength I had to roll him off me. His eyes were wide and full of fear and his mouth was open as he tried to scream.

In the dim light I could see the blood pumping out of his wounds, splattered everywhere, seeping into the floors. I thought about helping him, putting pressure on the wounds to stop him from bleeding out. Surely he was too injured to hurt me now. Or I could use this time to call for help.

I ran to the door, pushing the chair aside and undoing the bolt. I didn't care that I was naked. I opened the door and stopped short. We were in the middle of a field. It was still dark and all I could see were miles of emptiness surrounding us. I turned back around, grabbing my shirt from the ground to cover his wounds and stem the flow of blood. But before I could touch him I knew that it was already too late. He was dead. I had killed him.

Chapter 3

2014

Glancing into the rearview mirror, I scan the road for anything out of the ordinary. A red Polo zigzags through traffic before pulling up right behind me. Craning my neck, I try to get a glimpse of the driver but the weak sun is reflecting off the windscreen.

My panic is blaring almost as loudly as The Rolling Stones' *Wild Horses* on the car stereo. Hitting the off button and clenching my hands around the steering wheel, I take ten deep breaths, counting each one, synchronising them to my movements in a practised routine. A hot flush starts at my toes and makes its way through my body. Closing my eyes I try to blank out the image of the red juice spreading across the white countertop. I had contemplated walking out on the mess. Keeping my eyes closed as I navigated around the island. Leaving the sea of red behind me. Maya would be over in a few hours to watch the children and she could clean it up.

Instead I squared my shoulders and opened my eyes a fraction. Taking a deep breath, I swallowed the lump in my throat, reached behind me and grabbed the roll of kitchen paper. With my eyes only partially open, I crumpled a ball of Thirst Pockets on the countertop and winced as the white paper turned red. The sodden red towels made a squelching sound when they landed in the bin and I grabbed more clean, white sheets.

My heels felt unsteady as I walked to the garage. Sitting behind the wheel for a few seconds, I struggled to regain my composure. My hand inched towards my phone as I ached to tell my husband about this morning's nightmare, chide him for giving Leah red juice and leaving me to clean up. But his patience is wearing thin when it comes to my 'quirk'. He's begged me to talk to someone about it. But I know that's impossible. I cannot risk anyone, especially an expert, prying into my deepest thoughts and trying to uncover my secret. No, I just need to soldier on and continue avoiding any of the triggers I know will make me lose control.

Blocking out this morning's chaos, I focus on the road ahead as the conversation with Jennifer plays back in my head. The lack of information frustrates me as I filter what I know from what I don't. That familiar eagerness that always accompanies a new case bubbles inside me, the fascination of discovery, the desire to work out exactly what strategy is needed to win.

My personal phone does its jazz melody. I exhale in exasperation at the prospect of having to talk on the phone while driving, not wanting to lose focus, risk hitting a pedestrian or crashing into another vehicle. I don't want to hurt anyone else. But mostly, I want to avoid unexpected problems. My record needs to remain entirely clear.

But it's Mum. She's one of the few people I make an exception for; her, my husband and the babysitters.

"Hello." My voice is upbeat.

"Morning, Lizzy." Her joyful voice comes on the speaker, raised above a familiar whirring sound in the background. It's great to hear her. It always calms me, though I miss her straight away. It's been a few weeks since we were able to drive to the sleepy coastal town I grew up in to see my parents.

"How are you, Mum?"

"Great."

"Are you baking?"

"Yes. How do you know?"

A chuckle escapes before I can suppress it. "I can hear the mixer."

"Oh, sorry." The whirring sound stops. "I'm making a Devil's Food cake for the church bake sale and this afternoon I have my book club. We're reading *Breakfast At Tiffany's*. I bet you most of the others will just watch the film."

"Is that what you did?" I laugh, my mood suddenly lighter.

"Of course not," she says indignantly. "If I'm going to discuss a book, I'm going to *read* the book."

"How's Dad?"

"Good. We drove to Bristol to meet his cardiologist yesterday and he said he's doing well. He's out for a walk now. That heart attack scared him and now he's doing his best to keep fit and healthy."

We speak for a few minutes about everyday things while I manoeuvre the car through the morning traffic. The red car is still behind me. Despite the warm air blowing from the heater I shiver slightly.

"How's work?" Mum's question snaps me back to the here and now.

"Busy. There's a new case that I'm considering taking. A teenage girl accused of running someone over."

"Is this one of your usual pity cases?"

Rolling my eyes, I'm glad she can't see me: "Everyone deserves a solid defence, Mum, and not everyone can afford to pay for it." It's a statement I must have repeated a hundred times to different people.

"Just don't take on more than you can handle."

A few minutes later I step into the marble-clad lobby of our building. It always feels like stepping into a new dimension, the oasis before the cutthroat corporate world I've come to know, the modern surroundings in stark contrast with the City of London's narrow winding streets. Nodding at the receptionist, I head to the lifts, tapping my foot as I wait for one to ping open. When it finally does, I repeatedly press the button for the fifth floor. Stepping out into the sprawling space occupied by the law firm that I had opened a few years ago with an old university friend, I greet a few colleagues as I make a beeline for my office.

Jennifer is sitting at her desk, typing furiously on her keyboard. "Hello. Would you like some tea?"

"Please." I take the letters that she hands me.

"The case file we talked about is on your desk." She scurries off towards the kitchen.

In my office, I don't even remove my coat before opening the file, quickly skimming over the charge sheet. Chloe Wilson is being accused of attempted murder and causing grievous bodily harm to Ben Grant, as well as fleeing the scene of the incident. No additional information other than what Jennifer explained earlier.

There's a knock on the door and Jennifer walks in, with a steaming mug of tea. "Have you read it?"

"Yes." I take the mug from her and take a sip, wincing when the sweet liquid scalds my tongue. "There's not much to go on here. Can you get me

Sarah on the phone, perhaps she can share a few more details?"

Jennifer nods as she hurries out and a few minutes later my phone rings. "I have Sarah on the line for you."

"Elizabeth, thank you for considering Chloe's case," Sarah says immediately. "I'm swamped and really think she needs someone to focus their attention on her defence."

"I really don't know if I can take this one on," I warn. "It's a busy period and frankly there doesn't seem much to go on."

"I know her file is sparse, but I can fill you in on what we've got." I hear muffled chattering in the background and assume she's in court, waiting for her next case to start.

"Did she tell you what happened?"

"Barely," Sarah responds. "It was like pulling teeth, but she finally said she didn't mean to run him over. That she'd never driven before and hadn't realised the car was in reverse."

"So why did she leave if it was an accident?" I probe.

"She said she was scared and went back home," Sarah continues.

"Do you believe her?"

"I don't know. I want to, obviously, but she seems so controlled. She was so calm at the police station.

26

Anyone else would have been freaking out. But she just sat down, barely moving. The detectives said she didn't utter a word when they brought her in for questioning.

"Do you think she ran him over on purpose? That she knew what she was doing?"

"I wish I could answer that. I hope not."

"What about her parents? What's your impression of them?"

"See, that's the thing, she doesn't have a family. She's bounced from one foster home to another since she was a baby. She'd only been with these people for a few months and they say they barely know her."

"Is she still living with them?"

"No, they couldn't wait to get rid of her. They're friends with the young man's parents and looks like they're taking his side. Chloe is back in a children's home."

Sarah stops to catch her breath, giving me time to process the new information.

"She's completely alone in the world. Nobody seems to care about her. She came to see me on her own; her guardian didn't even bother to show up. She needs someone like you," Sarah presses. "If she goes to prison, she doesn't stand a chance of turning her life around." Those last words echo in my mind after I hang up the phone. Part of me feels sorry for the girl and wants to help, but my mother's words echo in my head. Am I taking on more than I should? Yet as easy as it might be to move on and forget about her, I can't bring myself to do that.

Reaching for my supply of sugar free mints in the drawer, my fingers brush the old newspaper clippings I know are there. Putting the clippings on my desk, I remember the first time I proved that a teenage girl accused of hurting someone else had been acting in self defence. I was so proud.

I'm so intent on rustling through the drawer, trying not to be overcome with memories, that I don't hear Jennifer walking in and jump slightly when I see her standing right in front of me.

My hand flies to my chest. "You gave me a fright."

"Sorry," she says. Then quickly adds: "How did it go?"

"I'm not sure it's a fit for our firm," I start. "And it doesn't seem like the right time to take on something like this."

Jennifer points to the clipping on my desk. "Isn't that your first case?" she asks. Nodding, I continue staring at the image of the girl, remembering her incessant fiddling with her long hair, her eyes darting around the room, following every movement as if she was scared of being attacked. The fear on her face had convinced me she'd been acting to protect herself and I made it my mission to find a way to defend her.

"Remember how you felt when the girl was acquitted?" Jennifer asks.

"Yes." I know where this is headed but I let it run. "Like it was a triumph for justice."

"And what if Chloe is telling the truth?" Jennifer inquires. "Wouldn't that also be a triumph for justice?"

For the rest of the day I battle to focus on the more urgent work in front of me. It's only when I leave the office that I allow my brain the indulgence of going over Chloe Wilson's case, making quick work of the drive home.

Rushing indoors in the hope that the children are still awake, I find the house is silent. The kitchen and living room are empty. Dropping my bag, I hurry upstairs, taking the stairs two at a time, the clicks from my high heels echoing in the stillness. At the top of the stairwell I pause, listening for any sound, until I hear soft voices coming from my daughter's room. Slipping off my shoes, I tiptoe towards them.

Through the open door I see Maya sitting in the recliner next to the bed. Julian is curled on the teenager's denim-clad lap, his head resting on her chest, his fingers tiredly twirling her long red hair. Leah is already tucked in bed and in the muted light I can see her chest go up and down in rhythmic breathing. Maya's face lights up as her melodic voice takes on different tones to highlight the various characters in the Dr Seuss story. Every fibre of my body wants to walk in, steal a few seconds with the children. But I restrain myself, not wanting to disturb the bedtime ritual. Despite the deep sadness at the thought of another evening where I won't spend bedtime with them, I make myself wait outside the room.

Finally, Maya finishes the story and closes the book, putting it down on the bedside table. She turns suddenly when I tiptoe in, unable to contain myself any longer. Maya sees me and smiles. Gently picking up Julian from her lap to allow her to stand up easily, I take him towards his bedroom. My son barely opens his eyes and I tuck him into bed and head back downstairs.

Maya is in the living room, putting away the children's toys. "You can leave them for me," I say half heartedly, glad she's still here. She has been a godsend and my most trusted sitter, always making sure that the children are not only safe but truly happy and enjoying themselves. She's not afraid to be strict when she needs to be, and only last week she cut Julian's television time after catching him bickering with his little sister. It helps that she lives down the road, making it easy for her to come over at a moment's notice and able to walk back home in the evening.

"It's ok, Mrs P. It will only take another minute."

Her smile lights up her whole face and warms my heart, reminding me of the first time I saw her, many years ago. Skimming over the letters sitting on the kitchen island, I throw out a few leaflets and put the bills to the side. A white, unmarked envelope catches my eye and my heart beats faster as I open it, only to find yet another advert. Bending over to help, I pick up an open book and one of Leah's dolls, putting them in the toy box. "How were they?" I ask.

"Good, as always. Leah was having a bit of a hard time falling asleep, kept asking about you and her dad." Maya's words are like a sword to my heart and I promise to try harder to get home earlier.

"Julian thinks one of his bottom teeth is loose," she continues. "There might be a slight wiggle, but I don't think it's going anywhere anytime soon."

"Guess it's time for the tooth fairy," I say, half sad at how quickly they are growing up.

"How are you doing?" I ask Maya.

"Great, I have my exams coming up so have been busy studying."

"I'm sorry to be keeping you so late." Unfortunately, it happens more often than I want and Maya is used to our schedule.

Maya shakes her head. "It's not a problem. I'm happy to help."

It strikes me that Maya is the same age as Chloe. Yet I sense that the two of them couldn't be more different. Maya has had a fantastic upbringing with parents who adore her and will do anything for their only daughter. Chloe hasn't been so lucky and I wonder how much her lack of family life has influenced her behaviour.

"Do you need anything else?" Maya's words snap me back into the present.

"No, you can go. Thank you."

"Mum gets antsy when I miss dinner," she says, rolling her eyes.

She picks up her leather jacket from the armchair and puts it on. As she turns to leave I am overwhelmed by an urge to keep her here a little longer, talk to her more.

"There's this girl I'm thinking of representing. She's about your age."

"Is she in trouble?"

"Yes, quite a bit." Taking a pause, I gather my thoughts. "She ran over an older guy and fled the scene."

"She must have been terrified of something," she immediately says. "I'd probably go rushing to Mum and Dad."

"That's the thing," I say, my mind adrift on the possibilities that might be true. "She doesn't have any parents."

And suddenly I know Maya must be right. But what was Chloe scared of? Why was she driving off in

Ben's car? Why was she in such a hurry to get away from him even after he was injured? I need to find out.

Chapter 4

1998

For a while I was frozen and had no idea what to do. I was numb, both from the pain and the realisation that I had just killed someone. I stared at him for a long time, waiting to see if he would all of a sudden wake up again. Maybe he was just holding his breath. But then I looked at the blood that had gushed through his two neck wounds and knew that I had struck the fatal point. He never stood a chance.

My body shook. I was not the squeamish sort and was addicted to crime series on TV, but never in my wildest dreams would I have thought that I would kill someone. That I even had the strength to.

I squeezed my arm to make certain that this was not a nightmare but the sharp pain assured me that I was awake. I wondered how long it would have taken for someone to notice that I was missing. I hadn't made any close friends at university, keeping to myself most of the time and focusing on my studies. I wasn't scheduled to speak to my parents until Sunday evening. It would have been days before anyone started wondering whether something had happened to me and who knew whether I'd still have been alive by then.

As the thoughts rushed through my head I realised that I had done the only thing that I could to protect myself. I could barely bring myself to think about the rape that had catapulted me into this situation. I felt sick at his violation of something so private.

I shook my head to banish the thoughts from my mind, and focused back on the dead man in front of me. Surely the police would understand. I looked down at my naked body and in the dim light I could see the angry purple wounds forming on my arms. My cheeks still smarted from his repeated slaps and my jaw felt swollen. I shuddered again at the thought of his hands all over my body, violating my privacy, but I forced myself to put my feelings aside and focus on the here and now. There was ample proof that he had assaulted me – my torn sports bra, the ripped shirt. And they would find his semen in me. I needed to call the police as soon as possible.

I walked towards the chair, where he had placed his mobile phone. I was about to pick it up when I realised that I didn't even know where I was. How long would it take them to find me? Hours? Days? Terry, whoever he or she was, might come over, and who knows what they'd do to me then. I needed to leave right now. My brain hurt from trying to think of a solution and then it occurred to me that I could take his van and drive into town for help.

I looked around for the keys, but they were nowhere to be seen. Perhaps they were still in his pockets, I thought, turning back towards his body. But when I caught sight of his bulk, I couldn't bring myself to touch him, or move him to look for the keys.

My only choice was to walk to the police station near campus. I picked up my clothes, which had somehow escaped the deluge of blood, and put them on. My body hurt as I bent down to pick up my knickers. I was going to be bruised for days. The small but sharp cut on my right hand, where the glass had dug in, smarted as I pulled the laces on my boots, making me wince. I left my torn sports bra where he had thrown it, wanting to preserve as much evidence as possible, and put on my flannel shirt. It felt cold against my skin and I shuddered as I struggled to do the three buttons that were still attached. Eventually, I picked up my jacket and zipped it up. The zip caught and I fumbled with the fabric to release it from the slider's grip.

With one last look around the room, I walked to the door. My heart was beating as fast as when I'd just sprinted a few miles and I stopped for a second to catch my breath. In those few moments, as I stood by the door, I started to doubt my decision to go to the police. Would they believe me? What if they thought I was the one to lure this guy to the middle of nowhere to kill him? Maybe he was an upstanding citizen, a contributor to society, someone whose record was beyond reproach? How would I cope with repeating my story, for all the world to point their fingers and doubt me, look at me as the bad person who had killed this man?

It was the fear that I wouldn't be believed that scared me, stopped me in my tracks, and made me change my mind. Suddenly, my priority shifted and I wanted to erase any sign of my presence in the room. I turned round and scanned the area, my eyes focusing on my sports bra. I walked towards it and picked it up, putting it in one of my jacket pockets. I picked up the shard of glass that I'd stabbed him with and wrapped it in the paper towels that I'd used to wipe my blood and stuffed them in the same pocket, zipping it up to make sure nothing fell out.

I took a step back and felt something crunch under my boot. Bending down I picked up one of the buttons that had been ripped from my shirt. Unzipping the jacket, I counted the number of missing buttons – five – and set out to find each one.

The mattress was covered in his blood, but I worried that there would also be some of mine mixed with it. It was too bulky to take with me, so I just removed the covering sheet, folded it and wrapped it around my torso, hiding it under my jacket.

Taking a step back, I sniffed back the tears that were pooling in my eyes. I wanted to scream, to sob my heart out. This wasn't me. In a few hours I had been changed from a normal person into a victim and then a killer intent on covering her tracks. The pit of my stomach churned with a hideous confusion of feelings. I felt sick just thinking about what I'd done, what I'd been subjected to, been reduced to, and for a moment I felt my resolve to walk away waver, started to wonder whether I should just report what had happened. But the thought only lasted a fleeting second. I knew that I'd gone too far now. The pains I'd taken to clean up the scene and erase any signs of myself would surely be noticed, pointing towards my guilt. No, I needed to leave.

Without a backward glance, I walked to the door and stepped outside, feeling the brisk air on my face. I had no idea what time it was, but it was still dark. I should have enough time to get close to college before sunrise.

I looked back at the place I'd emerged from and saw it was a shack in the middle of fields. I wondered what he used it for, but when the visions started getting darker and more horrific, I shook my head to stop them from scaring me further. I was out and I was alive, that's all that mattered at this moment. I spotted his truck parked under some trees nearby and remembered my damaged bike. It would be easier to run back to campus without having to carry it, but I didn't want to leave it there, evidence waiting to lead the police back to me. I hauled myself up on the truck bed and brought the bike down. It was dark and I couldn't see the wheel properly. Instead of wasting time trying to fix it, I lifted the bike up on its back wheel and started my trek back home.

Although I wasn't sure where I was, I could see lights in the distance, and started walking towards them. I'd reassess the situation once I stumbled on a familiar area. I started walking through fields, glad that it was still dark and nobody could see me. Still, I remained alert, listening for any sounds that could signify someone else approaching. I was terrified that the person on the other end of the phone was nearby, waiting for that call to come and find me. Who was he? Or she? Were they part of a violent gang? And what were they going to do to me? I hurried my pace and as I put more distance between me and him, I started to breathe more easily. My heart was still racing, but its rhythm had become more regular. I focused on putting one foot in front of the other, one step at a time towards my destination, towards safety.

It must have been thirty minutes before I began to see where I was. The lights were coming from the airport. I was thankful I knew how to get back to the university quickly from here.

Dawn had started to break, the light making my trek through the fields easier. I'd stumbled a few times in the gloom, and had to slow down my step for fear of tripping. Now that I could see where I was going, I started walking faster. The quicker pace, coupled with the exertion of pulling the bike, made me feel warm. The crusted sheet stuck to my torso and I wished I could just remove it. But I couldn't risk it being found by the police. I reached up to wipe the beads of sweat from my forehead and in the morning light saw streaks of blood on the back of my tan glove.

I stopped, put the bike down on the ground, reached into my pocket and took out my wallet. I looked at my face in the small mirror I kept inside. Blood was splattered all over my left cheek and forehead. I knew right then that it was from his horrific injuries, from the blood that had pumped out of his neck wounds. I should have known that I'd be covered in it.

Willing myself not to panic, I took out a packet of tissues and tried to wipe away the blood. But it had dried on. I didn't have any water, so I had to use my spit to wet the tissue and continued scrubbing at my face until every red streak had been removed. I knew that there would still be blood caked in my hair, but it wouldn't show on my red colouring. I took out my dishevelled bun, ran my fingers through the curtain of my long hair, and tried to straighten it out.

My cheeks were still red from the slaps and I could see bruises on each side of my jaw, but I knew there was nothing I could do to cover those right now. I had to wait to get back to my room.

Putting the mirror away, I started walking again, making my way towards campus. Anyone who saw me would think that I'd been out drinking, I tried to reassure myself. Still, when I got close to my residence I stopped and looked around, making sure that there was nobody who could see me and be prompted to ask questions about my battered appearance. I had escaped with my life, and now I needed to focus on getting back to my room without drawing attention to myself. Only then would I allow myself to concentrate on cleaning myself up and getting rid of the evidence. When I was sure that there was nobody around, I made a beeline for the bike rack just outside the halls of residence before heading to my building.

Being so close to safety threatened to overwhelm me and I swallowed the lump in my throat. I could not risk breaking down now. There was no time for emotion, for weakness. I just needed to get into my room and away from prying eyes. My hands were shaking, making it difficult to fit the key in the lock.

Just as I was about to try again, the door opened suddenly. Moving to the side, I looked up, as a guy who I'd seen before but never spoken to stumbled down the step, his legs buckling under him and falling with a thud on the ground.

I knew I should leave. Go up to my room and close the door behind me, try to shut out what had happened in the past hours. But I couldn't bring myself to leave him sprawled on the ground, his long hair fanned across his face. I'd already done enough harm today. "Are you ok?" I knelt next to him, inhaling the smell of cheap beer that seemed to be coming out of every pore of his body. He looked up, his eyes glazed over, and he opened his mouth to speak. But instead of words, a stream of vomit came out of his mouth, landing right next to me, missing my boot by a hair. The foul smell entered my nostrils, and for a second I thought I would be sick as well. Getting back on my feet, I took a step back, while he continued to retch. At last he stopped, wiped his mouth, smearing some sick across his thick beard and stumbled to his feet. "Cheerio," he said with a weak smile as he walked away.

Fear took hold that he might have recognised me. My red hair was hard to miss. But he seemed out of it. Perhaps he was too drunk to notice my dishevelled appearance or he might just forget about seeing me altogether. I dragged myself up the two flights of stairs as fast as I could and when I locked the door of my room behind me, sunk to the floor in relief, finally allowing the sobs that had threatened to escape for hours to take over my body. I let myself cry for a few minutes and then wiped the tears away and got to my feet again.

Careful to grab it from the plastic liner, I moved my rubbish bin out from underneath my desk and removed my gloves, throwing them inside. One of them was torn anyway. Standing in front of the full length mirror, I removed my jacket. I loved that jacket but it needed to go too. The inside was stained with blood from the sheet. It occurred to me then that I would have to wash my clothes, make sure to get rid of any link to him. But that was a problem for later. I dug out my wallet and keys, placing them on an open magazine that I'd be able to throw out as well. I was about to put the jacket in the rubbish bin when I remembered the shard of glass. I unzipped the pocket and took it out, unwrapping it from its nest of paper towels, and put it on the magazine, careful not to let it touch my other belongings. I took out my torn sports bra and put it on the other side of the magazine.

My shirt and the sheet were next to be put in the bin, followed by my knickers and jeans. I couldn't afford to throw out my boots, so I placed them aside, intending to scrub them later. First I needed a shower.

The warm water felt blissful on my aching body as I started lathering my hair. My stomach lurched as I saw the red-tinged water gathering at my feet before making its way to the drain. I scraped at my scalp until the water ran clear and I could feel my skin smart with cleanliness. Wrapping a towel around my head and another around my body, I walked back into the small bedroom and picked up the magazine, balancing all of the items on top of it, and carried it to the bathroom, putting it down on the closed toilet. Opening the taps in the sink, I picked up the shard of glass and put it under the running water, wiping away at the sharp edges with my fingers, touching it gingerly to avoid being cut. Next I put my keys under running water and then wiped my wallet.

I picked up the glass again and turned it in my hand, searching my brain as to what to do with it, where I was going to dispose of it. But right now I needed to go to my first lecture. I didn't want to miss it, to arouse any suspicion. From now on, every decision needed to be meticulously thought out to make sure that my actions remained concealed. I wrapped the glass in tissues and hid it in the back of my underwear drawer, shuddering at the thought of something so sinister in the sanctuary of my room. I removed the rubbish bag and tied the ends, putting it in the back of my wardrobe until I could think what to do next. Using what little makeup I had, I covered some of the bruises on my face and wrapped a scarf around my neck to mask the angry red marks before heading out.

I fumbled with the key as I locked my door, not wanting anyone to come into my room and find it contaminated with the blood of a dead man. I had to stop and compose myself before I was able to complete the task and move on. The fresh air hit my face as soon as I walked out of the building and catapulted me back to the moment I opened the shed door. The feeling startled me and I dropped my books. As I bent down to pick them up, I felt a sharp pain sear through my stomach and winced at the ugly reminder of what had happened last night.

Still, I forced myself to focus on moving forward, trying to remove the look of horror from my face. Every sound startled me but I needed to stop jumping at every single noise or I would draw unwanted attention to myself. I plastered a weak smile on my face as I walked into the room, stumbling to a seat in the back.

My mind wouldn't stay still. It leapt ahead to whether they'd found the body, whether his accomplice had raised the alarm, whether they were looking for the killer. My thoughts scared me and I was worried about someone rummaging through my room and finding the evidence they needed to throw me behind bars for the rest of my life. At this point I was sure no-one would believe what had really happened, that I was protecting myself from another assault.

Thursdays were busy days for me. I had five back-to-back lectures and only a short break before I had to go back in the afternoon. Instead of getting lunch, I planned to go back to my room during my break and try to wash the blood off the sheet. I wasn't hungry anyway. I thought getting rid of the blood would make it less likely to grab anyone's attention when I threw it out. But I couldn't risk taking it to the laundry room while it was still caked in blood.

My mind made up, I couldn't wait for one o'clock to roll around. As soon as my last lecture ended, I rushed to my room and into the bathroom, and started filling the sink with water. In the meantime, I took the sheet out and soaked it for a few minutes, before starting to scrub at the patches of caked blood. The water quickly turned red and I felt my stomach lurch uncontrollably. Bending over the toilet, I threw up, retching repeatedly when there was nothing else to get rid of. I felt light-headed when I stood back up, but knew that I only had a short amount of time to clean the sheet as well as I could. My knuckles grew red and raw from scrubbing, but I persevered, regularly changing the soiled water, until I realised that I would never be able to completely get rid of the stains. And then, I rinsed it again and again, until I was confident that there was nothing linking it to him. I draped it over the shower head, allowing it to drip, before locking my door again and running back to the lecture hall.

That evening I dug the sheet and my clothes out of the rubbish bag and took them to the laundry room, washing them repeatedly, waiting there to make sure nobody took them by mistake. I couldn't spare the money but I even ran the empty washer, to remove any remnants of my night of horror. As I walked back to my room, I realised that I hadn't eaten since the night before, but the thought of food made me nauseous. I shuddered as I closed the door behind me and took my clothes out of the laundry bag. They smelled clean, and for a moment I felt detached from what had happened last night. It was as if by cleaning up the evidence, I was slowly distancing myself.

Until bedtime. I climbed into bed, exhausted and certain that I would fall asleep without any problems, and closed my eyes. Then I saw him, crouching on top of me, ready to lunge into me as I lay helpless and terrified on the mattress. And then the image in my mind morphed into his contorted face as blood spurted out of his gaping wound as I readied myself to strike him again.

I sat up in horror. The image was more than I could bear and I burst into tears. What have I done? I asked myself repeatedly, horrified at the thought that this image was going to haunt me for ever. I had killed someone. And then I had covered it up. It didn't matter that I was defending myself, that I had acted out of necessity, that I was scared for my life. The fact that I had gone to such pains to eliminate any evidence of my presence in that room intensified the guilt. I should have gone to the police. But it was too late now. I could only hope that I had done a good job of scrubbing clean any links to him and would never be associated with the crime I had committed.

Finally I fell asleep, but he haunted my dreams. I could see his green eyes, going from friendly to terrifying as he prepared himself to rape me. I woke up drenched in sweat, having relived the fear that I'd felt at that moment, unsure what his plans were, whether he'd let me go or if he would keep me captive. Fear intermingled with the feeling of horror at what I'd done and kept washing over me in nauseating waves.

In the end, I got up and paced the room, then started reading. I had exams in a few weeks and needed to cram in as much information as possible. I had always worked hard to do well in school, driven by a powerful desire to get a good job and make something of myself. I was determined to make enough money to live a comfortable life, and also make my parents proud. I was not going to allow this incident to change the course of my future. Failing these exams wasn't an option and I tried my best to concentrate, not allow myself to dwell on the events of the night before, and instead immerse myself in my books, make the most of the time I had.

When I looked at myself in the mirror a few hours later, as I prepared for my day, I could see the impact of my two sleepless nights etched on my face. My skin looked grey. I had dark circles under my eyes and my normally fiery hair looked dull and lifeless.

I went down to the cafeteria before classes, both to get a cheap cup of coffee and, in a sudden panic, to read the newspapers that were always available. I needed to find out whether they'd discovered his body. But despite looking through every single column, I didn't find any reference to him. Somehow this made me feel better, giving me more time to get rid of the remaining evidence.

After class I went back to my room and dug out the piece of glass. I knew exactly how I was going to get rid of it. The supermarket had a large container where it disposed of glassware and as luck would have it, the pickup took place late on Friday afternoons. I just needed to get there before the container was emptied and put the piece of glass inside.

To be even more certain that it wouldn't be linked to him if anyone came looking, I decided to break the shard into smaller pieces. I took it into the bathroom and wrapped it in an old towel. Grabbing my toothbrush holder, I smashed it down on the towel, repeatedly, until I heard the crunch of the thick glass breaking. Tears smarted in my eyes again. I ran back to my room and dug out a Tesco carrier bag from my wardrobe, then unwrapped the towel and took out the three pieces of glass, putting them in the plastic bag. Wrapping the bag in some tissues, I put it in my rucksack and walked out.

Since my bike was unusable, I had to take the bus. I held my bag in my lap and stared out of the window for the short journey. I was exhausted but eager to rid myself of the horrific evidence.

When I got to the supermarket I went straight to the rubbish collection area. Closing the door behind me, I fished out the paper-wrapped plastic bag and shook out the three pieces of glass, careful not to touch them. It felt good to let them slip out of the bag and into the large container that housed a week of the supermarket's glass refuse. The relief was palpable and for the first time since Wednesday I felt myself relax slightly. I almost smiled with satisfaction as I walked towards the staff room, and then, when I realised, I was disgusted at myself. I'd killed someone. There was nothing to be smiling about. But nobody could stop the huge wave of relief washing over me when the recycling lorry came and I walked outside to see the vat of glass containing the shard I had killed him with being emptied into the large truck, on its way to be sorted, melted, and recycled.

My whole body trembled as I walked back into the supermarket, my knees weak from the anxiety that had become my constant companion. Try as I might I could not stop my hands from shaking. As I stocked shelves with jars of ketchup, one slipped through my quivering fingers. The glass shattered and the ketchup splashed everywhere. I saw it happen in slow motion, helpless to stop the jar from falling. It bounced on the ground, breaking into several pieces and the thick bright red dressing sprang upwards before splattering over the white floors. I heard the sharp scream and looked around to see people staring at me. It was then that I realised it was me who had screamed uncontrollably. The image of blood pulsing out of his neck flashed in front of my eyes and I clapped my hand over my mouth to stop myself from screaming again.

Chapter 5

Two days after Chloe's case was brought to my attention, I'm still veering from one possible course of action to another. Part of me knows I should let it go, allow myself to focus on my other clients, perhaps even manage to leave the office early every now and then. But Maya's immediate reaction upon hearing about Chloe's predicament keeps sounding in my head. The girl had to be terrified, and the question of why keeps me from taking the decision to pass on her case.

At the very least I have to meet her, get a first hand impression before deciding. Not long before she's due, I find myself pacing the length of my office when my business partner, Luigi Casato, walks in. "*Elizabetta, come va?*" he asks, putting on an exaggerated Italian accent. It brings back memories of our university days and I find myself smiling.

"Drop the Italian flirtation." There is no hint of his Italian heritage when he speaks normally.

"Who? Me?" he says in mock horror. "I'd never do that to my best friend." It was he who introduced me to my husband, acting as a modern day cupid while we were in law school.

As much as I enjoy our banter, I want Luigi's opinion on Chloe's case.

"Jennifer alerted me to a case that is being handled by legal aid." Luigi rolls his eyes, so I press on quickly. "There's this fifteen year old girl, Chloe, who's had a rough life, bumped from one foster home to another. She ran over a guy and left the scene. He's in hospital with pretty bad injuries."

Luigi rubs the stubble on his face as he digests the information. "Did she do it on purpose?"

Suppressing my frustration at his negative instinct, I tell him what I know. "She claims it was an accident, that she didn't realise the car was in reverse and he was just behind her."

"If it was an accident, why did she run away?"

"I guess she panicked."

"You *guess*?" Luigi exclaims. "You really should be more certain about the facts before even considering a case that's going to cost us money."

"Of course I'm going to find out all the facts before taking the case," I say indignantly. "This is not my first rodeo."

"Hold on, did you say she's fifteen? Whose car was it?"

"It was the guy's car."

"Why was she driving it? Did she steal it? Was he teaching her how to drive?"

"I don't know yet. Sarah didn't say."

"This is Sarah's case?" He puts both hands to his head in his trademark dramatic fashion, making me regret letting the name slip. For a second I'd forgotten that the two of them had been romantically involved, and just like all of Luigi's relationships – if you could call them that – it hadn't ended well, leaving Sarah the disappointed one.

"It doesn't matter who is representing her now," I quickly say. "This girl deserves a chance at a proper defence and legal aid is swamped."

"So are you! Don't you have enough on your plate? We have clients who are paying a lot of money for proper representation and we should both be focusing our energies on them. They're the ones who pay the bills."

I feel a pang of guilt as the truth in Luigi's words is driven home. Our clients include Luigi's very rich family, the ones who made it possible for us to start our own firm. Still, I want to be able to take on cases I feel strongly about. "We had an agreement," I remind Luigi. "You promised I could take on pro-bono cases when the firm was doing well. That's the reason I joined you."

"You *do* take pro-bono cases and I've never stopped you. But this sounds like a lost cause."

"She's a kid and deserves a chance. If she goes to prison her whole life is ruined and there's no way back." I try to remain calm and not get carried away by the girl's predicament. I hardly know a thing about it, after all, but I'm certain it's way more complex than it appears and justice doesn't always get beyond black and white.

Jennifer pops her head in, sparing me from further justifications. "Chloe is on her way up."

"Is Sarah with her?" Luigi asks.

Jennifer raises an eyebrow. "I don't think so."

"Better go, just in case," Luigi says, backing out of my office, his eyes widening as he mimes a hand slicing across his neck. Shaking my head at his drama, I go back to my desk. "Just think this through please," Luigi tosses over his shoulder.

A couple of minutes later Jennifer ushers Chloe in. A tall, willowy girl saunters towards me, chin held high, pony tail bouncing as she walks. She sits down across from my desk, crosses her legs, and her arms, placing her hands on her lap, her baggy sleeves hiding them from view. "Did you come alone?" I ask. Despite Sarah saying Chloe's guardian hadn't shown up for her meeting, I'm still surprised that nobody from social services accompanied her.

"Yes," Chloe says, fixing clear brown eyes on mine. "Shall we start?"

For a moment I stare her out, taking stock of the teenager in front of me. Her face is scrubbed clean, the lack of makeup emphasising the natural beauty of her delicate features. Her chestnut hair is glossy, well cared for, her nails neatly trimmed. But her clothes are evidently well-worn, probably hand-me-downs. The grey jersey is pilling in several places and the wool looks very thin over her elbows. Her jeans are clean but definitely not the latest fashion and the rips around her knees don't look like they were purposely made. Chloe doesn't seem to mind her less than glamorous wardrobe, but for a moment I'm reminded of my own teenage years, trying to make the clothes Mum bought me from Oxfam look less worn and feeling embarrassed when my friends flaunted the latest designs. To look at my life now, with the house, the car, the clothes, you'd never know it.

Years of experience meeting new clients kicks in and I assume a poker face, although I hate to admit that this one is just as unsettling as Sarah warned. She walked in here looking as if she knows exactly what she's doing. Even sitting down, her presence cannot be missed. She's rod straight, but instead of looking uncomfortable, perhaps even nervous, she seems totally at ease. Her head remains tilted up, giving her an air of arrogance, and her forehead is knitted into a small frown, enough to create a vertical line between her perfectly arched brows. She purses her lips and takes a deep breath before raising both eyebrows at me in a questioning fashion, challenging me to begin.

Taking a deep breath, I look at my notes, the neatly jotted questions that I'd prepared when, despite Sarah's report suggesting otherwise, I was still expecting a terrified girl to land in my office and almost beg me to take on her case. Her air of confidence could be a guise to cover the fear inside, I think, a shell she is used to wearing. Remembering how I had refused to allow my feelings to show in my actions, I am overcome by an urge to protect her and decide to go easy on her, take things slowly, make sure that she is comfortable speaking to me.

"Tell me about yourself," I say.

"What do you want to know?" She doesn't miss a beat, staring at me, not blinking, one eyebrow raised impossibly high.

"Tell me about school, the subjects you enjoy, what you like to do in your free time, about your friends…" I prompt, eager to know more about her.

"What does any of that have to do with the case?" she interrupts, an unmissable edge of sharpness in her tone.

"I want to get to know you better, understand who you are."

Chloe purses her lips, looking as if she's about to protest again. Instead she says: "I do very well in school, always top of my class. I don't have any favourite subjects; I do well in everything."

"What about your friends?"

"I don't have any close friends. It's not exactly easy when you move all the time, changing schools so often."

An expression flashes across her face as the corners of her mouth twitch downwards and she looks away. But she quickly regains her composure and assumes the same stoic look as before.

"Tell me about the incident."

"I didn't realise that I had put the car in reverse and when I pressed the pedal it lurched backwards and onto him."

She is economical with her words, making her explanation sound rehearsed, as if she's thought about it several times or been told what to say. "What did you do then?" I nudge.

"I got out of the car and left." She doesn't flinch.

"You didn't check on him?"

"No," she says, her voice suddenly shrinking. Then, regaining control, she continues: "I didn't realise he was badly injured. I thought he'd maybe have a couple of bruises."

"But neighbours said they'd heard him scream from inside their houses," I stress. "Surely you must have realised this was worse than that."

"I was scared and I wanted to get away."

So, Maya was right. Something had to have frightened this girl. Torn between wanting to know more and a fear that probing too much would cause her to completely clam up, I decide to sidestep her departure from the scene for now.

"Why were you in his car anyway?"

"I was just using it to get back to the party my foster carers were at."

"Ok, let's go back. How did you get to the Grants' house?"

"My foster carers took me to a party at a friend's house," she starts. "Ben and his family were there. His mum had forgotten to bring a trifle she had prepared and Ben was on his way out to fetch it. He asked whether I wanted to go with him."

"Were you friends with Ben? He's quite a bit older than you."

"No, I barely knew him."

"So why did you go with him?"

She shrugs. "It was better than staying at the party."

"Why?"

"Everyone was already drunk. Like my foster carers too. I just wanted to get away."

"Ok, so you went to Ben's home. Did he let you drive? Is that when the accident happened?"

"No, he drove. We got to his house and he invited me in to play video games."

"Had you been to his house before?"

"Yes, once, with my foster carers. Ben wasn't there that time."

"Does he have an Xbox or a PlayStation?" The details might derail her if she's lying.

"PlayStation," she answers quickly. "I'd seen them on television."

"What did you play?"

"I don't know what it's called, but we were killing zombies," she says.

"Was it fun?"

"Kind of," she answers noncommittally.

"How long were you there?"

"An hour maybe."

"Was Ben going to let you drive back? Is that why you were in his car?"

"I just wanted to go back to the party." A muscle in her jaw twitches slightly.

"Were you worried that your foster parents would wonder where you were?"

Chloe shakes her head and for an instant what seems like sadness flashes across her face. "They don't really care."

Perhaps she's right, but for now I cannot allow myself to feel sorry for her. "So why were you so keen to get back?"

She shrugs.

"You said earlier that you wanted to leave the party. That everyone was getting drunk, including your foster parents. Why were you suddenly so eager to go back?"

"It was a sunny day. The house where the party was being held has a big garden."

Taking a deep breath, I try again, unable to shrug off the feeling that she's hiding something. "Chloe, can you stop skirting my question and give me a straight answer?" Perhaps a tougher stance works better with her. "Why were you so keen to get back to the place you had wanted to leave just a short time earlier?"

Her eyes open wide as if the question startled her. She bites her lip and breathes deeply between clenched teeth. Seconds tick by. "I wanted to get away," she finally says.

"Why?"

She is silent, and looks down at her hands, which she's twisting in her lap. The confidence that was so apparent earlier has dissipated and in front of me I can only see a young girl who is hiding something.

"Why did you want to get away?" I ask one more time.

Again, no response. Her fingers fiddle with the hem of her sweater, twirling a piece of yarn that is hanging loose.

"Chloe, answer my question. Why did you want to get away?"

She doesn't say anything, doesn't even look up. Maya's words echo in my head. "Chloe, did he try to hurt you?"

She continues tugging at the loose thread, making it longer and longer, then twirling it between finger and thumb. "Chloe, look at me. Tell me what happened. It's the only way I can help you."

She finally looks up at me, and I can see the fury burning in her eyes, mingled with fear. Even before she speaks I can sense that what she's about to say is traumatic. "I wanted to get away from him," she starts. "Because he raped me."

Chapter 6

1998

The news that a body had been found just a few miles from campus broke on a Monday morning. I was running late getting to class and rushing through the corridors when I heard other students talking about the grisly discovery. I willed myself to keep going, not to make any changes in my behaviour that could draw attention to myself. I got to class and sat down at the back, wishing that I'd woken up earlier and gone to the cafeteria, like I used to right after the incident, so I could read the newspapers, listen to what others were saying. For a moment, after hearing about it, I thought about skipping class, but exams were coming up and I couldn't risk anyone being suspicious.

A girl came and sat next to me, twirling her long hair around her fingers. "Did you hear?" she asked me.

My initial reaction was to feign ignorance but I worried it would attract more attention. "Is it true that they found a body?" I asked her, rubbing the healing scar on the palm of my hand beneath my long sleeves. Her eyes widened, her lips curling with what almost looked like a smile. "I heard some people in the corridor but didn't know whether it was true." She was nodding at me. "Where did they find it?" I asked, reminding myself not to divulge any details that might not have been made public.

"Only a few miles from campus," she said, pausing for drama. "It's a man and he'd been stabbed. Apparently his body was all swollen and decomposed and he had been partly eaten by rats. Or wild dogs."

A shudder went through my body at the thought of that windowless place, him lying there for so long. I had told myself over and over again during the past weeks that I really hadn't had a choice and if I hadn't killed him, I would not be alive now. But I still hated what I'd done. I wondered whether he would have survived if I'd only stabbed him once rather than twice. Or if I'd tried to stem the flow of blood immediately rather than losing precious seconds wondering what to do next. I'd replayed the whole night in my head, trying to think what I could have done differently, but aside from not getting in his truck in the first place, I couldn't find another way out other than what I had eventually done.

And yet, despite knowing that I'd had no other choice, I still felt sick.

"Awful, isn't it?" I heard the girl saying.

"Do they know who it is?" I asked.

She shook her head. "No, apparently he's unrecognisable." She wrinkled her nose, looking disgusted. "But they did find his van just outside."

The lecturer entered the hall just then and the chatter died down. Despite my attempts to focus on what he was saying, my mind kept wandering back to that windowless room.

*

In the month since the incident in the woods I had been struggling. Part of me felt relief that nobody had come looking for the man's killer. Relief that with every day that passed, the more I could distance myself from him. I was starting to feel more confident that horrific night could not be traced back to me. I'd gone back to my usual routine, and was even managing to get a little sleep, despite the persistent haunting dreams that woke me up multiple times a night.

Then another part of me worried that nobody had reported finding the body. What about the person he had called? Hadn't he or she come looking for him? Hadn't they suspected that something was amiss when he didn't call back? Who were these people and what were their plans? The unanswered questions terrified me. I felt like I was constantly looking over my shoulder, expecting someone to come around each corner, ready to hurt me as he had done.

Each morning I would scour the newspapers for a missing person's report, any mention of a windowless room with a dead man on a soiled mattress. I knew I was becoming obsessed with him. I tried to convince myself that the longer it took for the body to be found, the better it was for me. Yet I couldn't help but worry about his family. Somewhere, somebody must have loved him.

On darker days I realised too that if nobody had found his body after weeks, the likelihood that anyone would have found me had I not managed to escape was remote. I wondered what would have been in store for me had my hand not landed on that shard of glass and had I not instinctively used it to kill him. I shuddered every time the thought crossed my mind.

To any outsider I remained my usual self, even though I felt constantly haunted by what I'd done. I studied hard, spoke to my parents each week and worked at the supermarket. But every unexpected sound, each sudden movement, startled me.

*

The minutes dragged eternally as the lecturer droned on. I twirled a lock of my long red hair around my fingers. I had considered dyeing it, removing any trace of the colour that reminded me of blood. I'd even bought a dark brown hair dye.

In the end, I couldn't bring myself to go ahead with it. I looked at myself in the mirror and saw the real me. My hair was who I was, who I'd always been, and who I knew I always wanted to be. I couldn't allow him and what happened that night to change me even more than it already had. I knew that I'd never be the same person. I knew that something inside me was different and would always be. I knew that even if nobody else found out what I'd done, I'd always consider myself a killer.

Instead I'd wear my hair with pride. It would remind me of that night, making sure I remained cautious so that I would never be caught.

Finally the lecture was over. With only a few minutes to get to my next one, I bid a hasty goodbye to the girl and ran off, hoping to get there in time to pick someone else's brains about what they'd heard.

As soon as my next lecture was over I rushed to the cafeteria, stopping myself from breaking into a sprint. Once I got there, I forced myself to get lunch before heading to one of the tables and picking up a newspaper. It was well worn, evidently handled by tens of other students eager to know what had happened. On the front page was a picture of the shack surrounded by police cars, their headlamps bright against the night. The headline read:

Dog Walker Makes Gruesome Discovery: Decomposed Body Found Close To Prestigious University.

The full article didn't have many more details than the girl had shared with me. A man walking his dog had come across a shack. His dog, which was not on a lead, entered the room and the man followed, to be faced with the decomposed body. He ran out horrified and rushed back home to call the police, who were now investigating.

My insatiable craving for more details shocked me. For weeks I had tried to block the incident out of my mind, especially at night when the memories came flooding back. At times I would get out of bed and jump into the shower, wanting to wash any remnants of the night off me. Even though time had passed since the attack, I felt dirty and broken and only the hot water almost scalding my skin would make me feel better, even if momentarily.

But now I wanted to know what leads the police had, what their theories were, and whether they'd found any evidence pointing to the killer. I noticed that the article didn't mention the two wounds or where he'd been stabbed and made a mental note to be careful not to divulge those details when I spoke to anyone. Neither was there any mention of an accomplice. I worried that they would track this person down through the last phone call the man had made. He knew my name, that I was a student, even that I had red hair. How long would it take the police to trace these clues directly back to me? My breathing became shallow, my fear becoming more intense. I felt slightly relieved that there was no mention of the man's mobile phone and wondered whether someone had gone there after I left and taken it.

Luigi, the Italian exchange student in my philosophy class, was standing in the middle of the room. We had plans to study together later that afternoon. He too wanted to become a barrister and we often shared notes and helped each other revise for our exams. He was in lively conversation with a group of students. I stood up and walked over to them, wanting to hear what they were saying, whether there was anything else that they'd heard, what the rumours were. Sure enough, they were talking about the state of decomposition.

"*Elizabetta!*" Luigi exclaimed as I approached. "Have you heard?"

I nodded.

"Horrible, isn't it?"

Everyone else nodded gravely. "Do they know how long he's been dead?" I asked, bracing myself for more of their gory curiosity.

Luigi shrugged and another guy, with spiky black hair, said: "Two weeks, maybe more."

This was all conjecture, I realised. Students making up facts to fill in the many blanks that the article had left. "How close is this place to campus?" I prodded, looking around the group.

Spiky hair answered again. "Very close, only a ten minute walk."

I remembered how my arms had hurt as I pulled the bike over the rough terrain. It had certainly taken more than ten minutes. But I had to act ignorant to anything that wasn't in the papers. "Eek, that's really close." We all shuddered in horror at the thought of something so awful happening close to a place where we felt so protected and safe.

We chatted for a while longer. Despite my thirst to hear more, I quickly realised that they didn't have any more information to share. They rehashed what had been written in the article over and over as I stood there, silently taking everything in, nodding my responses and agreement but not really speaking, terrified of saying anything that might throw suspicion on me.

After a while the crowd in the cafeteria started to thin. Luigi was the first of the group to bid his farewell. "*Arrivederci*," he said. The group dispersed in different directions and I picked up the sandwich I'd bought earlier, realising that I hadn't touched it. Reading about the discovery of the body sucked the appetite right out of me.

As I walked down the corridor, someone grabbed me by the arm. A scream formed in my throat and I clamped my mouth shut to stop it from escaping. I looked at the student, taking in his short brown hair and slight stubble. I didn't think I'd seen him before, and if I had, I didn't recognise him.

"I wanted to apologise," he said.

Confused, I thought he had mistaken me for someone else and was about to point that out.

"Don't you recognise me?" he said. "Wow, you must have been more drunk than I was."

Frowning, I struggle to remember. "Sorry. I think you must have the wrong person."

"No, I'm certain it was you," he insisted. "Don't you remember? You were sneaking into your building early in the morning and I fell right in front of you. You stayed with me while I puked my guts out. It had been quite a night."

Fear mounted as I looked at him. I vaguely remembered a guy stumbling over and vomiting, but my mind had not registered anything else. What else had I forgotten from that night that might come back to haunt me?

And what about him? I assumed he had been too drunk to remember anything, let alone me, and pushed the encounter to the back of my mind. But now I started to wonder whether he had spotted the blood in my hair. That he remembered how dishevelled I had looked.

"Oh." I was at a loss of how else I could answer, not wanting to talk too much for fear that my voice would start shaking.

"Are you ok?" he asked, looking at me through narrowed eyes.

"Yes, I'm fine," I said. "I'd forgotten about it."

I tried to walk away, but he held my arm. "Well, I haven't forgotten," he said. "Thank you for stopping to check whether I was ok. Especially since you didn't look too hot yourself." Our eyes locked and his grip loosened. "You look better now that the bruising has disappeared."

Blood roared in my ears. He had seen the marks on my face and might suspect I had something to do with the death of the man found in the fields. He could help the police work out the exact day it happened. He could tell them he had seen me in the early hours of that morning looking a wreck. I stood dumbfounded as my mind reeled with panic.

He started turning away, but then stopped and extended his hand. "I'm Miles Perkins, by the way," he said.

I shook the hand he offered me. "Elizabeth Phillips," I replied in a small voice. And he walked away, leaving me in the middle of the corridor wondering whether my shaking legs were strong enough to take me to class.

*

The next morning I left my room early and made it to the cafeteria an hour before my first class. My knees felt weak and my legs almost gave way when I picked up the newspaper and saw his blazing green eyes staring back at me. My hand flew to my mouth as my stomach turned and I looked around for a bin, terrified of throwing up right in the middle of the cafeteria. I forced myself to take deep breaths, try to compose myself. Fear, anxiety, anger and shame bubbled inside me in a cacophony of emotions and I couldn't stop my body from shaking as I looked at the large photo of him, smiling back at me. It was the smile I remembered when he had stopped after hitting my bike. The man I'd killed had a name – John Larkin, a thirty-five year old from a nearby town. Looking at him now, at his good-looking face, I remembered how I had trusted him to want to help me after damaging my bike. I had been so naive and for the thousandth time berated myself for my ignorance.

For the rest of the day I couldn't stop seeing his face. That smile and those beautiful eyes. Somehow that photo seemed to replace my memories of his contorted face as he attacked me, or how he stared at me blankly after I'd stabbed him. I went through the day in a daze, making time to talk to a few other students, trying to find out what else they knew. It wasn't much, but the sentiment about the case seemed to change from one of curiosity to pity for the victim of a gruesome murder. Girls commented how good looking he was and I found myself having to agree if only to make sure I didn't stick out.

The first opportunity I had I rushed back to the cafeteria, picked up the newspaper and locked my eyes on his face, as if his features could dissolve the fear in my heart. I kept staring at the picture, almost unable to put it down, going back to the cafeteria repeatedly during the day. I was the last one to leave that evening when the salad bar was already being cleared and the chairs stacked on top of each other. I gathered the books that were strewn on the table in front of me. As I was walking out, I looked at the newspaper one last time. It was crumpled from handling, and there was a grease stain on John Larkin's cheek. I picked it up and looked at the face that haunted my dreams. And then I looked around the cafeteria. One lone worker was mopping the floor, his back towards me. I could see the headphones covering his ears. Without thinking I tore out that first page, folded it and stashed it in my book, holding it securely against my chest as I rushed back to my room.

New information was disclosed the following day. Police revealed their suspicion that this was a sexually motivated crime. John Larkin was found with his belt open and trousers unbuttoned. This detail sent tongues wagging with theories that the killer had lured him to the shack for sex and once they got what they wanted, killed him. By lunchtime, the story had made its way around the campus and everyone seemed to be pointing their fingers at some awful predator.

I felt like screaming. The killer was not an awful predator, I wanted to say. The killer was the victim. I remembered how much I'd ached after the attack, how my cheeks smarted from his slaps, how long it took for my bruises to lighten. There was still a small mark on my right palm where the glass had cut through my skin. And those were only the physical marks. There were emotional scars that would never heal. The way he had forced himself on me, taking from me what I was not ready to give, was demonic. No, I told myself. I would not allow myself to feel pity for him, even if I had to pretend otherwise.

The media was making a feast out of the discovery. It was the top story on the evening news.

One of the reporters had interviewed John Larkin's mother who, in between sobs, sang his praises. "My son was such a good man, always looking out for others, finding ways to help those in need," she said, wiping the tears that had started rolling down her cheeks. "He would never hurt a fly, and someone just killed him…" Her voice trailed into a sob.

But even while watching her on television, I felt completely detached from what she was saying, reminding myself that her son was not the person she was describing, the person she knew and wanted to remember. No, he was a monster and if I hadn't protected myself in that moment, I wouldn't be alive.

Then, for a moment, the news almost had me swayed and I started wondering whether I'd been wrong, whether I'd imagined what he'd done to me, and whether I had killed an innocent person. But I knew that this wasn't the case and that I was a victim. I was the victim who had walked away alive.

I didn't need to fake my pity for too long. By the weekend the investigation took another turn when police found the bodies of three teenage girls buried in shallow graves near the shack. Despite Mrs Larkin's cries of outrage that her son had nothing to do with the macabre discovery, everyone started looking at him as a serial killer who was probably about to strike again.

For me the thought was sobering. Now I knew that I was not wrong to think that killing him was the only way I could ever walk away from that place alive. I was certain that I'd have ended up just like those girls, my body abused and discarded, buried in the middle of nowhere.

When autopsies on the girls revealed that they'd been tortured for what looked like days, and repeatedly raped, I knew that it would not have been an easy death. There would have been so much suffering, agony that was physical as much as mental. I wondered how long it took each of them to realise that he was never going to let them go, that they would be kept prisoner, continually abused, die in that place. I cried for them, for the life that they'd never know, for the suffering that they'd endured and which, I knew, I was the only person who could come close to imagining. I rubbed the scar on my hand and was grateful for the shard of glass that had saved my life.

A week after the body was discovered, the Police Commissioner gave a televised press conference, rehashing the details that had trickled out in the past days and outlining the investigators' belief that the killer was Larkin's latest victim, one who had managed to get away. "We urge her to come forward, to speak to us and help us better understand what happened," he said.

That evening I thought about speaking to a lawyer about what I should do. They could help me strike a deal with the police, help them understand that I had acted in pure self defence, that I didn't have any other choice if I wanted to live. They would help me explain why I had gone to such pains to remove all the evidence of my presence in the shack.

And I would be able to let them know that someone else was involved. Avoid the accomplice from going after more girls. It was my responsibility to speak up, stop him from hurting others.

But then I realised that even if I got away, even if I wasn't charged, I would still always be seen as a killer. Someone who had been stupid enough to end up in a windowless cabin with an unknown man. My parents would be horrified by this news. They'd be the talk of their small town when people found out what their only daughter had done. And then I thought about myself. Even if people hailed me a hero, I would still be a pariah. What I'd done was inconceivable, no matter that it was to save myself. Killing wasn't normal. It wasn't something you confessed to and got away with. Not only that, if I spoke up, my plans to go to law school and become a barrister would be over.

And there was one other thing that kept me from going to the police. Something that I had found out just days before the body was discovered. I was pregnant.

Chapter 7

The soft ticks from the clock on my desk are the only sound in the room. For a moment I'm unable to move, say anything, the familiar horror of Chloe's revelation sending shivers down my spine.

With effort, I swallow the lump in my throat and take a deep breath. "I'm sorry." I force my voice to remain calm. "Tell me exactly what happened."

"We were playing video games in his bedroom, sitting on his bed. He said he had to use the bathroom, so I continued playing on my own. The speakers were blasting the sounds of the game, guns firing, zombies screeching. I didn't hear him come back in until he tapped me on the shoulder."

She pauses for breath but I say nothing, afraid to interrupt her momentum.

"I didn't look at him, didn't want to take my eyes off the screen. But he turned my head around. He was completely naked and... you know..." she trails off.

"Aroused? Is that what you mean?" Her embarrassment saddens and surprises me at the same time.

"Yes."

"What did you do?"

"I stood up and tried to get to the door, but he was in the way and wouldn't let me through. I told him we should go back, that we'd be missed, but he just laughed and said that my foster carers wouldn't notice me missing," she says. "I'm sure he's right," she adds in a small voice, her head bowed, looking forlorn and alone.

"What happened next?"

"He grabbed me by the shoulders and threw me on the bed and pushed up my skirt. And then... he... you know... did it."

I'm frozen. Memories come flooding back of the moment *he* had forced himself on me. How violated I had felt, how alone, how desperate I was to get away. But I push the thoughts of the past out of my head and instead focus on the riddle in front of me.

"Why didn't you tell the police?"

As the words leave my mouth, the hypocrisy of them echoes round my brain. Why hadn't I gone to the police? Why hadn't *I* come clean? I rub at my right hand, where the small cut from that night has faded to a thin, barely visible line.

Chloe shrugs and almost seems concerned. For that passing instant she looks her age. A teenager, completely overwhelmed by the events that have shaken her life. Then her flash of regret is gone. She lifts her chin up, squares her jaw, and stares right at me. "I don't know. I thought they wouldn't believe me."

"Is that when you tried to run away?"

Chloe nods. "He rolled off me and I ran out of the room and down the stairs. I was running out of the house when I saw his car keys on the table in the hallway and grabbed them. I got out and into his car. I just wanted to get away."

The details roll off her tongue, but the way she tells the story is still devoid of emotion, as if she is relating an incident that happened to someone else.

"Had you ever driven before?"

"No. But I thought it couldn't be so hard. I'd seen others drive a manual car, knew how it worked. I just didn't realise I'd put the car into reverse instead of first gear. And when I saw him coming out after me, I panicked and pressed the pedal as hard as I could. That's when it happened."

"The car moved back and hit him," I finish for her.

"Yes. He flew into the air and fell down."

"Why did you run away instead of going to help him?" I ask her.

She looks at me, her eyes wide. "I was scared of him. I wanted to get away as fast as I could."

"But he couldn't hurt you if he was injured," I press. "You could have stopped to check on him, call for help."

Chloe shrugs, shaking her head slightly, her eyes properly leaving my face.

"Did you think he'd be able to get up again and come after you?"

Her eyes bore into mine again before flitting away. "I don't know," she finally says. "But at that moment I was terrified of him and wanted to get away. Be as far from him as I could."

*

The roads are glistening from the afternoon's rainfall, the lights from cars' headlamps bouncing off the puddles. Slowing down, I manoeuvre the car around the sharp turn, careful not to hit the red letterbox, and into our street, waving at my neighbour, Ellen. Her silhouette shifts in the bay window at the front of her house as she raises her arm to wave back.

Despite it being pitch dark already, it's early still and I've got away in time to put the children to bed. Maya has already fed them dinner and is giving them a bath when I walk in.

"I'll be downstairs," she tells me. It's like she senses how much I long to spend time with the children and leaves me alone.

We snuggle together in Leah's bedroom while I read them a book, enjoying the feeling of their soft warm bodies against mine. When they both drift off, I tuck them into their beds and head to the master bedroom. Changing into a comfortable pair of trousers and a soft jersey, I hang my suit in the walk-in closet. The gold-coloured box where my wedding shoes are stored catches my eye and I push it further back on the shelf, hiding it from sight, before going back downstairs.

"I didn't realise you were still here," I tell Maya when I spot her in the living room, putting away the children's toys and books, stacking everything neatly, just the way I would do it myself.

Her lips curl into a smile, lighting up her whole face. She runs her fingers through her long hair, her eyes sparkling in the dim light coming from the kitchen, as she puts the last book on the shelf. "I wanted to make sure you don't need anything else."

"Thank you." I clasp her arm and squeeze it, then quickly let go, almost as if her skin burns. "You're an angel to clean up."

"Of course. I'll be off then." She remains rooted to the spot.

"Would you like a glass of homemade lemonade?" I ask. These past months, I've been noticing her reluctance to hurry home. At first I thought I might be imagining it, but she always hangs back, clearing up even when I don't ask her to. Perhaps Ellen is being too strict. She means well, but sometimes can come across as somewhat controlling and Maya is too young to understand that her mother acts this way because she loves her immensely. Anyway, I could do with the company.

"Did you make it?" She follows me into the kitchen.

"Of course not! One of my clients did." Opening the cupboard, I take out two of the neatly lined tumblers, placing each in the dead centre of a coaster.

For a few moments we don't speak, surrounded by silence broken only by the crackling from the baby monitors and the clinking of glass on glass, as we lift and place our drinks on my hand-made, colourful coasters.

"Have you decided whether you're going to take that girl's case? The one who ran over someone?" Maya finally asks.

"Not yet." I pour more of the cloudy liquid into each glass, its pure sweetness moreish. "I did meet her today but I'm still undecided."

"Why doesn't she have parents?" She leans towards me across the kitchen island, resting her chin on her hand, nibbling at her already stubby nails. "Did they die?"

Her curiosity intrigues me. "Why do you ask?"

"I don't know," she says, shrugging. "Guess I feel sorry for her. She seems in big trouble. But it's all right if you can't tell me about it."

"It's no big secret," I respond, taking my time, wanting to keep her around for as long as I can.

"It must be hard not having anyone to turn to." She looks at me. Her lips are slightly open, her eyes glistening with all the neediness and compassion of a young teenager discovering life is much harder and more complex than first appears. Her words hit me in the stomach, and I feel her innocent anticipation weigh on me. Chloe is alone and I might be her one hope for a fair trial. But I force my thoughts into rational order, and focus on wording my answer to Maya. "She's a ward of the state and has been living in foster homes since she was a baby," I finally say, hoping that will satisfy her.

"But does anyone know who her parents are?" Maya perseveres.

"No. Well, yes, technically. But she was taken into care as an infant so we don't know her parents' identity."

Maya's face is completely still. "And she wasn't adopted?" she asks.

"No, unfortunately. There was an attempt but it didn't work out in the end. Not sure why."

Maya continues looking right at me. I stare back at her, mirroring her expression.

"But aren't there ways to track down her parents?" she asks, leaning further across the island until I can almost feel her breath on my arm.

Putting my glass down, I move the coaster until it's perfectly aligned across from Maya's. Seconds tick by as I take time to complete the simple task, allowing me to find the right answer. Maya's questions are out of character. She's not usually one to probe into my work, even though I have at times discussed elements of a case with her, especially when it involves someone her age. "Yes, there should be ways to find out," I start, twisting the glass from one side to the next. "She can unseal her birth certificate. And if that doesn't get her the answers she wants, do a DNA test and see if there's a match to someone in the system."

Maya doesn't say anything. She chews on her bottom lip, seemingly mulling over this information.

A crackling sound comes from the other end of the island. A light flashes on one of the monitors and the sound of a soft whimper comes through. "It's Leah," Maya says. "Want me to go check?"

I stare at the image on the screen and see my daughter roll over, pulling her toy elephant close to her chest.

"No, it's ok. She's gone quiet."

Maya downs her lemonade. "Better go before Mum throws a fit." She turns around, rolling her eyes in an exaggerated way while walking away.

My phone beeps the arrival of a text message. It's Ellen asking whether Maya is still here. "She just left. Was helping me clear up," I respond. Another message flashes. "She just walked in." Then, a few seconds later: "Let's do lunch soon."

For some time I don't move, sitting in the silent house long after Maya leaves. Finally I stand up and head upstairs. Opening Leah's door, I look at her small shape sprawled across the bed. She's uncovered, the blanket shoved to a corner of the bed. Approaching her cot, I pull the blanket over her. Leah stirs and pushes it away. Her face is flushed, as pink as the bright pyjamas that she's wearing. I kiss her softly on the forehead and tiptoe out of the room, closing the door behind me, and walk down the corridor to the next bedroom. Blue light is coming from the nightlight. Just like his sister, Julian is fast asleep, clutching his teddy close to his chin. I look at him for long minutes, my heart filling with love for my son. He barely stirs when I swipe a blond lock of hair away from his face. Part of me wanted him to wake up, allowing me to spend some more time with him. But I know that's selfish.

Back downstairs, alone in the silent house, I pick up Chloe's file, trying again to analyse the sparse information. Chloe's words come back to me, her hard looks, and sudden flashes of vulnerability. Her reluctance to tell anyone about the rape baffles me but I understand her contradictions at the same time. Still, I get the feeling that there's more to her story, that she's hiding something important. I just cannot figure out what, yet.

I am so wrapped in my thoughts that I don't hear my husband walk in. The sound of the garage door opening and the car door being slammed shut, that I'm usually so attuned to, don't register and I almost jump when I hear him behind me.

"Sorry, I didn't mean to startle you," he says, kissing me gently. I run my fingers through his hair. It's starting to get long, almost as long as the first time I'd properly met Miles Perkins as he lay on the ground in front of my dorm building, thick hair fanning his face, throwing up spectacularly.

I have Luigi to thank for reintroducing us. Occasionally I still reel at the fear that used to paralyse me whenever I thought of Miles Perkins, wondering whether he had been able to remember more than my bruised face that night, if he had also noticed the blood in my hair, my scared look, whether he realised that John Larkin's estimated time of death coincided with the night he'd seen me trying to sneak into the halls of residence. Two years passed before I saw him again. One evening Luigi dragged me to the pub after a marathon studying session. "Come on *Elizabetta*. We're going to turn into books ourselves if we don't leave the library." Luigi was ordering drinks when Miles walked in. The hairs on the back of my neck stood out in fear as immediate recognition took hold.

"We meet again," he'd said. "I promise not to get too drunk tonight."

Smiling weakly, I looked away, unwilling to engage with him. Yet as much as I wished he would leave, he stood his ground next to me.

"How have you been?" he asked.

"Good, you?"

"Better now that I've seen you again," he flirted.

Starting a relationship was the last thing on my mind, least of all with the sole other person I had seen, and who had seen me, that night. Getting close to anyone terrified me, risking having them see through my well-crafted facade and into my real self, filled me with fear. Anxiety that my secret would slip out led to my self-imposed isolation.

But somehow, as Miles talked, I started feeling myself relax and despite myself, I started giving him more than one-word answers. The next time Luigi started badgering me to go out, I didn't put up much of a fight. Miles was already at The King's Arms and I tried to keep the smile off my face. I came to see that he wasn't like all the other guys I'd met. He didn't try to push me into a relationship, barely asked me out on a date. We kept bumping into each other and I was transfixed by his kind voice and gentle behaviour. Somehow, without even realising it, I had started to fall in love, something I always thought that I would never be able to do. My conviction that I would remain alone started to weaken under Miles' caring, respectful attention. Even before any intimacy entered our relationship, we would spend hours talking, about important stuff but also about the most mundane things that happened in our lives. His jokes, even the bad ones, made me laugh harder than I had in years and gently started peeling away the layers of protection that I had built around myself.

But there was still a major hurdle to overcome. For months after we started dating, my body would stiffen up whenever he tried to be intimate. Each touch, every caress reminded me of that awful night and the man looming over me. John Larkin's contorted face kept flashing in front of my eyes. But stronger than my fear of intimacy was my absolute terror of losing Miles. I couldn't risk him slipping away. That night had cost me enough and it could not be the reason I lost this person I had become so fond of. Aside from Luigi he was my only real friend and quickly becoming more than that. Determined not to do anything that would jeopardize my blossoming relationship, I somehow found the strength to slowly start getting physically closer to Miles.

Despite our years together, I still fear that he knows that I'm keeping something from him, or that he knows there's something I've tried so hard to bury, that there is something distancing between us. Sometimes I catch him looking at me with an intense expression on his face, as if he's trying to drill into my head and read my thoughts. "What's your darkest secret?" he asked me once. I'd struggled to keep the fear that was bubbling inside me from showing on my face. "Sometimes, when clients give me chocolates, I bring them home, but eat them all in the car," I told him. He smiled, but said nothing, and I knew he didn't believe me.

"Have you eaten?" he asks, walking back into the living room, his hair still wet from the shower. As if on cue, my stomach grumbles loudly, the sound reverberating around the silent room. Miles laughs. "Pizza?"

"Yes, sure." I would have preferred Chinese but let him make the choice. "Can you order some garlic bread as well?"

While Miles orders our dinner, I reread my notes. "Working on anything interesting?" he asks, sitting on the sofa next to me.

Closing the file, I put it down on the coffee table. "There's a new case I'm thinking of taking." I summarize Chloe's story, including the new information that the teenager had divulged about the rape. "She's basically alone in the world."

"Jesus Liz, why are you so obsessed with these rape cases?" Miles exclaims.

"Everybody deserves a good defence," I argue. "This case is in the hands of legal aid right now, but they can't cope with it. She doesn't stand a chance."

"You cannot rescue every victim of abuse," he says, his voice hushed, almost as if he's speaking to himself. "And then you get so engrossed in these cases that you're barely recognisable."

"What does that mean?" My head thumps as a flash of anger rises.

"You know exactly what I mean. You end up spending every waking moment thinking about these girls and are never present."

"That's not true," comes my quick retort. "You're being unfair."

"I'm not being unfair. You're the one being unfair. To me, to the kids, and to your own firm. You focus so much on these cases that everything else becomes an afterthought."

"You can't be serious!" Hurt sears through me at his allegation that I'm putting him or the kids second to my clients.

"Why are you so obsessed with these victims? These young girls are nothing but a handful of trouble!"

"Do you even realise how unfair you're being?" I spit back. "This is my job, what I do."

"You're also a wife and a mother and you must never forget that," he says.

The doorbell rings as I am about to respond and Miles gets up to get our delivery.

Chapter 8

I pushed the fact that I was carrying a child to the back of my mind. There were way too many other things to think about. First were the exams that were just around the corner, and then the stress of the discovery trickling into the news a little piece at a time. My body had started showing signs of the stress I was under. My normally clear skin was breaking out in angry spots and every time I brushed my thick hair, I noticed more and more red strands falling out. I felt wiped out, like I hadn't slept in days, which I hadn't really. As for eating, I was picking at food like a bird. I'd always been thin, but in the past days I started to see my collar bones sticking out in a painfully angular fashion and my normally round cheeks had taken on a hollow appearance.

To the outside world, I was still the hard-working student, with no boyfriend or close friends, and only one real care in the world – to get through college. Forcing all thoughts of my current situation aside, I turned to prepping for my exams. The investigation had moved on from John Larkin's death to the girls who had been found. The bodies had started to be identified and police were trying to determine what had happened to them. News about the dead man started becoming more sparse. While I was still on high alert for every piece of information I could find, other students had started to move on, losing interest in the story. They talked about the end of term, their plans for the summer, what would happen next year. Everyone else was putting the horror at the back of their minds and focusing on what really mattered to them. Only I couldn't, I felt like screaming. Discussing the case had felt dangerous but liberating. As if I could somehow relieve the pressure in my chest that was caused by keeping such an enormous secret.

Focusing on my studies, I spent most of my time in the library, pouring over books and distancing myself further from other students. My job at the supermarket kept me busy but even there I kept to myself, spending my breaks reading in the car park now that the weather had improved. The fresh air was welcome and the books a distraction from my terrifying memories.

It was no surprise when I aced all my exams, placing me at the top of my class in almost every module, which earned me a scholarship for a year in the United States. It was an experience that I had longed for, especially now. I needed to put some distance between myself and this place.

My parents were thrilled with my results and the scholarship. They could never have afforded to pay for the coveted experience. Mum hugged me tightly when I got off the train and I felt myself startle at the sudden contact. Barely anyone had touched me since that night. I kept my distance. Most of the time my arms were crossed over my chest, and I would step back when anyone got too close. Even though I still thought about him and that night multiple times during the day, I was trying my hardest not to allow the incident to take over my life, and keeping people at bay was one way of trying to remain in control.

But how could I tell my own mother not to touch me? Not to hug me? I resolved to tolerate, even welcome, her embrace and hugged her back, breathing in her familiar scent. My eyes welled with tears as I thought that my mother could have lost her only daughter because of my stupid decision.

A soft sob escaped. She lifted my chin and wiped away my tears. "It's so good to see you," she said, looking at my dad and beaming with pride.

My parents had always struggled to make ends meet. My dad worked hard as a car salesman and my mother had a part-time job as a secretary. They lived in a small house on a middle-class suburban street. They counted their pennies and lived meagrely, saving just enough money to send their only daughter to a good college. They'd talked late into the night about how they could afford the fees after I got in. Thankfully my grades had won me a partial scholarship, taking some of the burden from their shoulders and making my dream of going to the university of my choice achievable.

Mum came to help me unpack. My bedroom seemed childish, with its pale pink flowered wallpaper and teddy bears lining the bed. I had few trinkets, but my heart skipped a beat when I caught sight of the red faux leather jewellery box, its deep rich colour pooling beneath the bedside lamp. Panic started rising in my chest, my heart starting to beat faster, my breathing becoming laboured. The feeling terrified me and I tried to shake it away, make sure Mum didn't notice. She was looking at me intently, her brain churning as she tried to figure out what was disturbing me and trying to determine how she should ask questions without being intrusive.

Picking up the jewellery box, I averted my eyes as I emptied its contents, before handing it to my mum, forcing a smile. "Here, I don't really want this anymore."

She took it and turned it in her hands. "Why?" she finally said, her eyes slitted.

I shrugged. "I guess I've gone off red." I hoped the explanation would suffice.

"What about your hair?" She reached out and touched my bright tresses.

"I'll keep it," I said with a watery smile.

That evening we had a quiet dinner. I picked at my mother's lasagne, a dish I used to love. But seeing the thick red liquid oozing out from between the sheets of pasta made my stomach turn. As much as I tried to force myself I couldn't bring myself to eat. My mother's eyes glimmered with disappointment as she saw me shredding the pasta with my fork, and taking tiny morsels.

After dinner she joined me in the conservatory. Closing my book, we sat in silence for a while, listening to the birds chattering through the open door. Then she asked about my year, my friends, my shifts at the supermarket.

It was a while before she broached the subject of John Larkin. I feared she might ask about it at some point. The shack was too near the campus for her not to worry. She'd asked about the case when I'd first spoken to her on the phone after his body was found and then when the other girls' bodies were discovered, and I had quickly changed the subject. "I don't know much," I lied. "Just what I've heard on the news."

"Those poor girls," she said, her voice drifting off in the night. "I wonder how he caught them."

I shrugged. From the corner of my eye I saw Mum looking at me. Then I felt her hand grabbing mine, squeezing tightly. "Promise me you're always careful," she said. At that moment I felt my heart break.

*

By the end of the summer I no longer jumped at every noise I heard, whenever a door creaked, or if someone walked towards me too fast, or jostled me in a small space. The nightmares persisted but I'd feel better soon after I woke up. I no longer spent hours in a daze of fear.

Most of my time I spent with my parents, enjoying quiet time at home with them, painfully aware that these moments might not have happened had I not found that shard of glass. Although I met up with some of my old friends, the ones I had growing up, I was constantly on guard, worried of letting anything slip that might blow my cover.

Dad had got me a job at his car dealership and I was genuinely grateful. It meant having something to do and being able to earn some money. It wasn't a great job, just a gofer, doing whatever small jobs were needed that day, from wiping the inside of the cars after a buyer went in to check out the interior to getting lunch for the salesmen.

I spent most of my other time at the library, reading everything I could. I borrowed books and read late into the night, focusing on making sure I was prepared for my year abroad, yearning to make a good impression.

It was Mum who commented on my weight gain one Sunday morning as I walked into the kitchen in my nightgown. "I'm glad to see you're finally eating properly," she said.

My face reddened and I looked down at my body. "Are you calling me fat?" I joked to dispel the tense atmosphere.

"Of course not!" Mum exclaimed. "You were just too skinny when you came back from university."

But I knew that this wasn't the whole truth. I'd noticed my belly growing all the time and it was becoming increasingly difficult to suck it in. Instead I concealed it underneath baggy t-shirts, while worrying that I wouldn't be able to hide my increasingly rounded form for much longer. I was thankful to be going to a place where nobody knew me.

But even as I saw my body change in front of my eyes, I refused to do anything about the situation, completely in denial. The baby was pushed out of my mind, as if it didn't exist, and I tried to convince even myself that the weight gain was due to my mother's cooking. The constant struggle to appear normal was as much pressure as I could handle and I feared that one more piece of stress would break me. Despite realising how irresponsible it was, I refused to see a doctor. The thought of having this pregnancy confirmed was more than I could handle. For now it was an abstract, something that I knew was true but refused to believe. It was all I could do to cope.

When the last weekend before the start of term rolled around, I woke up to find Mum crying gently at the kitchen counter as she prepared breakfast. Hugging her tightly, I arched my back so that she wouldn't feel my stomach.

On my last night at home, in my childhood bedroom, I lay in bed, wide awake, staring at the soft lights on the ceiling. Every time the curtain moved, the lights looked like they were dancing. Tomorrow I'd be boarding a plane to take me far away. And then I would have to deal with the problem that I had put off for so long. The thought terrified me but I knew that I couldn't will this situation away. I had to face it and find the best way to deal with it. My future depended on it.

Chapter 9

Chloe strides into my office, her head held up, her face steely. She is wearing the same shabby grey knit. The neckline has been stretched, making it fall over one bony shoulder.

"Sit down," I tell her, motioning to the chair across from my desk, before going back to finish an email, guilt eating at me for putting paying clients on the back burner while I considered this case. Minutes tick by as I concentrate on the right wording, the silence broken only by my fingers tapping the computer keys and Chloe's barely suppressed huffs.

Miles' disapproval and accusations are threatening to distract me. So is Luigi's resistance about me taking on this case. Only Jennifer seems committed. "I'm glad you're helping her," she said when I asked her to set up another meeting.

"I haven't decided yet," I warned.

But something about Chloe excites me and unnerves me. I want to be the one to find out what happened that day, dig deep into her story and determine whether she was really wronged. Ben's actions need to be exposed, if anything to protect other girls from him. Girls who he might hurt in the future unless he's stopped. Girls who, like Chloe, might have to hide their emotions under a sharp exterior and struggle every day with guilt, shame and fear. Just like I did. Like I still do.

Chloe's irritation is becoming palpable. But I keep her waiting for a little longer, knowing that I won't be able to fully concentrate before wrapping up my other work. Sure enough, her face is beginning to flush, and her crossed leg begins to twitch and then swing and shift with the other and back again. "Let's start," I finally say. She utters something indecipherable under her breath, but I ignore her. "Tell me exactly what happened that day."

"Haven't we already gone over this?" She arches her eyebrows and pulls the loose neckline over her bare shoulder. It stubbornly falls away again, showing a yellowing bra strap. She stares at me.

"And we're going over it again, as many times as I feel is necessary." I stare back at her until she shifts in her chair.

"I was at a party with my foster carers and Ben was there…" she starts. Despite knowing the story by heart, I pay attention to each word, alert to whether she deviates, even slightly, from her original account.

"Why didn't you fight him off when he attacked you?"

"Don't you think I tried?" she splutters, her face suddenly splashed with crimson. "He pinned me down until I could barely breathe. I can still feel him on top of me." Her body shudders, as if trying to shake off the despicable memory, and I notice how bony her collarbone is. She looks to her lap and I catch a glimpse of the vulnerability that she normally keeps well hidden.

"So, why didn't you tell the police when they questioned you?" I press. "Or the public defender?"

Chloe shrugs, pursing her lips until her mouth becomes a thin line. "Nobody asked why I was leaving the house," she finally answers. "Everyone was focused on him being hurt, me running away, me doing the bad thing. Nobody bothered to ask why I wanted to get away." She pauses to catch her breath. It's the longest she's spoken without prompting. "Nobody cared. Except for you."

The urge to go to the other side of the desk and hug her, tell her that I'm here for her, is strong. But I'm still weighing whether I should even take her case, so I resist. Exhaling slowly, I tap my pen absentmindedly on my desk, looking at her, still proud and stubborn against the odds, and feel how much it's costing her to try and trust me. This young girl has nobody in the world. Nobody to protect her or fight for her. Sadness creeps upon me as I think back to how alone I'd felt after I'd killed my attacker, how terrified I was of what I did catching up on me and having my life turned upside down. It could still happen and not a day goes by when I forget it. I could lose everything that I have built. She stands to lose everything that's still to come.

"Look, I might be able to help you, Chloe. But I'll need you to be honest with me. Tell me everything. No more half-truths or beating around the bush. I need all the details if I'm to present a winnable case."

A knock on the door startles both of us. Jennifer walks in, making her way quickly to my desk. "I'm sorry to disturb," she says, glancing towards Chloe. "But Mrs Spencer just called to say she's on her way over. She received a letter from her ex-husband's solicitor and wants to talk to you."

The small silver clock on my desk shows it's past five o'clock. This is going to be another long day. But Mrs Spencer is an important client, her constant legal battles with her rich ex-husband providing a good income for the firm, making it impossible for me to blow her off, especially for a pro-bono case.

"I'm sorry." I turn to Chloe. "We have to cut this meeting short. Come back tomorrow?"

For a second Chloe looks wounded, then stands up quickly, before falling back into the chair. Her face turns grey, the colour draining from her cheeks and lips. Her eyes, usually so fiery and bright, look broken, the rims reddened and circled in shadow.

Jennifer looks at me, stopped in her tracks. "Are you ok?" I ask, standing up and walking around the desk.

Chloe continues to sit there, still and hunched, her mouth working like she's suddenly chewing on air. "What's happening, Chloe?" I ask again.

She opens her mouth to speak, but no words come out. Instead, an expression of panic spreads over her face. Her eyes open wide and she slams her hand over her mouth, looking wildly around my office. Shooting out of the chair, she hurls herself towards the other end of my desk, pulling out the waste paper basket and throwing up inside it.

Jennifer rushes out of the room while I reach Chloe. She's slumped to her knees and is still vomiting into the bin. Pulling her long hair away from her face, I rub her back, feeling the jerking movements her body is making as she retches over and over. "It's ok, it's ok." I repeat the words like a mantra.

"Has this happened before?" I ask when she finally stops heaving. The suddenness of the episode is familiar but I can't quite articulate it to myself.

Before she can reply, Jennifer is back in my office "Here, I got tissues, and water." She puts one bottle of water on the floor, next to Chloe, and the other on the back of the girl's neck. "Do you feel any better?" she asks.

There's a small movement from Chloe and I think it's a nod. A short while later she straightens up, wipes her mouth with the back of her palm, and looks at me. "Sorry."

"Don't worry about it," Jennifer says before I can speak, handing Chloe an open bottle of water. "Here, drink this."

Glancing at the door, I wonder when Mrs Spencer will arrive and walk straight in on this scene. Sensing my worries, Jennifer grabs Chloe by the arm. "Let's go to the bathroom and get you cleaned up."

The paper basket half hidden behind her skirt, Jennifer leads Chloe towards the door. She looks frail and thin, and drags her feet with every step. And then, as if she regained some energy, she turns back and asks: "Are you taking my case?"

Two sets of eyes stare at me. Pros and cons that I've been evaluating for a couple of days rush through my mind. No need for a hasty decision; I can always tell Chloe that I still need time to assess the case. But deep in my subconscious, my mind is made up. I know what the right decision is. I can't turn my back on her. This could have been me.

"Yes," I say. "Come back tomorrow if you're feeling well enough."

The corners of her mouth curl into a weak smile and the muscles in her face relax. She nods and turns around. Miles is going to be furious and Luigi is not going to be happy. But I'm relieved to have made a decision.

ıapter 10

The bus let me off in the unfamiliar city and I lugged my suitcase down the steps. Although campus was not far, walking was not an option. Instead I'd have to take another bus. Totally exhausted after the long flight, I pondered a taxi. But I quickly quashed the thought, wanting to save as much money as possible.

Although classes didn't start for a few days, relaxation was not an option. I headed to the library and asked whether they had any jobs. I needed every penny I could scrounge and if the library didn't work I'd have to ask at the cafeteria, something that I wasn't keen on. But I was in luck, the library was looking for a clerk in the preservation unit and it suited me perfectly, allowing me to schedule my shifts around my classes.

Satisfied with the day's accomplishment, I decided to go for a walk, clear my mind. But my body was starting to change and before long I started to feel tired. My back was stiff and my legs hurt. Craving a glass of water, I headed to a café. I was sitting at a table outside, across from a small park, reading, when I felt a hand on my shoulder. My body stiffened. I lacked the energy to turn my head. "Elizabetta!" came the familiar voice.

Even as the fear fizzled, I felt panic bubble inside my chest. I was banking on a new start, where nobody knew me. At least for a few months. "What are you doing here?" The words were out of my mouth before I could think how rude they sounded.

But Luigi didn't seem bothered. "Same as you, I'd guess," he quipped, sitting down next to me. "Let's go explore," he begged. A summer spent backpacking across America had not tired him in the least and he had major party plans for this year. "I hear New Haven has a great nightlife."

"But we're underage. We won't be able to get into any bars."

"Oh, don't you worry about that. I know where you can get a fake ID. I already have one."

"Really?" My brain was going so fast that I almost felt dizzy. "How much would that cost?"

"Depends how believable you want it to be. A good one will set you back fifty dollars. That's around thirty pounds. But it's worth it. I haven't been turned away from a single place."

"All right, can you give me the details?"

Luigi's eyes sparkled. "Only if you promise to come partying with me."

*

Partying was the last thing on my mind. Once classes started, I immersed myself in my work. Any spare moment was spent at the library. It was there, as I sat hunched over a desk covered in books, that I felt the baby kick for the first time. At first I didn't know what it was. The weird sensation made me instinctively clutch at my stomach. When it faded, I dismissed it as gas. But then realisation hit and I knew that I had put off this decision far too long. I only had a couple of months to come up with a plan.

Although I had tried my utmost not to think about the baby, it seemed that my subconscious had done a fair amount of evaluating and knew exactly the steps I needed to take. Despite locating a nearby Planned Parenthood clinic, I hadn't gone to the doctor. I knew that I was too far gone for a termination to be possible, so what was the rush? There were moments when I regretted not ending the pregnancy before the summer break. Nobody else would have needed to know and I could have put this ordeal, this lasting sign of what had happened that night, out of my mind. But there was also a strange relief to have that decision pulled off the table. Sometimes I wondered whether I'd waited for so long because I wanted to try and give this child the best chance in life, if that was the only thing I ever did for it.

Yet I also knew that I wouldn't be able to take care of it. There was no way I could be its mother. Not only would it mess with my plans for my life, but a baby would link me to him forever. It would be a constant reminder of John Larkin and I worried that someone would somehow find out that the baby was his and piece everything together.

The ease by which I reached a decision surprised me. There was no need to think about it. I knew what needed to be done and I was driven by my belief in doing the right thing by the child. That was my only option. This baby would be put up for adoption the minute it was born, enabling it to have a life with a family who wanted it and could take care of it. Most importantly, it would never be connected to John Larkin. Or with me.

With my mind made up, I tried to distance myself even more from the life growing inside me, knowing that I could never allow emotions to cloud my judgement. It was imperative to make the right decisions for this baby and for myself. This meant not leaving a trail behind me and making sure that I could never be tracked down, even half way across the world. While open adoptions might be a good option for some people, I wanted the cord to be totally severed. There would be no looking back.

It was as if the baby knew how important it was that its existence was kept a secret and while my tummy was getting a little rounder, it was never big enough to be conspicuous. As the weather started getting colder, I cloaked my body under layers of oversized clothes, shielding myself from the snow and from prying eyes. "I'll find you good parents," I'd whisper to it sometimes in the night if I felt it kick or move, as if telling me not to forget about it and to start making plans for its future.

Although I was a virtual unknown in a new country, I still worried about being tracked down, then or in the future. So that weekend I dyed my hair dark brown, wanting to mask my most striking feature. I was almost unrecognisable, even to myself, and when I went to the cafeteria to pick up a bagel for dinner, I was able to walk by Luigi without him noticing me.

The following Saturday I packed the thick rimmed glasses that I'd bought and pocketed the address that Luigi had given me. I needed to give birth to this baby not as Elizabeth, but as somebody else, someone who would disappear again once the baby was born. Someone who would never be seen or heard from again. It was the only way I could be certain of distancing myself completely from the child. I took the bus to a house in the Connecticut suburbs where a guy just a few years older than me was sitting in a makeshift studio. Three hours later I picked up the finished ID card. Another piece of the puzzle was completed. I was now Laura Black.

Now it was time to find parents for the baby. It felt like a massive task, one of the most daunting I had ever faced and a complete unknown.

After days trying to find as much as I could about adoption, I was feeling apprehensive but hopeful. The ability to arrange a private adoption in the US should allow me to stay under the radar. The next step was to find a lawyer who could broker the deal, ideally someone who was more focused on his pay packet for a successful adoption than discovering as much information as possible about the birth mother. As much as it pained me to admit it, I needed a true transaction-focused mercenary.

Huddled in a telephone box in town, I started making calls. The first two firms would not put me through to a lawyer. A man answered my third call. "Yes, that's me. I'm Steven," he said. I asked if he had any clients who were waiting to adopt a baby. His enthusiasm could be felt through the phone line.

The following week I took the bus to Stamford to meet with him. I was glad his office was in another city, easy enough to get to but far enough that nobody would know me. His office was on the third floor of an old building in a narrow street. I was winded by the time I got there, my changing body making me less mobile and tiring more quickly. Steven went straight to business, asking question after question about my situation, why I wanted to give the baby up, whether I wanted to be in its life. "I want to find a good family, someone who will take the baby as soon as it's born," I explained.

After what seemed like an eternity, he sat back in his chair and took a deep breath. "Do you want the baby to stay in the US?"

What a strange question, I thought. "Uhm, I don't know. Why?"

He looked at me for what seemed like forever. "I have a great couple who would make marvellous parents." They had been trying to have a baby for many years with no success, he explained, adding that they had already been approved as adoptive parents. "They're English, like you. They might move back so the baby could be brought up there." I felt myself shifting in the chair, uncomfortable under his scrutiny. "Would you mind that?"

Quickly I shook my head. "No, that's fine."

"They'll pay for your medical bills and your delivery costs," he said. It was a relief to hear. Somehow, I had not even thought about that expense.

Steven wanted me to see a doctor immediately. When I balked at making the journey to Stamford on another day, he somehow managed to get me an appointment for that same afternoon. I gnawed at my nails as I waited at the clinic for Laura Black's name to be called, terrified that if something was wrong, I would be stuck with this child, unable to find a home for it and forced to explain myself.

There was no need to worry. Everything seemed to be going well and despite my lack of prenatal care the baby looked as healthy as could be. At least that's what the doctor said. I refused to look at the screen, staring straight at the wall ahead to make sure I didn't catch a glimpse of the life that was growing inside me. There was no way I was going to allow myself to get attached, to feel anything for this baby that would make it difficult to give it away.

As I left the clinic I wondered how other women would have rejoiced if they had been in my shoes, having been told by the doctor that the child they were carrying looked perfectly healthy. But all I could focus on was that I was a step closer to giving it up for adoption.

Two weeks later I was back at Steven's office signing documents. Diagnostic tests had confirmed that the baby – a girl – was perfectly healthy and Steven was keen to get the paperwork finalised before I changed my mind. A social worker was there, and went over my rights. I was barely listening, not really interested in what she had to say, not caring how she was involved. My decision to give up the baby was final. The weeks-long cooling period seemed unnecessary and I asked whether I could waive it, sign the documents when the baby was born. But the social worker shook her head and said that this was mandatory. Later, Steven went over the process hastily. I would continue seeing the doctor and the couple would reimburse my travelling costs. They were offering a stipend to allow me to buy healthy food, something that I was grateful for. Once the baby was born, they would make a generous donation to cover any future medical costs associated with this pregnancy. Steven went to great pains to underline that this was not a payment for the baby, but solely a voluntary action to help me out.

The baby was due at the end of December. My biggest worry was that I would miss classes if she was born late. But there was little I could do.

It broke my heart to know that I wouldn't make it home for Christmas, even though the scholarship included return flights for the holidays, which had already been booked. At the beginning of December I called my parents to tell them I was going to stay on campus for the holidays. "I have a lot of studying to do," I fibbed. My chest felt tight as I heard the disappointment in Mum's voice despite her words of understanding. It made me feel like I was the worst daughter in the world. I touched my belly and hoped that this child would never do that to her own parents. That she would always be grateful for their care, that she would return their unconditional love, that she would always make time for them, look forward to going home, talk to them about her dreams and her fears. And above all, that she would trust them enough to tell them when she needed help, if she ever got into trouble, and never feel forced to lie to them and suffer alone.

As luck would have it labour pains started when I was getting dressed on the last day of classes. It started with a dull pain in my lower back and I suspected what it was. I hadn't done much reading or preparation for labour, but instinct kicked in. I called the clinic, sharing my suspicions that I was in the early stages of labour. The nurse asked a few questions, probably to ascertain that I wasn't imagining things and wouldn't waste their time, then told me to head to the clinic.

By now my stomach was quite round. And yet I don't think anyone suspected I was about to give birth. People must have thought I'd simply gained weight. I hadn't made any friends and had mostly managed to avoid Luigi. He was too busy partying. I hid under increasingly large sweaters and wore coloured scarves to draw the attention away from my belly.

By the time I got on the bus, the pain had intensified. But at least it came in short spurts that weren't too frequent. It was difficult to lug my bag off the first bus and up to the second one, and the last leg of the journey was atrocious. It was getting dark by the time I got to the bus terminus, even though it was still late afternoon. At the clinic I was examined and admitted. The adoptive parents had splurged on a private room for me, and I was grateful. I flicked through the channels on the TV until I came across an episode of *Beverly Hills 90210*, thinking how excited the parents must be. Sometimes I thought it was odd that I thought of her as their daughter already, even though she was still inside me. I had declined the offer to meet them, but Steven had said that they were in their early thirties and had a heartbreaking history of infertility. The husband was an accountant and the wife was a former teacher who would stay at home with the baby. They had moved to the US for the husband's work but still owned a house in England, and Steven said they might return once the adoption was finalised. They seemed perfect, and a world away from me.

Three hours later and I was feeling less positive. This hurt. The nurse kept reassuring me that it would be over soon and the baby would be born before midnight. Midnight? That was hours away! But there was nothing I could do. Instead, I just pulled the gas mask to my face and took a deep breath, allowing the drugs to take the edge off the pain for a short time. It was the only thing I could do and damn right I was going to do it.

In the end the nurse was right. The baby was born just before midnight. I was exhausted and emotional, more from the pain of the past hours than anything else. Or at least that's what I kept telling myself. I didn't want to think that I was in any way upset about giving away this baby. I had tried my utmost to keep an emotional distance throughout the pregnancy and was not going to ruin it now.

Yet when the nurse handed me the little blood-covered human, I felt a surge of tenderness and my heart rose to her. I looked at her little face, crumpled and red, and at her tiny hands and feet, quickly counting her fingers and toes. Saw the fine hairs on her head, already with a tinge of red.

The sight of blood, the redness smeared over her small body, made me tremble. But what took my breath away were her eyes. As the nurse brought her closer, the baby opened her eyes. She looked at me, as if she knew exactly who I was and what I was about to do, and I caught myself staring into murky pools of grey. Eyes that were so beautiful and intense and I knew right away that they would turn green. Just like his, the person who was responsible for all this. And I was suddenly transported back to that unspeakable series of events. Seeing her brought back images of

John Larkin, his furious cruelty as he raped me and then lying in a pool of his own blood, his eyes open as he took his last breath.

It was at that moment that I knew that even if I wanted to, I would never have been able to raise this baby. I could never look at her every single day and be reminded of him. It wasn't her fault, but she would have been a constant reminder of what had happened, of the day that would change my life forever. The day I became a killer.

It was as if that whole night flashed in front of me, in fast-moving nightmare-inducing images, and I shook my head at the nurse. "You should take her to meet her parents," I said, looking away.

From the corner of my eyes I saw a look of pity come over the nurse's face. "You can have some time with her if you want," she said gently.

But I shook my head again. "I don't," I said with as much strength as I could muster, feeling my eyes welling up with tears and a lump starting to wedge itself firmly in my throat. "Please, take her away," I added before my voice broke.

I kept my eyes averted as I heard the nurse scurry away, the click of the door closing sounding so final. I knew that I had made the right decision and was certain that the pain I felt in my heart, seemingly crushing my soul, would one day go away. I asked for a sleeping pill and slept soundly for the first time in months.

Chapter 11

2014

George Winters is barely visible behind the files piled high on the desk in front of him. Sitting down across from him, I crane my neck to see him properly. "Excuse the mess." He clears a small space between the two of us.

Despite being a tough opponent, I've always known George Winters to be fair. Unlike some of his peers, he doesn't lobby for excessive sentencing and tends to give space for the accused to explain themselves. But his usual leniency doesn't extend to Chloe.

"Why didn't she say anything before?" he asks gruffly when I divulge Chloe's revelation of rape.

"George, she's a kid. She was scared and probably ashamed."

"She almost killed the guy," George says. "And now she's crying rape."

"You can't just dismiss it," I insist. "She's a minor. Aren't you going to take action against him?"

He shakes his head, looking completely exasperated. "Where's the proof? If she had spoken out when the police first brought her in for questioning, they would have investigated. Of course we'll look into it but it looks like she's coming up with excuses."

Proof. That's what this case lacks. That's what every case like this lacks. Chloe has provided no evidence that Ben raped her. And how could she, my inner voice retorts? It's nothing but her word against his, while his injuries are clear for all to see. Unless there's something she's not telling me.

"What if there's proof?" I ask.

"Are you going to manufacture proof? I would think that's beneath you," he says, eyeing me for a second too long. I flush, remembering a rookie mistake, when I had inadvertently encouraged a client to provide proof that didn't exist. It was a domestic violence case that we were losing when midway through the trial our client, the plaintiff, seemed to suddenly remember photos she had taken of her bruises from a beating she claimed happened a few years beforehand. Despite my suspicion that she had never mentioned the photos before, I pushed my mistrust to the back of my mind, knowing that they could help us make our case. I was so excited that this was the proof we needed to win, that I failed to do my due diligence. Thankfully my boss was not so naive and got our investigator to look into the photos. It hadn't taken him long to find that they had been taken recently, when the defendant was out of the country, saving us the embarrassment of presenting fake evidence in court. But the case file, with the photos, had already been shared with the prosecution, and I always wondered whether George was aware of the ensuing effort to retract the new details.

"You know I'd never do that," I retort. George doesn't need to know that there have been moments when I wondered whether there's something everyone had missed in Chloe's file, some small detail that can be magnified. "All I'm saying is perhaps the police should speak to her again and investigate the rape," I insist, before I leave.

The rain is coming down heavily outside and I struggle to find a taxi. My small umbrella is useless against the strong winds on Southwark Bridge but I try to hold it above my head as I struggle to open the taxi door while holding my bag. "Here, let me get that for you," a man says, opening the door for me. He seems familiar; I'm certain I've seen him before, but cannot remember where or whether I'm being paranoid. A shiver runs through me as I push the thought aside and get in the car.

Cursing my waste of time mission, I sit back in my seat, uncomfortable in my sodden clothes. The car moves a few inches, then stops, then starts again only to come to a jerking halt just seconds later as traffic clogs up the streets. There's nothing I can do but sit back and contemplate the bind I'm in. Cases like Chloe's seem to seek me out, almost as if destiny wants me to continuously relive my past. See if I can make up for my mistakes. Jolt me awake lest I get too comfortable in my seemingly perfect life and forget that there's someone out there who knows what I did.

Forcing myself to snap back to the here and now, I think about Chloe's upcoming trial and all the work that still needs to be done to prepare her, to make sure that she's ready, that she won't snap under the pressure.

My hair and clothes are still soaked by the time I get to the office, the leather at the edge of my soles darkening in a growing stain from the water. Chloe is already sitting next to Jennifer's desk. "Come into my office." I lead the way. I would have liked some time to dry myself, have a cup of warm tea, but don't want to keep her waiting

Her skirt rides up as she sits down and I notice the hole in her woollen tights. Chloe follows my glance and looks irate as she covers the offending rip.

"I need you to think back to the events of September the twentieth. Is there anything that we can use as evidence of Ben's assault on you?" I ask.

"Like what?" She suddenly looks even younger than her fifteen years.

Exhaling slowly, I wonder how far I can push her. "Anything you can think of. Did you leave any marks on him, maybe scratches as you fought him off? Could you have left something in his bedroom in your rush to leave? Was there any bleeding that could have stained the car seat?"

"I'm not sure, I can't think of anything, I can't remember." Chloe's mouth is still open, as if she's about to talk more but unsure of what she's trying to say.

Leaning against my desk next to where she's sitting, I put an arm on her shoulder. "I know this is hard, but I really need you to think. Any marks on your skin? What about the clothes you were wearing? Any tears or signs of force? We need evidence if we have the slightest chance of the jury believing he raped you. Tell me even the smallest, most inane sounding detail and then let me decide how to play it up."

*

"You need to look the part, Chloe."

"What part? I'm not playing a part."

"Don't smile when you talk about Ben," I say for the third time.

"I'm not smiling."

I take a few deep breaths to calm down, trying to forget the work that I set aside to concentrate on Chloe's case. Even though it's not her fault, it still irritates me when she doesn't follow my simple instructions. "Yes, you are." Walking towards the camera that's recording our sessions, I press rewind. "Here." I show her the offending footage, leaning towards her until our heads almost touch. "That was a smile and the jury won't like it."

She purses her lips and huffs.

"This is important," I insist, my voice softer. "If they don't like you, they're not going to want to acquit you, no matter what I say to try and convince them."

"Fine, I'll try not to smile," she says, rolling her eyes.

"I saw that. Don't roll your eyes either, irrespective of how much you disagree with what the prosecution, or especially the judge, says. It will backfire."

Glancing at my watch, I see it's late and feel a mixture of anger and disappointment. As much as I want to prove Miles wrong, show him that I can defend the girl without allowing the case to encroach on time with my family, I find myself getting home later every day as I struggle to juggle my other cases while still giving Chloe the time she needs.

"Let's wrap up for today," I say, gathering my bag and still wet coat. "We'll continue in a few days' time."

She stands up and steadies herself against the desk. For a few moments she doesn't move, but her forehead knots into a frown and her arms wobble slightly underneath her. Dropping my coat and bag, I'm by her side in a second. "Sit back down," I encourage, helping her ease back into the chair behind her. She looks ashen and I bring the paper basket closer to her. "Let me get you something to drink."

The look on her face is one I've felt myself. In the kitchen I raid the cupboard for some Jacobs crackers and a bottle of Sprite, hoping that she won't be sick in my office once again. My mind is whirring, wondering if she's hiding something under her ill-fitting clothes, proof we need that Ben raped her.

"Here, have some of these." Opening the packet of crackers, I put two in her hand. Chloe takes a small bite out of one and a gulp of Sprite. Her face is still grey and I keep an eye on her while sorting out some paperwork. She keeps glancing up at me, her eyes shifting from my face to the drink in her hand, almost as if she expects me to walk away.

"Thank you," she says after a while.

"How are you feeling?"

"Better." She gives me a watery smile.

"How many times has this happened?"

She thinks for a moment. "Only a couple of times, when I stand up too quickly."

"Have you been feeling any differently lately?"

"Not really. Maybe a little more tired, but that's because I'm staying up late finishing my homework."

"Perhaps you should see a doctor, get yourself checked out." I hate myself for hoping she's wrong, that the tiredness and nausea aren't due to the stress of the investigation.

"Yes, sure," she says dismissively, putting her jacket on.

Although eager to get home, I'm worried about Chloe and don't want her to take the bus all by herself. She seemed so fragile last time and I worry that she will have another episode while she's on her own. Anyway, it would be good to spend more time with her, pierce through her exterior and find out her story. I need her to trust me, to want to open up to me, to feel comfortable sharing even the smallest detail that might seem innocuous to her but might make the difference between winning and losing the case. The more I look at her, the stronger my determination to help her.

Even if I rush, by the time I get back Leah and Julian will be fast asleep. So I take the long route, aware of Chloe's reluctance to get back to the children's home.

For a while we drive in silence. I steal glances at her by my side, and I'm sure she does the same to me. The evening can't hold much fun for her, but if she's found guilty in this trial, this might seem like one of her happier memories. "Is there anyone your age at the home?"

"Yes, there are a couple of other girls."

"That's good. Have you tried to make new friends?"

She shrugs and looks out of the window, her face averted so that I cannot see her expression.

"Are they nice?"

"I don't know, they haven't spoken to me." Her voice is edged with bitterness. "I've seen them whisper among themselves and laugh when I enter the room."

"Have you tried talking to them?"

She shrugs again, but this time looks at me, sad, resigned. "Why bother?" She pauses, and her voice sounds harsh when she continues. "Anyway, I'm not good at making friends."

A wave of melancholy washes over me. Her loneliness is heartbreaking. "Perhaps you need to try harder." The irony doesn't escape me, having always been just like her. A loner. Making friends was never my priority. Even now, I don't have any close friends, anyone I can call to talk with. Except for Luigi and

Ellen. The only difference is that at least I have a family who love me.

"I was just like you." I decide to confide in her. Perhaps my experience will show her the error of her ways. "Always thought I'd be better off on my own. I focused on school, on getting the best grades, making sure I got into the best university."

Chloe shifts to look at me. She's paying attention, her eyes riveted to the side of my face. Turning quickly, I smile at her, before continuing: "It seemed like the best choice at the time. It got me where I wanted. But sometimes I miss having friends that I can share memories of our teenage years with. People who I have grown up with. Who know me well."

Tearing my eyes off the road, I look at her. There's a sadness in her eyes that pulls at my heart. Taking my left hand off the steering wheel, on an impulse I clasp hers and squeeze tightly. Her hand is cold and I feel a slight tremble. "It's not too late for you. You can make new friends, people who will be there for you when you need them, who you can share your thoughts and fears with. A proper support system."

Chloe's hand stiffens under my grasp and I think she's about to pull away. I'm about to let go when she relaxes, then turns her hand over and clasps mine tightly, like she's thirsty for human contact. But the vulnerability is only momentary. Her hand soon slips out of mine. Her lips are pursed in a thin line, muscles on each side of her mouth twitching as she clenches her jaw tight. But as her gaze drifts to the window, it's her eyes that strike me, full of sadness, and completely resigned.

*

The Spencer's case starts dominating my time, forcing me to cancel my upcoming sessions with Chloe. My eyes are bleary from staring at the fine print in their divorce papers, trying to find a small loophole that would allow Mrs Spencer a portion of her husband's recent inheritance. Despite numerous readings, nothing has caught my eye and I'm starting to lose hope. But the firm cannot lose her as a client. She is easy money for us, racking up several billable hours of usually straightforward work each month. We need her. And she was also one of our first clients. Somehow I feel we owe her our best efforts.

There's a knock on the door and I look up, squinting my tired eyes. Jennifer walks in and closes the door behind her. "Chloe's out there," she whispers. "She's insisting on seeing you, even though I told her you're busy and can't be disturbed."

The gladness I feel takes me by surprise, but I chalk up my feelings to relief at being able to take a break from the toxic divorce documents I've been poring over all day. "Show her in, but come back to get her in ten minutes."

Chloe walks into the office and takes a seat across from me. Her face is flushed and her breath is coming in quick gasps. She looks like she's been running, or about to pass out. "Chloe, what happened? Are you ok?"

"Yes. Well, no, not really," she splutters the words.

"Chloe, I have a mountain of work to do. Please tell me what happened."

For a moment she almost seems about to burst into tears and I immediately feel bad. Quickly I stand up and walk towards her, leaning against the desk next to her chair and put my hand on her shoulder. The bone is jutting out. "Tell me how I can help."

Vulnerability is soon replaced by her regular strong look as she squares her jaw and looks me straight in the eyes. "I was sick at school and they took me to the nurse." she starts.

"Are you ok?" My heart's pace increases and I realise I'm holding my breath.

"She ran some tests."

Nodding, I continue rubbing her shoulder, urging her to continue, not wanting to say anything that gives her more opportunity to pause. When she doesn't say anything, I smile to encourage her.

"She said I'm pregnant."

Her words float in the silence that follows them. Neither of us says anything. I try to put on a look of surprise. "Are you?" I ask after a while.

Chloe shrugs. "They ran the test twice. That is what they said."

"How far along are you?" Quickly, I work backwards to the date of her incident with Ben. By my calculations she must be around ten weeks pregnant. I dare not hope that the timing works in our favour.

"They didn't tell me. But I know that it could only have happened that time, with Ben."

"And you're sure of that."

"Of course I am," she fires back, shrugging her shoulder like my touch burns.

"And you didn't know until today?" She must have at least suspected that something was happening.

"I've been feeling a bit strange, but I put it down to stress. I suppose I had some suspicions, but just hoped that I was wrong. There was nobody I could ask if this was normal."

The scar on my hand tingles and I rub it gently. "You can always come to me." Even as I say the words I realise that I have still to prove I mean them. Despite recognising Chloe's vulnerabilities, I have done little to make her trust me, see me as more than her legal representative but someone who wants the best for her beyond the case. I need to try harder to make her feel comfortable talking to me. It's the only way she will really open up and we can stand a chance of winning this case. I need every bit of information that can help us. "My door is always open."

There's a knock and Jennifer walks in. "Your next meeting is here."

My mind goes blank and then floods with the question I've asked myself again and again over the years. If I had had the courage to come clean about what I had done back then, I wonder how different life would be. Jennifer returns my stare, tipping her head knowingly towards Chloe, forcing back my memory. "Reschedule," I say. "And hold my calls."

The click of the door closing is the only sound in the room as I fix on the teenager in front of me. The corners of my mouth twitch upwards. "This is good." Chloe's blank expression tells me she's not yet thinking what I'm thinking. "This is the proof we need that Ben raped you."

*

The drive home is a blur. I can't forget the horrified look on Chloe's face at my excitement about her pregnancy and wish I had been more subtle. Yet this is the breakthrough we've been waiting for, I'm sure of it.

As soon as Chloe leaves my office I pick up the phone to call George Winters. Surely a more thorough investigation would have to take place now that she is pregnant. But before he can answer, I'm assailed by doubt. If the nurse got it wrong, or if Chloe misunderstood, if the timing doesn't fit and the baby was someone else's, it might destroy my whole case. Hanging up, I decide to keep the information to myself until I can get more answers, until I am certain that this development can work in our favour.

When I get home, I try to put Chloe at the back of my mind while I turn to my family, building Lego towers and reading books with the children. Back downstairs after putting them to bed, I find Miles reheating yesterday's leftovers.

"How was your day?" he asks as I sit down at the kitchen island.

"Ok, busy."

"Were you in court today?"

"Yes, just this morning though. I spent most of the afternoon buried in paperwork. Poor Jennifer was still at the office filing motions when I left. How about you?"

"Same as always. One surgery after the other and then a ton of patient files to complete. I feel like I have no time for research anymore and hate the feeling of not being completely up to date with what's happening." Miles takes the chicken vindaloo out of the microwave, transferring it into mismatched bowls.

"We should go away somewhere," he says suddenly. "Just take a couple of weeks off and go somewhere sunny, lie on a beach. Maybe even invite your parents; that way we can have some time on our own while they look after the children."

The thought of lazy days on the beach, licked by the sun's rays, reading something that's not a legal document, not trying to be in three places at once, overwhelms me for a second. I can almost smell the saltiness of the water, hear the waves crashing. But I know that neither of us can just up and leave. Miles might be making the suggestion, but every trip we take has to be perfectly planned out so that none of his scheduled surgeries have to be postponed.

"I'd love to," I say.

"Is there a 'but' coming?"

"I have a trial starting in a few weeks, just after the New Year."

"Is this that girl's case?"

"Yes." When I don't elaborate he asks how it's going.

"She's been feeling unwell, actually threw up in my office just last week." Miles has a concerned look on his face, the one he always gets when someone starts talking about a health problem. "She was sick at school today and the nurse told her she's pregnant."

"Whoa, that's awful!" Miles exclaims. "She's just a child herself."

Despite the horrified expression on his face, I cannot keep my enthusiasm at bay. "Yes, it's not ideal. But it could help the case, provide proof that the guy she ran over raped her. If it is him."

"Oh my God, Liz! Why does everything have to be about the case? This is going to ruin her life."

"Going to jail will also ruin her life," I answer indignantly. "I'm trying to see the bigger picture."

Shaking his head, Miles digs his fork into his bowl of vindaloo and we eat in silence for a few moments. "What's she going to do?"

"I don't know. I don't think she knows herself. It's all been a shock to her."

"I can imagine. But perhaps this is the push she needs to turn her life around."

"Maybe. Unless she decides to terminate."

Miles looks at me, his eyes searching my face. "Is that what she wants to do?"

"I really don't know. This all just happened. But there are other options as well."

"What? Giving the baby up for adoption?" he asks. Nodding, I look down at my food, uncomfortable under his scrutiny. "Is that what you're advising her to do?"

His eyes bore into mine and I shuffle in my chair. "It's not my place to give her advice on that," I say, staring deep into my bowl.

"I've never been able to understand how a mother could abandon her child."

His words are like daggers to my heart. I want to protest. Explain to him that sometimes it's the only option. That it is not a selfish choice, but one meant to give the child a better life, and one of the hardest choices a mother can make.

"And what will she do then? Continue living her life as if the child never existed? Refuse to acknowledge what happened to her? Even to the people she's closest to?"

He glares at me. Anger distorts his face and I cringe, remembering his old questioning about my past. I know he suspects that I had a child before Julian; he's a doctor after all and his suspicions were provoked even more when my doctor questioned me. I'm transported back to the examination room when I was pregnant with Julian. "So, this is your first pregnancy?" the doctor had asked, disbelief evident in his voice. Miles' head had shot up. He'd quizzed me about the same exact issue so I knew that he had his suspicions. But I'd remained steadfast in my denial.

"What's the next step?" he finally asks.

"I was about to tell the prosecutor, but had second thoughts. I want to have this pregnancy confirmed."

"Have you spoken with her doctor?"

"No, she hasn't seen one yet. I need to arrange that for her, determine the length of the pregnancy so we can find out whether the timeline fits in with the rape."

"Don't you believe her?"

"Who knows! People lie all the time. I want to be sure before acting on this information, find a way to confirm whether the guy is really the baby's father."

"That's easy to do," Miles says.

"It's not just that," I continue. "I'm worried that if Ben is not the baby's father, this pregnancy will make her seem easy and her rape claims will lose their intensity." I pause to try and eat. I'm surprised Miles is letting me talk this over, so I hazard another of my conundrums about the case.

"I just wish there was a way to do the test without informing the prosecution. Or Ben."

Miles looks at me, narrowing his eyes until they look like slits in his face. He drops his fork and pushes the bowl away from him. His right hand forms into a fist and he bangs it on top of the island, causing the bowls and glasses to clatter.

"No, Liz!" His voice is raised. "We're not doing this again."

"Doing what?"

"I know he was at my hospital. I'm not going to look for his file for you. Or try to dig out blood samples."

"I never asked you to!"

"You didn't have to. I know what you're thinking. That was a one-time thing. I'm never again accessing a patient's file for you."

"Hey, that was years ago. Why do you have to keep bringing it up?"

Picking up my glass, I take a sip of water, wanting to cool down before saying something that I will regret. But Miles is still staring at me, his face tinged with the regret that is always apparent when he is reminded of his role in that case several years ago. My client was contesting his mother's will and I was desperate to find more information about the elderly lady's state of mind before she died, something that was not written in the official hospital documents but might be hidden in the copious notes that nurses take and which Miles could access.

"I was not going to ask you to do anything unethical," I say, wanting to diffuse the argument.

"You've done it before. It was the wrong thing to do and I still regret it." His eyes still blazing with anger, Miles stands up and leaves the kitchen. I make a feeble attempt to continue eating but each forkful is more difficult to digest than the one before. Throwing out the rest of the meal, I rinse both bowls and put them in the dishwasher, before going in search of my husband.

Miles is sitting up in bed, a medical journal open in front of him. In the dim light coming from his bedside lamp I can see his forehead knotted in a frown and his mouth set in a thin line. We haven't talked about the incident with the medical records for some time and I had no intention of bringing it up. Miles has been clear many times that he'd never do it again and now that I'm older and more mature I won't ask him to jeopardise his reputation and a job he loves to help a client.

Yet there's a small part of me that hoped he would offer a solution. That he would have been willing at least to think it through with me. That he recognises how important it is to prove that Ben is the father. That he understands, like I do, that Chloe's future depends on this.

In the bathroom I change into my nightgown and scrub my face clean, wishing I could wash away the tension between us so easily. Opening the cabinet, I look at the neatly lined face creams and take out my favourite lotion, applying it liberally to my face and neck. My bare feet sink into the carpeting when I walk into the bedroom. Standing at my side of the bed, I pull my hair into a pony tail. Miles doesn't look up, not even when I get into the bed and inch my way towards him.

Not wanting to go to sleep without making up, I touch his left hand. It takes a few seconds before he looks at me, his face still scrunched in anger. "Let's not fight," I say gently.

"You still don't understand that what we did was wrong," he spits out.

"Of course I do." My voice threatens to break at his accusation.

"You'd do anything to win a case, irrespective of who else gets hurt." It's as if he hasn't heard me. "You lose sight of reality when you take on these cases. That's why I begged you to give this one a miss."

"That's not true!" I hiss back, not wanting to shout in case I wake up the children. "I never asked you for help. You simply jumped to conclusions."

"Did I? Or were you paving the way to ask me to get my hands on Ben's file?" He pauses, looking at me pointedly. "I know you well Elizabeth, perhaps better than you know yourself. I could sense what you were getting at."

A hot flush makes its way through my body as hurt is replaced by anger. Perhaps there was a small part of me that hoped Miles would help, but I'm still angry at his accusations. "If you knew me so well you'd have known I was not going to ask you for anything," I insist. And then, I can't help unleash, "You need to get off your high horse sometimes. It's not like you never made a mistake in your life."

Miles' face changes in front of my eyes. His pursed lips open slightly and his brows shoot upwards in shock. "Don't bring my mother into this," he throws back at me.

"I never mentioned your mother. You're the one with the guilty conscience."

"I did what I had to do." This time his voice is softer and I can barely hear him. "She was suffering and it was only going to get worse. At least she died with dignity."

Throwing the covers off himself, Miles gets out of bed and starts leaving the room. He turns back and says: "We only get one big mistake in our lifetime. That was mine." Then, he walks out, slamming the door behind him.

His bare feet make a pattering sound on the corridor's hardwood floors. Moments later I hear cupboards downstairs being opened and the clink of ice hitting a glass. I strain for more sounds but cannot hear anything through the closed door.

For what seems like hours I lie in bed staring at the ceiling, playing our argument over and over in my head. I don't move, not even to turn off Miles' lamp. Part of me wants to go and find my husband, but his harsh words still echo in my ears, the hurt they caused stronger than my desire to make amends. Closing my eyes, I try to let sleep take over.

But I can't. Just like I often do, I lie there, asking myself again and again how things would have panned out had I not run away all those years ago. If instead I had gone to the police. How different would my life be if I had come clean?

The mattress bows under his weight when Miles gets into bed. Opening my eyes, I glance at the clock on my bedside table. It's past two o'clock. The lamp is no longer on, but the sliver of light coming from the window allows me to see my husband's face. His hair is dishevelled, as if he's spent the past hours continuously running his hands through it. His expression is resigned, his eyebrows and mouth both sloping downwards. Moving towards his side of the bed, I reach out for him, and when he turns towards me I can smell the alcohol on his breath. In the dim light I can see that his eyes are glistening with unshed tears and I hug him tightly.

It breaks my heart to see him upset, knowing that what he did was intended to stop his mother's suffering yet that his guilt still eats at him in his darkest moments. And I'm sad that while he confided in me his biggest secret, I have never found it in my heart to tell him mine.

Chapter 12

1998

I was to stay at the clinic for two days to recuperate. The next morning passed quickly. The doctor came to check on me, telling me that I was doing well. I spent the time watching TV and napping. Physically, I was feeling better, with just a few pains that were well managed with mild painkillers. But my heart felt heavy, and as much as I tried to focus on reading, I was unable to get the baby's sweet face out of my mind.

By early afternoon I wanted to go for a walk, even if it was along the hospital corridors. I was starting to feel cooped up. I tightened the drawstring on the black yoga pants, pulled on a hooded fleece over my t-shirt and tied my long hair in a ponytail. I remembered to put the glasses on and left the room.

The hospital was buzzing with activity. I had not noticed the day before, but there were festive decorations everywhere. The Christmas tree was wrapped in twinkling lights, while candles flickered on a Menorah stood on the reception desk. Everyone was smiling, looking extremely happy. Men walked around with beaming faces, heavily pregnant women paced the corridor, their eyes sparkling with joy despite the painful grimaces on their faces. You could feel the pulse of excitement, the joyousness of new beginnings.

I walked along the corridor, trying to keep out of the way of the scurrying nurses. I looked at the cheerful cards attached to the notice board covering a large wall. There were notes of thanks from delighted parents. Photos and photos of smiling babies met my gaze. I looked at each of them, wondering whether next year her parents would send a photo of the baby I'd given birth to last night, whether her image would be stuck on this same notice board.

Despite not wanting to think about her, wishing more than anything to put all that had happened behind me, I couldn't help but wonder how she was doing. Was she healthy? Did I do things right? Did I take care of her well enough while she was inside me? I felt this incredible urge to know. And without even realising what I was doing, I started walking towards the nursery.

I followed the signs and as I approached the end of the corridor, I saw a couple huddled together, staring through the large glass panel into the nursery, where babies were lined up in cots, dressed in shades of blue and pink. The couple was unaware of anything else that was happening around them, but just gazed right ahead, barely moving. The man was dressed in a perfectly tailored dark suit and had his arm around the woman, probably his wife. She was very slim, the large belt accentuating her tiny waist. There was no way she had given birth and I knew instinctively that it was them, that they were the people who were adopting her.

Alarm bells rang in my ears. "Walk away," they warned, getting louder and louder. But I just couldn't help myself. I kept walking slowly towards them. As I approached, the husband removed his arm from around the woman's shoulders and whispered in her ear, before kissing her on the cheek, taking a last glance through the glass panel and walking away. She didn't even look at him, continuing to stare through the glass, as if she was mesmerised.

I walked towards the woman, who didn't move. I felt bad intruding on this special moment. But I just couldn't help it. I looked at her. Her eyes were red and puffy but her lips were curved into an unmistakeable smile that revealed how she was bursting with happiness.

Following her gaze, I looked at the crib she was staring at. Even without that guidance I would have known which one she was. The fine strands of red hair could be seen escaping her woollen hat, contrasting against her pink skin. She was fast asleep, peaceful. The woman tore her eyes away from her daughter for a quick second to look at me, and smile, before returning her gaze to the person who really mattered.

"Which one is yours?" I heard myself asking, surprised that I was talking to her. She pointed at the crib where I knew she was.

"First row, third one from the left," she said. "It's a girl," she added quickly.

I continued staring at the baby. "She's beautiful."

"Thank you." A tear escaped the corner of her eye and started the rushed journey down her cheek, before she stopped it with her hand, blinking hard to stop others from forming.

We stood there, both staring at the same baby. I knew I should go, leave her alone to bask in her happiness. But I found myself unable to walk away, wanting to prolong this moment for as long as I could, knowing that I would never see her again. I wanted to etch the memory in my brain, allowing me to remember her like this, sleeping peacefully in the crib.

The woman turned to look at me. "Are you visiting someone?" she asked gently, as if she realised that it was only polite to make conversation.

"My sister," I lied.

"Ooh," the woman said. "That must be so exciting."

I shrugged noncommittally. I needed to leave. I looked at the baby one last time, drinking in every inch of her. The curve of her cheek, the cute nose, the bow-shaped lips. "Goodbye," I said to the woman.

"Good luck to your sister," she said, reaching over to clasp my hand. As she stretched, the small bag that she had been holding under her arm slipped from her grip, falling to the ground, opening and spewing her belongings all over the corridor. Coins – both pounds and dollars – spread across the tile floor and a tube of lipstick rolled towards the corner. A packet of tissues cartwheeled to my feet and pieces of paper fluttered to the floor. We both bent down to pick up her belongings. She put her bag on the floor, and we both put the items back inside. I picked up her mirror, which had miraculously remained intact. She reached out for her wallet, but it was open, and when she picked it up all its contents dropped out. We looked at each other and laughed, starting again to pick up everything. I was putting a few coins inside the zip compartment when I noticed her British driving licence peeking out. Without even thinking, I reached out, took it and put it in my pocket.

Chapter 13

2014

Maya is sitting at the kitchen island, reading, when I get home that Friday. She looks up and smiles, her eyes glistening in the light coming from the overhead lamps. Putting my bag down on the island, I sigh deeply that this week is finally over.

"Hello, Mrs P." She closes her book and sits straight on the stool.

"Hi Maya, are the kids asleep?"

"Yes." Then, looking at her watch, she adds: "I put them down around forty-five minutes ago."

Although her answer was expected, it's still depressing. By six o'clock I'd been ready to leave, to rush home and start off the weekend. But then the phone rang and I had to deal with a work crisis. "I kept them up a little longer, but in the end they both were too tired," Maya says.

"Did they give you any trouble?"

"Not at all. Julian wanted to finish his homework. I took a peek and it looks like a good job. They helped me make chicken nuggets. There's some left that I put in the freezer."

The kitchen is pristine. The sparkling white countertop doesn't look like anyone has just done any cooking, let alone with the help of small children. The utensils are lined up on their magnetic strip; the floor is immaculate. Sometimes Maya seems to know how my mind works. I pick up a small jar of white pepper that's next to the sink and put it in the alphabetised spice rack.

"Thank you so much."

"Mum brought over a chicken casserole. I put it in the fridge."

The grumbling in my stomach makes Maya giggle, a lovely sound that brings a smile to my face. "Thank your mum, she's a life saver."

A staccato ring comes from the dishwasher. Maya jumps off the stool and starts emptying it, putting all the contents away. I catch my breath as I watch her line everything up, the mugs with their handles facing to the right, bowls and plates separated according to their size and colour. Just the way I would do it.

Pouring myself a glass of water, I stand across from Maya, taking small sips.

"What's new with you?" I ask her.

"Not much, it seems that all I do is study these days." She gestures towards the book she put down earlier.

"*Introduction to Philosophy*," I read the title. "Thrilling!"

"Yeah, right." She makes a face like she's been cast in cement from boredom, and before we know it, we're both laughing, the offending book lying on the countertop between us.

"I should go," Maya says after a while. I feel a pang of disappointment. But before she leaves, she takes the casserole out of the fridge and spoons a portion onto a plate. "You can put this in the microwave when you're ready to eat."

Upstairs, I check on the kids. Opening the door to Leah's bedroom, I look at her small shape sprawled over the bed. She's uncovered, the blanket shoved to one corner. With her legs and arms wide open, she looks like a starfish. Kissing her softly on the forehead, I tiptoe out of the room, closing the door behind me, and walk down the corridor to the next bedroom. Blue light is coming from a nightlight, projecting Star Wars characters onto the walls. Just like his sister, Julian is fast asleep, clutching his blanket close to his chin. My heart fills with love for my five year old son as I look at him for long minutes. I kiss him softly and walk out of the room, longing for the morning when he will be awake.

The master bedroom is at the other end of the hallway. Sitting on the edge of the bed, I crane my neck from side to side and arch my back to stretch in the hope that the stiffness, caused by hours slouching in my chair poring over documents, will go away. Then I try one of my breathing exercises, inhaling through my nose and pushing the breath loudly out through my mouth.

There's a knock on the front door. For a second I think I've imagined it, and am just about to go back to changing out of my suit, when I hear it again. I contemplate ignoring whoever's at the door. But perhaps it's Maya and I rush downstairs, barefoot. Opening up, I see it's my neighbour, Ellen, on the doorstep. "Maya said you're alone. Would you like some company?"

"Come on in," I say, holding the door wide and hugging her tightly as she steps in.

"Feels like I haven't seen you in ages," she says.

"I know. I'm sorry I had to cancel lunch these past few weeks. I've been so busy."

It was around a year after we moved to the neighbourhood that I bumped into Ellen on Regent Street. She was out of breath, lugging several shopping bags. "Here, let me help you," I'd said, taking some of her load. As she thanked me I smelt the alcohol on her breath. "I was going to grab something to eat," I said. "Why don't you join me?"

We'd popped into Fortnum and Mason and I sat back as Ellen told me hilarious stories about the other neighbours. By the time we finished our sandwiches, we'd made plans for weekly lunches in the city.

"Thank you for the casserole," I say now.

"Have you eaten?" she asks and as if on cue my stomach grumbles one more time. I take the plate Maya had prepared and put it in the microwave.

"A glass of wine?" The words are barely out of my mouth before I start to regret them. There was one time when Ellen confided in me about a period of heavy drinking many years ago, before Maya was born, when the pressure of repeated failed fertility treatments got to her. But although she's sometimes tipsy, she seems in control, the only effect of alcohol being her increased chattiness.

"Please."

Reaching for two glasses and a corkscrew, I pop open the bottle.

"Did you put the kids to bed?" she asks.

"Maya did." Holding it from the stem, I twirl the glass round and round, looking into the golden liquid swishing inside. "I'm missing out on so much time with them." The thought never leaves me but I rarely say it aloud. I wasn't there when Julian crawled for the first time. Or when Leah said her first word.

The microwave pings, interrupting my thoughts, and I tuck into the meal, sighing my satisfaction as I swallow the delicious dark thick sauce sticking to the chicken and vegetables, covering them with sweetness.

Sitting around the kitchen island I am transported back to the day Ellen walked into my life, the first person to knock on my door to welcome me to the area. The memory of that Saturday morning is as clear in my head as if it was yesterday and not five and a half years ago. On my own, I was surrounded by boxes that needed to be unpacked, unsure where to start. Miles was at work and I was left with the overwhelming task of turning the empty rooms into a home. Opening a box, I'd stopped, unable to bring myself to start unpacking. So, I moved on to the next box. And the next. When Ellen showed up at my door with a chicken pie, I burst into tears. Within seconds, she'd put the dish down on an unopened box and was hugging me. I'd cringed at the close contact with someone I didn't know, but she held me tight. "It's ok, everything's going to be ok," she'd said softly in my ear, rocking my body gently as if I was a child.

Ellen gets up from her stool and walks towards the far end of the kitchen. She tears out two sheets of paper towels from the roll on the countertop and hands them to me. "Careful you don't get your clothes dirty."

Tucking one into my shirt's collar, covering the front of my silk blouse, I shrug out of my jacket, hanging it over the back of the stool. Laying the other towel on my lap, I take another spoonful. Ellen beams her approval.

It had taken me some time to stop sobbing when we first met, but when the tears had finally dried up, Ellen released her grip and I blushed in embarrassment at my outburst. "Second trimester," I'd explained and Ellen smiled. "Let's get you all moved in," she said. Walking into the house, she started to unpack a box. For the next few hours, we worked together, taking items out of boxes and putting them away, Ellen fussing over me like a mother hen and taking care of anything that she deemed heavy.

Picking up my wine glass, I clink it against Ellen's. "These are the glasses you gave me after we moved in."

I had been stocking the shelves in the pantry when I heard the sound of glass shattering followed by a piercing scream, making me jump in shock. "What happened?" I asked rushing towards Ellen. "Are you hurt?"

She was standing still looking at the floor. Next to her feet was a box of wine glasses, or what remained of them. "I'm so sorry," she finally said, bending over to pick up the box, which had luckily contained the broken glass.

"Don't worry about it," I responded. "Those came from Ikea, and anyway, it's not like I'm drinking much wine these days."

But Ellen would not stop apologising and the next day she had turned up at the house with a beautifully wrapped box. I'd invited her inside, but before she stepped in, she looked to her left and summoned someone.

Maya skipped into the house, her red hair bouncing up and down as if it had a life of its own, the thick white hairband barely containing it. "Hello," she'd said, cocking her head to one side and politely extending her right hand.

My feet felt glued to the floor and I stood there, transfixed, looking at the young girl, taking in the delicate red brows, her small upturned nose, cheeks that still held a childhood chubbiness, and eyes the colour of emeralds. "This is Maya, my daughter," Ellen said, breaking the spell.

"Hello, Maya." Shaking her hand, I marvelled at her strong grasp, so unusual for her age.

"We've come to help you with the rest of the unpacking," Ellen said. "Maya can start on the books and we can continue with the breakables."

"Thank you." I showed Maya into the shelf-lined room that was to become our office and watched for a few minutes while she started taking books out of boxes and lining them neatly on the shelves.

In the kitchen, Ellen put the box she had been carrying on top of the island. "This is for you." I removed the wrapping paper to uncover a box of crystal wine glasses. "I wanted to replace the ones I broke," she said.

Miles found us sitting on the sofa when he got home from the hospital that evening. Maya had left shortly beforehand, but Ellen had stayed to keep me company. We'd kicked off our shoes and were chatting about everything and nothing. The house had started to look like a home. I'll always be grateful for Ellen's help and the friendship that had started forming that day.

What Ellen doesn't realise and what I would never tell her was that we'd met before. Soon after her life changed forever. It had been a short meeting that she surely didn't remember, as she had much more important things to think about. And even if she did, she'd never think it had been me who stood next to her at the clinic as she looked at her newborn daughter.

Chapter 14

Ellen takes a long sip out of her wine glass. She tucks a glossy strand of hair behind her ear. Her brown eyes stare into the depth of the glass as she twirls the stem round and round.

She has worn the same hairstyle all these years, a neatly parted brown bob that I now know to be expertly coloured every six weeks. Back then, behind the door of my hospital room I turned the driver's licence over in my hand, gazing at her photo. The sophisticated air and the kind brown eyes – her face had already been committed to memory from our brief encounter. Even without the help of the photo on the driving licence, I knew that I would never forget it. The happiness, so clear in her eyes as she stared at her baby daughter would remain in my mind forever.

At first, I didn't know what to do with the driving licence. At the dorm I put it in my underwear drawer and eventually forgot about it. Or at least I told myself that I had. I focused on my studies and tried not to think about the baby I'd given away. Whenever I caught myself wondering what she was doing, whether she had smiled for the first time, if she was happy, I tried to shake the thoughts out of my head. I wanted her to be part of my past, a past that was never to be relived. My only focus was doing well in my studies and getting into law school, earning the money to pay for it, and then earning enough to pay back my student debt. That was my way out.

It was as I was packing before returning back to England that I found it again. I turned it this way and that in my hand, trying to decide if I should throw it out, forget that I'd ever had it and make myself move on. But I couldn't bring myself to do it and in the end I stuffed it in the inside pocket of my duffel bag, where I had hidden everything that reminded me of the attack and its aftermath, unwilling to leave the newspaper cutting at my parents' house. I've since thrown out the bag, hiding everything under my wedding shoes, where I know Miles would never look.

"Have you noticed anything different about Maya lately?" Ellen asks, interrupting my thoughts.

"I don't think so," I respond. Ellen's love for her daughter is intense and leads her to scrutinise every minuscule turn her daughter makes and reads volumes into insignificant actions. Last year it was a new friend that Ellen was not sure about and two months ago all she could talk about was Maya's short-lived vegetarianism. "She seems the same to me. Why do you ask?"

Ellen inhales deeply before taking another sip of wine. "I don't know. She seems different. Distant. Almost as if she can't wait to be out of my sight."

Hiding my face behind my glass of wine, I take a long sip to buy myself some time, consider my words, as I try to control a pang of jealousy and instead focus on what a great mother Ellen is and how much she loves Maya. Still, deep inside there's a desire to tell her to chill out, stop being on Maya's case, stop obsessing about her daughter's results and who she's friends with, start giving her some autonomy. I want to tell her that Maya needs space to be a teenager; to make mistakes, and not have her mother constantly within arm's reach. She's not a baby any more, but Ellen seems not to have noticed. I've seen her looking at her daughter, analysing every small movement, telling her to stand straight, picking non-existent lint off her already spotless sweaters, using her fingers to comb out imaginary knots in the teenager's hair. It feels that whenever Ellen opens her mouth, it's to tell Maya what to do and what not to do.

But I don't go into any of that. It's not my place to give Ellen parenting advice. She will take offence. She spent so many years struggling to become a mother and once Maya came along she seemed terrified of making a mistake. "I only want the best for her," she's told me so many times.

Had I known just how obsessive she is, I might not have made that first trip to the street, back when Miles and I were living in our first flat in Clapham. That Saturday morning, I had no plans for the day. Miles was doing a double shift at the hospital and I had the day to myself. It was a gorgeous day with not a cloud in sight. I needed to leave the tiny flat, get some air. But instead of going for a walk, I got in the car. I told myself that I didn't know where I was going, but that wasn't true. I knew exactly where I was headed, a place that I had looked at on a map many times. An address I'd committed to memory so that I no longer needed to take out Ellen's driving licence to check the details.

For years I'd been resisting the urge to make the trip. I forced myself to push the baby out of my mind. I focused on my studies, on getting the necessary grades, on securing the right internship. I was too busy to think about her. And yet I could never get her sweet face out of my mind. The image haunted me. A desire to see her grew deep inside, one that I could not explain. Instead of fading over time, it grew stronger than me, and I was unable to repress it, like I managed to stifle so many emotions that were inconvenient.

Again and again, I almost turned back. As the car inched forward in the afternoon traffic, I kept telling myself that they might have decided to remain in the

US. Even if they had moved back to England, what were the odds they were still living in that house? I argued with myself that if Ellen recognised me, I could get into serious trouble.

But still, I kept driving, as if pulled by a magnetic force, until I found the right street, lined with big houses and manicured front gardens, with expensive cars parked outside.

I almost drove past Ellen's house without even realising. It was just like all the other houses in the street. Colourful flowers bloomed in pots outside the bright red door and ivy climbed up the brick walls, almost covering the iron house number. Looking at the large structure, I wondered if they'd had any more children.

The next time I had a few hours to myself, I got in the car and headed towards Richmond. I drove with determination until I got to the now familiar turning and then up the street where the house was. I drove at a slow pace, scanning the house, and turned around in the spacious area at the end of the street and left. I made the trip again and again, whenever I had the opportunity.

It was a few months later, during one such trip, that I saw her. She came jumping out of the house as I was driving by, her red hair flying everywhere. My heart skipped a beat. I tried not to stare, but looked at her from the corner of my eyes, yearning to take in every single detail. The white knee socks and the shiny patent black shoes. The light blue dress with a white Peter Pan collar. Most of all, I wanted to get a good look at her face. I wanted to know what she looked like now. But she turned around too quickly, looking up at the house where her mother was standing. Ellen looked past her daughter at the unfamiliar car and I kept on driving.

Ellen is staring into her wineglass, some unsaid anxiety eating at her.

"She's a teenager," I tell her, squeezing her hand.

She bites her lip, twirling the stem until the golden liquid swirls around the glass causing some bubbles to rise to the surface.

"Ellen, is something wrong?" I ask, suddenly worried that there is more to her questioning than her harmless worrying.

She shrugs and takes another sip of her wine. Her glass is quickly emptying and overcome by a sense of protection, I instinctively move the wine bottle slightly further away from her.

"I'm scared of losing her," she finally says, bringing the glass to her mouth again automatically.

"What does that mean? How could you lose Maya?"

When she doesn't respond, I feel a fluttering of panic. "Ellen, what's wrong? Why are you talking about losing Maya? Where would she go?"

"I've always worried that one day Maya will want to track down her birth mother and that I will be cast aside."

"Oh Ellen, you need to stop with these negative thoughts."

Ellen's eyes are downcast and she's back to twirling the wine glass in her hand, round and round and round until a fat drop streams down the side of it. She finally looks up and I see that her eyes are glistening with the threat of tears. "What if she finds her birth mother and they hit it off?"

"Oh, come on, that's never going to happen." As I say the words I secretly hope that Maya wants to find me, even though I could never allow that to happen. "Even if she did find this woman and they do forge a relationship, you'll still be her mother."

"You don't know that."

I want to reassure Ellen, tell her that I have gone to extremes to make sure that the child I gave away would never track me down. That this is what I've promised myself. That even though there are many times when I want to tell Maya who I really am, I never will because I cannot have the past catch up with me. I've got too much to lose. The life I've built for myself could be gone in an instant if my secret was uncovered.

"Maybe her birth mother doesn't want to be found," I say. "Perhaps she's moved on and doesn't want to dwell on the past."

But Ellen is not convinced. "Who wouldn't want to meet their own child? What if she's always regretted giving Maya away? If she's been waiting for her daughter to get in touch?"

"Ellen, I think you might be imagining problems that don't exist?"

And yet, even as I try to reassure her, I know there's truth in her fears. After all, I fought hard to move close by. I still remember the day Miles put down his toothbrush and asked me where I wanted to make our permanent home. I knew exactly where I wanted to live and was more than happy to show him. We got into the car and I drove us straight to the area that was always on my mind.

It took us two years to get the funds together to buy a house. Twice a house on that street came on the market and we had to pass. Each time I tried to convince Miles to take on a bigger mortgage than was prudent. "I love this area," I'd begged. But he remained firm, telling me how irresponsible we'd be to stretch ourselves so thin financially.

We might not have been able to afford it had it not been for Miles inheriting money following the death of both his parents, months from one another. His father was first to pass away. The suddenness of his death following a severe stroke rattled Miles. The situation was made worse by his mother's frail state. She had suffered from dementia for several years; her mental state deteriorating even more after Miles' brother was killed while serving in Afghanistan, until she could barely recognise her own son, her only remaining child. His father had been her caregiver, preferring to keep her in the house they had so many joyful memories of, hoping that the familiar settings might one day help her remember, even if only for a moment. Now we needed to find a place for her, somewhere she'd be taken care of, where she would be kept comfortable and safe. It killed Miles to see how fast she deteriorated after his father was gone. "I'm a doctor and I can't do anything to cure her," he said over and over. We tried to visit as often as we could, but each visit would depress Miles further. "She doesn't even know who she is. What sort of life is this?" he said one day as we were driving back from the nursing home.

Despite the sheer grief, there was some relief when she overdosed on her medication, only hours after we'd last visited her. She was in peace now, I told Miles as he wept the evening we received the news.

A few weeks later, when the rush of daily life started taking the place of the sorrow that filled our hearts, Miles raised the subject of his inheritance. "We should buy a house."

But none of the homes close to the McBride's were for sale. Miles started getting impatient. "Why are you so obsessed with that one street?" he asked in exasperation. Our agent kept pushing other options, and Miles was insisting we make a purchase. "I feel we owe it to my parents to buy a house." I was reluctant. I'd dreamed about living on that street for so long now and refused to consider anywhere else. But I finally had to agree that we couldn't wait forever, especially since we had just found out I was pregnant.

And then, just like a miracle, on the day when we were about to make an offer on another property, the agent called. "A house is coming on the market in the street you love. Do you want to see it?"

I was running out before I even hung up the phone. Miles couldn't make it, and warned me not to get too excited. "We're on the verge of making an offer. Why change course now?" He made perfect sense. Except I knew I could not pass on this opportunity to live so close to her.

The house was perfect, as I knew it would be. It was large and airy, with a sweeping staircase and a big garden. The kitchen needed to be modernised and there was some painting that needed to be done, but I didn't care about the cosmetics. The asking price was right too, less expensive than the one we were thinking of buying. "Nasty divorce," the agent whispered, even though we were alone in the house.

Standing in the doorway, I looked around the spacious hall. It couldn't have been a coincidence that it came on the market just as we were ready to make a purchase. I knew this was the house I wanted to live in, the one I wanted to turn into a home, where I wanted to raise my new child. I called Miles. "I love it. Please come and see it and let's make an offer quickly before anyone else pounces."

"Why are you so adamant to live there? What is it about that street? Is there something you're not telling me?"

I laughed nervously and shrugged off his questions. "Of course not. I just like it."

Reluctantly Miles agreed to see the house that evening and I went back with him, knowing that he might need some convincing. "Isn't it perfect?" I gushed.

He was noncommittal, walking around the rooms pointing at the work that was required. The paint was peeling and the garden was overgrown. But even he could spot a good deal. "The sellers are very motivated," our agent said.

"Please, I love this house," It was one of the few times I wouldn't let him have his way.

His eyes were kind as he looked at me for a long time before nodding. "Ok," he said. "Let's make an offer." I jumped up and hugged him tightly, kissing him on the lips, oblivious of the agent still in the room.

Just three months after I first saw the house, it was ready to move in to. We had dug into our savings to get it exactly the way we wanted it. It was perfect. New furniture was delivered and we packed up our small flat and hauled our multiple boxes to the new place. And then an angel by the name of Ellen came to help me unpack.

Over the years I'd grown to know her better. Ellen has the uncanny ability to always be there when I need her. I will always be grateful that she dropped everything to stay with me the first time Julian had a fever while Miles was away at a conference. The first time she popped over after I got home from work took me by surprise. I didn't know what to make out of it and had feared that she had figured out who I was. But I've started to look forward to her impromptu visits. Beside the company, it gives me the opportunity to find out more about Maya.

She's still twirling her wine glass, stopping every now and then to take a sip. "Every time I see a woman looking at Maya, I think it's her, coming back to take her away."

She pauses and inhales deeply. "I think Maya is actively looking for her birth mother," she finally says.

The need to know more bubbles inside me, making my heart beat faster. I grip the counter edge as I try to stop myself leaning in too close to Ellen. "How do you know? Has she told you?"

Ellen continues toying with her wine glass, taking small sips every few seconds. I'm holding my breath, waiting for her to answer my question, to tell me what has fuelled this suspicion.

But she doesn't. We sit in silence, me replaying Maya's questions about tracking down Chloe's birth parents in my head, and fighting the urge to confide in Ellen.

"What's been happening?" I probe instead.

Ellen's eyes fill with tears and she purses her lips, "She's been researching online for a while now."

"How do you know?" Fearing that Ellen will see my flushed face, I stand up, busying myself filling a glass of water. I take it down in one gulp. The cold liquid steadies me for a second. Then panic bubbles up again and I take deep breaths to try and control my escalating anxiety as the fear of being found out for who I am intensifies. It was crazy to walk in to this, yet I did it consciously and I use that prop as I struggle to remain calm.

Ellen's hand is shaking as she grips her wine glass. Reaching over, I take the glass away, clasping her hand tightly. "Ellen, what's happening?" My overarching need to extract more details is intensifying and Ellen looks like she'll collapse under the pressure any moment.

"How do you know that Maya's been searching for her birth parents?" I dig when she doesn't respond. "Tell me; maybe I can help."

"I was using the computer and saw her browsing history," Ellen says in a small voice. "She was searching for ways adoptees can contact their birth parents."

My heart skips a beat and I turn around so that Ellen cannot see my face, fiddling around with another glass of water. Conflicting emotions rage inside me. The weird pleasure in her wanting to find me is overshadowed by my fear of what Maya will discover, and Ellen, and Miles. That she will find out about my link to John Larkin, uncover the secret I've been guarding right in front of her. "Has she mentioned her biological parents?"

"No." Her voice is so small that I have to strain to hear her. Then she looks up and stares me right in the eyes. "Has she said anything to you?"

"No, why would she tell me?"

"She spends so much time here. And she looks up to you, is always going on about how you manage to balance your career with two kids. Thought maybe she'd tell you what's on her mind."

I shake my head, glad it's the truth. "She has mentioned her biological parents a couple of times, but not recently." And it always seemed very superficial, just mentions in passing.

"Maybe she was just exploring the possibility and isn't really thinking about doing anything," I add. "You know, like when I look at a Chanel handbag online. I'm never going to buy it, but I still catch myself looking." I'm trying to relieve the tension, lighten the moment.

Ellen gives me a watery smile, but I can tell that she doesn't really believe me. "This was not a one-time search." She lowers her eyes, but not before I can see the complete and utter devastation behind them, the fear of being replaced.

When she looks up, her eyes shine with the tears she's been holding back. "The thing is, she has the right to know. I can't stop her."

Part of me is desperate to change the conversation. But this is the opportunity to find out what Ellen knows. "Do you know anything about the biological parents?" I look at her expectantly, then away, fearful that she can see through me. My heart is beating wildly, and I channel my court professional self as I wait for her to answer.

"Just that she was twenty-one and in college. She didn't want to meet us and we didn't ask any questions, risk jinxing everything. It felt like the stars had aligned perfectly with Tom getting that job in New York and us starting to pursue adoption there. We could barely believe it when our lawyer told us about the birth mother."

I catch my breath to stop myself from sighing in relief. Taking small sips of water, I hide my face behind the large tumbler.

After a pause Ellen continues. "I never told you about the girl at the hospital," she says, and the hairs on the back of my neck stand up again in fear. Putting the glass down, I don't even bother to look where it lands on the coaster as I stare intently at her, willing her to continue but not wanting to say anything lest my voice betrays my fears. I know exactly what she's going to say, but wait patiently until she continues.

"I was looking at Maya through the window. They hadn't let us hold her yet, just pointed at her in the nursery. I was standing there, mesmerised that this was my little girl. That I was finally a mother." Ellen takes a deep breath before continuing. "And this girl came and stood next to me."

Every detail of the short encounter bears down on my memory. Ellen had barely looked at me, her eyes riveted on the baby. But maybe she remembers more than I hope, just like Miles remembers how I looked that night on campus.

"She stood next to me, staring through the window," Ellen continues. "She told me her sister was having a baby. I dropped my purse and she bent down to help me pick up my things and I saw the hospital bracelet on her right hand."

My eyes are wide open. Ellen stops. My head is about to explode until I remember to breathe again.

"I've always thought it was Maya's birth mother, coming to take a last look at her baby. And what was even stranger is that she sounded English."

Chapter 15

"Are you ok?" Miles asks, a worried look on his face, as he bends to pick up the sharp pieces of the plate I had just dropped.

Nodding, I squat next to him, gingerly picking up a shard of shattered porcelain. "I'm fine, just got startled. Why don't you get the door while I clean this up?"

Miles sits back on his heels, looking at me. For a moment I think he's going to assault me with questions, but then he stands up and walks out of the kitchen. "Hello, thank you so much for coming at such short notice," I hear him say to the babysitter.

This Monday morning is more frantic than usual. Leah woke up with a fever, her skin scalding hot to the touch. I longed to stay home, nurse my daughter back to health, make sure she has everything she needs. But I cannot miss work. Knowing Maya would be at school, I'd quickly called a replacement.

All weekend I haven't slept for worry, perturbed by Ellen's revelation. Even though she doesn't remember what the girl at the hospital looked like, I'm terrified that one day something will jog her memory and she'll realise it was me. I might have changed my name, dyed my hair, worn glasses, but I couldn't change my features.

How could my younger self have made such a stupid mistake? Even back then, when I stood next to Ellen at the hospital, I knew that I was risking getting caught. But I needed to take one last look at the baby. A crazy, deep down part of me wanted to say goodbye.

Shaking my head, I try to rid myself of these thoughts as I throw the debris in the bin, I straighten my suit, then pick up my bag and briefcase and follow Miles outside.

"I'm so late," he says.

"Shit, shit, shit," he shouts, banging his fist on the top of his car.

"What happened?"

"A fuckin' flat tyre," he groans.

"Get in, I'll drive you to the hospital." A glance at the dashboard clock confirms that we're running late. Despite my hatred of speeding, I press my foot down. As I'm about to switch lanes, I hear a horn blast in my ear and another car whizzes past. Gasping loudly, I quickly turn the steering wheel in the other direction, veering dangerously into the other lane.

"Liz, what the hell?" Miles shouts.

"It's ok," I respond in the most soothing voice I can muster.

"What's happening to you? You're really jumpy this morning."

"Nothing," I lie. "Just worried about Leah."

"You've been like this all weekend." I can feel Miles' eyes on me but I don't turn to look at him. Instead I concentrate on breathing, allowing the air to fill my lungs and calm me down.

"No I haven't." But I know it's true. Despite my fears, my mind is running wild with imagining a future where Maya is so much more than my neighbour's child.

*

"How did the doctor's appointment go?" I ask Chloe as we ride in the lift. I found her standing in the lobby of my office building looking lost and slightly shifty, her hands twisting in that same baggy grey knit.

"That's what I came to speak to you about."

The lift seems to take forever to get to our floor, making several stops to let people in or out. Finally, Chloe is seated opposite my desk. She doesn't look well, and I recognise the pallor in her face. "Are you nauseous again?"

She nods, then reaches into her bag and takes out an almost empty packet of crackers and starts nibbling on one. Pouring her a glass of water, I wait for the colour to return to her face.

"I went to the doctor yesterday," she finally says. Nodding, I cock my head to one side, willing her to continue. "Well, I'm pregnant."

"Did the doctor say how far along?"

"Three months. The doctor gave me this." She hands me an envelope.

It's exactly what I was hoping to hear, the length of the pregnancy fitting with the rape timeline. Chewing on my lower lip, I force myself not to say anything that shows I'm pleased at the development. She is still sitting motionless, looking right at me, and I feel the weight of her expectation. "Ok, that wasn't a complete surprise," I finally say.

"Yes, I was certain." Then, her tone changes, becoming sharper. "Perhaps people will believe me now."

Pulling a chair close to her, I sit down and squeeze her arm. Right now she needs the parent figure she's never had. "I know this pregnancy has come as a shock to you," I tell her as gently as I can. "However, this will hopefully back up the rape allegations."

"What do you mean 'hopefully'?" Her voice rises with every syllable.

Taking a deep breath, I look for the best way to word my reply. "We need to do a paternity test to confirm that Ben is the baby's father," I explain.

"So, you still don't believe me!"

"Chloe," I start gently. "It doesn't matter whether I believe you or not. What's important is that the jury believes you. We cannot go to court and say that you're pregnant with Ben's baby without having unequivocal proof of this."

"Whatever." She purses her lips and turns her head to stare out of the window.

Returning to my desk, I open the envelope, finding a detailed report about Chloe's examination. I'm still reading through it when she says, in a small voice: "I'm scared."

The confession takes me by surprise. She always seems so invincible, as if nothing gets to her, and her outside self is a stranger to what's really going on. But as I know from my own experience, self-control is deceptive.

"What are you scared of?" I ask as kindly as I can, remembering that she is barely more than a child.

"Having a baby, looking after him by myself. Am I even able to do that? What if I'm a horrible mother? It's not like I've had any role models." The fiery sparkle that's always in her eyes seems spent.

"Why would you think that?"

Standing up, I again walk towards her, leaning against the desk next to where she's sitting. "It's normal to be scared. Every woman worries about being a good mother. But you'll do great." I move closer to her, put my hand on her arm. "Did the doctor explain your options?"

"Yes, he talked about termination for ages," she answers.

"And what do you think?" I'm transported back to the time when I was the one faced with a similar decision. Only, unlike Chloe, I had pushed the problem out of my mind until it was too late to act on it.

She doesn't respond and I realise I'm holding my breath for her answer. "I don't know," she finally says. "It just doesn't seem right to me. And anyway, wouldn't that be getting rid of the proof we need?"

Our eyes meet and I feel a kinship with her. She is being pragmatic, seeing the full picture, refusing to allow emotions to cloud her judgement. Not many people I know are able to separate their feelings and look at how they can work a problem to their advantage. It fills me with hope that we can win this case.

"Take some time to think about it." I take a pause, trying to find the best way to verbalise what I need to say next. "But please talk to me before you take action so we can do whatever tests are necessary to establish Ben is the father. And keep this to yourself for now until we've agreed on the plan."

*

Any compassion I felt for Chloe flew out of the window two days later.

"It was only a photo. Why are you being so mean?" Her accusatory words shock me. I thought we were on track now, I thought we were finally working together, but she has gone way off course.

Clenching my fists, I squeeze them in my lap. The heat rises to my face. "Mean? You don't know what mean is. If you don't listen to me and end up behind bars, you'll soon experience what mean is."

"See," she answers, her tone calm, seemingly unbothered by the prospect of ending up in prison. "That's mean."

It takes me a few moments to regain my composure. "I specifically told you not to have any contact with Ben, to tell me if he tried to as much as look in your direction. I could not have been more clear."

"It was no big deal, just a photo." Closing my eyes, I bite my lip, stopping myself from snapping at her.

The day had started on a bad note. Jennifer called me this morning as I was heading into work. "George

Winters wants to see you in his office urgently." As I headed to his office I prayed he was finally persuaded to drop the charges.

"Sit down," George said as I was ushered into his cluttered office.

"How are you, George?" I asked, taking a seat across from him.

"Pissed off."

I said nothing while waiting for him to elaborate.

George sized me up as though I'd truly disappointed him. "Why didn't you tell me Chloe Wilson is pregnant?"

A lump formed in my throat when I realised that my plan to keep Chloe's pregnancy quiet for the time being was ruined. "I only just found out about it myself."

"When exactly did you find out?"

"She had the pregnancy confirmed by a doctor two days ago and told me yesterday."

George didn't respond but continued to look at me through narrowed eyes, as if he was trying to decide whether to believe me or not.

"May I ask how you found out?"

Grunting, he opened one of the files in front of him, closed it again and handed it to me. "That's a copy of the text message she sent Ben yesterday."

Reaching over, I took the file. Inside was a sole sheet of paper with what looked like a screen shot from a mobile phone. An ultrasound photo of what I could only assume was Chloe's baby was plain to see under the words "Meet your child".

Closing my eyes, I inhaled deeply, counting backwards from ten. I didn't want George to sense my anger at Chloe's irresponsible move. "I was planning to officially inform you of this." The lie didn't bother me as much as how Chloe's revelation would impact my strategy. "Now that you know, what's the next step?"

"I need proof of this pregnancy," he responded gruffly.

"Fuck!" I exclaimed under my breath as soon as I walked out of the prosecutor's office. But once behind my desk I forced myself to focus on the rest of my caseload, looking for a distraction from the morning's frustrating turn of events.

"Why did you send that photo to Ben?" I asked Chloe as soon as she walked into my office.

She stared at me for a few moments before shrugging. "Oh. I wanted him to know what he did," she finally said.

"Why would you do that? I told you not to say anything. Can't you listen to me for once? I'm only trying to help you here."

Her forehead knotted into a frown and I readied myself for her to strike back. Instead, she'd simply asked: "Why is it so wrong to tell him?"

Burying my face in both hands, I shook my head in exasperation. "I was working on a plan to use this to our advantage." I gesticulated towards her stomach. "I can't believe you texted him. You've ruined my strategy."

"Why all the secrecy? The prosecution is going to find out eventually. Why is it such a big deal for them to know?"

My nostrils flared as I glared at her through narrowed eyes. Despite my anger, I felt this overpowering instinct to protect her. I needed to be there for her. She couldn't see the consequences like I could. She couldn't be left all alone, like I was fifteen years ago.

*

The letterbox is full. A couple of thick magazines take up most of the space. A bunch of marketing materials. Coupons for the new pizza place. An advert for a new childcare centre. An estate agent offering his services in case we decide to sell the house.

And among all the junk, a plain white envelope with my name and address written on it in black ink. I don't need to open it to know what it is, who it is from. My hands trembling, I slip it into my bag, pushing it towards the bottom, underneath everything else.

It is hours later, once the children are asleep and Miles is sprawled on the sofa reading, that I dare take it out of its hiding place. Holding the bag tightly against my side, I rush upstairs and go straight into the walk-in closet. Sitting down on the stool we use to put our shoes on, I rummage in my bag and fish it out. The envelope is crumpled from my hasty attempts at concealment. But still, there is no doubt what it is.

Fiddling with the corners of the envelope, I consider not opening it. Throwing it in the bin. Tossing it out of my life. It will be like all the others.

The first letter had arrived five years after John Larkin's death. Miles and I had just moved to a new flat. We were so busy that we rarely bothered to check the letterbox. It was a new beginning and I was walking on air, like I hadn't for years. Until one day the building superintendent stopped me while I was walking up the three flights of stairs and handed me an enormous pile of mail. "The postman said there's no more space," he said.

Miles wasn't home yet. Inside our tiny living room, I sat down and started sorting through the post. A couple of cards wishing us well. An invitation for a university get together. A discount voucher for my favourite clothing store. Then there was the crisp white envelope with my name written in a handwriting I didn't recognise and no sender's address.

Tearing open the envelope, I'd taken out the plain sheet of paper.

I FINALLY FOUND YOU,

was written in block capitals.

I KNOW WHAT YOU DID AND YOU'RE GOING TO PAY.

Immediately I knew what this was about. It had to be him. Or her. Terry. He, or she, knew what I had done. And they had found me. I wasn't safe. Neither was Miles. What else did they know about me? They must have been following me if they knew where I lived. I had not even changed my driving licence yet.

The fear was so intense that for a moment I considered confiding in Miles. Finally telling him everything. Perhaps I should go to the police, report the threat. Tell them about that night and the phone call to someone called Terry.

But instead I put the letter back in the envelope and folded it into square after smaller square. Standing on shaking legs, I had gone into the bedroom and dug in the back of the wardrobe for a hiding place. I found my wedding shoes box. Taking them out, I stared down at the newspaper clippings that I had saved and Ellen's driving licence.

Now closing my eyes tightly, I take a deep breath. Before I can change my mind, I tear the envelope open and take out the plain white sheet.

YOUR TIME IS RUNNING OUT.

Tears sting my eyes as the fear that someone, somewhere, knows my secret overwhelms me once again. But there is nothing I can do. I put it in the box with the others and push it out of sight.

*

The redness is blinding. It's everywhere. I look around and everything is red. I strain my eyes to take a closer look. The red is not uniform. In some places it's dark, more like crimson, in others it's very light, pink. It looks like paint has been smeared everywhere. In thick brush strokes, each movement leaving its marks. I try to focus on different parts to get a better idea of what I'm looking at. But I can't concentrate. It seems like everything is spinning. I'm falling into a sea of red. The liquid is warm, and bubbles around me. I reach out, my arms flailing around, trying to grab at something that will stop me from falling. The liquid is so thick it feels like it's enveloping me, sucking me in. I hear a laugh. I look towards where the sound came from, but now it's coming from the other side. I turn my neck. I want to scream but no sound comes out. I hear the laugh again. And again. And again. It's surrounding me.

And then I see a pair of green eyes looking at me. Filled with sneering and hate. I can feel them drilling right into my soul, letting me know that I will never be free from the torment that I'm experiencing right now. That anywhere I go he will find me. And he will make me pay. He laughs again and I scream.

"Lizzy," I hear the voice in the distance. Hands on my shoulders. I scream again, louder, in desperation, wanting to shake them off, not wanting him to touch me. But I can't move, can't run out of his reach and I'm starting to panic. "Lizzy, wake up!"

Miles is hovering above me when I jolt awake. In the dim light coming from the open window I can see the look of concern on my husband's face. He is staring at me, stroking my face. "You're ok," he says gently, taking me into his arms and hugging me tightly. "You just had a bad dream."

Craving safety, I surrender to his embrace. But I'm still rattled. Beads of sweat cling to my chest and I'm trembling in fear, the stress of the previous day reaching a crescendo with the dream, leaving me exhausted from the paralysing fear I feel.

"Mummy?" Snapping out of my thoughts, I turn around and look at the small form in the doorway. It's Julian. He must have heard my screams. Waves of guilt wash over me for having scared my son.

"Come here, baby." I reach out for him. He clambers into the bed next to me, looking at me with inquiring eyes. "Mummy had a bad dream. But I'm ok now that you're here." Hugging him closely, I savour his warm body against mine.

Miles returns with a glass of water. I hadn't even seen him leave the room. "She's asleep," he answers my unsaid question. Taking the tumbler from his hands, I mouth my gratitude and take a gulp of water. I realise I'm parched and drain the glass.

Julian has fallen asleep next to me. He's snuggled close to my body and I don't have the heart to wake him up and take him back to his room. Looking at Miles, I attempt a shrug. He smiles, and gets into bed, on the other side of Julian. "Are you ok?" he whispers.

I nod. But I'm not. I'm rattled. The dream always terrifies me, reminds me of my weakness, of all I've concealed and how the longer I bury it the darker the hole I've dug for myself gets. I know I won't be able to go back to sleep, but don't want to get up in case I disturb Julian.

"You're safe, I'll make sure of that." Miles clasps my hand across Julian's chest.

"I know," I respond softly. "I just hate the darkness."

For hours I lie in bed, rubbing the scar on my hand, staring up at the ceiling, wishing the time to pass. For the sun to rise and for the darkness to be replaced by light. More than sixteen years have passed, and there's not one day that goes by when I don't remember that night. It's etched in my memory like carvings on prehistoric walls that have endured centuries. And I know that it doesn't matter how much time goes by, how many changes I make to my life, I will never forget that horrible night.

Neither do I want to. Every decision I've taken in the past decade and a half has been carefully weighed to ensure that what happened back then can remain my secret. It is, I know, the only way I can continue living the life I have built for myself, continue being seen as a loving mother, daughter and wife, and as a professional in the law.

The moment the darkness outside starts to dissolve, I get out of bed, careful not to disturb Miles and Julian, knowing that the odd weekend off is the only time my husband can sleep in. Wrapping a robe around me, I glance at the two of them, marvelling at the way they sleep in the exact same pose, their right arm curved above their heads, their legs spread wide.

I tiptoe downstairs. I fire up the coffee machine and make myself a large cup of coffee.

Leaning against the counter, I take sip after scalding sip. A noise comes from outside and I spill coffee as I turn, burning my hands.

It's unlike me to be this clumsy. My favourite dressing gown is stained, meeting a couple of old stains I made when I last had a rough patch several years ago, when already overwhelmed by the stress of my first proper legal job, I had started feeling my resolve to never share my past start to weaken. The feelings of desperation and loneliness threatened to overcome my rational mind and I came close to confiding in Miles. We had just started living together and I longed for our lives to be as perfect as I dreamed they could be. I desperately needed an outlet and remember thinking attending AA meetings might help. Anxiety ate at me when I walked in that first day, my hands shaking so much that I spilled coffee all over the front of my white satin shirt. Flustered, I'd sat at the back and listened to others tell their stories. It took a while for me to muster the courage to stand up in front of my peers.

"I'm Elizabeth, and I'm an alcoholic," I said. Because I couldn't tell them I'm a killer.

Chapter 16

Miles walks downstairs yawning and stretching. His brown hair is sticking up and he has two parallel sleep marks on his right cheek. "You ok?" he mouths from behind the kids and I nod.

"Was it the same nightmare?"

"Yes," I say softly, looking at the children, not wanting them to hear the conversation.

He moves towards me. "Please, speak to someone. You look exhausted, completely drained. You need to sleep without nightmares."

"I'm fine." It's the same mantra over and over.

"No, you're not. People who are 'fine' don't wake up in the middle of the night screaming."

"I don't want to talk about this now," I hiss back at him. Instead I turn towards the children, sitting at the kitchen island eating their breakfast. "What do you want to do today?" I ask. It's a beautiful day." There's a mist in the air that's a prelude of warm weather in a few hours.

"Disney World!" Leah exclaims, rocking forwards and backwards excitedly.

"Not today, sweetie," I say. "What about the park?"

We spend the day at Richmond Park, running around, looking for deer. My phone beeps and I sit on a bench to answer an email. Leah's laugh interrupts my thoughts and I look at my family, feeling my whole body relax. The weak sun feels blissful on my face and I close my eyes for a second. I must have drifted off because the cold hand on my arm jolts me upright. It's Leah, looking at me with big brown eyes.

"Mummy, I'm hungry."

"Little hungry or big hungry?" I ask, pulling her towards me.

"Big hungry."

We head to our local pub for lunch. The waitress brings our food and Leah reaches out for the ketchup bottle, turning it on top of her plate, and squeezing with both hands. The red liquid squirts out, hitting the plate and splashing across the table and onto my white shirt.

Taking a deep breath, I will myself to remain calm, trying to stop the scream that's threatening to escape my throat. My breathing is quick and shallow and I can feel my heartbeat speeding up. It's just ketchup, I tell myself. But as I look down at the dense red liquid splattered all over my chest, I start shaking. My mind goes back to that night and I see his face in front of me, his green eyes open in shock. I feel the warm blood pulsing from his gaping wound and I'm transported away from the here and now, from the happiness of being with my family, back to the place of my nightmares.

It must only have been a couple of seconds, but the panic feels like it lasts for hours. Miles' hand reaches out for mine, reminding me that I'm safe. Closing my eyes tightly, I work on composing myself. When I open them I see Leah staring at me, the plastic bottle still held upside down in her hands, dripping ketchup onto her plate. Forcing a smile, I take the ketchup bottle from her, trying to steady my trembling hands. Then, I excuse myself and go to the bathroom, wanting nothing more than to remove my sodden shirt. I have a thick cardigan in my bag I'd removed earlier. Locking myself in a stall, I try to avoid glancing at the mirror but my eyes go exactly where I don't want them to and I look at the angry red spatters all over my chest. My stomach lurches. I quickly take off the shirt and throw it in the bin. I wipe a few drops of ketchup from my neck and arms and put on my cardigan, buttoning it up with fingers that are still trembling. Taking a deep breath, I walk back to the table and sit down, intent on continuing to enjoy our meal and the rest of our day.

Nobody mentions the incident and we finish our food and go back to the car.

Later that evening, when the children are in bed, Miles orders Chinese. We sit on the sofa watching comedy reruns. Miles laughs loudly at something on the TV and takes a swig of his beer.

We're relaxed so I'm caught completely unawares when Miles mutes the TV and turns towards me. "Liz, you need to do something about your phobia of red."

I freeze, the chopsticks midway to my mouth, and remain immobile for a couple of seconds, before I force myself to snap back into the here and now and lower the utensils back into my bowl.

"We're having a nice evening," I say. "Why do you always have to bring this up?"

"It's not healthy to live with constant fear. It was just ketchup, Liz. You acted as if someone was being murdered in front of you."

"Oh come on, you're being overly dramatic."

"I'm not." Miles' voice is softer. "You should see the fear in your eyes. It frightens the kids."

I remember Julian's scared face when he heard me screaming last night and Leah's concern that I'd be mad when she spilled ketchup. I want to scream at the unfairness of his comment. He's using the children to make me see sense, guilt trip me into taking action.

"Don't threaten me with the kids!" I exclaim, leaning away from him.

"You're the one who wakes them up when you start screaming in the middle of the night. You're the one who freaked out at the sight of ketchup."

He stands up and storms out of the room, leaving me sitting there. Shame and sadness engulf me. Tears well in my eyes and I blink vigorously to stop them from rolling down my cheeks, not wanting to appear so weak.

I have to resolve to change. To overcome this fear of red. To try my best to be normal again. I've allowed myself the indulgence of this fear for far too long, and yet my secret is still safe from the people I love. Ellen has told me as much. It can't be beyond me to take action to put my fears behind me.

Chapter 17

"Maya is here to see you," Jennifer says, poking her head into my office.

"Maya? What's she doing here? Let her in, let her in."

Saving the document I was tweaking, I stand up and walk to the door, anxious to find out what brought Maya to my office. My body erupts in goosebumps as soon as I see her, standing there, leaning against Jennifer's desk, her red hair contrasting against the mostly monochrome office colours.

"Maya, what happened?" My mind is whirring with different scenarios. "Is everything all right? Why are you here?"

She continues looking around, taking everything in, her eyes skimming every corner of my office. "Sorry Mrs P, didn't mean to intrude."

"It's ok, here, come in and sit down. What happened?"

"Nothing happened." She follows me to the sofa in the corner of the room and takes a seat. "I wanted to see where you work."

Sitting next to her, I turn round to face her and take stock of her appearance, examining her for any clues. Her flaming red hair is escaping from the thin Alice band, soft tendrils falling around her face. Her dark green sweater has clearly been ironed. Her skinny black jeans fit her flawlessly. And her black boots have been buffed to shiny perfection. She is the image of a privileged girl.

It strikes me that I rarely see her outside the confines of our little street. Sitting here, in my office, she seems different. More grown up, more sophisticated. It's almost as if she left her real self back in the suburbs. Or maybe this is her real self. Despite my attempts to get close to her, I still don't feel like I know her properly and my heart aches at what could have been.

Maya doesn't flinch as I examine her. She cocks her head to one side and grins at me. It's the innocent smile that I'm accustomed to. But somehow, in this setting, it seems different and it bothers me that I cannot put my finger on what's really going through her mind.

"What brought you to the city?"

"I came shopping with some friends. I've never seen your office so I decided to swing by, come see you in action."

Why do I get the feeling that there's more to this visit?

"Does your mum know you're here?"

"No, well, yes, she knows I'm in the city, not here specifically. It was more of an impromptu visit." She crosses her legs at the heel, a gesture I've seen Ellen do a million times, I note with an irrational stab of jealousy. "I hope you don't mind," she adds quickly, biting at her nails.

"Not at all." I feel a simple joy to see Maya. I always do.

She continues looking around my office, taking her time to glance in every direction. Her eyes settle on the big mahogany desk, normally perfectly organised, but right now scattered with documents, stationery and coffee cups. Books are open on my desk instead of neatly lined on the shelves. The clutter embarrasses me. I don't want Maya to see me in any way less than perfect.

"So, this is where you work." She stands up and walks to my desk, picking up a glass paperweight, a gift from a client. There are no other trinkets, family photos, good luck charms on display. I keep it sparse and impersonal. I follow her with my eyes as she continues to look through the piles of paper on my desk.

For a moment I allow myself to think about what could have been. Maya stopping at my office after school, talking about our days, before heading back home together. But I quickly shake my head to get rid of the fantasy. Our lives would have been nothing like this had I decided to keep her. Even with Mum and Dad's help, the odds of finishing university and going to law school were remote. Chances are I would have an entry-level job, probably two, and still be struggling to make ends meet.

Her green eyes glisten as she continues to look around my office and I'm transported back to the first time I saw him, when he seemed so kind and helpful rather than the monster he turned into. A shiver runs down my spine, but instead of pure fear I also feel regret. How could I be so naive as to think that I could walk away from a baby and never look back? Never want to see her again. Not long to know what happened to her, how she's doing.

Maya is still circling my desk. She leans over to touch one of the documents and I cringe, not wanting her to change the page, disrupt my train of thought. It's almost like she senses my apprehension, as if I somehow managed to communicate my fear without saying anything, because she backs away and turns around to face me.

"What are you working on?" she asks.

"I have a few cases right now. That's why there's all this mess."

"Are you still working on that girl's case?"

"Chloe? Yes. We're preparing for trial."

She comes back to sit next to me, closer than she was earlier. The smell of soap mingled with washing detergent enters my nostrils and I feel this enormous urge to hug her. Take her in my arms and stroke her face. Play with her red hair, twirl the strands around my fingers. Be close to Maya in a way that I have never been, probably never will be.

"Do you think I'd make a good barrister?"

"Is that what you want to be?" Maybe genetics is stronger than I thought, perhaps my love for the law was passed on to her. Without wanting it I feel a surge of pride.

"I don't know. Maybe. I don't really know what I want to do yet. Figured this could be an option."

"So, you don't want to take over your dad's firm?"

"What? Be an accountant? No way! I'm awful with numbers."

"What about a teacher like your mum? You're good with kids."

"Meh, I don't know. I'm good with your kids because they're great. But to be with new children every year. Don't think that's for me."

I sense an opportunity that I cannot let slip, a way to spend more time with Maya. "You could come and spend a few days at the office, shadow me, understand how we do things, see if it's something that excites you."

"Really? I could do that?"

"Yes, of course." Inside I'm bursting with excitement and disbelief at the fantastic opportunity. Surely even Ellen will understand that this is for Maya's benefit, help her make decisions for her future. She wouldn't read more into it.

"Maybe I can come in the summer holidays, when I'm not watching Julian and Leah…"

My hands are almost trembling and I swallow hard to make sure my voice is steady. "That would work. Or even before, maybe after school? Perhaps when my parents are visiting and are watching the children."

It seems like there's another question on Maya's lips, perhaps the one she came here to ask me. But a knock comes at the door. "Your three o'clock is here," Jennifer says.

My heart sinks as reality calls, cutting short this unexpected visit. I fight the urge to brush off my next meeting, indulge this new idea of Maya shadowing me here, and me helping her learn the ropes. She's still leaning against my desk, in no apparent hurry to leave. But I know it's not a good idea to seem too eager.

"Give me two minutes," I tell Jennifer and she closes the door behind her.

Standing up, I walk towards my desk. "I'm sorry but I have to get back to work now," I tell her. "Let's figure out a day when you can come over. If you like it, you can come back. I can even see if there are any internships for the summer."

"Sure." She straightens up and starts to leave. "See you soon."

As she opens the door, she comes face to face with Chloe. Maya pauses as she walks past the other teenager and looks at her, a head to toe sweep that takes in every inch of the other girl, something I've seen Ellen do on countless occasions as she evaluates every person she meets. Chloe's chin goes up another millimetre, a gesture so subtle that anyone else might have missed it. The two look at each other, squaring each other up in an instant. I can't help but notice the differences as well as the similarities. Chloe's clothes look nothing like Maya's expensive ones. But somehow she makes up for her old garments with not a hair out of place. Although certainly not manicured, her nails are neatly trimmed, as opposed to Maya's jagged edges. Her posture is straight and regal in contrast to Maya's slightly slouched shoulders.

"Goodbye Mrs P."

Maya gives me a smile, and I'm left with the uncanny feeling I've no idea what she's thinking. I nod at her and summon Chloe into my office.

*

"This was just delivered for you," Jennifer says as she walks into my office the following Monday and hands me a large envelope marked 'urgent'.

"Thank you. It's Chloe's paternity test." My breathing quickens slightly as I rummage in my drawer for a letter opener. Impatient when I'm unable to find it immediately, I use a pen to tear the envelope open, pulling out the stapled sheaf of papers. Looking up, I see Jennifer sitting upright in her chair, her neck craned towards me, her eyes wide open as she bites her lower lip. Taking a deep breath, I start reading the report.

"Aaaaah," I sigh loudly. "Thank God."

"Is it his baby?"

"Yes. Can you get me George Winters on the line?"

Nodding, Jennifer stands up and leaves my office, and I take the time to read through the document again, careful to digest every word. My phone beeps.

"George. I just received the paternity report."

"Yes, I got it as well."

When he doesn't elaborate further, I continue: "Now we know it's his baby. Surely this changes the whole story."

"I still have to consult my medical experts," he says.

"George, what are you talking about? You chose the lab that ran the test and the results are unequivocal. You cannot decide to question its authenticity now."

"I need to consult the experts," he repeats.

"George, this proves she wasn't lying about the rape."

"No, it doesn't," he says firmly. "This only proves that they had sex, but not that he raped her."

"What about the fact that she's only fifteen? And he's an adult. That's a crime." My voice is inching higher with each syllable as the urge to fight for Chloe threatens to overwhelm me.

"Elizabeth, for the third time, I'm going to consult with the medical experts before determining the next steps."

Hanging up, I put my head into my hands. That's how Jennifer finds me a minute later. "Your ten o'clock is here."

Nodding, I stand up and walk towards the door, ready to greet my next client.

*

Despite my schedule, I am still determined to keep my promise to Miles and overcome my fear of red, if only to get him off my back. I even go as far as watching gory movies, to try and desensitise myself to blood.

The next step is to face my aversion to red food and master a proper Italian tomato sauce. On Friday I leave work early and stop at Whole Foods on the way home.

Maya is cross-legged on the floor, her back resting against the sofa. Leah is sitting in her lap and Julian is cuddled next to her, his hand on her knee. She's reading to them and the three are so absorbed they don't hear me walk in. It gives me a few seconds to look at them without being noticed. Maya's soft voice is calming even to my tattered nerves, the singalong tone making me, for a second, forget the constant fear of being found out. The worry that's never far from my brain, any small trigger bringing it to the fore.

The clouds shift and a burst of light comes in from the window, catching Maya's red hair and creating a halo around her face. Julian is staring at the book, following the words that Maya is pointing to as she reads. Leah is transfixed, her lips slightly open as she stares at her sister.

The thought begins to bathe my mind in a familiar fantasy, and I have to physically shake my head to shrug it off, forcing myself to think of Maya as the neighbour's daughter, my children's sitter.

Maybe the carrier bags rustled or perhaps I'm breathing too heavily because three pairs of eyes turn to look at me, interrupting my silent observation. A grin spreads on Leah's face and she screams: "Mummy you're home!"

Julian is more subtle in his enthusiasm. I sit down on the sofa behind him and ruffle his hair. "What are you reading?" Maya makes to hand me the book. Shaking my head, I encourage her to keep going.

Watching Maya's lips open and close as she continues to tell the story, her free hand stroking Leah's cheek, I have a momentary urge to tell Maya everything, to try and have a bigger presence in her life. I know this is impossible. The reality of the situation fills the pit of my stomach with desperation and anger, a familiar cold knot that lives there. Not wanting them to see the expression on my face I turn around and head into the kitchen, bracing myself in readiness to start cooking the sauce. Folding out the recipe I've printed out, I place it on the island, then unpack my bags and take out a large pot, careful not to make too much noise. Once all the ingredients are lined up neatly in front of me, I busy myself chopping onions and mincing garlic.

In front of me are three tins of cherry tomatoes. I'm psyching myself for the moment I have to open them and pour the red liquid into the pot. "You can do this," I whisper to myself.

Maya has finished reading the story and stands up, leaving the kids on the floor leafing through the book.

"How did everything go?" I ask her.

"Good. Julian fell at school and has a hole in his trousers. He only had a few scratches on his knee, and I put a plaster on it."

"Did he seem ok?" I ask.

"Yeah, he almost sounded proud of his injury, as if it makes him a badass." Maya throws her head back and laughs. The sound warms my heart and I join her, any concerns about Julian's small injury waning as I allow myself to get lost in the moment of camaraderie.

"Oh yeah, I meant to tell you. A man approached me while I was walking back with the children. Said he's looking for gardening work, left a card." She digs deep into her jeans pocket. "Terence I think his name was."

My heart stops and my breath starts coming in quick pants. Terence. Terry. Could this be him, the person John Larkin had called? Is he getting closer, fulfilling the threats in the letters?

"Clarence, sorry," Maya says, putting a flimsy business card on the counter. My eyes can barely focus as I pick it up, turn it over in my hands, the fear making my ears pound.

"What are you making?" Maya asks, her left eyebrow raised.

"Pasta sauce."

"Wow, that's a first!"

"Easy! I cook sometimes."

Maya cocks her head to one side and looks at me. She purses her lips together but I can see the smile trying to break through. Finally, when she cannot keep her stoic look any longer, she bursts out laughing.

I frown at her. Or at least I try. But I know she's right and soon I join her.

"Need any help?"

Delighted that she wants to spend time with me, I struggle to hide the smile sneaking onto my face. "Sure, can you measure out the spices?"

Maya finds the measuring spoons, careful to wipe them before putting them into the next spice jar. I get back to chopping the onions, glancing at her every now and then, relishing the moment. She must do this with Ellen all the time, I think, and feel the irrational sting of a wound caused by their closeness. At least she's here now.

"What's next?" she asks, interrupting my thoughts.

Picking up the recipe, I place it between us and we both spend a few moments reading the instructions. Bracing my shoulders, I pick up one of the tins of tomatoes. But I put it back down on the counter, not yet ready to open it. Although don't want to backtrack, I'm suddenly wondering why I'm putting myself through this.

Maya is regarding me closely, almost as if she's worried about me.

"Do you want me to open them for you?" she asks.

It would be so easy to accept the help. To succumb to the realisation that this is too big a step. But as I look at Maya, standing before me, I feel a wave of embarrassment at my vulnerability. I want her to see me as strong, determined, completely in control, like I usually am. It's just tomatoes and there's nothing to be afraid of. I can do this, I tell myself, and seize a tin and tear the top open, dumping the contents into the pot.

Exhaling, I look at Maya. She smiles at me in encouragement. Picking up the second tin, I repeat the process, then move onto the third. I smile, feeling the elation of success.

"There, that wasn't so hard," Maya says, sounding older than she is.

"Guess not," I respond, picking up a spatula and stirring the sauce. I curl my lips in disgust and Maya laughs loudly, a sound that warms my heart.

"Wanna stay for dinner?" I ask.

She shakes her head. "No, Mum is expecting me. But if you've got some extra sauce left…"

"You bet," I say, making sure my voice doesn't betray my disappointment. "There'll be some in the fridge with your name on it."

She leaves but I can't stop thinking about her, how much I enjoy the little time we spend together. The trace of an almost serene feeling blooms inside me; pride to have finally made this step, and happiness at having shared the moment with Maya.

Chapter 18

"I'm not dropping the charges against her," George Winters says when I walk into his office.

A few choice words come to mind but I stop short of hurling accusations. "George, you're being unjust. Can't you see that she's the victim? That she was running away because she had been abused? It was an accident."

But he doesn't budge and there's no use continuing to argue with him. I can see that his mind is made up and I'm not going to get anywhere on that tack.

"What about the fact that she's fifteen? Are you going to let that slip?"

"You should know me better than that Elizabeth," he says, a scowl plastered on his face.

I had been clinging to the hope that Chloe's case would be dismissed, allowing me to go back to my busy schedule and avoid more conflict with Miles. As much as this case drives me, I'm starting to wish I hadn't become involved. But it's too late now. It would look even stranger to drop Chloe now. No, I have to see it through, make time for her, work harder and longer.

"When can I carry out a pre-trial interview with Ben?" I ask him instead.

"Someone from my office will get it on the books. You can use our conference room."

"That's a kind offer, but I'll hold the meeting at my office." I need to be on familiar ground, able to retain control.

Jennifer greets me with an expectant look, leaning forward in her desk as I walk by. "How did it go?" she asks.

"Not good," I say, shaking my head. "Give me five minutes and come into my office." Closing the door behind me, I drop into my desk and turn in my chair to look out of the window. Why can't we catch a break?

"They're not dropping the charges," I say, when Jennifer comes in.

"What are you going to do?"

"The outcome is going to pivot on Chloe's testimony. She needs to be properly prepared or she'll do more harm than good. We have to increase the prep sessions, meet daily if possible. We need a proper outline of exactly how she will answer each question."

"Surely the paternity results should help," Jennifer says.

"Nothing is certain," I say. "Right now, it could equally go against her. We need to be prepared for any eventuality."

Tapping my fingers on my desk, I concentrate on sorting through the facts. This case needs some extra help from somewhere, for someone to dig into Ben's life and uncover some dirt, give me ammunition to use against him. I've resisted this for as long as I could, not wanting to tap into the firm's finances. It's a last resort, but I can't postpone what now feels inevitable. I need to know everything about him, even the slightest indiscretion. I just hope that there's something in his past that we can use.

"Get me Luke Ross on the phone," I tell Jennifer. "We need him if we're to stand a chance."

*

"Why did you leave the scene of the incident?" Luigi asks. I've convinced him my case is stacking up well, and Chloe could use some of his tough training.

"I was afraid," Chloe repeats.

"That's not what you told the public defender?" stresses Luigi. "You said, and I quote, 'I didn't realise he was injured.' Why are you changing your version of events?"

"I was scared of what he'd do and wanted to get away," she says, before adding: "I didn't care if he was injured."

"No." Fixing on her face, I bang my hand on my desk. "Never, ever admit that you're indifferent to his injuries. That's what the prosecution wants, to make you seem cold and cruel."

Chloe squares her jaw and nods, before trying to stifle a yawn. There are dark circles under her eyes and I can see that she is exhausted. Looking at my watch, I stand up. "Let's wrap this up. I'll see you here on Monday. Make sure you're on time." Walking out of the office, I ask Jennifer to call a cab for Chloe.

"What do you think?" I ask Luigi when she's gone.

Scratching the stubble on his face, he looks at me for a beat too long.

"She's not ready," Luigi says.

"Not even close."

"The rape offers a reasonable defence. If they believe her. But even then, I'm not sure that will matter if she comes across as inconsiderate of the harm she has caused," he goes on. "I'm not sure the jurors will be convinced that he raped her. There's no proof and it can easily be depicted as a lovers' quarrel. That's what I'd do if I was in George's shoes."

"No doubt."

"When are you interviewing Ben?"

"On Tuesday." Picking up a thick folder, I put it in my briefcase. "Fun weekend reading."

"I'll try to sit in."

Packing my bag, I leave soon after, wanting to get home with enough time to spare for a shower before going out to dinner with my parents who are visiting for a few days.

Maya has agreed to babysit and she is already at the house when I get back. She's sprawled on the floor, Julian and Leah next to her, poring over a book. Mum is standing against the door, looking at them. "Maya reminds me so much of your aunt Jill," she says. Still staring at the teenager, she continues: "I'm not sure what it is about her, but she looks just like Jill at her age."

There's a lump in my throat and I feel like I cannot speak. "It's the red hair. Everybody seems to think all redheads look alike." Then, before she can argue, I head upstairs to get ready for dinner.

Chapter 19

"You're late. Again," Miles says accusingly on Monday evening, as I walk into the living room and put down my briefcase.

Closing my eyes, I start counting to ten, trying to compose myself and avoid snapping back. I'm exhausted after spending the last six hours in trial preparations with Chloe.

"My last meeting ran late."

"It's almost ten o'clock."

"I know." I sound calmer than I feel. "And I'd have loved to be here earlier. I'm exhausted and have a pile of documents to go over before going to bed."

"You cannot let work be your priority," Miles lashes out. "Don't forget you have a family."

His words feel like swords to my heart and hurt mingles with anger as I try my best to remain calm, refrain from telling him that he too tends to come home late on many occasions. Remind him how I put work on the back burner to spend the weekend with my family, only picking up my case files after everyone had gone to bed.

But I don't want the confrontation. "I'm sorry. I've had one of those days."

Miles' nostrils flare as he exhales in anger. "I'm going to get changed," I say, turning towards the staircase. I hear him mumble something under his breath but don't have the energy to argue. His accusations are adding to my mental strain and I can feel the start of a headache.

Upstairs I pop into the children's rooms and look in on them. They're both fast asleep. I cover Julian up and tuck Leah's curls behind her ear before tiptoeing towards our bedroom. The hot water feels blissful on my tired body. I stand underneath the shower for so long that the tips of my fingers start to wrinkle. Wrapping a soft towel around me, I sit at the edge of the bath and allow my mind to drift.

Work has been sucking all the energy out of me. But the tiredness is nothing compared to the sheer disappointment of not seeing Maya tonight. I wanted so badly to be home earlier, to be the one to step in and relieve her from her babysitting duties, to savour a few minutes talking to her alone at the end of the day. That life could have been ours had I taken a different decision all those years ago. Instead, she goes home to Ellen and I have to settle for stolen moments, while constantly looking over my shoulder.

My phone flashes the arrival of a text message. Ellen's name flashes on the screen.

I'm going to be in the city tomorrow. Fancy a late lunch?

My day is full but I haven't spent much time with Ellen lately. I miss my friend. And I won't lose out on an opportunity to hear about Maya.

Sure

I text back.

How are the birthday preparations going?

Lines of text fill my screen as Ellen rambles on about the specially ordered napkins arriving with a spelling mistake, and her fear that Maya finds out about the upcoming surprise.

This could have been me, getting ready for Maya's sixteenth birthday. Instead I'm sitting on the sidelines, a spectator, as Ellen prepares to shower the child I'd given birth to with love and gifts.

"Are you ok?" I hear Miles on the other side of the door.

"Yes, I'm fine," I snap out of it. I dry my hair and put on my nightgown before unlocking the door and going back into the bedroom.

Miles is sitting at the foot of the bed. "I'm sorry I snapped," he says in a gentle voice.

It's a little too late for an apology, I want to tell him. That he started a fight despite knowing how stretched I am. I want to scream and throw things, tell him that he's being unfair, that I never complain about his long hours when he's stuck late at the hospital, that my job is also important. But I don't, not wanting to make matters worse, give him any more reason to complain. "It's ok," I say instead, the lie sounding hollow to my ears.

"I'm going downstairs," I say, putting on my dressing gown and tying the belt tightly around my waist.

"Ellen sent over shepherd's pie," he says. "I can warm some up for you."

"It's ok, I can do it," I respond, walking towards the door. I stop and look back. "I have some documents to go over." I turn around, blocking out the disappointment and irritation on Miles' face.

*

"Ready for this?" Luigi asks the following morning as he takes a seat next to me.

In the conference room, the camera rears its ugly head for Ben's pre-trial interview. Facing the seat where he will be asked to sit. It's designed to intimidate and help force out the truth, and I hope it does.

"Of course," I respond, taking a sip of my coffee. I'd been up until the early hours preparing for this meeting and I need the caffeine.

Jennifer pops her head in. "They're on their way up." A few minutes later she is back, opening the door wide. Carrie Young, one of the assistant prosecutors, pushes Ben's wheelchair into the conference room. A sense of panic escalates in my head. I hadn't thought he'd still be using a wheelchair. This might gain him sympathy with the jurors. Luigi hurries around the table to help, moving chairs out of the way to clear a path. The brakes on Ben's wheelchair squeak when he stops at the table. He stretches his arm for the jug of water but doesn't quite reach it, making a low growling noise as he leans back in the chair. "Here you go," I say, filling a glass for him.

While everyone finds their seat, I take a proper look at Ben. It's the first time I've seen him and I use the few seconds to take stock of the young man in front of me. Even in his seated position, I can see that he's tall, probably close to six feet if not more. Muscles can be seen rippling under his light sweater as he takes the glass of water and I notice that his hands are impossibly large, the veins protruding ominously.

"Are you comfortable?" I ask him when everyone has taken their seat.

Ben shrugs but doesn't respond.

"We will be recording this interview." I signal to Jennifer to switch on the camera.

"Can you please state your name for the record?" I ask.

"Ben Grant."

"How old are you Mr Grant?"

"Twenty-two."

"What do you do?"

Ben stares at me blankly. "What's your job?" I ask.

"Uhm, I'm an actor."

"What movies or shows have you been in?"

Ben looks at Claire and she nods. "I've been in some adverts," he responds. Then he quickly adds: "But I had just secured a recurring role in a new TV series."

"Congratulations," I say in a flat tone. "What's your relationship with Chloe Wilson?"

Again Ben looks at Claire. "Look at me Mr Grant and answer the question," I tell him.

"Uhm, we don't have a relationship. I barely know her."

For the next two hours I question Ben, trying to poke holes into his story. Yes, he had sex with Chloe, he admits. He didn't know she was fifteen. The idea that he raped her is laughable, he insists. "Why would I do that? I've never had any trouble getting girls." He never loses his cool, raises his voice, makes an inappropriate expression. We're in trouble. Next to him Chloe is going to appear a bag of nerves and everyone is going to think she's the guilty one.

But then, as he's being wheeled out, he twists his head to look back at me. "I didn't rape her," he says, a little louder than necessary. "She wanted it. They all do." I can hear Claire shushing him and hope that the camera caught that last exchange.

Chapter 20

Ellen is already sitting in a booth when I walk into Barbecoa. Stopping for a second, I look at her. She's leafing through a magazine, pausing every now and then to take a sip of her coffee. There's a slight tremble to her right hand as she holds the cup.

We haven't seen each other since she told me about Maya looking for her birth parents. Coming from behind her, I put a hand on her shoulder. She turns round, her brown hair flying around her face like a satin curtain. "Have you been waiting long?" I ask, kissing her on the cheek, squeezing her shoulder.

"No, I only got here a short while ago." Ellen puts away the magazine and straightens her purple cardigan. Not that it needed straightening up. It's just her habit.

"Can you ask Maya to babysit on Saturday afternoon?" she asks after we've ordered.

"Yes, of course." Then, worried my quick answer will make me sound too eager, I add: "Any particular reason?"

"She was supposed to spend the day at a friend's while I prepare for her surprise party. But the girl has gone and got chickenpox. I desperately need another excuse to get her out of the house."

"Ok, don't panic, I'll be glad to help." My mind is already leaping ahead, trying to think of something to do with Maya, use the opportunity to spend time with her. "How are the preparations going?"

Ellen runs her fingers through her hair and I am transfixed by how every strand falls back into place as if it is governed by some magnetic pull. "Oh, I don't know. I'm trying so hard to make sure she doesn't find out. I've been hiding decorations in my wardrobe and always worrying she'll go in there and find them. That would be such a disaster."

A wave of sadness washes over me and I allow myself a moment to imagine what I would have done for Maya's birthday party. How I wish I was in Ellen's shoes right now! As if she can read my thoughts, she stops. "Oh, listen to me going on. I should be grateful I have a child to organise a party for. There was a time when I thought we'd never be here."

Shrugging off the thoughts of what might have been, I return my focus to Ellen. Time and time again I've felt extreme gratitude for the series of events that led Maya to be adopted by the McBrides. Ellen loves Maya fiercely. Yet, she still hasn't quite got over her ordeal; the years trying to have a child have left their mark on her. Even though she brought it up herself, it's a sensitive subject and I'd rather not focus on it. Better try to help. "I regularly invite

Maya to stay over for dinner, but she's under the impression you'll be mad if she's late."

Ellen purses her lips so tight that the skin around them turns to white. "I just want us to have dinner as a family. Is that so bad?"

"No, of course not," I respond hastily.

"So, will you ask her to babysit on Saturday?"

"Yes, sure. But your house is clearly visible from our kitchen window," I say, fiddling with my napkin. I don't tell her that I often linger longer than necessary at the sink, staring at their house, hoping to catch a glimpse of Maya, even though her bedroom is on the other side of the property. "What if she sees people coming in and out? Won't she suspect?"

"Ugh, I didn't even think about that!" She lowers her head in her hands and doesn't move for a while.

Then I have an idea. I force myself to appear calm. I can't sound too excited. I have to make it seem like I'm doing her a favour, like this is the best way to keep Maya occupied and stop her from suspecting that her mother is up to something. "Ellen, I know how to get Maya out of your way. You know how she's always complaining about her red hair?"

Ellen grunts. "Oh, she told you about that?"

"Yeah, she might have mentioned it a couple of times." I look away from her searching eyes. "What if

I took Maya to my hair salon to get her hair coloured? It would get her out of the house for a few hours and she won't be able to peek."

Ellen stares at me, her eyes looking right into mine. "You think she should change her hair colour? That's a little strange coming from another redhead."

My cheeks burn and I take cover behind the large water glass. "I think she's beautiful," I start. "It doesn't matter though, does it? It's what she thinks that counts. And it would get her away from our street for a few hours. But only if it's ok with you." I find myself holding my breath. Hoping that she'll say yes. It has already become the most important thing for me to make this happen.

"Oh, I don't know," she starts.

"Come on Ellen, it's just her hair. It will grow back. It's not like I'm taking her to get a tattoo."

For a few seconds she doesn't respond and I wonder whether I've offended her. "I love her hair. But it's a good excuse and I'm desperate to get her out of the house," she says after a while, a sudden sadness washing over her eyes.

There's a spring in my step as I leave the restaurant, and walk back to the office. As soon as I'm back behind my desk, I call the salon, hoping for the perfect appointment time.

"You seem in a good mood," Jennifer says when she brings me a document to sign.

"I am," I answer, handing her some signed papers. Then, as she's walking out, I ask: "I don't have any more meetings, do I?"

"No, there's nothing on the books."

"Then I'm going to leave early today."

*

"Can you stay a little longer? Prepare dinner for the kids while I go over some paperwork and help me give them their baths?"

"Yes, sure Mrs P," Maya answers.

Although I try to convince myself that I'm doing this for Ellen, to buy her more time to prepare for the party, I cannot deny that any extra time to spend with Maya feels like a gift. Taking a seat at the kitchen island, I boot my laptop and start going through a document. Every few seconds I look up and watch Maya. Her head is bent and her eyebrows knitted together as she concentrates on cutting carrots into uniform batons. There's an illogical fear that she would turn me down, not want me to take her to the hair salon. I want to ask her so badly but find myself dillydallying.

She looks up and cocks her head to one side, an inquisitive smile spreading across her face. "Are you free on Saturday afternoon?" I ask her.

"Yes. What time do you need me?"

Shaking my head, I try to inject an air of mystery into my words. "I don't need you to babysit. It's your birthday present."

Her eyes open wide and her mouth forms into an O. It's the exact expression Leah makes when she's surprised. Maya takes a couple of steps towards me "Really? What is it?"

"I'm taking you to my colourist. You get to choose your own hair colour."

Her mouth drops open as our eyes lock. "That'd be awesome. But Mum will never allow it."

"Don't worry about your mum. I've already spoken to her," I say conspiratorially. "We have her blessing."

"You're kidding! How did you get her to agree to that? I've been asking her to take me for ever and she always says no."

Her eyes are sparkling and I feel a surge of emotion at her evident joy. "I have my ways," I respond.

"This is fantastic. I can't wait." She takes a step towards me. My arms ache for her hug. But she stops when Julian calls out for me.

*

"Are you ready for this?" I ask Maya as she gets into my car on Saturday morning. The rest of the week had dragged, but finally the much-anticipated day is here.

"Yes, I can't wait." She's bouncing in the seat as if unable to control the energy that's building up in her body.

"I'm glad you're happy," I say, smiling at her exuberance.

"I can't believe that you convinced Mum. I've tried so many times but never managed to get her to agree."

"Stick with me, kid." I don't tell her about Ellen's incessant phone calls, making me promise not to allow Maya to do anything too drastic. She was so close to changing her mind, and it took all my energy and imagination to convince her otherwise. "Think about Maya's face when she walks in," I'd urged her. "You don't want her to suspect and ruin the surprise."

The day couldn't come soon enough for me. This was a rite of passage for any teenager. I was the one taking Maya for her first hair colouring. She might think this is simply a gift, a way of thanking her for her help with the children. But for me it's much more. This day is special beyond words, even though only I know that. The opportunity to spend time with Maya, just me and her, without the distractions of the children, is priceless, especially since we have not managed to schedule a day for her to spend time with me at the office.

The roads are mostly empty, just as I'd suspected. "I thought we'd hit traffic," I lie. "We should have an hour or so to spare before the appointment. How about we go for lunch?"

"Yes, sure."

"I know this little cafe. I go there all the time during my lunch break. It's tucked into a side street and not many people know about it. I'll take you there if you promise not to tell everyone about it."

"Ooh, a secret haunt. Exciting!"

Both of us burst out laughing. This feels so normal.

"How's school?" I ask when we sit down at a corner table in the empty cafe.

"Good, I guess." She pauses. "It's getting harder though. There's so much competition, everyone fighting for the same top spots. I have to do more work to be anywhere near the top of my class."

My mind drifts back to when I was her age and how determined I had been to ensure I got the best grades and was placed top of my class. Anything but a perfect score irritated me because I expected so much more of myself. Maya must be the same.

"Feel free to bring your books with you when you're taking care of the kids. You've got to use any opportunity you can to catch up on your studies.

And if you need time to study, don't hesitate to tell me you can't babysit."

"Thank you, but I love spending time with them," she says. "I've always wanted a brother or sister. I missed that experience growing up. I've known Julian and Leah since they were born. They're the closest to siblings I'll ever have…"

I force myself to keep my eyes fixed on the menu, blinking rapidly, afraid that she might see the emotion clouding over my eyes.

*

"How's that girl's case going?" Maya asks, taking a bite out of her steak and kidney pie, something I'd almost insisted she order. "They're renowned for this. It's amazing. Trust me," I'd coaxed.

"Chloe?" I know who she's referring to but I'm nervous about how to answer her questions.

"Yes, the one from the hit-and-run."

Maya's green eyes are wide with curiosity, fixed on me, waiting for answers. I could avoid going into details, give her a generic response. Or I could be honest and tell her about Chloe. At least as much as I can.

"There's been a development." I decide on the latter. "She is having his baby."

Maya stares at me, jaw dropped. "So, they're a couple? Did she run over him because they'd had a fight?"

"No, she told me in the beginning that he sexually assaulted her. There was no proof but now there's this baby..."

"How do you know it's his baby?"

"We had tests run to confirm that."

"Really? How old's the baby?"

"Not born yet." When I see her confused expression, I say: "Science!"

Maya pops a piece of the piecrust into her mouth and munches quietly. "How do they do that?"

"The test?" When she nods, I continue. "It's just a blood test really."

"They take blood from the baby?"

"No, no," I say, smiling at the shocked look on her face. "The blood is from the mother and they got a DNA sample from the father."

"They can do that?" Her mouth is wide open again.

"Quite incredible isn't it?"

Maya nods and continues eating. I'm about to change the subject, when she says: "So if they can do this with a baby who hasn't even been born, I imagine it's much easier after birth."

She's staring at me, her brows knotted, her head slightly tilted to one side. I know that I'm treading on thin ice, that especially after what Ellen told me I should stop the conversation now. I'm not naive and I suspect that Maya's interest stems, at least partially, from a personal desire to find her own parents. Yet, I cannot stop myself.

"DNA testing is very common nowadays. I've ordered quite a few for work and they tend to be pretty accurate."

"So, you have to order blood tests?"

"There's not even a need for that. A swab from the inner cheek is enough," I say, pointing to my mouth.

"That's incredible." After a short pause, she adds: "So anyone can use DNA to track down their family?"

Taking a deep breath, I exhale slowly. I should back off, change the subject, hope that Maya will forget this exchange. Ellen will be furious if she finds out I discussed DNA testing with Maya, especially after what she told me. Not to mention that if she starts digging and uncovers my secret, I'd be in big trouble. No, that cannot happen. My world would come crumbling down if she finds out who I am. I swallow hard before opening my mouth, intent on changing the subject. A couple of D-list celebrities have sat down at a corner table, providing me the perfect opportunity to deflect Maya's attention.

But this is my chance to try and find out what Maya is thinking, what she's planning on doing. Perhaps she'll confide in me. "Well, no not really. But the DNA database is growing so there's an increased chance of finding a match." I say.

Maya doesn't respond, but continues to look at me, willing me to continue with my explanation. And looking at her, I'm flooded with the memory of the moment I saw her for the first time. The moment when I took the final decision to give her up. I feel my chest squeezing and my breath suspended. But, for now, I've said enough. Turning round slightly, I add: "See that guy in the leather jacket sitting next to the window with the blonde in the Manchester baseball hat? Aren't they in that new crime series that's on TV?"

*

Maya keeps smiling and fidgeting with excitement as we wait for our coats to be brought out almost four hours later. She has chosen to mute down her natural colour but agreed to add some lighter highlights. The result is young and vibrant and contrasts beautifully with her all-black outfit.

"Thank you so much Mrs P," she says, looking at me with sparkling eyes as she runs her fingers through her hair.

"You look amazing," I say.

"You don't look too bad yourself. Do you always go to the salon dressed up like this?"

A flush creeps up my face and I look down at my tailored black dress with a deep V-neck. I had splurged on a new outfit for Maya's party but didn't realise she would notice. "Oh, I just put this on in case I don't have time to change before going out later," I lie. Then, I quickly change the subject. "Hope your mum approves."

Maya looks at me and I see a fleeting expression of panic cross her face. "I hope so. Although I'm sure she'll find some fault with it." Then, in a barely audible whisper, she adds: "She always does."

One step after the other I continue walking, as if I haven't heard her. I would never agree with any criticism of Ellen. Looking at my watch, I realise that it's still early and I need to kill a few hours before taking Maya back home. "Hey, do you want to come with me to the shops?" I ask her.

"Sure."

"I used to hit the shops during my break but I've been too busy recently and I need to get some clothes for the children."

Not wanting to move my car, we hail a taxi and head to Covent Garden. We sit in silence. But instead of feeling awkward, it seems right. It feels like two friends spending an afternoon together, two people who know each other well, who are so comfortable in each other's company that they don't need to fill each moment with conversation. Maya keeps glancing into the car window, looking at her reflection and smiling. Joy fills my heart to have been able to make her happy.

Once there we make a beeline for Gap Kids. "Isn't this adorable?!" Maya exclaims, holding up a newborn sleep suit. She looks right at me with her still button-cute nose, and says: "I can't believe that I was this small at some point."

I can almost hear and taste the force inside me that wants to tell her exactly how small she was, exactly what she looked like. How she used to kick the right side of my stomach whenever I ate chocolate and how she'd move around whenever I listened to jazz. The image of a just born Maya flashes in front of my eyes, the tiny peaceful face all crumpled up and her hair already so flaming red. But I cannot tell her any of this. Because I shouldn't know.

We walk by a makeup shop and I stop to look around, telling myself that I want to give Ellen enough time to get ready but know that I'm stalling for my own selfish reasons.

Maya follows me around as I pick up a few items, studying the labels instead of making conversation. "Hey, why don't we get our makeup done," I say, finally finding an excuse to extend our time together. She hesitates for a second, but I insist. "You need to give your mum a full reveal with hair and makeup."

Within minutes Maya is sitting in a chair with a makeup artist fussing over her, lining her eyes with subtle shadow and perfecting her pout with a light pink lipstick.

"I'll buy whatever she's using on her," I tell one of the sales assistants.

"Your daughter is going to be so happy," the girl says.

My heart feels like it's being squeezed, but I still manage to utter: "No, she's not my daughter. She's my neighbour."

The girl is astonished. "You look so alike," she exclaims.

She's right. I see it too. Even Mum saw the family resemblance. But I try hard not to think about it, never dwell on how the shape of her face has the same roundness. How her nose is slightly upturned just like mine. How her earlobes attach to the side of her neck in the same way mine do. "It's the red hair," I tell the woman now, wanting to get her off my back.

Maya joins us as I'm paying. "I thought she was your mum," the sales assistant tells her, motioning towards me.

The smile fades from Maya's face and her eyes cloud over, the change in demeanour so obvious that even the sales assistant looks at me questioningly. But then Maya smiles and her whole face lights up. "She's more like an older sister," she tells her.

*

My heart is beating fast as I pull into the McBrides' driveway. We've made good time getting back from the city and I hope that the party preparations are finalised. I'd managed to sneakily send a text to Ellen, letting her know we were on our way.

The McBrides' house doesn't look like a party is in full swing inside. It's mostly dark, except for the kitchen. Ellen must be beside herself with excitement and anticipation for her daughter to walk in the house and find a party in her honour. This should have been me.

Parking in front of the house, I start getting out of the car. Maya looks at me inquisitively. "I'm not going to miss seeing your mum's face when she sees the new look," I say. It's not a complete lie.

Maya puts her key in the lock but Ellen pre-empts her and cracks the door open. She proceeds to open it slightly wider, enough for her head to fit through, and she looks at her daughter. I can see Ellen examine every inch of Maya's face and then she smiles. I realise at that point that I'd been holding my breath, hoping that Ellen would approve of Maya's new hairstyle and that she doesn't think I've allowed her daughter to go too far, or crossed the boundary between them and me.

"I love it," she says, opening the door wide.

We're greeted by a deafening sound that startles even me, despite expecting a warm welcome. "Surprise," shout some thirty people in unison, all crowded in the entryway of the McBrides' house. My eyes scan the crowd until I find Miles and the children. Leah looks adorable in the tartan dress I picked for her, even though the bow in her hair looks a little lopsided. Julian looks older in his new jacket. My heart hurts a little as I remember that I gave up spending the day with my two children to be with Maya.

"You were in on this?" Maya's voice jolts me back to the here and now. When I nod, she continues: "Darn, you're good. I didn't suspect a thing."

And then she reaches out and hugs me, her arms tight around my neck, her head nestled against mine. For long seconds she doesn't let go and I put my arms around her, not wanting the moment to end, smelling the sweet scent in her hair. Tears sting my eyes and I blink away furiously. "Thank you Mrs P," she says when she finally lets go. "This was a great day."

Chapter 21

"It looks pretty," Leah exclaims. She's standing with her small legs wide apart, her hands on her hips, looking at the Christmas tree.

"You did a great job," I say, patting my little girl's head. "You all did."

Turning around, I look at Maya. "Thank you," I mouth.

She smiles, bending to pick up boxes that are strewn all over the floor. Her hair sweeps across her face, covering it from view and I have to fight the urge to tuck it behind her ears, stroke the glossy strands. Instead I clench my hands together, glad the mess is making her stay for a while longer.

As I help her pick up bubble wrap, I accidentally touch her hand. Squeezing it tightly, I smile at her. Maya smiles back and for a moment I'm lost in her beautiful eyes.

"Miles can put these back in the attic." I motion towards the boxes piled haphazardly in one corner of the living room. "Would you like something to drink?"

"Do you still have any of that homemade lemonade? That was pretty good."

"No, but I have the store-bought stuff."

She follows me into the kitchen and I pour us both a glass of lemonade. "Had it not been for you the tree would never have been decorated," I say.

The Christmas when Maya was born seems so far away. I'd told my parents that I wouldn't make it home for the holidays, but at the last minute I decided to make my flight and surprise them. Only when I got there, there was no sign of Christmas, none of my mother's over-the-top decorations, no smell of food being prepared in readiness for the big day. Years later, when the movie *Christmas With The Kranks* was released, I remembered how my parents hadn't bothered to do anything as their only daughter wasn't coming home.

"It was fun. The kids loved it," Maya says, sipping her lemonade. "Well, I definitely had a good time."

We gaze at the bright lights, lost for a moment in the promise of Christmas. "My friends are so jealous of my new hair," she says at last.

"I bet they are. It really suits you."

"I had a lot of fun last Saturday. Thank you for taking me."

"It was my pleasure." I'm so close to asking her to go out somewhere with me again, but worry it would sound too eager. Instead I savour the moment, racking my brain to start a conversation that will make her stay longer.

Maya shifts on her feet. She picks up her glass, but puts it down again. She looks at me, then away. I remain mum, fearful of scaring her off. Finally she opens her mouth and I find myself holding my breath, eager to know what's on her mind.

"Mummy, mummy, can we make the lights twinkle?" Leah asks, running into the kitchen.

"Uhm, yes, I think so," I respond. "We can ask Dad later."

Maya finishes her lemonade. "Gotta go."

"Why don't you stay a little longer?" I ask. "I'll make hot chocolate."

But Maya shakes her head and makes a face. "I have homework." The moment is gone and I might never find out what she was about to say. I want to cry in frustration and run after her but instead fix a smile on my face and follow Leah into the living room.

The following day marks the start of my annual hiatus from the office. Luigi had insisted when we first started out that we should close our office over the Christmas period. "Give the staff time to celebrate," he said back then, even though the staff consisted of the two of us and an elderly secretary. Over the years, as the company grew, we became more flexible and although it's still more than a week to Christmas, I decide to stay home.

That doesn't mean that I don't have any work to do. After dropping the kids off at school, I boot up my laptop and start going through my emails. Most are holiday greetings or other companies sending notices of their office closures. Scrolling down I come across an email from Luke Ross, the private investigator, sent in the early hours.

I think I've found something. Call me.

Picking up my phone, I quickly dial Luke's number. We had worked together on a number of cases and his thoroughness has often helped the firm win a case. The drumming sound of my fingers tapping the dining room table makes me even more anxious as I wait for him to pick up.

"Hello," he mumbles.

"Luke, it's Elizabeth Perkins. Did I wake you up?"

"No…. yes…. give me a second." The creaking sound must be his bed.

There's a clanking noise coming from the other end of the line, and the swish of a tap being turned on.

"Ok, so your Chloe Wilson case," he finally says.

"You said you found something. What is it?"

"One second, I'm looking for my notebook."

There's a sound of papers being flipped and I chew on the end of my pen. "Yes, here it is," he finally says.

There's a pause. "What is it?"

"Hold on, my kettle's boiling." There's more clattering, the sound of a cupboard being opened and slammed shut, the bang of a mug being placed on the counter, and the swish of water being poured, followed by the clinking of a teaspoon.

"Ok, here we go," he says, when I'm about to burst with frustration. "I've been looking into Ben Grant. Quite a ladies' man, not sure what they see in him. Anyway, there's one girl from his acting class who wasn't too keen about his amorous approaches. She filed a written complaint with the coach."

"Do you have a copy?"

"Elizabeth, how long have we worked together? Of course I have a copy. I will scan it and email it to you."

"How long ago was this? Can you find the girl?"

"I'm working on tracking her down but this was three years ago. Don't get your hopes up; I only have her name and not much more to go on."

"Luke, I need this," I stress.

"Just be realistic, ok?"

Putting down the phone, I stare at my computer screen, unable to focus on the words. "Don't get too excited," I say loudly to myself.

With tremendous effort, I force myself to concentrate on work, preparing questions for Ben's interrogation during the upcoming trial, trying to think of how he would answer and coming up with additional questions.

The alarm startles me and for a moment I'm disoriented. Then I remember. School will be out shortly and I need to shift my attention to the children. Putting on my coat, I head outside, looking towards the McBrides' house as I walk to the top of the driveway. The front door is no longer red, as it was when I first drove through the street. They changed it the year after we bought the house, sometime in August. Ellen had pansies planted to match the dark blue door.

A battered black Ford comes chugging along, starkly out of place. The windows are tinted and I cannot see the driver. It goes round to the end of the street and turns. It slows down as it drives past me again and even though I cannot see the driver, I feel his or her eyes on me. I cower under the scrutiny, my heart beating fast.

Forcing the thoughts out of my head, I walk to the school, enjoying the crisp air, the sun shining weakly from among the clouds. Outside the school I make small talk with a few other parents. The kids' faces light up when they see me waiting for them and I feel guilty that my stress messes with my enthusiasm for what they want to do. We take the long way home, meandering through the streets, as the children excitedly tell me about their day, what they've learned and what they've done. Normally it would be Maya picking them up, or our other sitter. I was lucky if I got home early enough to spend time with them, and even then, they're already tired.

Back home I put the stereo on and blast Christmas music around the house, while the kids make Christmas cards, covering the white countertop in stubborn crayon marks. Leah sways with the beat as she glues paper flowers to her card, her light brown brows twisted in concentration. Her tiny fingers are covered in glitter. Julian cuts his card into an oval shape and it amazes me how steady he is with the scissors.

They are reluctant to go to bed; the dramatic change in the weather making them both scared of the thunder roaring outside and the rain making a heavy drum on the windows. It took some coaxing but finally they're asleep, Julian holding on tight to his dinosaur book. It's his latest obsession, started by a school trip to the Natural History Museum, and he wants to know everything about the extinct creatures.

Back downstairs I plan to do some more work on Chloe's case before Miles gets home from a late shift and accuses me of obsessing about her. Making myself a cup of herbal tea, I get comfortable on the sofa. I'm not hungry, having nibbled from the children's plates, and will eat with Miles later.

I'm focused on work when I hear the frantic knocks on the door. Looking up from my paperwork, I hear it again. Putting the file down I walk through the dimly lit hallway. Maybe Miles forgot his keys. A gust of wind blows in when I open the door. But it's not my husband standing in the puddles of rain. It's Ellen and she's crying hysterically.

"What happened?" Opening the door wide, I reach out for her arm and pull her in. Her light t-shirt is soaked through and she's shivering in the cold December weather. She walks in, still shaking uncontrollably. I'm not sure whether it's from the crying or the cold. A puddle starts forming in the hallway.

"It's Maya." Her voice breaks as she speaks.

My heart stops. "Is she hurt?"

She shakes her head. "No, no, not that."

Heaving a sigh of relief, I put my arms around her shoulders and walk her to the living room. "Here, come in." She sits hunched over on the sofa and continues to cry. Standing in front of her, I'm at a loss. Should I sit next to her or give her some space? Put pressure on her to tell me what happened or allow her to take her time? "Shall I make you some tea?" I ask. Ellen nods without looking up and I hurry into the adjoining kitchen and put the kettle on before rushing into the bathroom to get a towel. "Here, dry yourself up."

Putting a steaming mug of tea on the side table next to her, I run upstairs to get a blanket, draping it over her legs. Her head is bowed. She's still trembling. Fat tears are rolling down her cheeks.

I've never seen her as distraught as this. The thought that Maya might be sick or in trouble scares me and I rack my brain to think whether there was anything different about the teenager these past few days.

"Ellen, what happened? Please talk to me," I implore, sitting down next to her.

She turns towards me. Her eyes are red and puffy, wrinkles that I'd never noticed before spreading across her face like dark cobwebs. Her lower lip quivers when she opens her mouth to speak. "Can I trust you?" she asks.

"Yes, yes, of course," I say hastily.

Ellen's sniffles cut through the silence. She dabs at her eyes with a soaked tissue. Finally she speaks. She looks at me through swollen eyes that are shining with tears. There is a hurt so deep and a fear so big that it scares me. This is the look of a woman who's terrified by what has just happened and has no idea what's next.

"Maya's out with her dad, visiting his parents," she starts. "They left early this morning and I'm not expecting them until later tonight. I think they set off an hour or so ago, so with the traffic..." Her voice trails off. "I was just watching TV, had just poured myself a glass of wine, when there was a knock on the door." The hairs on the back of my neck stand up in fear.

A roll of thunder reverberates through the house. Ellen snaps her head up. "It's ok, just the weather," I say in the same calm voice I would speak to Julian or Leah.

"There were two people outside, a man and a woman," she continues. "At first I thought they were collecting money for some charity or were looking for a different house, for a holiday party or something. But then they said they're detectives and needed to speak to me." She takes a sip of tea.

Come on, come on, I mentally urge her as horrible scenarios rush through my mind. Ellen looks at me with haunted eyes. "I thought they were at the wrong house. When they said they needed to speak to Ellen and Tom McBride, I just got scared that they were impostors and would rob me. But they showed me their badges and they looked genuine. So, I let them in." She starts crying again, her willowy frame shaking with the intensity of her sobs, pausing for what seems like forever.

"Maya is trying to track down her biological mother," she finally says, her voice breaking down as soon as the words are out of her mouth.

A wave of heat rises through my body, starting at my toes and making its way to my head. I try to sort one problem from another. Why would the police be involved in a paternity issue?

"She sent a DNA sample to a testing company in the US. They found a strong familial match in their database."

My heart speeds up, each beat merging into the next. My temples feel like they're about to explode. How did she even know to do this? Where did she find the money?

Am I the one to blame? After all I was the one who told her about the use of DNA in reuniting families. But I never thought it would come to this.

And then my fear intensifies as Ellen's words boom in my ears. The familial match had to be to me. But who could have got their hands on my DNA? Still, fear overtakes rationale. The police must have told Ellen that I'm Maya's birth mother. She's going to take Maya away forever so that I never see her again. She must be here to tell me that she's going to take me to court and accuse me of stalking her family. That she's going to tell everyone what an impostor I am. That I've spent years acting like a friend when I was really this awful person who didn't think twice about abandoning her baby in another country only to come and live next door. I wait for Ellen to start hurling accusations at me, about my lies and my false pretences. She'll tell me she never wants to see me again. That I'm never to get close to Maya. That she's already requested a restraining order and that the police are outside ready to question me.

Staring at my hands, I try to think hard. How am I going to explain this? How can I spin this story? Help Ellen understand that I gave up the baby because I wanted her to have a better life. I need to find the right words to make her believe that I'm not here to take away her daughter. That I moved next door only because I wanted to see Maya grow up. Asking her to babysit my children was meant for her own good, to help her out. That I have not intentionally tried to keep her here longer each night and don't mean any harm.

When I look up, Ellen is shaking her head. "It gets worse," she says.

Warmth creeps up my body. My head spins and I feel faint. Here it comes. I'm scared. Terrified really of what's going to happen next. Of what Ellen's going to say or do.

"The match triggered an alert and the DNA company notified Interpol. They tracked it down to some guy who was found dead almost seventeen years ago in the fields close to Cambridge," Ellen says.

My head jolts up. Have I heard right? The connection was to John Larkin and not to me. Does this mean I'm safe? Or is this just the beginning? Ellen is looking at me, waiting for me to say something. Swallowing the knot in my throat, scared that my voice will betray my fear and confusion, I ask: "So they tracked down her biological father?" It's more a statement than a question.

Ellen nods. She rummages in the pocket of her tracksuit trousers and takes out a crumpled piece of paper. She opens it and reads something. "His name is... was... John Larkin."

Familiar survival instincts lock into place. My brain whizzes with the chaos of thoughts rushing through it. Protecting my secret, continuing to keep it hidden, becomes of paramount importance. One false move, one word out of place, and I could be caught. Ellen must never suspect that I knew anything about John Larkin's link to Maya. Rubbing the scar on my hand, I make small circular movements meant to calm me down. My best response right now is to feign ignorance. "How did he die?"

But Ellen shakes her head vehemently. "No, you don't understand." She starts to cry again. "He was murdered. Stabbed in the neck and left to bleed out."

"And it gets worse," Ellen continues. "The investigators found the bodies of three girls buried around the area. They believe he'd raped and killed them and his attacker was to be another victim."

A sense of relief spreads inside me. She doesn't seem to know about me. This is horrifying, but perhaps I am safe. For now. But I have to remain alert. I can't let the cover-up that started all those years ago slip now.

"This story rings a bell," I say, feigning calm over the beating of my heart. "I think it happened when I was at university."

Ellen looks at me and then nods. "I had forgotten you went there."

"I don't remember much," I lie. "Just that everyone was really scared when they started to find the bodies.

"What did the detectives want? Were they simply letting you know about the connection?"

"No," she wails. "They want to unseal Maya's birth certificate to help with the investigation into his death." Then in an increasing pitch, she adds: "They want to use my daughter in a murder investigation."

My heart stops. Then it starts beating so fast and loud that I'm sure Ellen can hear it. The thumping in my chest escalates to a crescendo and I wonder if this is how people feel before a heart attack.

This has always been my greatest fear. Back then, I had heaved a sigh of relief when the investigation into John Larkin's death had fizzled out. There had been no fingerprints, no clues as to who had killed him. It only took a few months before the detectives gave up. Once the girls were found, he stopped being a victim and became the perpetrator, not deemed worthy of police time. It didn't matter how much his mother appealed to the authorities, how many letters she wrote to newspapers. What mattered was that he was no longer a living threat.

Yet I never stopped being afraid. I have always worried I'd be caught. Especially since someone out there knew my name. Would some twisted turn of events link John Larkin to me? Right now Maya is that link. The moment she is connected to me, my secret is out.

And now that the case is being reopened, I know that I'm facing a ticking time bomb. At any moment I can be found out. Made to pay for my actions. Probably even sent to jail. I try to compose myself, to focus on what Ellen is saying rather than the fear bubbling inside my chest.

"… they said the timing seems just right."

"Sorry Ellen, can you repeat? I didn't catch what you said."

"The detectives said that Maya was born almost nine months after he was killed and perhaps her birth mother killed him when he attacked her."

I decide to act as ignorant as possible as to what happened "But Maya was born in the US. How is her biological mother connected to someone found dead here?"

Ellen narrows her eyes. "I asked the exact same thing. But they said she could have been here on holiday when he was killed. Or travelled to the US to give up the baby."

"I thought that case was closed." I am clutching at straws.

Ellen shrugs. "Apparently they think they can solve it now they have this new lead."

I'm in trouble. Once the case is reopened there's no saying what they will find. Whether they will uncover my secret. The life that I have built over the years will fall apart. The one that I've worked so hard to make as perfect as I can. My parents and my husband will never look at me the same way. My children will know that their mother is a killer. There will be a long, drawn out court case and I might end up in jail.

"Liz, are you ok?" I hear Ellen say. Her voice seems so far away.

I need to snap out of it. I need to find out every single detail that can help me determine the extent of the risk I'm facing. "Yes, I'm sorry." I reach out for her hand across the gulf between us. "I guess I'm just in shock at what you've just told me. Did the detectives say what they want from you?"

"Just permission to unseal Maya's original birth certificate." Her shoulders shake as she starts crying again.

Digging deep into my memories, I try to remember the details on the birth certificate. But I cannot picture it after all those years. Aside from the surreal memory of signing the birth register as Laura Black, everything else is fuzzy.

Snapping back to the present, I ask Ellen: "Are you going to tell Maya?"

She shrugs. "I don't know. I need to speak to Tom."

"I need your help." She faces me. "I want Maya to have a legal representative to protect her interests."

"Yes, of course," I quickly say, even though my mind is still catching up with Ellen's intentions, why she ran over to me before even telling her husband.

"We need to go and talk to the detectives after the holidays. Can you come with us? We'll pay your regular fee of course."

"I'll be there." The irony that this situation will allow me to get first-hand knowledge of what's happening is like a form of torture. It also means that I need to compose myself. Not give away any indication that I'm closer to this than as just their lawyer. A family friend.

Ellen puts her mug down and stands up. "I need to go. I want to be home when Maya and Tom arrive."

I walk her to the door. "Are you telling Tom tonight?"

"I don't know. Part of me wants to wait until after the holidays."

She opens the door and disappears into the dark night, engulfed by the pelting rain and raging winds. It's freezing cold but I stand in the doorway for a while, rooted to the spot, unable to move. When I do, I feel as if I'm about to collapse.

Chapter 22

When Ellen leaves I pace through the maze of rooms, going over these revelations. My stress levels are escalating rapidly and I can't keep still, overwhelmed by the fear that I'm finally going to be found out.

The feeling of safety in the knowledge that Maya's birth certificate won't bear my name is soon replaced by panic. The police are immediately going to find out that Laura Black never existed. For years I had forced myself to believe that giving birth in another country, finalising the adoption there, would further distance me from John Larkin. But it was not going to take the police long to figure out what happened, that the killer travelled to the US soon after. And that was going to narrow down their search. Until it led them to me.

Making my way into the kitchen, I pour myself a glass of whisky. This is unlike me. I don't even enjoy drinking. Certainly nothing this strong. Bringing the glass to my lips, I take a sip, making a face at the burning sensation in my throat. Taking a second sip I make an effort to shift my concentration to the strong taste of the alcohol instead of what has blown up tonight.

"Liz, is something wrong?" My head shoots up when Miles comes in.

Putting the glass down, I walk towards him and put my arms around him, nestling my face in the crook of his neck, savouring the rock of his body as he holds me against him. I wish I could speak to him, tell him what happened. Tell him the whole truth. Have someone else help me carry the tremendous burden that I feel on my shoulders right now. But I don't know how to do that. I don't know what I'm going to do, but I'm not going to give my secret up unless it's uncovered. And most importantly, I'm not going to ruin Christmas. I'm going to cling to it in case it's the last one we will ever have as a family before the truth comes out to ruin us.

He walks into the living room and sees my case notes still strewn on the coffee table, where I'd left them when Ellen came to the door. "So, this is why you're upset." His voice is tinged with impatience. "You've got to stop letting this case get to you."

"Don't jump to conclusions!" I retort, stress transforming into anger. "I'm worried about the McBrides." Then, knowing that I have to give my husband some proper information, I add: "Ellen was here."

Pausing, I wonder how much I should tell him. I decide to be as honest as I possibly can, all the while swallowing my dread at how closely I am skirting the truth I've withheld from him.

"Remember that guy they found dead a few miles from campus when we were in university?"

"Who?" Miles asks. "That Larking guy?"

"Larkin," I correct, shuddering slightly at the mention of his name. "Maya tried to track down her birth parents and the investigation led to him."

Miles' mouth drops open, his eyes open wide. "What do you mean?"

"She sent a DNA sample for testing in the hope it would lead to her birth parents, and it led to him."

He doesn't speak for a few seconds and I'm about to continue when he says: "Is he her father? The man in the woods?"

"It appears so."

Miles continues to stare at me, the frown still plastered on his face, his head making minuscule back and forth movements as he digests the information. "But didn't the McBrides adopt Maya in New York?"

"Connecticut," I correct. "Close enough."

Miles runs his hand through his hair. Once, twice, three times. "So, was he in the US before he was killed?"

I bite my tongue before I can say too much. Give one detail too many. Get into the timeline that I know intimately. "I don't know," I say instead.

The silence that ensues makes me uncomfortable. "And how did Maya even know how to go about tracking her father?" he finally asks.

"She looked it up online. Ellen told me a few weeks ago that Maya was looking for information on tracking down her birth parents."

"But... It's a big step from doing research to actually acting on it. Didn't she tell anyone?"

"I don't know. She's smart." There's no way I'm going to tell him I talked to Maya about DNA testing.

Miles shakes his head from side to side, as if he's still trying to make sense of all of this. "How did Maya take the news?" he asks.

"Maya doesn't know yet. The police were alerted to the link and they want to unseal Maya's birth certificate to track down her birth mother and question her."

Miles rubs his forehead, as if he's trying to smooth out the frown. "Why would they need to speak to Maya's birth mother?" And then, before I have time to respond, he realises the implication. "Do they think it was her who killed him?"

Nodding, I avert my eyes, afraid that Miles will see the fear in them. "That's what the detectives told Ellen."

The seconds tick by and I force myself to look at Miles, hoping that he doesn't see how terrified I am. His lips are pursed and he is staring at me, a new questioning look in his eyes. "So, they think she was American and went back to the US after she killed him?"

Wanting to avoid more conjecture, I simply shrug. "Ellen was a mess, so upset and so lost. She hadn't even told Tom yet, just came here," I say instead. Miles doesn't respond. He seems to be mulling over the information I've just given him, going through it in his head, trying to piece together the sparse details. "What are you thinking?" I prompt when I feel that I cannot take the silence any longer.

Miles takes a deep breath and finally says: "I don't know what to make out of all this. I am still trying to wrap my mind around the strange coincidence that a person who was killed next to campus while we were in university happens to be linked to our neighbours."

My stomach lurches and the hairs at the back of my neck stand on end. I don't want to talk about John Larkin. I don't like the direction of Miles' thoughts. His eyes lock onto mine, he looks exhausted, and I can't read the expression in their depths. "Yes, it's quite a coincidence," I say, looking away. "Small world."

Suddenly, he grabs me by the shoulders, turning me to look at him. "What is really happening, Liz? What are you not telling me?"

The severity of his look scares me. There is suspicion in his eyes. Real doubt about my story. It looks like he's putting together all the scraps of information and building the puzzle that I never want him to complete. Swallowing hard, I say: "I told you what Ellen told me."

Putting the whisky glass on the counter, I busy myself taking plastic containers with yesterday's leftovers out of the fridge. My hands are trembling and I almost drop the sweet and sour chicken.

Chapter 23

I'm walking along a narrow pathway, with tall trees lining each side. There's nothing else around me. The path keeps going until it disappears into the distance. Behind me is the same – a long narrow street that dissolves into nothingness. The leaves rub against each other in the light wind, making a swishing sound. I hurry my pace, wanting to get out of there, to reach my destination, wherever that might be.

But the more I walk, the longer the road ahead seems. It's as if I'm being followed. I know someone's watching me. I can feel their eyes on me, surveying me carefully, probably waiting until the perfect moment to pounce on me. I don't know where I can go, what I can do to get away from them.

It seems like the road is narrowing. I have to walk sideways to make it between the trees. I'm not sure how much farther I'm going to be able to go before I can't walk any longer, before the road becomes too narrow for me to go through.

Opening my eyes with a jolt, I take a deep breath. And then another, as if I'm climbing out of an abyss. Remaining still, I force myself to calm down. I stare at the ceiling until my heart has stopped racing and my breath's no longer coming in short pants. It's only five o'clock but I know that I won't be able to go back to sleep. The dream has rattled me, like bad dreams always do. I need to be awake and in control, able to take the right decisions and understand the consequences.

Quietly, I get up from the bed and wrap a robe around me. I walk out of the bedroom, careful to close the door softly. Popping my head into both children's rooms, I listen to their soft rhythmic breathing. There's a lump in my throat as I consider how my past can ruin their perfect lives.

Downstairs, I make a cup of coffee. Standing by the kitchen sink, I look towards the McBrides' house. The windows are dark; everyone's still asleep. Why did Maya have to bring up the past?

Shaking my head, I move to the kitchen table and boot up my laptop. Work is the only way I know how to stop the thoughts that are running through my mind. The fears that have been brought to the surface. Putting headphones on, I watch the video of Ben's interview over and over, hoping to catch any minuscule sign of what will trigger discomfort, force him to stray from his scripted responses. Identify which buttons to push for the best impact. I focus on his eyes, noting the times he looks away, lowers his glance, changes his blinking pattern. I concentrate on his hands, looking for a pattern in his gestures. Then I direct my attention to his facial expressions, observing when he purses his lips, or sighs, or fiddles with his hands. Some questions triggered longer than normal pauses, others made him shift uncomfortably. A few hours later I feel I know better what ticks him off, what can get me the reaction I want. It's only then that I continue working on my questions for the trial, tweaking my verbiage for the highest impact.

My phone rings. The caller's number is blocked. My heart misses a beat and I hold my breath as I answer.

"You're gonna love me," comes the booming voice on the other end of the line.

"Luke?"

"I found her."

"The girl? Please tell me it's her!"

"Who else would it be? Her name is Mary Beth Hayes."

"Will she talk?"

"I don't know. I just found her. The rest is up to you."

"Yes, of course. This is fantastic news. Where does she live? Can you send me her address?"

"It should hit your inbox any second. She's in Sutton, so not that far from you."

"I'm going to head there now." I jump to my feet, already half way up the stairs before I hang up.

*

An hour later I'm knocking on the door of a small semi-detached house. It opens a crack and a young woman peeks through the small gap. "Can I help you?"

"Yes, I think so." I smile, trying to appear as friendly as I can. "I'm Elizabeth Perkins, a barrister…"

"Oh, we're not interested."

"Please hear me out. I need your help with a case I'm working on. It's about Ben Grant. You filed a complaint about him."

She opens the door another inch. "How do you know that?"

"It came up during the investigation. Mary Beth Hayes, right? Can we talk?"

"I don't know, it was a while ago, I just want to forget about it."

"Please, you'd be helping a teenager. Just let me speak to you."

"Ok." Her voice is hesitant. "What do you need?"

The door is still cracked and she makes no move to open it further. I will need to tread carefully so as not to freak her out or she will slam it shut.

"Ben was run over…"

"What does that have to do with me?"

"That part doesn't. But the teenager who ran him over is being prosecuted and could end up in jail. She insists that he raped her and she was trying to get away."

"Oh God!" She says and opens the door another inch until I can see her whole face. "I'm trying to establish precedent," I continue hastily. "Show that this was not the first time Ben tried to assault someone. That's why I need you."

She twists her lips as she bites the corner of her mouth. "Look, why don't you come in." She finally opens the door. "I don't have much time though. I'm meeting my husband in an hour."

"Does he know?" I follow her into a small living room.

"Yes, we were dating when it happened. He was the one who persuaded me to file the complaint."

She sits down on the checked sofa. "What do you need from me?"

"I need you to testify in court."

"No way." She shakes her head vehemently.

"Please, Mary Beth," I plead. "She could go to jail and she's only fifteen."

"I don't want anything to do with him. I put this behind me and moved on. I don't want it haunting me again."

"He got her pregnant. She's only fifteen."

She exhales loudly. "Oh God."

"She's basically a child herself and she's risking being locked up. You can help her."

"But what would my testimony do? I haven't seen him in years, barely knew him even then."

"Even better. He barely knew the girl either, it was the first time he'd met her," I explain. "Your testimony can show that he's a predator, that Chloe had every reason to be scared of him."

"And I have to testify in court? Can't I write a letter?"

"No, I'm afraid not. You will need to be questioned. But I will prepare you, help you tell your story, make sure that you have all the answers."

"I don't know. I really don't want anyone to know."

"Can you tell me what happened? The complaint didn't say much."

She looks away, towards the window, sitting motionless. "I was stupid," she starts. "He was nice and offered to drive me home one evening after class. I was running late to meet my husband. Well, he was my boyfriend then. I wanted to get home in time to change my clothes. When Ben said he could drive me, I thought he was being nice.

I got in his car and gave him my address. He drove off and we were talking about the class, about the other students, why we want to be actors. I didn't realise that he missed the turn towards my street.

And then he stopped and I looked out of the window and realised that we were at an abandoned construction site."

She takes a pause and closes her eyes. Then she opens them again and looks at me. "It happened so quickly. Within a second he was on top of me, forcing his hand up my skirt, squeezing me against the passenger door. I tried to push him away, but he was strong. My arms were pinned between us. I could barely move."

"Did he say anything?"

"Yes, he said I wanted it. That I'd been begging for it all afternoon. That I should lie back and enjoy it. Or something on those lines, I don't remember the exact words."

"Did you say 'no'?"

"Of course I did! I screamed and shouted but he wouldn't get off me. Then, somehow I managed to free one arm and punched him in the face. I think I hit his nose because suddenly blood started gushing out. I didn't stop to check. I got out of the car as quickly as I could and ran towards the main road."

"Did you call for help?"

"No, I just ran home. My boyfriend was already waiting and saw that my shirt had blood on it so I told him. He tried to get me to go to the police, but all I wanted was to take a shower and forget all about it."

"I'm sorry this happened to you."

"I just wanted to forget all about it."

"Why did you file the complaint?"

"I went back to the class the following week and he was there. When someone asked him about his bruised face, he said he had been punched when he went to break up a fight. After what he tried to do, he wanted to be the hero. He wasn't even ashamed to say it in front of me. And the others were lapping up his every word. I told my boyfriend and he was so angry, I thought he'd go and find him and end up in trouble himself. He said he'd only stay put if I filed a complaint, so I did."

"I need you to say this in court. It can make the difference between this young girl being found guilty or not."

She shakes her head. "I don't know if I can do it. Even speaking to you is hard, let alone repeating the story in front of a roomful of people."

"Please, it might stop him attacking someone else."

"Ahh, that's not fair," she says.

"It's the right thing to do. Please think about it at least."

"I'll have to speak to my husband first."

"Please. And I can come back and talk to both of you, explain the process." I dig into my bag and take out a business card. "This is my phone number, call me anytime."

Chapter 24

"Mrs P, you seem distracted."

The voice seems to come from nowhere. Slapping a hand to my chest, I turn around to see Maya next to me. The smile fades from her face. "Oops, sorry for startling you."

"Oh, it's no problem." Pulling myself together, I smile at her.

It's two days before Christmas and with my parents in town and watching the children, I took the chance to dash out to Westfield for some last minute shopping.

She motions to my bags. "That's a lot of stuff."

"Yes," I admit sheepishly. "I've gone a little overboard this time."

"Just this time?"

"Ok, I've gone overboard as usual."

She laughs, a sweet sound that is contagious. She looks exactly the same as she always does, with no hint that she might know about the detectives talking to her mother.

Her bold move still troubles me. Never would I have suspected Maya to go behind her parents' backs like this. The realisation that I don't know her as well as I thought saddens me but I'm consoled by the fact that Ellen didn't see it coming either. Still, I'm overcome by a compulsion to find out more. I just don't know how.

"Have you come to finish your Christmas shopping?" I ask before the silence becomes awkward.

"Yeah, need to get something for Mum."

"What are you looking for?"

Maya shrugs and makes a face. "I don't know. She's a little fussy."

That's an understatement, I think, suppressing a laugh. Ellen is what you might call strait-laced. Her clothes are prim and proper, her wardrobe mostly made up of perfectly tailored trousers and skirts and twinsets that would have looked fashionable in the 1940s. Her jewellery, while expensive, is demure. And she hasn't changed her hairstyle since the first time I saw her. It works on her.

"Hey, do you want some help?" My offer spills out before I know what I'm doing. This little moment of conspiracy with Maya is exciting. Now that she's looking for me, for her mother, it seems like an even worse idea, but at the same time even harder to resist. There's a force greater than me that makes being with Maya more important than anything else.

"Do you have time?" she asks.

"Yeah." Then, moving closer to her, add: "I'm playing truant today."

Maya gasps and giggles. "Thanks, I'd love that."

We stand in the middle of the atrium surrounded by shops. People flock in and out, walking fast, laden with colourful bags. Everything is brightly lit, decorations blinking from the overflowing shop windows. Maya follows my gaze. She is biting her nails. I want to slap her hand away, tell her she's messing up her pretty hands. But even Ellen has been unable to quash that habit. She'll get over this phase, like I did when I was a few years older than her.

"Anything that she needs? Perhaps something that she's mentioned recently." I say ignoring the state of her nails.

"I really have no idea. Was planning to wander through the shops until something catches my eye. But everywhere is so crowded that I started to give up."

"It's two days before Christmas. Surely you didn't expect to have the whole place to yourself!"

"No, but it's a little overwhelming."

"You shouldn't have left it until the last minute, kiddo."

The jolt to my shoulder takes me by surprise and I take a step forward to steady myself. Looking back I see a man staring back at me. It's a familiar face. I've seen him before but cannot remember where.

"Sorry," he says boring down on me with dark eyes. The corners of his mouth twitch. A knowing smile. As if he knows me. Or knows about me.

I feel suspended in time. The carols blaring from the speakers, people talking, children shouting; it all feels muffled. As if I'm under water. It could be him. Terry. Fulfilling his threats and coming to get me.

He keeps going and I stare after him. "Do you know him?" Maya asks. With major effort, I tear my eyes from him and turn to her. Her brows are knitted together, her lips pursed.

"I... I don't... know," I stutter. "Maybe someone I met in court."

Turning back, I try to find him, but he's lost in the crowd. He could be anywhere by now. My hands shake and I grip the bags tightly. It's probably nothing, I try to convince myself. Just another shopper rushing through. Nobody important.

Chapter 25

The McBrides' house is bustling, as it always does at their annual Christmas Eve party. Decorations glimmer in every nook. Garlands have been hung along the banisters, mistletoe in every doorway, and there are festive cushions strewn everywhere. Ellen's Christmas tree puts mine to shame, standing majestically in the corner of the entryway, the branches alight with baubles.

Miles is talking to one of our other neighbours, also a surgeon. They're discussing some new study about the best way to make an incision for quicker recovery. "Reducing blood loss is paramount." My stomach churns and I look away, making a face. Although I've made strides forward in overcoming my fear of red, the thought of blood still terrifies me. Miles puts his hand on the small of my back.

"I'm going to look for Ellen."

Walking through the house, I stop to talk to other neighbours. Marion Lexington's overdone curls bob around her head as she waves me over. "How are the babies?" she asks.

I resist the urge to point out they're hardly babies any more. "Great, they stayed home with my parents." Taking out my phone, I show her a few recent photos of Julian and Leah and my heart warms as she oohs and aahs over them.

It takes a few minutes to extract myself from that conversation and I head towards the back of the house, thinking that Ellen must be in the kitchen ordering the caterers around. But instead I find Maya leaning against the kitchen counter, typing furiously into her phone. She pauses to snatch an hors d'oeuvre from a tray, popping it into her mouth. Her face is averted and she cannot see me standing in the doorway. I wonder who she's texting or emailing. What's going through her mind.

I don't know how much time has passed. Whether it's mere seconds or minutes. I am lost watching Maya, taking in every inch of her. My mind wanders back to that first Christmas after she was born. How I tried to smile despite the deep sorrow in my heart. I had thought it would be easy to give her up. Sign the papers and move on. But it wasn't. It isn't.

One of the caterers slams a tray on the counter. Maya's head jolts up, looking around, grinning when she sees me.

"Hey Mrs P. Want some of these?" She gestures to the tray in front of her.

"Sure," I respond, taking one of the crab puffs and nibbling at it slowly, wanting this moment to last forever. "Did your mum make these?"

"Nah. But don't tell anyone. She wants everyone to think she's a modern day Julia Child."

"Well, she's certainly closer to her than I am," I laugh.

"You have your strengths, Mrs P," she says, wiggling her eyebrows.

One of the caterers takes a tray from the fridge. Maya cranes her neck. "What are those?"

"Stuffed olives," he says.

Maya makes a face. "Yukk, I cannot stand olives."

"Madam?" the caterer asks, looking at me.

"No, thank you."

"Don't you like olives?" Maya asks.

"Can't say I'm a fan."

"I never noticed. Have you always been like that?"

"Yeah, I can't remember a time when I liked them."

"Me too. Mum loves them and always tries to convince me to try again. She says they're an acquired taste. But they make my stomach churn."

We both eye the tray of stuffed olives on the counter. Maya wrinkles her nose and I grip the counter tightly to stop the urge to hug her. "Are you going out tonight?" There's an overwhelming desire to know exactly what Maya is doing, how she will be spending her time.

"No, Mum wouldn't let me." She shakes her head in resigned desperation. "She said there would be too many weirdos out and about. At least she allowed me to invite a couple of friends. After I begged."

"That's fun."

"Whatever, I'm used to her now." She shrugs and takes another crab puff. "Bet you won't be as strict with Julian and Leah."

Maya's phone beeps, saving me from having to answer. "Oh, they're here," she says, straightening up. "Merry Christmas if I don't see you."

"Merry Christmas, Maya." I stand there, staring at the doorway, long after she's gone, wishing that I'd had the courage to hug her.

Guests are milling about in every room as I wander around looking for Ellen. Neighbours stop me to talk, asking me about work, about the kids, my plans for the break. I need a moment to gather my thoughts. I walk towards the closed office door, hoping for some privacy. It isn't locked.

As soon as I walk in I see her. Ellen is sitting in one of the wingback chairs next to the window. She's barely visible in the shadows. Not wanting to disturb her, I take a step back, about to walk away, when she calls my name softly.

"I'm sorry, I didn't realise there was anyone in here," I tell her.

She shakes her head and brings her wine glass to her mouth. She's been drinking more lately and I worry that she's going to have another full-blown relapse. As I walk towards her, I see that she's crying. A tear rolls down her cheek, catching a ray of light coming from the dim lamp that turns it into sparkling silver. Leaning over, I take her free hand into mine, almost pulling away when I feel how cold it is. Instead I warm it between both of mine. She continues taking one sip of wine after another until her glass is empty. I wonder whether she should be getting help. But I don't dare say anything, not even when she bends down and picks up a bottle of wine from next to her chair, filling her glass again.

"I haven't told Tom yet," she says in a voice so faint that I have to strain to hear her.

"Do you think I should have?" she adds when I don't answer.

"Why didn't you tell him?" I ask her gently.

"I didn't want to ruin Christmas."

"So, you've decided to carry this burden all by yourself?"

"Well, you know."

"He'd want you to tell him, to be able to discuss this with you, have a say in the way forward," I say.

She nods her head so slightly that the movement is barely visible. But I can feel the vibration going through her body. "Do you think he'll be angry?"

Part of me wants to protect her, help her get over this. But I also know that I have to keep a level head, keep my distance, make sure I let nothing slip.

Squeezing Ellen's hand, I say: "Of course he won't. This isn't your fault."

Our quiet corner is disrupted by Tom who walks in looking for his wife. "The caterers are asking what time you want to switch from savoury to sweet." He looks bewildered to find Ellen and I locked in this sombre mood. Ellen nods, stands up and walks out of the room. But I remain in the study, not yet ready to face the rest of the crowd, wanting to remain hidden in the darkness.

Chapter 26

Two days later I'm home alone. My parents have taken the kids to watch a film and Miles is at the hospital. I should be working but instead I'm going through the bags of wrapping paper, deciding what should be thrown out and what can be salvaged and reused. The former pile is much bigger, I notice, smiling as I remember the sheer exuberance with which Julian and Leah tore through the colourful paper to uncover the gifts the previous morning.

The doorbell rings. "Are you alone?" Ellen asks as soon as I open the door. She is frowning deeply, her face slightly flushed under her expensive makeup.

"Yes." My heart starts beating faster as immediately the fear of what Ellen has found out about me and Maya rises to the surface. "Did anything happen?"

"I told Tom." Relief flows through me.

"Come on in." Leading the way into the kitchen, I arrange the documents on the island into a neat pile.

"What did he say?" I ask.

She sits down with a sigh. She looks different, older, and I'm worried about the impact of this ordeal on her health. "He freaked out, accused me of hiding important things from him." She pauses to catch her breath. "He doesn't get it."

"I guess it's quite a big thing to keep from him. Even if it was only for a few days."

"Not you too! Why is everyone ganging up on me?" After a beat, she collects herself. "Anyway, at least he agrees that we shouldn't say anything to Maya."

"So, you're not telling her?"

"Don't you agree? She's too young and we don't want her thinking that she has anything to do with this Larkin guy."

"Well, it's obviously your decision."

"Ok, spit it out." There's an edge to her voice and her face is slightly red. "What would you do?"

Ellen's hint of aggression takes me aback, but I pause without showing it, thinking about the right way to answer. It feels so hypocritical to want them to tell Maya about her paternity when I have kept such secrets from her since I've known her. But for some strange reason I want her to have some of her questions answered, unwilling to connect this with how much more danger it could put me in.

"I don't know. It's a difficult decision obviously." Then, to deflect the tension, give myself some time, I offer to make tea. We are both silent while I put the kettle on then take mugs out of one cupboard, teabags from another, and teaspoons from the drawer, lining them up like surgical tools, allowing myself the chance to think.

"I wonder whether they will be able to unseal Maya's birth certificate even if you deny them permission," I muse.

"How can they do that?" Ellen's voice rises sharply.

The kettle whistles and I busy myself making tea, using the interruption to gauge Ellen's reaction, and think ahead of how to guide the McBrides to a decision that still protects me from being exposed. "They might take the matter to court and petition a judge to overrule your wishes," I say as I hand her a mug.

"They wouldn't dare!" Ellen puts her mug down with such uncharacteristic force that she spills tea over the white countertop. Leaning over, she grabs a handful of paper towels and wipes it off.

"Ellen," I say gently, seeing a plan more clearly now. "I think you should collaborate with the detectives. Or at least give them reason to think you're going to be helpful. It's the only way you can keep informed of what they're doing, where the investigation is going, whether they've found out anything."

She doesn't say anything. "That's what *I* would do," I add.

"Anyway, even if they were forced to stall the investigation, Maya will be eighteen in less than two years and they will go directly to her then without consulting you."

Or me, I think. The thought that detectives could continue looking for Maya's mother, for me, without me knowing what stage the investigation is at, whether they're getting closer to finding me, looms inside me. I need to know what's happening, whether I'm in danger. Will Terry come forward this time? Or perhaps the police will find him or her. This person knows my name, where I live. It will not take long for that trail to lead to me.

On the other hand, who knows what will happen by the time Maya turns eighteen. Perhaps the detectives will no longer be interested in reopening the investigation. Terry might not be found. He, or whoever she is, might remain underground, especially if any revelations about Maya and the John Larkin case go public.

Both options have risks and I don't know which one is best. But for some reason I feel this enormous need inside me to know what's happening, for the case to be resolved quickly. I'm terrified I might crack under the constant pressure of not knowing my fate for two whole years. Somehow I need to convince the McBrides to allow the detectives to unseal Maya's records. The quicker they finalise the investigation, the quicker I'll know where I stand.

"Let's focus on the meeting with the detectives. Try to get as much information as possible out of them. Hopefully I can help you with that. Seeing that you have legal help might push them to collaborate more. Then you can decide what to do based on the information they give you and how you feel after the meeting."

Ellen nods, looking down at her mug, staring into the depths of the liquid as if it held the answer to all her questions.

Chapter 27

"Don't twirl your hair," I tell Chloe, trying to keep my voice even. "Try to avoid fidgeting,"

She rolls her eyes and crosses her arms. "Don't cross your arms either; it makes you look antagonistic."

"What do you want me to do with them?"

I sigh, my patience starting to wear thin. It's the same argument every single time. "Relax your arms and place your hands on your lap," I say in my calmest voice. "We've gone over this already," I add in exasperation.

A hand presses on my shoulder. Luigi is right behind me. "Let's take a ten minute break," he says.

"Five minutes." I turn towards Chloe. "Do you need to use the bathroom?"

She walks out of my office and I hear her mumble something under her breath. Exhaling deeply, I shake my head, half wanting to go after her. "Calm down for a second." Luigi's voice is soothing. "Don't let her get to you."

"Ugh, she can be so frustrating," I say, rubbing my temples. "She seems intent on doing exactly the opposite of what I tell her. Doesn't seem to realise that I'm trying to help."

"She's a kid and she's acting like one. You need to remain calm and continue coaching her," he says. "Losing your temper is not going to do anyone any good."

"I know."

Changing the subject, I broach the topic of the McBrides. "My neighbours need some help. It has to do with their daughter's adoption."

"Yeah? Which neighbours? Have I met them?"

"Yes, actually. Tom and Ellen. They were at Leah's first birthday party."

"The accountant?"

"Yes," I nod as Chloe walks back in. Her face is flushed, her cheeks rosy and she averts her eyes when I look at her. It looks like she's been crying. "Let's continue. We'll start from the beginning, from when you're called to the stand. Everyone will be looking at you, examining every detail, the way you walk, how you sit down, where you look. It's important that you look as natural as possible."

"Ok." She takes a seat next to me in the makeshift courtroom we've created in an unused office.

"The defence calls Chloe Wilson to the stand," I say. Chloe stands up and walks over to the witness stand. Her head is not held as high as usual and her face seems relaxed, softer. She sits down and rests her hands in her lap, glancing over at the seats where the jurors would be sitting, before turning her head and looking straight ahead. "Good," I mouth, pleased that she's followed all my suggestions.

For the next two hours we rehearse a mock trial, Luigi acting as the prosecutor and asking Chloe the difficult questions. "Am I boring you?" Luigi asks.

"No, no," she responds.

"So why are you yawning?"

"I'm sorry, I'm just tired," she says, looking down.

"I think we've done enough for today," I interject. "You've done really well. Let's continue tomorrow."

When Luigi leaves, I ask Chloe to sit down. "What are you going to wear to court?"

She shifts uncomfortably in her chair, looking down at her lap. "I... I'm not sure," she finally says.

"It's imperative that you choose the right outfit. It's all part of the image we're trying to portray. It needs to be neat but demure. And you're starting to show. Let's see your bump, but not too much flesh."

Chloe doesn't say anything. Instead, her eyes dart around the room, as if she's trying to find a way to escape. Of course, I think. She cannot afford to buy new clothes. All her outfits look worn, some of them with small holes, most totally out of shape, and those jeans definitely won't last the pregnancy.

"I'd like to get you an outfit for court."

Her head shoots up and she looks directly at me. Then, when the realisation of what I'm saying hits, her face flushes deep red. "It's ok, I'll figure something out."

"I insist. Let's go."

As we get into a taxi, I think of the times I would have gone shopping with Maya if the situation was different. How I would have picked up things for her during my lunch break. Or ordered cute outfits online. There's a tightening in my chest as I realise how much I've missed out on and how much worse there could be to come.

*

By the time I get home I'm feeling totally washed out. Returning to the office after taking Chloe shopping, I'd buried myself in work. The mental exhaustion, brought on by the hours spent trying to prepare Chloe for the trial, is matched by sheer physical tiredness. Pulling into the garage, I don't get out of the car immediately. Turning my head from side to side, I pull my chin to my chest and crunch my shoulders back. I take deep breaths, in from my nose, out from my mouth, and repeat.

After a few minutes I take one last deep breath in and exhale slowly before opening the door and swinging my legs out of the car. Taking my handbag and briefcase from the passenger seat, I head into the house, stopping on the other side of the door and propping myself against the wall as I remove my high heels.

The house is silent and dark. It's hours past the children's bedtime and I wonder whether Miles has gone for an early night. He has been working long hours, performing more surgeries to cover for a colleague who needed time off while his wife undergoes chemotherapy. My heart sinks at the thought of not spending any time with him, but I know he needs the rest.

Heading towards the kitchen, I navigate my way around furniture with only memory and the dim light coming in from the windows to guide me. Putting my briefcase down, I reach for the light switch and turn it on.

And then, as I turn around, my right hand flies to my mouth and I suppress a squeal. There, on the kitchen island, is something I never wanted to see. A sight that instils fear inside me. I've long dreaded this moment, hoped that it would never happen. And yet I did nothing to prevent it.

Chapter 28

"What the hell is this?"

Miles' hair is dishevelled as if he's been pulling at it for several hours, like he always does when he's worried. There is a pallor in his face, his cheeks look drained. He is staring squarely at the entryway where I am standing, sitting bolt upright on the stool, his arms propped against the island.

He purses his lips and flares his nostrils, staring at me with eyes that are full of anger. But there is something else in his gaze. Fear. And incredulity. As if he still cannot believe what he's just found out. As if he still cannot fully comprehend what his discovery means.

The gold-coloured cardboard box is open, the lid upside down a few inches away. The crisp white tissue paper is crumpled next to the box. My wedding shoes are sitting on the kitchen island. I cringe as I think of the dirt from the soles on the usually pristine surface. Looking at them, I notice the scuffs in the white satin, the dent in the heel where it had been caught between the tiles as I danced the night away. One of the diamanté embellishments has fallen off, leaving a blob of glue in its place.

Tearing my gaze from the once-worn shoes, I look into Miles' blazing eyes. He stares at me, and I see a muscle in his jaw twitching as he clenches his teeth. Cowering under his glare, I look away from him and at the evidence of our past, and the secrets I have kept from him.

John Larkin's eyes look right back at me, his face distorted by the creases in the newspaper page that I have kept for all these years, hidden underneath my wedding shoes, the box tucked in the back of the closet. There are other newspaper cuttings strewn across the island, the headlines screaming back at me, reminding me of the fear I felt as I read the unfolding details of the investigation into John Larkin's death. I'd kept them all, never wanting to forget what the police had revealed, scared that I might one day divulge a detail that would expose me.

Miles moves his hand and picks something up. He stands up slowly and walks towards me. I cower back, wanting to run away, to turn the clock back so I can undo the damage. But I know I cannot escape what's coming. The consequences are reeling me in, dragging me down in the terrible aftermath of what I've done.

"What are these?" he asks in a voice unlike his usual tone. There's a harshness that is never present. His right bicep ripples under his sleeve as he waves a small pile of envelopes in my direction, their torn edges jutting out messily. Our home address is written in block capitals on the envelope on top, and I know it's the last letter I received, not too long ago.

"Elizabeth, why is someone threatening you?" His voice has risen a decibel and sounds sharper, as if he's about to lose control.

I swallow hard, trying to clear the lump in my throat, but am unable to talk. Miles takes a sheet of paper from one of the envelopes and unfolds it. "Your time will come soon. You'll pay for what you did," he reads.

Miles lets the sheet flutter onto the island and picks up the second one. "I know what you did and I'm watching you." He looks right at me. "Who is this? Why is he threatening you?"

Tears sting my eyes as the familiar dread takes hold of me, and worse, as I sense the fear that is palpable in Miles right now.

"Stop reading those," I tell him, reaching out and snatching the rest of the envelopes from his hand.

Anger flashes in his eyes as he glares at me. He picks something else up and the plastic glistens as it catches the light. "Can you explain what this is?" he asks. "Why do you have Ellen's driver's licence?"

I desperately rack my brain to try and come up with a story, spin a tale to avoid telling the truth. Some seemingly innocent explanation that he will want to believe. But I know it's too late, especially when he brings his other hand in front of me. His knuckles are white with the force he's using to clench the small strip. The writing on the hospital band is faded but still legible.

"What is this?" Miles spits at me. "And who the hell is Laura Black?"

"I… I can explain." I look around, searching for something to do to buy time. To think of an excuse. Some way to get out of having to tell Miles the truth.

He grabs my arm with such force that I'm taken by surprise. "You'd better start." His voice has a sharp edge to it. "And you'd better tell the truth. I'm fed up of your lies."

Biting my lip to stop my quivering chin, I look straight into Miles' eyes, reach out and take the hospital band from him. I remember the moment it was secured around my wrist when I was admitted, how I clawed at it when the plastic edges started rubbing against my skin, trying to stretch it. As soon as I was discharged I'd asked the nurse for a pair of scissors to cut it off. I should have thrown it away, left it in the hospital. But instead I'd put it in my pocket.

"It was a long time ago. I was in hospital." Perhaps he will stop asking questions. He always has. Almost as if he is scared of what he will find out if he delves too deeply into my past.

But not today.

"Elizabeth, one lie and I'm taking this box to the police. Then you can spin your tales to them, see if they believe you."

"Please Miles, leave the past in the past, where it belongs," I implore.

He continues to stare at me, his eyes narrowing into slits. His face is red, the veins on his temples throbbing. There's a glisten of sweat on his brow. I've seen Miles angry before, but not like this. At least not at me. We've had fights, long arguments, gone to bed without speaking. But this is different. It seems like there's no longer any love in his eyes. Just anger and fear.

"It's no longer in the past. Surely you cannot be so deluded not to realise that. You've dragged us all into it, so you'd better start explaining."

Where do I even start? The rape? Maya? The letters? Miles seems to sense my confusion. Reaching behind him, he picks up the newspaper page and lifts it in front of me. "What happened with this guy? You were involved?"

"He... I was riding my bike back to campus and he hit me. And then... I was an idiot... I got into his car. And he drugged me, took me to this room." The tears that I'd been trying to hold back start flowing down my cheeks. Fear is intermixed with the relief of finally telling my story to someone.

"Was it that night? The night I saw you?"

"Ye…" The incomplete word comes out in a rasp as a lump closes my throat.

"Did he attack you? Was it you? Did you…" He trails off, as if he cannot utter the words, talk about my unspeakable actions.

Again, I nod. Swallowing hard, I try to clear my throat. "He attacked me, was about to rape me again. I found a piece of glass and hit at him. I didn't mean it, didn't want to. I just had to stop him, get him off me, give myself the time to run away…" My voice breaks down and I find myself sobbing.

"Oh, my God." He closes his eyes for a few seconds, inhaling deeply. "Why didn't you go to the police? Tell them what he did to you?"

I shake my head. "I was afraid. Afraid that they wouldn't believe me."

"Even when they found the other girls?"

"Yes."

"You were raped. And you were pregnant."

I nod.

"Oh God. Is Maya your daughter?"

"Miles, please," I plead, burying my face in my hands.

"Is she your daughter?" he asks again. Then, in a voice that sounds sharper: "Look at me, Elizabeth."

Prying my hands away, I force myself to meet his eyes. And I know at that moment that he will not give in, that he will continue quizzing me until he is satisfied I'm telling him the truth, until all his questions are answered.

"Yes," I say in a small voice.

"Oh my God, Liz, how could you keep this from me? I knew you'd had a child before. I'm a doctor for fuck's sake. But Maya? What the hell?" He turns away and clasps his head. "This explains so much."

There are no words. No explanation. For years I've feared this would happen, the moment that my secret stops being a secret, when someone else finds out. I should have got rid of those letters, the cuttings, Ellen's driver's licence, the hospital bracelet. They were a trap set in wait for me to be caught.

"How did you find this?" I ask before I can stop myself.

"What does it matter?" Miles snaps back. He pauses and I see his Adam's apple bob up and down. "Is that why you went to the US? So that nobody would know you? So you could keep this a secret?"

"I guess. It was a convenient opportunity."

"So, this is why you were so adamant to live in this house," he says after a while. "How long have you been stalking the McBrides?"

"I wasn't stalking them," I defend myself. "I just wanted to make sure she was ok. That she had a good life. Was well cared for."

"You could have done that from a distance. We didn't need to move to the same street."

Swallowing the lump in my throat, I look up at my husband. And the desire to tell him the truth, to explain my feelings for Maya becomes so important after my years long need to keep any connection to this hidden. "I wanted to be in her life. I wanted to get to know her, find out who she is. I wanted to make sure I did the right thing by giving her away. I couldn't help myself."

Miles purses his lips as he continues to stare at me, seeming to judge me for how bad a person I really am. "Does she know?" he finally asks.

I shake my head. "No, she has no idea. I never wanted her to know. I only wanted to make sure she was ok. I couldn't stop thinking about her. I tried. But I couldn't."

Miles exhales loudly and rubs his forehead. He pulls a stool and sits down, resting his elbows on the island. He looks at me as if he's seeing me for the first time. I cannot read the emotions on his face. Is he angry? Surprised? Scared?

Then, when I think I cannot stand his silence any longer, he says: "What were you thinking? You have two other children. *We* have two other children. Have you forgotten about them? Don't you realise that you've put them in danger too?"

The words escape me. It almost feels like part of my brain has been paralysed and no longer able to form coherent thoughts. Instead there's a jumble of emotions. Among them is regret at the series of actions that have led me to today. I had been so adamant after the incident to get as far away as possible from where it all took place. I wanted to make sure that the past never caught up with me. I packed everything related to that night and its aftermath and tried to push it out of my mind.

But every night, when I went to bed, I dreamed about the little girl that I had given up. I could not get her out of my mind. Her face shone just behind my eyes and I longed to hold her. Sometimes I'd rummage in the back of my closet until I found the hospital bracelet, its clean cut edges a stark reminder of our severed relationship. I wondered how she'd grown, what she was doing, who she had become. And I felt a need to be in her life, making the move to this street essential to my happiness. I needed to be near Maya, to see her grow up. It was a force bigger than me, one that I couldn't resist.

A buzzing sound forces me back to the here and now. Miles looks at his phone and stands up. "It's the hospital."

The slam of the front door sounds final. It feels like the door closing on the life I've built, the life I love so much. I don't know what tomorrow will bring, what Miles is going to do. Will he help me continue to cover up my past or is he going to turn me in? Does he hate me for what I did, and for lying so much? What I'm sure of is that things will never be the same again.

Chapter 29

For long minutes I sit at the kitchen island, staring into the dim room, trying to wrap my head around what happened. But it's too much for me. My brain doesn't want to process the events of tonight. It keeps whirring and whirring without focusing on anything in particular.

When the door goes, I know it must be Ellen. With effort I force myself to get up from the stool. Bracing myself, I open the door. "I saw Miles drive off. Figured I'd pop by, see if you felt like a chat."

Ellen's holding a bottle of wine, looking far less breezy than she sounds, and her company is the last thing I need. But I can't find the courage to send her away, tell her I need some time to myself. Instead I swing the door back automatically. "Yes, of course."

She starts following me into the kitchen. Then, two steps away, I stop in my tracks. The box is still open on the island, its implicating contents spread over the white marble. Ellen will take one look at her driver's licence, my hospital band with Maya's birth date written on it, the newspaper cuttings, and she'll know what I did. That it was me all along.

"Is everything ok?" She's right behind me. I can smell her expensive geranium face cream, the minty breath, the laundered clothes. She's going to find out. She's going to hate me. Probably go to the police. She'll never agree to keep my secret. Not when it involves Maya.

I need to send her away, come up with an excuse, tell her I have work to do. She'll understand. But my brain is frozen and I cannot think of anything. Of a way out of this.

Think, think, I urge myself. Quick. There are no seconds to spare. I need a solution right now. Squaring my shoulders, I almost collide into her and we both step back. "I'm sorry Ellen, I just remembered some paperwork that I need to finish tonight. Can we take a rain check?"

Her face crumples, her shoulders stoop. "Yes, of course," she says. "I should have called." She's already turning around, then she shifts the bottle to her elbow as she digs into her oversized bag and takes out a large brown envelope. "I wanted to bring Maya's adoption paperwork. They're copies – the originals are in the safe."

"Thank you. I'll look at them later. Is there anything that was said · or done that's not documented?"

Still standing awkwardly in the entryway Ellen looks down at her hands, pursing her lips into a straight line. Her face is ashen, her eyes wide open, fear etched into every pore. She takes another deep breath before continuing. "We paid the lawyer a lot to keep us top of mind with any clients."

*

One after the other, I look through the documents that Ellen brought. Opening the file is like stepping into the past, back to the last time I visited Steven in his grey office. On the bus I'd thought about the extent of what I was going to do, the fact that this was the absolute last chance for me to change my mind. For a fleeting second I had considered the possibility of taking her back, of flying back to England, going to my parents and telling them the whole story, of asking for their help to bring up my child.

But I quickly shook off the thought and signed the documents without hesitation, knowing that I was doing the right thing both for myself and the baby. And for the couple who had adopted her.

I'm startled by the sound of the garage door opening. My heart lifts at the thought that my husband is back. That he hasn't abandoned me. At least not yet.

Miles looks haggard. It's like he's aged years in the space of a few hours. His face is drawn, his lips pale and there seem to be new wrinkles around his eyes. He stands next to the sofa, staring down at me, the silence between us becoming more uncomfortable by the second.

Closing the file, I put it on the sofa beside me. "What is that?" Miles asks, motioning to the folder.

"Maya's adoption papers. Ellen brought them over."

He reaches out and picks it up. He fiddles with the cardboard corners. He's never touched any of my work documents, knowing the importance of confidentiality. He looks as if he's going to open the folder, but at the last second puts it back down.

"Do you know who has been sending you the letters?"

I shake my head. "No," I say in a small voice. "But he called someone that night, told them my name. That must be how they found me."

"Are you being followed?"

Part of me wants to tell him that I've seen the same car on my way to work, pulling in behind me. That sometimes I see the same man on the bench right across from my office, just sitting there, staring right ahead. That sometimes I feel I can't tell the truth from its opposite any more. But I cannot bring myself to share the depth of my paranoia. "I don't know," I say instead.

Miles pinches the bridge of his nose between his thumb and forefinger, rubbing the area slowly. "Has there been any other contact?" he asks.

Shaking my head, I'm grateful that for once I'm able to tell him a fact I'm certain of. "What if they tell the police about you?"

Blood rushes to my head and I feel faint with fear. It's a scenario that I've considered many times, always shoving it to the back of my mind, too terrifying to conceive. When I don't answer he continues. "And what if they try to harm you? Or try to harm our children? Have you thought about that?"

"Yes, of course, I think about it every day," I say, my voice trembling. The fear of this anonymous person has stayed with me since the first time I received a letter. Especially when we moved and the letter arrived at the new address. But I still lacked the courage to talk to the police.

He sits down next to me, putting the file on his lap. "Tell me everything. What do the police know? How much trouble are you in?"

"I don't know. It's been so long, almost seventeen years. The case was closed and I thought it was over. That it was only there in my nightmares, in my phobias. I knew what I did would always haunt me. That would be my everlasting punishment."

"And what about the letters? Surely you couldn't have thought you were fine with someone else out there knowing what you did?"

"Of course I'm worried. But I thought since they hadn't said anything yet, maybe they wouldn't."

"That's a big 'maybe'," he says, his lips curled into a snarl.

"And I thought maybe whoever was threatening was also afraid their wrongs would catch up on them too, if they were some sort of accomplice."

"And what about the evidence on the scene?"

"I don't think I left anything that would link me to him. I cleaned the place well. At least I think I did. I was in shock and acted on my instincts."

Miles' face bears an expression I cannot read. He shakes his head, small jerking movements from one side to the other. "How did you even manage to do that? Know what to do? Have the concentration needed to cover everything up?"

Shrugging, I look down. It's a question I've asked myself many times, wondering why I had not panicked and been unable to do what needed to be done, and how on the thin line I've been treading, I haven't slipped before now. "I don't know. My defences took over. I wanted to erase what happened, and make sure I was never caught."

Miles nods slowly and I hope that he can sympathise. But then he asks: "Have you ever thought about turning yourself in? Coming clean?"

This is the reaction I'd been dreading. It's the main reason I never told my secret to anyone. I never wanted to be forced to do something I wasn't ready for. "Do you think I should?" I ask, wanting to know what's going on in his mind.

"I don't know what to think. How could we have been together for all these years and you never told me? Not about the rape, not about Maya. Who are you?" He looks confused for a moment, and my heart bleeds for him and for us. "I'm not even sure I want you around my children."

The last words cut through me, a veiled threat that he'll take away the kids.

"I'm their mother," I try, my jaw set.

"Then start acting like it!"

*

For hours I toss and turn, my head bursting with thoughts and fears. Miles' reaction was worse than I expected. And with the investigation underway, who knows whether I'm going to be found out. Every time I close my eyes I see Maya's face. It pains me to think how lonely she must be feeling, unable to speak to her parents about her desire to track down her biological mother. I wonder whether we'd have had a closer relationship had I kept her.

Julian and Leah's sweet faces flash in front of my eyes as Miles' words reverberate in my ears. How is this going to affect them? What will their lives be like if I'm caught? The risk of losing them, just like I'd lost Maya, sends shivers down my spine and I shiver despite the warm blanket.

The house is empty when I go downstairs the following morning. The kitchen is devoid of the clutter Miles always leaves behind him. Silence surrounds me. There are none of the sounds of our usual morning routine. The children eating their breakfast noisily. The swish of the newspaper as Miles turns the pages. The smell of coffee.

My heart starts beating faster, my breath coming in short gasps. Kicking off my heels, I run upstairs, taking two steps at a time. The children's rooms are empty. Their pyjamas are on the floor of the Jack and Jill bathroom.

"No!" The word comes out in a strangled squeak as I run back downstairs, almost slipping on the top step. But I don't slow down. I need to get out of here, find them. He can't take away my children. I lost a child once and I won't let it happen again.

Rushing into the kitchen, I pick up my phone from the island and dial Miles' number. It rings once. Twice. A third time. My pulse quickens. Finally he answers. "Hello."

"Where are you?" I struggle to keep my voice even.

"Uhm, I took the kids to breakfast before school. I left you a sticky note on your phone."

"I didn't see it… You should have woken me up. I woke up and there was nobody in the house. I thought…"

"What did you think? That I went behind your back? I'm not you Liz. I don't keep secrets."

His words cut. I don't know how to respond. "Gotta go. I have to drive them to school," Miles says instead.

The line goes dead and I'm left in the empty kitchen, all alone. The few minutes I spend with the children in the morning are precious. I want to cry. But I don't have time. I'm already late. With shaking hands I pick up my bag and briefcase and head to the garage.

Hours later I'm still shaken, the panic from this morning's episode mingling with worry about meeting the detectives searching for Maya's birth mother. "Nothing's going to happen. This isn't about you." I repeat the mantra in my head as I walk out of the office and flag down a taxi.

Tom and Ellen are already waiting outside. Their nerves are plain to see even from my cab window. Tom is pacing in a circle and Ellen is standing upright, twisting her hands. We discussed the case a few nights ago and they are not seeing eye-to-eye. Tom wants to tell Maya about the developments. Ellen is adamant that she doesn't want her to know.

The hairs at the back of my neck prickle as we leave the bustling Westminster street and set foot in the police headquarters. Sweat begins to creep from my pores. The click of my heels on the white tiles sounds like the ticks of a clock, each second bringing me closer and closer to being discovered for who I am.

"That's them," Ellen says, indicating a large man with a bushy moustache and a petite blonde woman. They walk towards us and introduce themselves as Detective Brown, the lead investigator, and Detective James.

"You didn't need to bring a lawyer," Detective Brown tells Tom and Ellen when I introduce myself. We've been shown into a cramped office, the large desk covered with files, and invited to sit on mismatched chairs.

Tom opens his mouth to respond, but I quickly jump in. "I'm here to help them make the best decision for the wellbeing of their daughter. As you can imagine your visit last month was a complete surprise to Mrs McBride. Mr McBride and myself would like to hear the whole story straight from you."

Detective Brown rolls his eyes and for a second I think he's about to dismiss my request. Tell me that he doesn't have time to waste. But instead he motions to his colleague.

Detective James sits straight in her chair and takes a deep breath. "The DNA company alerted us about the match…"

My concentration wavers despite the importance of knowing exactly what the police are saying. Detective James drones on in the background as my mind swims. Being here, in the police station, discussing John Larkin's death feels surreal. This should have happened sixteen years ago. We shouldn't be here right now. I shouldn't be going behind Maya's back.

"We want to find Maya's birth mother so we can question her, determine whether she knows anything about the murder," Detective James continues.

"Do you think she's involved?" I ask before I can stop myself.

The detectives look at each other before Detective Brown replies. "We don't know. It's a working theory and we want to find her to answer some questions."

"Do you think she's still in England?" The question escapes before I can stop myself. "Maya wasn't born here."

The two detectives look at each other, a confounded expression on their faces. "We don't know yet," Detective Brown says. I need to be more careful, appear less eager to find out more, make sure nobody suspects I have any other agenda other than supporting the McBrides through this.

"What do you need from us?" Tom interjects.

"We need your permission to unseal Maya's birth certificate so that we can track down her birth mother." Detective Brown looks straight at Tom and Ellen. "That's the only involvement you have in this case."

"Will you keep us… uhm… Mr and Mrs McBride informed about the progress? Whether you're close to finding Maya's mother?"

"It depends. This is a police investigation after all, spanning across two countries," he says gruffly.

"Of course," I respond. "But detective, as you can imagine, Mr and Mrs McBride's main concern is their daughter's wellbeing. Maya is still young and we fear the impact of finding out that both her biological parents are suspected of murder might have long-lasting negative effects on her. That's why it's important for them to know how the investigation is going. So they can prepare Maya. Otherwise they will be reluctant to allow any action that can impact on their daughter."

"She's the one who tried to track down her birth parents," Detective Brown replies. "Anyway, this is a murder investigation and we will leave no stone unturned that might lead us to what happened. If need be, we'll petition the court to overturn their decision." He motions towards Tom and Ellen.

"So, your request was a courtesy. Mr and Mrs McBride have no choice in the matter?" This conversation needs to get back on course. I need to find out what information they have.

Detective James interjects. "We want to get their permission. But we don't think we can wait another two years for Maya to turn eighteen to continue with our investigation. That's why we want access to her birth records immediately."

Ellen is playing with the strap of her handbag, nervously twisting it around her other hand. Tom is sat upright as if there's a rod going through his torso. They both look shellshocked.

"As I mentioned, Mr and Mrs McBride are adamant that Maya's privacy is respected and very concerned that her identity might be leaked and splattered across the media. We cannot have a sixteen year old's life turned upside down. Maya needs to be protected at all costs."

Detective Brown doesn't speak. He chews on the end of a pen as if he's mulling over what I've just said. "Is there anywhere I can speak to my clients in private?" I ask.

He stands up. "Use my office," he says, circling his desk. "We'll be back in ten minutes."

For a few seconds after the detectives leave, we sit in silence. Tom and Ellen look ashen, their eyes shifting around.

"What do you think?" Tom speaks first.

"I don't think you really have a choice. You either give them permission now and hope they will inform you of any developments or risk them petitioning the court and everything being made public."

Ellen starts crying softly. She takes a pristine white handkerchief from her handbag and blows her nose.

"What would you do?" Tom asks.

My head throbs, a sharp pain searing between my eyes. Blinking, I will it to go away, allow me to concentrate. I don't know what would be best for all of us. Maya's interests must come first but I also need to think about myself. How can I live knowing that detectives are re-examining all the evidence from John Larkin's death, looking for more, getting closer to finding me?

"Let's ask for a week to mull over your options." This will give me time to come up with some sort of plan for myself. "In the meantime, you can speak to Maya."

"Do we have to tell her?" Ellen asks.

"Well, not necessarily. But telling her now will give you control over the message, what you tell her and how you tell her," I explain.

Tom nods. "And can you protect her? From a legal perspective?"

"Yes. I will do everything that the law allows to make sure that Maya is never harassed or has her name associated with this case."

The irony doesn't escape me. Sixteen years ago I gave up a tiny baby because I wanted to protect myself and her. Now I'm using my knowledge of the law to continue to protect her. But I'm wondering if I got it wrong then and I'm still getting it all wrong.

Chapter 30

"Cancel my afternoon meetings," I tell Jennifer as I pass by her desk. "Hold my calls." I close my office door behind me before she has time to respond.

The mountain of paperwork on my desk looks daunting. There is so much to do, trial preparations to continue, tens of emails that require a response. But as much as I try to concentrate, my mind keeps wandering. I can only think of Maya. And myself.

Now that Miles knows, the situation is complicated further. I'm no longer able to take decisions on my own, but have to take him into consideration. Taking the children out of the house without allowing them to say goodbye is so unlike him. It's like he was trying to prove a point but I can't bear to think what it is.

Leaning back against the cushioned chair, I close my eyes as I shift to try and find a comfortable position. My life feels like it's starting to unravel and I need to wrap my mind around it.

The McBrides have promised to think about my recommendation. "We can meet you later, discuss the issue further," Tom had said.

A voice inside me screamed "no". I wanted to spend time with my family, try to understand what's going through my husband's head.

"Why don't you sleep on it and we can meet in a day or two?" I told the McBrides.

"Sleep?!" Ellen spat out. "I haven't slept for weeks. But if you don't have time for us…"

"No, of course I have time," I said quickly. The risk that they would look for another lawyer, that I will be cut off and unable to find out what's going on is too great. I need to be part of this, not only to make sure I'm always a step ahead of the investigation but also because I want to know how this is affecting Maya. I know that I'm treading a fine line, bending all the rules, risking losing my licence. But the need to learn more is bigger than my fears.

An hour later I am still staring at the documents in front of me, unable to focus on the words. Shaking my head at the hopeless task, I pack my briefcase and pick up my coat. "I'm leaving," I tell Jennifer. "I'll be on my cell if you need me."

Instead of heading home I drive straight to the children's school, calling the sitter on the way and asking her to meet us at home. A gust of wind greets me when I step out of the car. My mind goes back to that night, his body pressing me down, the blood gushing out of his neck, the look of surprise mixed with fear in his eyes as he took his last breath.

Leah hops out of the building, her skirt swishing around her legs. "Mummy!" She runs into my arms and I pick her up, holding her tight, inhaling the sweet smell of her hair. A few minutes later Julian walks out with his friends. His face lights up and he runs towards me. "Hey, kiddo." Putting Leah down, I squat next to Julian and pull him towards me. "I missed you this morning. Did you have fun with Daddy?"

We pile into my car, stopping at the bakery on our way home. The children ooh and aah as they flatten their noses against the cake display, pointing at the different confections. We return home laden with boxes of cakes and sit on the sofa tasting different goodies.

As much as I wish to spend more time with my family, as soon as Miles comes home I head to the McBrides.

"We're speaking to Maya this weekend," Ellen says as soon as she sees me.

"Have you thought about my recommendation?"

"We didn't have that much time." Ellen's hand is shaking around her wine glass. Judging by the half empty bottle on the table, this is not her first glass. Perhaps I should talk to Tom, try to find out more about Ellen's drinking habits, tell him that it's important for me to know everything if I'm to represent them.

"We asked for a week. So you can have a few more days if you need."

"No!" Tom glances at his wife in irritation. "We haven't stopped talking about it since we left you and our decision is to give the investigators permission to unseal Maya's birth certificate as long as they guarantee to protect her privacy. We don't want anyone else to know about this."

Jumbled thoughts rush through my head. Allowing the detectives access to Maya's birth certificate is another step towards me being found out. But the name on that document is a blind alley. And despite the risks, I cannot imagine waiting years for this investigation to continue. Anyway, this choice is out of my hands. I look at Ellen and she purses her lips and looks away, but finally nods. "I completely agree. It's the best choice in the circumstances," I say, even though I'm not so sure. "We can demand that they guarantee to protect Maya's privacy, make that a condition of the agreement."

"Yes, that's a good idea," Tom says. "Anything else we should ask for?"

"Yes. You should insist that the detectives share any information they uncover about Maya's birth mother."

*

It's pouring with rain. It hasn't stopped all day. Pulling the car into the garage, I take a few seconds before getting out, needing some extra time before facing my family.

Maya is sprawled on the sofa playing with the children. The three of them giggle conspiratorially, and for a few moments I stand and look at them, before Maya sees me. "Hi Mrs P, you're home early today."

"I guess." I look at my watch. It's not yet six o'clock. Despite my busy schedule and almost daily prep sessions with Chloe, I've somehow managed to carve out time to draft the McBrides' contract, not wanting to lose any time since yesterday's meeting with the detectives. They want to meet this evening to go over it.

But for now I put them out of my mind and sit down. Work can wait. "What are we playing?" I ask the children, picking up a few Lego blocks and starting to build a tower.

"How are you, Maya?" I ask her later, when Julian and Leah are busy with a jigsaw puzzle.

"Good," she answers. Her eyes are twinkling, the smile on her face that of someone who's truly happy in a way I cannot fathom. "We had a fun afternoon, went for a walk around the neighbourhood since it was so sunny. Before it started pouring, that is. I was just about to make them supper. Can still do if you want me to."

"That'd be great." I know it's selfish to keep her here, but I'm steeped so far into this surreal situation and her presence is one of the few rays of light, making her offer impossible to refuse. Following her into the kitchen, I perch on one of the stools and watch her prepare cheesy pasta. She works fast, knowing exactly where everything is. She looks like she belongs in this kitchen, more than I feel I do right now.

She is still cooking when Miles walks in. He stops in the doorway. I follow his gaze even though I know exactly what he's looking at. His eyes are riveted to Maya, looking at her as if he's seeing her for the first time.

Maya doesn't look up. She is spooning portions into two colourful bowls, working methodically, making sure that both have the same amount to avoid any ensuing fighting.

Miles' throat vibrates as he swallows. For long seconds he remains in the same spot, immobile, almost as if he is made of stone. Still looking at Maya he opens his mouth and I fear that he's going to say something to her, that he's going to reveal my secret. But no words come out.

"Hello, Dr P," Maya's cheerful voice interrupts the moment. She looks towards me. "Dinner's ready.

Is it ok if I go now, Mrs P? Or do you want me to wait until they've eaten?"

"Yes, yes of course. Thank you for preparing dinner."

"Bye, Dr P," she says as she walks past Miles, who is still standing in the doorway, his bag in his hand. I don't know what he's thinking and don't want to ask. Instead I tell him that Tom and Ellen are coming over to discuss the case.

"Is it wise to represent them?" he asks. "To be so close to this case?"

"That's the whole point. I want to know what's happening, how close the police are to finding Maya's mother."

"Finding you," he says in a low voice. Then, when I don't answer, he asks: "How are Tom and Ellen doing?"

"Scared. Exhausted. Full of uncertainty."

Miles' phone beeps and he reaches behind him to get it. "Sh…" he starts, catching himself in time. "Gotta go back to the hospital." He doesn't look back as he goes.

*

It's late when Miles returns. Sitting in bed, I'm propped up against the pillows trying to read through a file on one of my easier cases, making margin notes to discuss with the client at our next meeting. I hear him rummaging downstairs, the sound of the cupboard opening, the clink of a glass being put down on the counter, the swish of the refrigerator door. Then the squeak of his rubber soles as he walks up the stairs.

The door opens and he walks in. Smiling at my husband, I close the file, putting it aside. "Are you ok?" I ask as he sits down at the foot of the bed and removes his shoes.

"Great," he says, sarcasm dripping from his voice. "Absolutely fantastic."

"Did anything happen?" I find myself holding my breath as I wait for his answer.

He bends forward and rests his elbows on his knees, his head in his hands, covering his face with his long fingers. "You have some nerve asking me that," he finally says, not looking at me. "Like finding out my wife killed a man and made us move next door to the child she gave up is not enough."

He eventually lifts his head up and turns towards me. His lips curl up like they do when he eats something sour, his nose wrinkled, his eyes slitted. There is none of the love that used to be so evident on his face.

"I should have known. That night... all those bruises on your face... and then the body found just outside campus. But I refused to believe that you could do something like that. And then that you'd keep it from me. Something that could ruin our lives, impact the children forever. I still can't understand how you've managed to keep this hidden for so long. The fact that you covered all this up and managed not to get caught scares me. I feel like I don't know you anymore. Who are you?"

Tears sting my eyes. "I'm still the same person."

"It's nobody I know." His voice is flat. "I didn't marry a killer. I knew you'd had a child, and it hurt that you would never tell me, open up about it. But I thought it was because it was too painful a memory. I even thought that your fear of blood had something to do with the baby. This though. This changes everything."

Alarm bells ring in my ears. "What do you mean?" I'm scared to ask but need to know.

"This is a lot for me to take in. I need time to wrap my head around it. I need to figure out what's best for our children." He walks to his side of the bed and picks up his pillow. "I'm sleeping in the spare bedroom."

Jumping out of bed, I run towards him. "Please don't do that." My voice breaks as I plead, my hands on his chest, trying to stop him.

He stops for a moment and I wonder if he's going to relent. His eyes are shimmering with sadness. But then he pushes my hand away. "I need time." There's a hoarseness in his voice and he clears his throat. "I need space."

There's a thumping sound in my ears and tiny flecks of light cloud my vision. "I didn't have a choice. He would have killed me," I try to explain. "I made a spur of the moment choice back then and I have to live with it."

"Well, I need time to figure out if I can."

Chapter 31

"Are you ready?" I ask, closing my laptop and getting up from my chair.

Chloe nods as she exhales sharply.

"It's going to be ok." I put a tentative arm around her shoulder. "You're prepared and I'm going to guide you." She leans against me, as if she craves human touch.

Jennifer pops her head into my office. "Your Uber's two minutes away."

In the car I go over my opening statement. Although I've done this so many times before, I still always fear getting stuck, that my mind will go blank. Chloe is silent, looking out of the window. "Try not to chew your lip. It makes you look nervous and it's not the image we want to portray." She nods, relaxing her face, but her eyes are still full of fear.

The drive to the courthouse is short. Chloe gets out and straightens the new clothes I'd bought her. Under her jacket she's wearing a light pink sweater and a knee-length dark grey skirt that shows her baby bump. Her legs are covered in opaque black tights and she's wearing black flat shoes. She's followed my instructions and her hair is in a neat ponytail, her face scrubbed clean of any makeup.

She stands next to the car, staring at the building in front of us. Only her eyes are moving, taking it all in. Steering her by the elbow, I guide her towards the steps, making our way through the crowds that are coming in and out of the courthouse.

Inside, I nod at a few peers but don't stop, leading Chloe through the milling building and straight to the courtroom. We take our seats at the defence table and I feel Chloe shiver next to me. Judge Kerns always keeps his courtroom Arctic cold as if to freeze out the truth and today is no exception. Putting my arm around her, I pull her towards me and rub her skinny arms, trying to warm her up.

A few minutes later we hear a commotion coming from the rear of the courtroom. Looking back I see Ben being wheeled in, George Winters close behind him.

The judge walks in and makes a few remarks, mostly to the jury. It is then George's turn to make his opening statement. He stands up and clears his throat. Walking towards the jury, he turns around and points at Chloe.

"On September the twentieth of last year Chloe Wilson ran over Ben Grant. She took his keys, got into his car, and reversed over him. Then, instead of stopping to check on him, to see how bad his injuries were, to try and help him, she ran away. Mr Grant's screams of pain brought the neighbours out from their houses, but didn't stop Ms Wilson from continuing on her way.

She went home and carried on with her life.

In the meantime, Mr Grant was being rushed to hospital with injuries so severe it is doubtful whether he will ever walk again. His acting career had to be put on hold. His livelihood is under threat."

He pauses for a few seconds, walking up and down in front of the jury, looking each of the members in the eye. Then he stops, and leans forward.

"Ms Wilson never apologised. She would not even talk to the police. Then, weeks later, when she realised that she'd been caught, Ms Wilson came forward with a story about rape."

"But this was nothing other than a lover's quarrel. Ms Wilson went to Mr Grant's home, had sex with him, and then took flight, running him over, heartlessly leaving him sprawled on the street. She never turned back, but kept going with her day. The defence will try to make excuses for her actions. But what she did is inexcusable. She has irrevocably changed a man's life, robbed him of his dreams, left him for dead. This is why we're here today, to make sure that justice is done."

George stands still for a few moments, then turns around and walks back to his seat, patting Ben on the back as he passes behind him.

It's my turn and I feel my head pound with tension. It's my job to convince the jury that Chloe is not only innocent, but is the victim. Mary Beth Hayes has left me hanging in doubt about whether she'll testify. She said she needed more time to think about the repercussions. And now she's not even answering my phone calls.

Standing up, I take several deep breaths, close my suit jacket and walk over to the jury stand. Pacing in front of them, I look each in the eye. I want them to trust me, to stir their emotions to believe what I'm about to tell them.

"Chloe Wilson has just turned sixteen. She should be in school, spending time with her friends, going out on first dates. Instead Ms Wilson is sitting here. And it's all because she met Mr Grant on September the twentieth and agreed to go to his house. That was her mistake, a mistake that she's paying dearly for.

As you will hear in the coming days, Ms Wilson has not had an easy life. She has never had a stable home, but spent her life bouncing between one foster home and another. But her misfortune didn't stop her from working hard, hoping to turn her life around. Her school record is impeccable, always at the top of her class. She wants to stand on her own two feet, make a better life for herself, ensure that her future is bright."

Looking at each juror, I try to connect with them, convince them to understand and sympathise with Chloe.

"Perhaps it was her lack of family and friends that left Ms Wilson exposed. Mr Grant preyed on this vulnerability when he invited her to his parents' house with the excuse of playing video games. Ms Wilson didn't want his sexual advances. She struggled with him. But he was stronger than she is. He pinned her down and raped her."

Pausing, I walk up and down in front of the jurors, allowing the words to sink in.

"At the first opportunity, Ms Wilson ran away. She wanted to put as much distance between her and Mr Grant as possible. So, she took his car keys and got in the vehicle. She panicked when she saw Mr Grant coming out of the house, running towards her. She was scared of what he was going to do to her. She was terrified he was going to attack her again. So, she turned the ignition trying to escape. She'd never driven a car before and put it in the wrong gear. As she pressed her foot on the accelerator pedal, it lurched back and hit Mr Grant.

It was an accident, driven by her fear and panic. This is a girl who was trying to run away because she was terrified. None of this would have happened if Mr Grant had not attacked Ms Wilson.

The prosecution is trying to demonise Ms Wilson for leaving the scene. But as you will hear straight from her, she left in shock and self-defence, because she was terrified of what Mr Grant would do next, and that he could attack her again."

Turning around, I walk towards Chloe. She's sitting bolt upright in her chair, her hands on her lap. I smile at her, hoping to ease some of her anxiety, before turning towards the jurors.

"The prosecution will be focusing on Mr Grant's injuries, how they are going to impact on his life. But Ms Wilson has not left this ordeal unscathed. She is pregnant with Mr Grant's child, and we will present proof of this. She is a top student, and had a very promising future. But she will now have to juggle her studies with taking care of a child.

Ms Wilson's mistake was getting in the car with Mr Grant. Trusting him. She should never have done that. But that doesn't excuse Mr Grant's vicious attack and the repercussions it will have on the rest of her life."

Taking a deep breath, I stop in front of the jurors, studying the expressions on their faces. On some of the bigger cases the firm would have hired an analyst to help read the jurors' reactions, but there are no funds for this case. So I'm trying my best to assess their response. One of the jurors, a woman in her thirties, seems to be sympathising with Chloe, looking at the teenager with a soft expression in her eyes. But another juror kept frowning throughout my statement. I cannot read the others and will need to work harder to keep my eye on them as the trial unfolds.

*

Chloe stifles a yawn in the taxi. She looks exhausted. Her face is drawn, and there are shadows under her eyes. Even her new plumpness now makes her only look puffy and dull. "Tired?" I ask her.

"Shattered," she says.

"It's been a long day and I'll have you on your way soon," I tell her. The taxi stops in front of my office building and I pay the fare before getting out and leading Chloe inside.

She doesn't say anything. She looks down as we get into the lift, her shoulders hunched, in stark contrast to how tall and straight she held herself when I first met her. She flinches slightly when I put a hand on her shoulder. "The next few days are going to be tough, but keep what I told you in mind and you'll be fine."

"Do I need to be there for Ben's testimony?" she asks, looking at me with eyes that are full of fear.

"Yes, it wouldn't look good if you're not there," I tell her. "And don't forget – call him Mr Grant when you take the stand. We need to make sure the jury understands that you barely knew him."

Chloe nods, and as the lift pings our arrival, follows me through to the offices. "The parcel's on your sofa," Jennifer says as we walk past her.

In my office, I look at the large Next box and turn towards Chloe. "I took the liberty of ordering you some more clothes for court," I tell her. She cannot afford new clothes and I need her to look the part every day. Despite being so tense and rushed, the task was easy and I took guilty pleasure in it as I have so often imagined the clothes I would have bought for Maya.

Chloe stares at me, not saying anything. And then, just when I think she might protest, that I have somehow offended her pride, tears start filling her eyes. She looks away, blinking furiously, her mouth set in a thin line, as if she's trying to control herself. "Thank you." There's a genuineness in her voice that makes clear how emotionally fragile she is right now.

"Well, open it," I say, wanting to defuse the tension.

Chloe sits down on the sofa and opens the parcel, and starts taking out clothes. She fishes out a pair of jeans and looks at me inquisitively.

"Those are not for court, obviously," I say. "I added a few maternity clothes. You're going to need them."

Her eyes flit between me and the clothes, her face contorting with emotion, until she squares her jaw and lifts her chin up. "Thank you."

Chapter 32

Ellen's name flashes on my mobile screen. She has been calling me constantly, asking questions that are impossible to answer and wanting reassurance that I cannot provide.

For a second I contemplate not answering the call so I can concentrate on work, attempt to get home early, spend time with the children before they go to bed, try and get through to Miles. It feels like our marriage is on the line. We need to talk. I need to make him understand why I did what I did if I have any chance of saving my marriage, keeping my family together.

On top of everything, with the preparations for Chloe's ongoing trial adding to my workload, it's been a few days since I've seen Maya, the long hours making me arrive home later each day. My heart aches with desire to spend time with her, but Miles sends her home as soon as he arrives, almost as if her presence is too much for him, too sore a reminder of what happened. What I kept from him. Perhaps he'll get stuck at work tonight, which would give me time with Maya. Time to talk to her. Try to understand what's going through her mind. Whether her feelings towards her birth mother have changed now that she knows about the potential link to John Larkin's killing.

Shaking off my thoughts, I reluctantly pick up the phone, readying myself to reassure Ellen, go over what we know, tell her they've made the right choice in giving the detectives access to Maya's birth certificate. Our conversations are always the same. She's scared and worried. But so am I. The only difference is that I can't show it.

"There's an old lady here," Ellen says in a panicked voice before I have time to say hello. "She's insisting on seeing Maya. She won't leave."

"Who is she?" I try to keep my tone even.

Ellen's whisper is barely audible. "She said she's John Larkin's mother."

Mrs Larkin. Amidst all my other concerns, I'd completely forgotten about her. Assumed she posed no threat, and would be dead by now. She must be very old. Her hair was snow white, her skin wrinkly even when she had appeared on television after his body was found.

"Where's Maya?" I ask.

"She's still at school but will be home soon. What am I going to do?"

My brain goes into overdrive. A raging need to protect Maya engulfs me. But this requires me to be level-headed, to push my feelings aside and take properly thought-out decisions. Especially if Ellen is falling apart.

"Where's Tom?"

"At work."

"Ok, you stay there. I'm going to call Tom and tell him to pick Maya up and keep her away." I get up and grab my coat.

Tom picks up straight away. I quickly tell him the story. "I should go home and be with Ellen," he says.

"No, go and get Maya. We don't want her going home."

The drive to the McBrides' house seems to take forever as I battle the afternoon traffic out of London. My foot is heavy on the accelerator as soon as I hit the A4, and aches at the stops and starts, the urgency to find out why his mother turned up at the McBrides' overtaking my fear of a collision or being pulled over.

"Get out of the way!" I shout angrily at the two cars going at a snail's pace in front of me, blocking both lanes. Clenching my fists around the steering wheel, I try to focus on the road rather than Mrs Larkin's haunting face as she appealed for help finding her son's killer. It starts to come back to me, the grief carved in every wrinkle creating shadowy circles around her eyes. I never thought I would come face-to-face with the woman whose life I had forever changed. I'm scared. Not only because seeing her might escalate the guilt that has never released its grip on my heart. But because I don't know what she might do, whether she's going to hurt Ellen, whether she'll even act out some form of revenge on Maya. Or I could be walking into some kind of trap.

But there's also a part of me that's curious to meet Mrs Larkin. The woman who raised a monster. Did she know what he was doing? Was she in some way complicit?

I try to remember her name. Nina? No. Nelly? No, that wasn't it. Nora. Yes, that was her name. Nora Larkin.

Pushing harder on the accelerator pedal, I weave the car through traffic. Finally I get to the McBrides' house, vigorously ringing the bell, my heart thumping, afraid of what might have happened to Ellen.

She opens the door, her face devoid of all colour and a haunted look in her eyes.

"Did she leave?"

Ellen shakes her head. "She's in the living room. She was making a scene outside and I didn't want the neighbours to see."

Walking past Ellen, I head towards the McBrides' living room.

At first I don't see her. She's so small that she seems to be swallowed by the McBrides' enormous sofa. A small movement catches my eye and I glance in its direction. She straightens up a little with what seems to be a lot of a struggle. And then she looks at me, her eyes as green as Maya's. As green as John Larkin's. For the first time I'm looking straight at his mother. I'm looking at the woman whose son I killed.

Chapter 33

My breath escapes my body. The moment seems never-ending as I look at Mrs Larkin, taking in every detail. The woman in front of me is ravaged by age. Her grey clothes seem too big for her, as if they belong to somebody else. Her shoes look worn, the leather cracking where she bends her feet. Her white hair is pulled back in a bun and her face is crossed with deep lines.

But there is a fire in her eyes as she looks past me towards the door. Her eyes widen with expectation as she stares at the empty doorway. Then, when she realises that nobody else is walking in, she looks right at me and asks: "Where is she?"

Her voice is hoarse, either from emotion or a lifetime of smoking.

"Where is Maya?"

Locking eyes with her, I walk further into the room, approaching Mrs Larkin but keeping some distance between us. Maybe she's dangerous. She could be here to hurt us. My hands are shaking and I grip tightly at the strap of my handbag until my knuckles turn white. A shiver runs through me as I take another step into the room. A voice inside me begs me to stop. To get out of there. But I shake it off and move closer to her, the need to know how she found the McBrides suffocating all other fears.

"Maya cannot meet you today."

Mrs Larkin's face clouds with disappointment, pain flashes through her eyes. But quickly she clenches her jaw, the movement almost completely masked by her sagging skin.

"Where is she?" Her voice shakes and her chin trembles. She bites her lip in a childish gesture that reminds me of Maya.

Snapping back into reality, the need for self-preservation takes over. "You can't see Maya." My voice is gentle but firm. "Not today."

Her eyes droop slightly and the corners of her mouth turn down. She slumps a little more in her seat like a balloon deflating, as if she's lost the struggle to keep upright. She looks vulnerable and worn out.

"But she wants to meet me," Mrs Larkin says very softly.

Glancing at Ellen, I narrow my eyes questioningly. But she shrugs and shakes her head.

Turning back to Mrs Larkin, I see her sliding to the edge of the sofa and sitting upright in her seat, staring at me and Ellen. Her eyes are blazing, her mouth a firm line. Her nostrils flare as she puts her hand in her pocket.

Ellen emits a strangled scream behind me but I stand there, terrified, not knowing what she is going to take out. The seconds go by endlessly. The sound of Ellen's heavy breathing echoes in my ears. My eyes are riveted to Mrs Larkin, watching her rummage inside her pocket, looking for something.

Tearing my eyes off her for a second, I glance behind me towards the door, calculating how long it would take us to run away. Perhaps she's stronger than she looks and will come after us.

I should have called the police. I should not have come here on my own to help Ellen. Miles would tell me how reckless I have been, opening us up to danger like this. I see the loving way he looked at me as we exchanged vows on our wedding day. The way he sleeps with one arm over his head. How he gobbles down his food as if someone's about to steal it from him.

And I think about the children. Julian's constant questions that sometimes threaten to drive me crazy. His incessant curiosity and love of the outdoors. I see him running in the garden, barefoot in the summer. Then I think about Leah. Her cherubic face as I tuck her into bed. How her arms hold me tight when she hugs me and her hair smells of orange and vanilla.

As I stare at the old lady, I feel like I'm falling into a deep hole from which there's no way to claw myself out.

She starts to take her hand out of her pocket. Her every tiny gesture has me transfixed in fright. I'm waiting for the glint of a blade, the shine of a weapon. But instead all I can see is a piece of paper, its rustle breaking the silence.

"She said she wants to meet me," Mrs Larkin says, motioning with the folded envelope.

"This is the first I've heard of this," Ellen tells me in a barely-audible voice, staring blankly at the intruder in her living room.

Mrs Larkin holds the paper towards me, and I take a tentative step in her direction, leaning forward until I can take it from her hand. "She wrote to me," she says, just as she lets go of the crisp white envelope.

My hand is shaking as I open it. I stare at the neat paragraphs written in blue ink. Words merge into one another as I skim over them and I have to shut my eyes tight to bring my eyesight back into focus. Opening them again, I read the short letter, which has the McBrides' address written at the top of the page.

Dear Mrs Larkin,

You don't know me, but I recently found out that your son is very likely my biological father.

My name is Maya and I just turned sixteen. I was given up for adoption when I was born so I never had the opportunity to meet my biological mother. I was instead raised by fantastic parents who I love very much.

However, I've always wanted to know more about my biological parents and would like to meet you to learn more about your son since he's no longer alive. I want to hear from you who he was as a person and what he liked.

Best regards,

Maya McBride

"Is this Maya's handwriting?" I ask Ellen. She nods.

Handing the letter back to Mrs Larkin, I notice the care she takes in folding it and putting it back in her pocket. Sitting down across from her, I lean forward.

"We understand that you want to see Maya," I start, speaking gently. "But she's not here right now and you cannot meet her today," I repeat.

She stares at me, wringing her hands in her lap and finally says: "But she said she wants to meet me."

She sounds like a young child, grasping at a shred of hope, wanting to use it to get what she wants.

"I know. But this is not the right moment. Maybe another day."

For some time she doesn't speak. She stares down at her lap, looking defeated, as it dawns on her that her wish will not come true today.

"How did you get here?" I ask her.

"I took the bus."

It must have taken her forever to get here, I think, remembering the address on the envelope. "Let me drive you home before it gets too dark," I say before I can stop myself.

She looks up and opens her mouth, and I fear that she's about to protest, to insist on staying until Maya gets back, leaving me with no choice but to call the police. But then she just nods.

"Let's go." She struggles to her feet and I feel pity but am unable to help her.

The muscles in Ellen's face relax as she sees this nightmare is about to end. Guiding Mrs Larkin to my car, I open the passenger door for her. She's frail, limping when she walks. She fumbles with the seat belt, her hands trembling.

"What's your address?" She gives it to me and as I type it into the car's navigation system fear takes hold and I consider backtracking. I should call her a taxi, get myself out of danger. But I shrug off my feelings and start the car, wanting more than anything to take this woman as far away from Maya as possible.

She doesn't speak, but looks out of the window. Every small movement startles me. She shuffles in her seat, keeping me on edge. At one point she puts her hand in her pocket and I almost career into oncoming traffic. Relief sweeps over me when she takes out a handkerchief and dabs at her eyes.

"Can you tell me about her?" she asks about thirty minutes into the drive.

Focusing on the road ahead of me, the myriad possibilities of what I could say about Maya threaten to overwhelm me. But I feel I have to answer her. A little information won't harm, I tell myself.

"She's a great kid," I start. "She does well in school, is very smart, is gentle and always wants to help others."

She's silent for a few seconds, seemingly digesting the information I've just given her, even though it's not much. "What does she look like?" she then asks.

"She's very pretty. Her eyes are green, like yours. And she has red hair."

"Like you?" she asks.

"It's a different shade," I say, desperate to play down even the hint of a resemblance. "A little deeper."

Mrs Larkin doesn't speak and we drive in awkward silence for a few more minutes. "Why don't you tell me about your son?"

The words are out of my mouth before I can stop myself. Before I can think about what I'm asking. My own question makes me cringe. Why would I want to know more about him? Why would I want to listen? It's a mistake. I know this. Revulsion fights with the guilt that I've been carrying for all these years, and my fear is this will only be intensified if I start seeing his human side.

"John was such a good boy." Her voice is so soft that I have to strain to hear. "He didn't have a good life. His father wasn't the best of men. First he beat me but when John came along, he turned his attention to him. Thankfully he left when John was six, found another family. Poor John found that very hard."

Taking another look at her, I realise that the deep lines crossing her face are not all wrinkles. Faint scars mark her face, a stark memory of her abusive marriage. My guilt deepens. This woman had a rough life and I took away something she cherished. Her only son.

And I cannot help but wonder whether John Larkin's aggression was triggered by his early exposure to his father's violence. Whether being raised in that toxic environment, and being abandoned so young, caused him to become the monster he was. Perhaps he was a victim of circumstances, of his unfortunate childhood. And then he met me and his life was over.

No. I cannot allow myself to think that way. To come up with excuses for his actions. He killed those other girls and would have killed me too. There was no other way out.

She pauses for a while, and then takes a deep breath and continues. "He wanted to be a teacher and he'd have made a great one. But he left school at sixteen because he wanted to help out with the bills. I begged him to keep on studying. But he dropped out and found a job."

There's pride in her voice as she continues. "He was always smiling, always happy. He wasn't the horrible person everyone made him out to be."

His monstrous face, his eyes blazing with hatred, his mouth curled into a snarl, flash in front of me. This woman didn't know the real him. What her son did. I cannot allow her version of him to make me feel even worse than I already do.

She sniffles and I reach behind me to grab a box of tissues and hand it to her. She takes one and dabs her eyes with it, then wipes her nose. Every few seconds I glance at her, unable to properly concentrate on the road ahead. Despite my practised techniques to keep focus, I feel like I'm having an out-of-body experience.

"Did he have any friends?"

"He was close to his cousin. John was two months older. My sister lived down the road and the boys grew up together. They remained best friends, even as adults, always going out together."

"Yeah? What was his name?"

"My sister's son? Terry."

Terry. The person he had called. The one who's been sending me the letters. A shiver runs down my spine and my insides flip. "Where's Terry now?" I ask.

She shakes her head. "He got into some trouble soon after John's death and ended up in prison. But he should be out in a few months."

So, he couldn't be the one sending me the letters. He wouldn't be able to get them past the prison guards reading the inmates' mail. They would have flagged them as threats, probably launched an investigation. Unless he's bribed someone. Which means that someone else knows about me. Maybe more than one person. Could it even be her? Could the old woman in my car know I was the one who killed her son?

"Yeah? What trouble?" I try to keep my voice even, needing to know more about this person, how long he's been in for.

"Oh, some girl he was dating lied about him, said he assaulted her. It was a lie of course. He wasn't that type."

"Of course," I say, trying to keep the sarcasm out of my voice. "So, he was jailed for sixteen years for that?"

She looks at me and narrows her eyes at my calculation. I need to be careful not to sound too interested. "No, it was only a few months. But something else happened, not sure what." She pauses. "Why do you ask?"

"Oh, no reason."

We continue driving in silence. As we approach her Luton address, the streets start getting grubbier. Less trees line the pavements and instead there are metal bins, some toppled over and spilling their contents onto the street. The paint is peeling on the houses, a few windows have cardboard taped over their broken glass. Small groups stand talking at street corners. They all look up and stare as I manoeuvre the car along the narrow street, making me feel self-conscious, my fear increasing with every second. Feeling like a fish out of water in this neighbourhood, I shudder.

The navigation system beeps, indicating our arrival, and I pull up in front of a small house. It's better kept than most on the street. The yellow paint might be peeling in places, but it's clean. Curtains hang in the window and the two plants on each side of the door look well cared for.

"Thank you for driving me here," she says. But she doesn't get out of the car. Instead she turns to me. "Do you have kids?" she asks.

Her question is unexpected. "Yes, two. I need to get back to them."

She removes her seat belt, then starts to open the door. But she turns, looking at me with pleading eyes. "When can I meet Maya?"

This is all she cares about, I realise. Reaching into the glove compartment, I fish out a piece of paper and a pen. Handing them to her, I say: "Write down your telephone number. We'll give you a call." She takes them and with trembling hands scribbles down her number.

"Do you promise you won't forget?" she pleads, her voice full of anguish.

"You have my word." I dig into my bag for a business card. "You can call me, but don't try to see Maya without letting us know or we'll have to take the matter to court." It's a flimsy threat, but it's the only thing I can think of.

*

My foot is steady on the accelerator as I drive away from the neighbourhood, wanting to put distance between myself and the place. Mrs Larkin's revelation about Terry being in prison drives my fear up. Does this mean he told someone else about me, what I did, who I am, where I live, where I work, about Miles and the children? Has someone else been sending me the letters? A shiver goes down my spine as fear grips me that perhaps Terry has not acted on his threats because he was in prison. But if Mrs Larkin's right and he's going to be out soon, he might come after me, get revenge for his friend.

My phone rings. It's Ellen.

"Liz, are you ok? Where are you?" comes the frantic voice from the other end of the line.

"I'm ok, just driving back."

She gives an audible sigh of relief. "Thank God, I've been so worried."

Focusing as best I can on the busy road in front of me, I respond: "I just dropped her off, warned her not to try and see Maya again, that we'll be in touch. I don't know what she'll do though."

"She can't come close to my daughter." Ellen's voice is shrill.

"What if Maya tries to see her?"

"I'll make sure she doesn't. I'll ground her if need be."

For once I cannot disagree with Ellen's rigidity. "Why don't we talk in person?"

"Ok," Ellen says. "We can come to your house when you get back. I don't want to talk in front of Maya."

My mind shifts to the work I dropped earlier, the work that I still need to do. I want to tell her to come another time, that I'm too busy, and that I need to spend time with my husband. But I don't.

*

Miles is in the kitchen flipping through a medical journal when I arrive home. He looks up when I walk in and eyes me with a look of irritation.

"Working late again, I see," he says.

A bubble of anger rises inside me. Pausing, I take three deep breaths, not wanting to respond without thinking. Instead I pour myself a glass of water, focusing on the small task, taking tiny sips. "I wasn't at work." My calmness surprises me. "John Larkin's mother came looking for Maya today. Ellen called me and I came to speak to her. I just drove her back home," I say in one breath, wanting to get the words out of my mouth as quickly as possible, before I change my mind and go back to my old habits of hiding the truth from my husband.

"You did what?" he asks. His face is reddening and I cringe under the look of anger that's forming. "How do you know she's not a crazed person?"

"I didn't think it through. I wanted to get her away from Ellen."

"This isn't like you, Elizabeth." He rarely calls me by my full name. "Does she know who you are?"

His expression has changed. The disdain of earlier has been replaced with care and worry and my heart fills with hope that we're going to be ok. That he cares enough about me to allow our marriage to survive.

"She knows I'm their lawyer." I look away, not wanting him to see the fear in my eyes, the doubt that perhaps she knows more.

"What were you thinking? If you're not scared for yourself, can you pause for a moment and think of your two children? What if something happened to you? How do you expect me to explain that?"

The corners of my eyes sting with tears. I want to lash out at Miles, tell him that he's being unfair bringing the children into this. But I know that he's right. Guilt eats at me that in my rush to get Mrs Larkin away from Maya I had not really thought what the impact could have been on the rest of my family.

The doorbell rings. "It's Tom and Ellen," I say. "They want to speak about next steps." And then I add: "I'm sorry this is taking over our evening."

Miles purses his lips as he shakes his head. "This has taken over our lives, not just our evening."

"Do you want to go to the office or would you prefer the living room?" I ask Tom and Ellen when I open the door. Tom nods towards the living room and then walks into the kitchen and starts talking to Miles.

"How are you?" I ask Ellen when we're left alone.

She shrugs. "I'm a mess. I want to be so mad at Maya for writing to that woman and not saying anything. But at the same time I can't help but feel sad for how she must be feeling." Then, she quickly adds. "Maya, I mean."

We head into the kitchen and I busy myself making tea. We talk for a few minutes and then Miles starts to excuse himself. Tom stops him. "Can you stay, Miles? We'd like your take on it too."

"Have you spoken to Maya?" I ask.

Tom nods. "I had to tell her why I picked her up from school and didn't want us to go home." I look at him expectantly, wanting to hear more. He obliges. "She's being quite stubborn, refusing to realise how wrong it was to contact this woman, to try to meet her before we know more about her."

Maya's face flashes in front of me, her light smile, yet her eyes glistening with determination. Pride surges through me at her independence, her ability to go after what she wants. She must be feeling alone, unable to speak to her parents and I wish I could be there for her.

"We told her we're disappointed in her." Ellen's voice interrupts my thoughts.

"Do you think this woman could be dangerous?" Tom changes the subject.

Three sets of eyes turn to look at me. Although I'm the one who spent most time with her, I'm ill equipped to give judgement. Her son had also seemed harmless when I first met him. "She didn't seem like it, but I really can't say for sure," is all I can muster.

"I don't care if she's the nicest person on the planet. She cannot come near Maya," Ellen says, her voice raised.

Remembering Nora Larkin's pitiable face, all her hope set on the chance to meet Maya, I am overwhelmed by a strange desire to make up for the pain I caused her by killing her son by finally helping her meet her granddaughter, the one I kept from her for all those years.

"But Ellen, surely you understand that if Maya wants to meet Mrs Larkin, she will find a way. And unless we organise a meeting between the two, you won't have any control over this encounter."

A fat tear rolls down Ellen's cheeks and Tom hugs his wife. "Whose side are you on?" she throws at me.

Her words hurt. "I'm on your side. I want you to do what's best for Maya. But perhaps we're still rattled by today's incident and need more time to think about the next steps."

Looking over at Miles, I see his forehead creased in concentration. He hasn't said anything yet. As if on cue, Tom turns to him. "What do you think about all this?"

Miles' forehead knots even tighter, the lines between his brows deepening. "I have to agree with Liz. Organising a meeting means that you can control it, that you can choose the time and place. You can prepare Maya for it. It's better than it happening behind your backs and taking you by surprise."

"I can see your point," Tom says. "What do you think?" he asks his wife.

We all turn to look at Ellen. She's sitting bolt upright on her stool, her head held high, her lips tensed in a thin line. "We don't know anything about this person," she finally says.

Tom looks at me questioningly.

"We can hire an investigator. Have him look into her, give us more information," I say.

Ellen doesn't move. "What do you think, Ellen?" Tom coaxes.

"Whatever," she shrugs, still sitting stiffly on the stool.

Mixed emotions rush through me. The fear of finding more about John Larkin's past, of intensifying my guilt mingles with an insatiable curiosity to find out more about the man who haunts my dreams.

When the McBrides leave, I sit down next to Miles, anxious to get a few moments together. But he stands up, his face pinched, like he cannot stand to be around me. "I'm going to bed," he says.

My legs wobble as I stand up and take a step towards him. He moves back before I can reach him. "Please come back to our bedroom," I beg.

He stares at me. His eyes blaze and suddenly the expression changes to something softer. Pity. "I cannot be around you. Not yet." The sound of his shoes on the hardwood floors are like daggers in my heart.

Chapter 34

I must have fallen asleep because when I wake up, it's pitch black in the bedroom. The light from the lamp just above our front door, that creeps in from the sliver of space between the curtain and the wall is not visible. Staring at the wall where the window is, I wonder at the absence of light coming in. Maybe the bulb's out, I think. I'll have to get Miles to look at it tomorrow.

Realising that I'm thirsty, I reach over to my bedside table, rummaging in the darkness for my water bottle. But I cannot find it. I must have forgotten to bring it up to bed with me. Swallowing through my dry throat, I wonder whether I can fall back to sleep. But my throat feels like parchment.

Getting out of bed, I feel for my robe. It's draped around the back of the chair sitting in front of the dressing table and I pull it around me, shivering slightly in the chill of the bedroom. Not bothering with slippers, I tiptoe barefoot out of the room.

The whole house is really dark. Strange, I think. There's always at least a little bit of light coming through the windows. The street is pretty well lit, even at night, a decision that residents had taken before we moved in, wanting to make it extra safe. Not that this neighbourhood is anything but safe.

Feeling for the bannisters, I hold tight as I walk down the stairs. A glow of light comes from the kitchen and I walk towards it. It's strange that there's only light in that area of the house and nowhere else. I look towards the front door but the hallway is in pitch darkness.

A chill creeps up my bare legs as soon as I enter the kitchen, making me wonder whether we've left the window open, although I didn't think we opened any last night. It's still quite cold and the alarm would notify us of any downstairs windows or doors that aren't locked. Something feels strange, but perhaps Miles made some changes to the system and forgot to tell me. Or didn't bother. It's not like we've been talking much these days.

Eerily, the light that I'd seen from the hallway has now somehow disappeared. In the darkness I reach out towards the wall and feel for the light switch. It takes me a few seconds to find it and I flick it on. But I'm still surrounded by pitch darkness. I flick the switch again but nothing happens. It seems like we're having a blackout; only that would explain the lack of light inside and outside.

Shivering, I tell myself it's from the cold. But I know that it's something else that's making me feel so uncomfortable. Something doesn't seem right.

Part of me wants to go back upstairs and wake up Miles, but instead I square my shoulders and walk further into the kitchen, bumping against the island and manoeuvring around it. Feeling for the drawers, I open one and rummage inside for a box of extra long matches. Taking one out, I flick it against the striking surface.

The flame bursts alive, throwing a dim pool of light around me. Looking at the window, I see that it's wide open, the fine curtains billowing outside. I pull them in and close the window, bolting it shut. The flame is licking my fingers and I blow it out, quickly striking another match. Turning around, I start making my way to the fridge and stop in my tracks. I feel like I can't breathe. I feel like I can't move. I feel like I'm glued to the ground. There, standing right in front of me, is Nora Larkin.

I open my mouth to speak, but nothing comes out. Swallowing through my dry throat, I wet my parched lips with my tongue before trying again.

"Hello?" It's more a question than a greeting.

She doesn't move, doesn't say anything. She's standing on the other side of the island, looking at me intently. I wonder how long she's been in here. She must have got in through the window, although I never thought she'd be strong enough to climb up and over the kitchen counter. And how does she know where I live?

"What are you doing here?" I finally ask.

She doesn't say anything, but her lips twist into an evil smile, the corners of her mouth contorting upwards. I don't want to show her I'm terrified. Instead I need to remain calm and think what to do next, talk to this woman just like I did yesterday. "Mrs Larkin, what are you doing here?" I repeat.

She continues staring at me, with eyes that look as cold as I feel, and I shiver under her gaze. "You know why I'm here," she says. At that moment I realise that she knows. I know that she's come here for revenge. And I'm terrified. For myself but above all for my family sleeping upstairs.

I feign ignorance. I resolve to deny whatever she accuses me of. "What do you mean?" I try to keep my voice as steady as I can, but hear it crack in a high pitch.

And then she laughs. It sounds sinister and so loud that it makes me wonder whether Miles will hear her and come downstairs. But I don't want him involved. I want her gone. Surely I'm stronger than her and shouldn't be afraid. I can ask her to leave, and if she doesn't, I will simply push her out. I don't want her in my house, certainly not while my children are sleeping upstairs.

"Look, it's late," I start. "Why don't you come back in the morning and we can talk properly." I'm holding my breath for her answer, hoping that she doesn't cause any trouble.

But she doesn't say anything. I start to take a step towards her, but she shouts at me. "Stop," she says.

Then she lifts her hand and I see the glint of a blade. She waves the knife at me menacingly. "Don't you take one more step," she says. Her voice is no longer that of an old woman. Instead it sounds like that of a person on a mission to get what she wants. Someone who's thought about what she's doing and is determined to see it through.

My body erupts in goosebumps. My heart is beating so fast it feels like it's about to burst out of my chest. The fear that I've withheld for so long is bubbling to the surface. I don't know what she's going to do next and am terrified that soon I'm going to find out. This is my worst nightmare coming true. Standing still, I look at her, imploring her with my eyes not to hurt me. "What do you want?" I ask.

She keeps staring at me, then she says: "I know you're the one." Her voice drops so low that I'm not sure that I've heard correctly. Shaking my head slightly, I try to let her know that I didn't understand her. "I know you killed my son," she repeats, louder this time.

There's no escape, I've been caught. But I cannot admit to it. "What are you talking about? I didn't know your son."

"Don't you dare deny it." She takes a step towards me, her hand shaking slightly but her fingers tight around the knife's handle. I take a step back and find myself wedged against the kitchen counter, with nowhere to go. "I know you did it. You heartless bitch."

I don't know what to do. I'm shaking. After all these years, I've been found out. She knows I killed her son. Maybe she's known for a while. Terry must have told her. She could have been the one sending me the letters. I wonder whether she's going to the police or whether she's already spoken to them.

"You stabbed him and left him to bleed to death, alone," she says.

I want to tell her that it's not true. That he died immediately. That I'd tried to look for help but it was too late. That even though he'd hurt me, I still didn't want to kill him. I want to tell her that it had been a horrible accident. That I reacted without even thinking to stop him from hurting me again. And that I've never stopped regretting what I did.

But I find that I cannot speak. She's inching closer to me, the knife pointed in my direction. There's nowhere to go and I feel as if my feet have been glued to the floor. I wouldn't be able to run away even if I could get away from her.

She's right in front of me now, and brings the knife to my chest. She's shorter than me and has to lift her arm up to reach. The point of the blade digs into my skin and when I look down I see a bead of blood slither down the glistening metal. Perhaps I can grab her arm and twist it until she drops the knife and then hold it against her throat and scream for help. But I don't want Julian and Leah to come down here and put themselves in danger. What if she's not alone? What if there's someone else in the house? No, this is my problem and I'm going to see it through.

We continue staring at each other for what seems like forever. "I'm not going to kill you," she finally says. And I find myself heaving a sigh of relief. But I'm not safe yet. Not while this crazy person is in my home. Not while she's holding a knife so close to my throat.

"I'm not going to kill you," she repeats. "That would be way too easy." Again she laughs and I hear my fate in her voice. I know that she's not going to leave here without getting her revenge. I know that my time has come to pay for what I'd done so many years ago. "I want you to live and feel what it's like to lose a child," she says. "I'm going to take from you exactly what you took from me, and you're going to watch."

The room is spinning so fast that I cannot keep up. I feel that my world is coming to an end. And the only thing that I can do is scream. Scream as loudly as I can. Until my ears ring with the sound that's coming from inside me and surrounding me. But I continue screaming even though I'm out of breath.

And then, when I can't hold my breath any longer, I take in a gulp of air and start screaming again, my eyes shut so tight that they hurt. Until I feel my body shaking so badly that I fear I'm about to burst.

Forcing my eyes open, I see Miles hovering over me. He has worry etched all over his face. His eyes are wide open and his lips parted. I see them moving but don't hear the sound. "Where is she?" I ask him, turning my head to look around me, looking for her, making sure she hasn't gone for Julian or Leah.

But I'm no longer in the kitchen. Instead I'm surrounded by light blue sheets and I feel the soft pillow under my head. I look at Miles in confusion. "You had another bad dream," he says softly, leaning over and placing a hand on my brow like a sick person.

It was a dream, I tell myself. Just a nightmare. It wasn't true. Mrs Larkin wasn't in my kitchen with a knife. She didn't threaten my children. It was just a horrible dream. I'm ok. The kids are ok. Miles is ok. We're fine.

For now. Once the detectives figure out who I am, it can't be long before Mrs Larkin finds out that I killed her son. Then my nightmare might come true.

She might come for my children. Maybe this wasn't just a dream, but a warning. Perhaps my brain is looking into the future and telling me what I need to be afraid of, what to avoid. I need to protect my family at all costs.

Miles lets go of me and takes a step towards the door. "I'm going to check on the children," he says.

I feel guilt and shame. If Miles heard me from the spare room, chances are that the children did too. And I'm also overcome with fear of being alone. "Please come back. I'm scared," I say in a soft voice.

He looks at me for long seconds. Then he nods. "Just for tonight."

Chapter 35

"Why did you invite Chloe Wilson to go home with you on September the twentieth?" I ask Ben the following afternoon. He'd taken the stand earlier, answering the prosecutor's questions with a well-rehearsed story about Chloe seducing him.

Ben shrugs. "She looked bored and I thought she'd enjoy a quick trip."

"And when you got to your parents' house you invited her inside."

"Yes."

"Why was that?"

"I didn't feel like going back to the party and neither did she. I thought we could play video games."

"How long did you play video games for?"

He shrugs "Maybe half an hour."

"Who was winning?"

"I was," he smirks.

"And that was when you went into the bathroom and removed your clothes."

"It wasn't like that…"

"Mr Grant," I interrupt. "Did you or did you not remove your clothes and walk towards Ms Wilson naked?"

"They were dirty. I wanted to change."

"So why didn't you take a change of clothes into the bathroom with you? Surely, you wouldn't want a girl you'd just met to see you naked."

"I didn't think."

"Weren't you embarrassed?"

"I didn't have a reason to be."

"Quite the confident one, aren't you?"

"Objection," George Winters shouts.

"Withdrawn," I say. Turning back to Ben, I ask: "What happened next?"

"She reached out and touched me. It was obvious what she wanted."

"Did she tell you that? What were her exact words?"

"I don't remember."

"Did she ever say that she wanted to have sex with you?"

"I don't know, I don't remember exactly," he says, his eyes darting across the courtroom.

"Are you saying that you don't have a clear recollection of what happened that afternoon, when Ms Wilson was in your bedroom?"

"Yes." He nods enthusiastically.

"Perhaps then your memory of Ms Wilson touching you is also mistaken."

"No, I remember that."

"So, you only remember parts of what happened, the parts that fit within your story."

"Objection," shouts George Winters. "Counsel is testifying."

"I'll rephrase Your Honour. Mr Grant, how come you only remember parts of what happened that afternoon?"

"I was injured, remember?" he says with a smirk.

He's been coached well, I think. "Mr Grant, the accident in which your injuries were sustained happened after the events in question."

My work phone flashes with the arrival of a text message, distracting me momentarily. It's Luke Ross. I've asked the investigator to look into Nora Larkin, check her background, help us determine whether or not she's dangerous. Knowing more about her is the only way the McBrides will ever consider allowing Maya to meet her.

I'm on it

it says.

Turning back to Ben, I continue: "Mr Grant, do you distinctly remember Ms Wilson agreeing to have sex with you?"

"Yes, definitely."

"And what did she say? Can you tell us her words?"

Ben tries to look around me towards the prosecutor but I'm in his way. The seconds tick by, the clock in the courtroom tracking the stillness. Ben shifts in his chair. "Answer the question, Mr Grant," I say.

"I don't remember the exact words."

"Mr Grant you said just now that you definitely remember Ms Wilson agreeing to have sex with you. How did she verbalise her agreement?"

"I don't remember, ok." His voice is shaky, less convincing. I know that I have an in.

"Mr Grant," I continue. "Is it possible that Ms Wilson did not want to have sex with you that afternoon?"

When Ben doesn't answer, I continue. "Is it possible that she tried to get away from you, that she asked you to stop?"

"I don't think so."

"So, you cannot be certain," I say, looking at the jurors.

"I think I'd remember that."

"But you're not sure. So, it's possible that Ms Wilson tried to fight you off, tried to push you off her, but you don't remember."

"I guess that's possible."

"No further questions, Your Honour," I say, returning to my seat.

Jennifer follows me into my office when I get back. "Maya, your sitter, called about an hour ago," she starts. "She said it was not urgent but I didn't want the message to get buried among the others."

My heart is beating fast as I dial Maya's familiar number, my mind filling with scenarios of Julian and Leah being injured, or getting into trouble at school. Or perhaps this is about Maya. What would she need to tell me that couldn't wait until I got home?

"Hello?" comes her voice from the other end of the line.

"Maya, it's Elizabeth. Is everything all right?"

"Oh, hi Mrs P. Everything's great, nothing to worry about."

"You called earlier, left a message."

"Yes." She pauses and I feel the seconds dragging tortuously. "I was hoping I could come and talk to you in your office."

"Yes, of course, you're welcome to come. Has something happened?"

"No, no, it's just that I'd like to talk to you."

"I can leave the office now. Why don't we talk at home, save you the trip into the city?"

She doesn't say anything. I can hear Julian and Leah's muffled voices in the background as I wait for

Maya to respond. "It's just that I want to get some advice," she finally says.

"Has something happened?" I ask her again.

"No, nothing new at least. It's just that I need to talk to you. In your legal capacity."

"I'll still be a lawyer at home," I tell her. Looking at my watch, I realise it's rush hour and I will be stuck in traffic. "I'm leaving now."

Chapter 36

The drive home seems endless as I manoeuvre the car between traffic. At every stop I feel my heart start beating faster as I rack my brain to try and figure out why Maya would need legal help. What has she done? My mind goes through a myriad of possibilities, different types of trouble that she might have got herself into. Has she been caught cheating and is being thrown out of school? Did she steal something? Or is it more sinister, a secret like I've been harbouring for all these years.

Tightening my grip on the steering wheel, squinting my eyes against the weak sunshine, I desperately try to convince myself to wait until I know more before starting to panic. This has to be about her adoption and a chill runs down my spine despite the warmth in my car. By the time I run inside the house, I'm churning with adrenalin.

The scene that greets me calms me down a notch. Julian and Leah are sitting at the kitchen island, drawing. Maya is across from them, chopping vegetables. "I'm making dinner for the kids," she says. "Chicken fajitas. Would you like some?"

"Uhm, no, it's ok." Leaning over, I hug the children. Maya turns her attention to the red pepper she's chopping.

Sitting down next to Leah, I stroke her hair back, looking at the jumble of colours on the paper in front of her. "What are you drawing?"

"A garden," she responds.

Julian is so engrossed in his work that he barely looks at me when I speak to him. As much as I'd love to spend more time with the children, I have work to do. Opening my briefcase, I take out a document and try to read, but I keep looking towards Maya, willing her to hurry up. I'm clawing to find out what she wants to tell me. "I'm going to the study to finish some work. Come and find me when you're done."

Maya nods and I walk away. In the study, I go over my notes for Chloe's testimony, reading my questions, tweaking here and there. I'm so immersed in my work that I don't hear the door opening.

"Oh, dear God, you startled me," I tell Miles, who is standing right in front of me.

"Maya said you're in here. Is everything ok? You rarely use the study."

"Yes, yes. Can you shut the door?"

Miles squints at me, but closes the door, before sitting on the other side of the desk.

"Maya said she wants legal advice. I figured the study would be more private," I say. "I'm waiting for her to finish feeding the kids."

"Do you know what this is about?"

"No, she wouldn't say."

"Do you think she suspects who you are?"

"I don't know." I raise my shoulders in a slow shrug.

"Miles," I call after him as he turns to leave. "Thank you for staying with me last night. I needed you."

"Yeah, sure," he says, walking away.

*

"Come in." Closing the file in front of me, I brace myself for whatever Maya has to say.

She is still standing next to the door. Her face is flushed. She brings her right hand to her mouth and starts biting her fingernails. I motion to the chair across from me. She walks in small jerky movements, her head down, her long hair framing her face. Sitting down across from me, she finally looks up. But her eyes keep flitting away, seemingly unable to look right at me.

"Is everything all right?" I ask when she remains silent.

"Yes, yes." The colour in her cheeks deepens to crimson.

Still, she remains silent and for a few seconds I can feel the awkwardness intensifying. Miles' words echo in my ears and I cringe at the possibilities of what might be going through her mind.

"I need your help," she finally says, her eyes firmly fixed on her lap.

"Sure, what do you need?"

"Will you be my lawyer?"

"I already am," I try a smile.

She finally looks up and stares straight at me. "You're my parents' lawyer." Her tone is harsher than I've ever heard it. "That's different."

"Not really. Your parents are trying to do what's best for you, making sure you're protected."

She takes a deep breath and exhales slowly, as if she's frustrated. "See, that's the problem. I don't need protecting. What I need is to be told the truth instead of being kept in the dark. I'm not a little kid anymore. It took my parents weeks to tell me about John Larkin. Is it going to be the same when they track down my mother? Do I have to make do with snippets of information instead of the whole story? I don't want to continue like this. I don't want to look at every red-headed woman and wonder whether she's my mother. I just can't go on like this." Her eyes look directly into mine. Her hands are clenched in fists on her lap. Her earlier timidity is gone and instead I am faced with a determined young woman.

"Why do you want to find your mother?" I snatch the opportunity to learn more.

"Wouldn't you? I want to know who she is, why she gave me up, whether she still thinks about me. And now I also want to know whether she killed him. How it happened. Why it happened. If he hurt her. I have so many questions and I don't want to wait until my parents decide to tell me what's happening. I want everyone to stop treating me like a child."

"What do you need from me?" I try to quash the thoughts that are racing through my head.

"I want you to tell me the truth. My parents don't."

And then, before I can respond, she carries on: "And I want to meet Mrs Larkin. My parents don't want that, they're coming up with silly excuses. But I want to meet her, get to know her, find out about her son."

"I don't know if I can do that," I say.

Maya stands up. "Then I'll have to find someone else. I came to you because I thought you cared about me, but evidently I'm just your babysitter."

Tears well in her eyes and start running down her cheeks. She wipes them furiously with the back of her sleeve. I want to stand up and hug her, hold her close to me, tell her that I will do anything for her. But I know that despite my best intentions, I can never be there for Maya in the way I really want. I gave up that right as soon as she was born and have to live with the consequences.

Yet, she's giving me an opportunity to do something for her. To help her in a way that she needs. To make a difference in her life. I cannot let this go.

"Sit down, Maya," I say. "Let's not make any rash decisions."

She takes her seat back and stares at me, her eyes boring into mine. She fiddles with the hem of her shirt and shifts in the chair, like she's trying to find a comfortable position.

"I can continue trying to convince your parents to allow you to meet Mrs Larkin."

Another expression flickers through her eyes. Disappointment. Resignation. She brings her hand up and twirls a strand of hair around her index finger. Round and round and round. "You know that won't be enough. It might work with Dad but Mum is just too stubborn."

She fixes me with a look that suddenly reminds me she is almost an adult. The recent events have pushed her to grow up faster than she should. It's my fault for creating this situation. "I want you to arrange the meeting with Mrs Larkin."

"Maya, I need to think about this. I'd be going behind their backs."

Her expression softens. "Ok. But please don't keep me waiting for nothing."

Standing up again, she remains next to her chair for a few seconds, then turns around and leaves. The sound of the children playing drifts through and I catch snippets of their conversation. But I don't move. Toying with a pen, clicking the nib in and out, I replay the conversation with Maya in my head. There is no right decision. Whichever way I decide to go I will be letting someone down. I don't know if that can be Maya.

Chapter 37

Chloe shuffles in her chair, shifting her small bump this way and that. "You're going to be fine," I tell her, putting one hand on her arm and squeezing slightly to reassure her.

We're in the courtroom, waiting for the judge to walk in, and today is her turn to testify. "Just remember what we discussed. Answer my questions as you did during our preparations and when the prosecutor starts interrogating you, stick to what he's asking. Don't give additional details.

"Don't talk fast. Take your time, use it to think about what you're saying."

When she is called to the stand, Chloe walks with ease, keeping her paces straight, her head slightly bowed. When she sits down, she puts her hands in her lap, relaxing her arms, and looks straight ahead. She answers my questions about that afternoon, relating in detail how Ben had attacked her, how she tried to push him away, how he was too strong, and how she finally managed to escape.

"Why did you take Mr Grant's car?" I ask.

"I was scared."

Her voice is wobbly and I worry that she won't be able to handle the questions.

"What were you afraid of?"

"I thought he was going to catch up with me. That he'd drag me back into the house. That he would attack me again."

"Did it occur to you that driving could be dangerous for someone who'd never done it before?"

"I didn't think that far ahead. I saw the car as a way to escape, get away from him." She looks at the jurors and then back at me. "I wanted to get away as quickly as I could. I wanted to be as far from him as possible."

"What happened next?"

"I switched the ignition and moved the gear stick. I thought I'd put it in first, but when I pressed the accelerator the car jerked backwards."

"So you put the car in reverse by mistake?"

"Yes, I think so."

"Did you press the brake?"

"I don't think so. It all happened so quickly. I didn't have time to think."

"Why didn't you stop to check on the extent of Mr Grant's injuries after you hit him? Did you hear him cry out in pain?"

"Yes, I did. But I was still scared. I didn't realise how injured he was and thought he might be faking, and might get up and attack me again."

"So, what did you do?"

"I got out of the car and ran away." She looks up and her eyes are glistening. "I wanted to be somewhere where he couldn't get to me."

Taking a short pause, I look at the jurors, studying the expression of each one. They are looking at Chloe, drinking in every word. A young woman is biting her lip while an elderly man has the same kind of expression my dad has when he looks at Leah. They believe her, I think.

"Where did you go?"

"I ran to my foster home."

"What did you do then?"

"I took a shower and washed my clothes," Chloe answers.

"Did it occur to you that you were destroying evidence of the attack?"

"No, I didn't think about that. I wanted to wash him away, get any remnants of him off me. I felt dirty and ashamed."

"Why didn't you tell the police that he had raped you?"

"I was embarrassed. It felt like he had destroyed my privacy and I didn't want anyone to know what happened. I was ashamed, and I didn't want to relive what happened."

She continues answering my questions convincingly and I can feel that the late nights preparing for this testimony are paying off. She talks about the shock of finding out about the pregnancy and how it will impact her life.

"Why did you decide to keep the baby?" I ask.

She lifts her shoulders in a small shrug. But it's not a smug gesture. Instead it shows resignation. "It's not the baby's fault. He, or she, deserves a chance." One juror dabs at her eyes and another sniffs audibly.

When it's George Winters' turn to question Chloe he confronts her about inconsistencies in her story. "You lied to the police, said you didn't realise Mr Grant was injured. Why should we believe what you're saying now?"

It's at that moment that Jennifer taps me on the shoulder and hands me a note. She wasn't supposed to be in court so I know this must be important. My hands are trembling as I open the folded piece of paper.

Mary Beth Hayes has agreed to testify.

Relief floods through me and I scribble a note back to Jennifer, asking her to set a meeting for that afternoon.

Jennifer nods and leaves the courtroom. For the rest of the afternoon I try to focus on the prosecutor's questioning and Chloe's responses, objecting often when I think he's crossed the line. But part of my brain is already working on my questions for Mary Beth.

It's almost four o'clock by the time George Winters finishes questioning Chloe and the judge wraps up for the day.

"Let's talk," the prosecutor tells me when the judge walks out. "We're ready to offer you a deal. If she pleads guilty to involuntary grievous bodily harm, we will recommend probation and community service."

"But she'll still have a criminal record." I glance at Chloe still sitting upright in her chair.

"She'll be spared jail and can take care of her kid."

"That's not good enough, George. A criminal record will be a black stain for the rest of her life."

"That's the best you're going to get."

"I'll speak to her, but I can tell you right now that I will be recommending that she refuses your offer."

"Suit yourself."

In the taxi back, I tell Chloe about the offer. "But he raped me," she cries. "I didn't mean to run him over, to hurt him this much."

"I think the case is going well and we have a good chance of winning," I tell her. "But it's still a gamble. You have to be ready for an unfavourable outcome if we don't take the deal. That means several years in prison. You won't be able to see your child grow up. But if you take the offer, you will always have a criminal record. That might impact your future opportunities to find a job and livelihood."

*

Mary Beth is waiting in my office when I get back. I have purposely not told Chloe about her. It seems cruel to raise her hopes before making sure that the new witness will work in our favour.

For the next two hours I go over Mary Beth's story, talking about the incident, questioning her over and over, making sure that her story remains consistent. We focus on the details, the description of the construction site where Ben had pulled over, how she felt when he pinned her against the seat, how she finally managed to escape.

"Thank you for doing this," I tell her.

"I couldn't let the girl go to jail. He's a horrible person and needs to be stopped from ever doing what he did to us again."

"I'll see you tomorrow morning," I tell her, squeezing her hand.

*

That evening I get home late and for once I'm glad to have avoided Maya. I'm still troubled by the conversation we had the day before, her insistence that she gets the information first hand from me. I'm struggling with my decision. I don't know what the right thing to do is, whether to betray Ellen and

Tom's trust and give Maya the information she wants. Or tell them about her request. As a mother I would want to know if one of my children went behind my back. But this is Maya and I'm rarely rational when it comes to her.

Miles has dinner ready. The children are playing on the living room floor. My husband hands me a plate of stir-fry noodles. My stomach churns. Although I'm hungry the thought of food makes me feel sick. But I take it gratefully and start fiddling with my fork, pushing the food around the plate, staring at the small cut vegetables. I feel Miles' eyes on me and look up to see him staring in my direction. "Have there been any developments in Maya's case?" he asks.

Swallowing the lump that has formed in my throat, I reply: "No, I haven't heard back from the detectives and am waiting for the investigator's report into Mrs Larkin."

"I always wondered whether it was one of the other students who killed him. Someone we knew." He exhales through pursed lips and shakes his head. "Surely the detectives must suspect that too. It's a college town after all."

"I don't know. They haven't said where they're focusing their investigation."

"Does Maya being born abroad help you? Or does it make things worse?"

"That's been on my mind. I think it will make it easier to track me down if they start looking at student records. It will narrow their search."

Miles takes a deep breath and exhales slowly. "From a legal perspective, what is likely to happen if you are caught?"

I focus on the chip in the nail polish on my left thumb.

"I would be prosecuted. The fact that he killed those girls should work in my favour, somehow justify my actions. But I will get slammed for covering everything up instead of trying to get help. And I'm quite certain I'm going to be disbarred so I'd have to quit the firm."

"Jeez Liz, this is bad. You'll need the best legal help you can get."

"Yes."

"We'd have to protect the children as much as possible. They're young, won't be able to understand."

I don't like the direction he's going in, almost like it's a given that I'm going to be caught.

"This might blow over," I say.

"What are the chances of you getting away with this?"

"I don't know. If nobody else knew I'd say they were pretty good. But the fact that there's someone out there who knows my name, knows where I live… Well, that's not good."

"So, best case scenario would be acquittal but losing your job?"

"More or less."

"And what if you turned yourself in? Tell them about this Terry guy and try to strike a deal?"

"I don't think I have any leverage. All I know is that he made a phone call to Terry, but I have no proof of his involvement."

"Still though, if you confessed you won't have to continue constantly looking over your shoulder, waiting for something horrible to happen. Especially with someone threatening you. What if they come after the kids? I can't believe how irresponsible you've been keeping that to yourself, knowing that there's someone out there who knows what you did and might try to seek revenge. So reckless."

His tone is final.

"You need to step forward, Liz. Or…"

"Or what?"

Miles raises the palms of his hands at me as if he won't be responsible for his actions. I realise he's giving me an ultimatum. I know at this moment that if I want our marriage to have any hope of surviving, I'm going to have to start making arrangements to confess.

Chapter 38

"What the hell are you doing?" George Winters spits at me, his face so close to mine that I can smell his tobacco breath.

"I don't know what you mean." I motion to Chloe to sit down. We've just entered the courtroom to find him already there.

"You know exactly what I mean," he hisses. "Why are you adding a last-minute witness when we're already discussing a deal?"

"The witness just came forward and as for the deal, we graciously refuse it."

"You're going to regret this."

The colour drains from Ben's face when Mary Beth takes the stand. He whispers something in the prosecutor's ear, nodding his head widely at Mary Beth. "Your Honour, we object to this last-minute witness," George Winters says.

The judge summons us over. "We were not given enough time to evaluate this witness," the prosecutor complains.

"Your Honour, we alerted the prosecution about the existence of Ms Hayes during disclosure. However, she only agreed to testify yesterday," I argue.

"The defence has buried the document amongst tens of others. How convenient!" George Winters says.

"Hold the sarcasm, Mr Winters," the judge says. "I will be allowing this witness."

Answering my questions Mary Beth tells her story. "Why did you decide to come forward?" I ask her.

"I couldn't bear another person suffering because of him. I felt it was my duty to speak up and tell the court what he had done to me."

Mary Beth is the last witness and after her testimony, George Winters and I make our closing arguments. The trial is almost over.

"What happens next?" Chloe asks me as we walk into my office.

"We wait for the jurors to finish deliberating."

"How long will that take?"

"I don't know. It could be a couple of hours or longer. It really depends whether they all agree on the verdict."

She doesn't respond, but sits across from me in silence. "Why don't you lie down for a bit, try to get some rest?" I ask her, noticing how exhausted she looks.

"Ok."

She walks over to the sofa but I stop her.

"Let me take you to an empty office where nobody will disturb you." I lead the way. Chloe removes her shoes and lies down on the sofa, her body sinking into the cushions.

"Thank you," she says in a small voice.

"Get some rest." I wish I could do the same, close my eyes and relax into oblivion, but my mind is overloaded with thoughts. I'm concerned about Chloe. The next few hours are going to seal her fate. I fear that if she is found guilty Luigi will resist me representing her in an appeal.

And when I force myself to stop thinking about Chloe, Maya's face flashes before me. I've surrounded myself with a web of lies, woven over many years, and I'm terrified that once one thread is pulled away, the whole fabric will come apart.

Shaking my head vigorously I try to shift my focus to my work. Opening my laptop I start scrolling through the tens of emails, deleting junk and flagging the ones that need to be replied to. I work diligently for a while before going to check on Chloe. Opening the door a crack I see she is lying on the sofa, her eyes closed, her hands cradling her growing stomach. Taking care not to make any noise, I close the door again and walk away.

Back in my office I stand next to the window, taking in the city traffic, people walking fast, dodging other pedestrians, crossing the road without looking.

But my attempts to distract myself fail. My mind keeps going back to the investigation and Miles' look of mistrust whenever he glances at me.

For a while I pace back and forth, walking between my desk and the window and the door and the desk again in an endless triangle. We haven't heard from the detectives, have no idea what's happening with the investigation into Maya's birth mother. Despite Ellen's daily calls asking about the case, I have stopped short of contacting Detective Brown. My justification that I've been too busy is just an excuse. I'm scared of what he'll tell me, worried that he will see through me and realise that my eagerness is due to my involvement, especially if he already has the slightest suspicion of who I really am.

But every night I lie awake in the empty bed, staring at the ceiling, wondering how close I am to be discovered. I think about Mary Beth, coming forward to do the right thing. And Maya, standing up to her parents. I cannot ward off Ellen's questions for much longer. With shaking hands I pick up the phone and dial Detective Brown's number.

"Hello," he says in his usual gruff voice.

"Detective Brown, this is Elizabeth Perkins. I'm working on Tom and Ellen McBride's case."

"Yes, yes. Hello."

"I'm calling to see if there have been any developments in your investigation. Mr and Mrs

McBride are eager to know." Clutching the phone between my ear and chin, I shrug out of my jacket, suddenly feeling uncomfortably warm. "Maya keeps asking them," I add.

"Yes, of course. Give me a second." There's a long pause and I hear the shuffling of papers on the other side of the line. My heart is beating faster and faster. There's a lump in my throat that makes me feel like I'm about to choke. "Here it is." I hear him whisper.

In a louder voice he continues: "We received Maya's birth certificate from the US. Her biological mother is called Laura Black. We're currently working on tracking her down but haven't had any luck yet."

My hand trembles around the pen I'm clutching. I tighten my fist around it, trying to steady the shaking. They know the name. How long will it take to find out it's a fake? I don't dare say anything.

"Do you think she's still in the US?"

"We don't know; we're looking in both countries. We also spoke to the McBrides' adoption attorney and he gave us the few details he had. Looks like she was a student and wanted to give up the baby so she could continue with her studies. She was British actually, which reinforces our belief that she might have been involved in Larkin's murder. The lawyer insisted that she seemed like a normal girl. He thought she had just found herself in a sticky situation and wanted to give up the baby to continue with her life. He thinks he might have her file somewhere in storage, with copies of her identity card, and promised to look for it."

The photos. That is likely to be my unravelling. Despite changing my hair colour and wearing glasses, the resemblance is still there. They will easily see it. Still, I force myself to remain calm. "So, no real leads yet?"

"No, unfortunately not. I understand that this can be frustrating, especially for Maya, but these things can take time... Especially since we have to involve law enforcement in the US."

There's a knock and Jennifer puts her head round the door. "The jury's back," she mouths when she sees me still on the phone.

"Ok, thank you detective." Standing up, I put my jacket back on. "I'll check back in a few days. Hopefully you'll have some more information."

Hanging up I go to get Chloe. She's lying on the couch staring at the ceiling. "We need to go back."

"Did you manage to get any sleep," I ask her in the taxi.

She shakes her head but doesn't say anything. Her hands are shaking. She clasps them tightly in her lap until her knuckles turn white. Her face is as pale as can be, her eyes sunken and rimmed with dark circles. She looks at me, her face distorted in fear. "I'm scared," she says.

A surge of affection for her rushes through me mingled with regret at having considered turning her away. I don't know what the next hour will bring, but I know that her case never stood a chance in the hands of the public defender. I've done my best and normally that's good enough for me. Yet, seeing her so helpless, so terrified, I wish I could give her assurances. But everything is out of our hands now. I cannot tell her not to be afraid for fear of raising expectations I can't fulfil. We sit together and I squeeze her hand.

We walk into the courtroom and it seems to take ages for the jury to be brought in. Chloe is standing rod straight next to me. The judge is handed the verdict and I see him nod. The head juror stands up and starts reading the charges. As we wait for those words that will determine Chloe's fate, it feels like a vacuum where time has stopped. I find myself trembling and can only imagine how she feels.

The head juror's mouth moves as if in slow motion. I strain to hear above the sound of blood pumping in my ears. Then I hear a scream. It's not loud, but sounds like the cry of a wounded animal. Looking around I see everyone staring right past me. Behind me Chloe is crumpled on the chair, her face buried in her hands.

Chapter 39

Luigi is sitting on the sofa in my office when I get back. Standing up, he breaks into a theatrical loud clap as I walk in. "*Brava*! That was amazing. You won the unwinnable case."

"We got lucky." And I believe it. Without Mary Beth's testimony I'm not sure Chloe would have been acquitted. Instead of being over, her ordeal would only be just beginning.

He cranes his neck to look behind me and through the open door. "Where's Chloe? Thought I'd take you girls to a late lunch. Hawksmoor?"

"Oh, she went home. She looked drained."

"She must be relieved though. This could have gone very differently. Thanks to you it didn't."

Leaning against my desk, I nod slowly, remembering the first time I met Chloe and my reservations about taking her case.

"What about you? Fancy lunch? Couple of cocktails? You deserve to celebrate."

The idea is tempting. Luigi is fun to be around and I could do with the distraction, a break from the incessant worry. But anxieties press in on me, and a quick glance at my overloaded desk stops me. "I'd love to but have so much work to catch up on."

Then, seeing Luigi's disappointed face, I add: "Why don't you come to dinner sometime soon? I know Miles would love to see you."

Once Luigi's gone I bury myself in paperwork, wanting to catch up on my other cases. There's a knock on the door and Jennifer walks in. "Detective Brown just called. He said they've uncovered something about Maya's birth mother and wants to speak to you immediately. He's asking whether you can go down to the station."

Shock spreads across my whole body. I feel like I cannot move. I can barely even breathe. I realise after a while that I'm holding my breath and notice Jennifer looking at me strangely. "You don't have any meetings scheduled for this afternoon if you want to go."

Nodding, I wait for her to leave. Alone in my office, I allow fear to overwhelm me for a few seconds. They must have made the link to me, that's why he wants to speak to me urgently.

Putting my head in my hands, I lower it towards my desk, as my desperation continues to intensify. My heart is beating so fast that I fear it's going to do some serious damage. Asking me to go to his office, rather than speak to me on the phone, sounds menacing. Am I going to be arrested? There's no doubt that they've uncovered something important. I know I'm in deep trouble and there's nothing I can do about it. I square my shoulders and put on my coat.

*

Detective Brown is in a meeting when I get to the police station and I'm shown to a dingy waiting room. The minutes tick by and I keep glancing at the clock in one corner of the empty room. Picking up a magazine, I try to read but the words dance in front of my eyes, blurring into each other. I cannot think about anything other than what Detective Brown is going to tell me. I close the magazine and put it back on the rack and just stare in front of me.

Finally, after what seems like an endless wait, I am shown into the detective's office.

I sit down on the chair across from his desk, anxiety eating away at me. My hands are shaking and I hide them behind my bag, twirling its strap around my fingers. Taking a deep breath, I clench my jaw and look at Detective Brown. This is it. This is the moment of truth. In just moments I am going to find out whether he knows about me. He's going to tell me how the investigation led them to me. How my careful plan to hide my identity fell apart under their scrutiny.

I wonder whether he's going to press charges immediately. Or will he give me a chance to tell my side of the story? Am I going to be interrogated right now? Will he be questioning me or is he going to get someone else?

Perhaps I should have gone home, said goodbye to Miles, spent some time with the children. Their innocent faces flash in front of my eyes. They don't deserve to grow up without a mother. They shouldn't be paying for my mistakes.

"What did you need to speak to me about?" I have to know. This wait needs to be over right now. I cannot take it anymore.

"Yes, yes," he says. "I know you must be busy." He opens one of his desk drawers and rummages inside, taking out a green folder and opening it in front of him. He takes his time scanning it. I crane my neck to see what he's reading but cannot make out the words from my position. Finally, when I think I'm about to explode with anxiety, he looks up at me.

"I wanted to speak to you before I shared the news with Mr and Mrs McBride," he starts. "I felt it was important to give you the opportunity to speak to them yourself since you seem to be friends."

Here it comes, I think. This is exactly what I've been fearing for all these years. It is finally happening and I cannot do anything to stop it. It feels like a train careening on the tracks towards me. All I can do is stand there, wanting to move away, wanting to do something to stop it from hitting me, but knowing that I am powerless. I cannot move from my position, even though I know that in just a few seconds I'm going to get hit and killed. I cannot change my destiny.

"I told you already that we unsealed Maya's birth certificate and discovered her biological mother to be Laura Black. We strongly believe in a link between her and John Larkin's death and we really want to find her and have her answer some questions..."

His voice trails off. I can feel the bad news coming soon and I sit stock still as I wait for it.

Detective Brown is staring at me with a strange expression on his face, as if he doesn't really know how to continue. Is that pity in his eyes? Could he be feeling bad that he's about to change my life forever?

"We've searched for Laura Black. Both here and in America. We've tried everything to find her. But we can't."

Why is he telling me this? Why does he keep wasting time on inane details? Why doesn't he get right to the point? I know that Laura Black doesn't exist. She never did. When is he going to tell me that they found out Laura Black is me?

"This ID card is fake," he continues. "We tried to see if the clinic had any other details of her, maybe they took a DNA swab or something similar, but even if they did, those records have been discarded."

"Laura Black doesn't exist and we have hit a wall."

His words reverberate in my head. Could it be possible that they were unable to make the link? That my efforts to hide my tracks were successful? Or is this a trap? Is Detective Brown trying to lure me into a false sense of security so that I let my guard down and blurt out the information he needs to nail me?

"What does this mean?" I need to understand exactly what he's saying.

"Whoever Laura Black was has covered her tracks so well that she's managed to disappear into thin air."

The room is spinning around me and I am afraid that I'm going to faint. Swallowing hard, I ask: "So what's the next step?"

"We're going to continue looking, but it doesn't look good. I wanted to be upfront about this, especially since there's a child involved."

"So, the investigation isn't closed?"

"No, no. We don't really have much to go on, but we're re-examining all the evidence and hope to find some way to track this woman down."

My head feels heavy as I walk out of the police station. Who knows what they will find once they examine all the evidence. Forensics have made great advancements. There could be something hiding in plain sight that will lead them to me.

My work phone flashes. The investigator's name pops up on the screen:

Just emailed you that report.

Not wanting to go back to the office, I duck into a coffee shop and log into my inbox, opening the report and skimming it fast for new revelations. Mrs Larkin wasn't lying when she talked about her aggressive husband. Luke had uncovered reports of regular hospital visits. Every bone in her body seemed to have been broken or sprained. There were reports of gashes on her face. Why did nobody take action? And why did she not walk away from the cycle of abuse?

I cannot help but feel sorry for her. She never had a break. Instead, her life has been a constant struggle. Then the unspeakable happened. The nightmare that every mother fears. She lost her son.

No wonder she is obsessed with meeting Maya. She wants, needs, some happiness in her life.

There's no reason why Maya should not hear this story. Tom and Ellen might not want her to, claiming she's too young, and won't understand. They'll come up with some excuse to keep her in the dark, unless I take matters into my own hands.

I wish I could tell her everything. Tell her exactly what John Larkin did. How gullible I was to get in the car with him. How I managed to escape. Why, in a moment of panic, I decided to cover up my tracks. And why I decided to give her up, how I've come to regret my decision.

But I cannot do that. Instead, I'll let her find out about the grandmother she never knew she had.

*

Traffic is light, allowing me to get home in record time. As the car speeds forward I think about Mrs Larkin. The years of covering up for her husband, telling everyone that the dark bruises, the broken bones, were caused by clumsiness. The hospital records showed multiple miscarriages and I'm certain that they were caused by the beatings. Why did she have to be cursed with such horrible men in her life?

Maya's head is bent over the book she's reading, her hair falling in front of her face, covering her features. The seconds trickle by as I stand in the doorway, motionless, looking at her. With a quick movement she flicks her hair behind her left ear and I can see her lips moving as she reads.

Don't look up, I will her, wanting to absorb this moment, make sure I don't forget even the smallest detail.

Too soon she finishes the story. "Are you hungry?" she asks the children, her beaming smile warming my heart. Before she sees me watching her, I walk into the room.

"Can you come into the study for a few minutes?"

Maya's head shoots up. She nods and gets to her feet. She looks scared, like a little girl sent to the headmaster's office.

*

There's a moment when I almost change my mind. As Maya sits across from me, I find myself re-evaluating my decision, questioning whether I'm doing the right thing. If I'm being selfish.

It's not too late to backtrack. I can tell Maya that I will not be breaching her parents' trust and giving her information about the investigation. That I will not go behind her parents' back to arrange a meeting with Mrs Larkin. Warn her that I will tell Tom and Ellen about our conversation.

But then I look at her. She is biting her nails, nervously nibbling at the skin on her fingers. She is looking at me with eyes full of expectation. And I cannot bring myself to let her down.

"This document doesn't leave this room, but I want you to read it." I hand her a copy of the investigator's report.

She takes the stapled pages and turns them over in her hands. I see her eyes move quickly from one side to the other as she skims over the words. Her hand shoots to her mouth and she keeps it there. I cannot see what she's reading but wonder whether finding out about Mrs Larkin's constant beatings will traumatise her, leave a permanent mark.

The rustling of the pages is the only sound in the room. While I don't want to interrupt her reading, I need to set the ground rules. What I'm doing right now is wrong on so many levels. I'm going behind my clients' back, against their wishes, and speaking directly to a minor. I could get into trouble, more than I already am. Someone might suspect that I have a vested interest in this case. That my actions are more than those of a lawyer and a friend. That perhaps I'm further involved.

"I am still working for your parents and will continue discussing the case with them, advising them on the best way forward," I explain. "That won't be changing. But I will consider giving you information about the investigation."

"Thank you," she says.

Closing my eyes, I take a deep breath. There's no way back now. I've crossed a line. "This will work as long as you don't tell your parents. Once you do, I will no longer share any information with you. Do you understand?"

"Yes, yes." Her answer comes quickly.

"I'll leave you alone to read it."

With that, I walk out of the study. My breathing is fast and I stop just outside the room, leaning against the wall. This was a mistake, I think. How do I know I can trust Maya to keep this a secret? Deep inside I fear that this will start a cascade of consequences which will uncover my hand. I should have thought this through better, acted in my own best interest rather than get carried away by my feelings for Maya. I wouldn't have acted this way if it was anyone else, risked my career.

"Mummy, are you all right?" a small voice asks.

Looking down I see Julian standing next to me. "Yes, of course," I say, straightening up. "Where are you going?"

"Nowhere," he says, looking away.

Bending over, I pick him up, marvelling at how heavy he's become. "Wanna watch TV?"

He nods enthusiastically and I walk back into the living room, where Leah is playing with her dolls. Putting Julian down next to her, I switch on the television. Removing my suit jacket, I lower myself to the floor, not caring that my dark woollen trousers will get covered in the carpet's cream threads.

The three of us are immersed in the television program when Maya walks into the living room.

"Thank you, Mrs P." Her face is flushed and her eyes are red. It's obvious that she's been crying. But I cannot afford to let my guard down. "You're welcome. Where's the report?"

"I left it on your desk."

Scrambling up, I walk to the study, panicking for a moment about having left her alone in there with the report. My sudden mistrust shocks me. But there it is, the stapled sheaf of papers where Maya left it.

Chapter 40

The following day I ask Jennifer to hold my calls and bury myself in paperwork. But I cannot concentrate. With Chloe's case over I should be getting my life back, spending time with my family. Instead I'll be going home to a husband who can barely look at me. Who has gone back to sleeping in the spare bedroom.

Shaking my head I try to focus on the document in front of me. But my eyes keep clouding over, the words dancing in front of my eyes. In the end I close the file and pack my bag. I have to get out of here, get some air, go home early. Show Miles that I'm making an effort to be around more.

Popping my head into Jennifer's cubicle I ask whether there were any important messages. "I was just typing up an email," she says, handing me my work mobile phone. "Nothing pressing but you did get a call from Detective Brown."

"Yes?" I respond, trying to keep my voice steady as my pulse starts racing. "Did he say what he wants?"

"No, he wouldn't, said he'd like to speak to you directly. All he said was that there's been a breakthrough."

"Ok, thank you." My legs feel like jelly as I walk the few steps back to my office and close the door, leaning against it as all the energy seeps out of my body. My feet feel rooted to the spot as shock spreads across my whole body. I feel like I cannot move. I can barely even breathe. I realise after a while that I'm holding my breath.

Long moments go by until I feel strong enough to push myself upright and gingerly take a step into the room, hoping that my legs won't buckle beneath me. Taking small steps, I make my way to my desk.

My world stops spinning every time Detective Brown calls. Is this it? Does this mean that they've made the link? That all these years of keeping such a big secret are coming to an end and the future is completely unknown. I'm overcome by fear for myself but also for my family. The children will grow up without a mother. My parents will have to come to terms with what I did. The embarrassment that this will cause Miles.

My hands are trembling so much that I keep hitting the wrong button as I dial Detective Brown's number. One ring. Two rings. Three rings. Four rings until the machine picks up. But I don't know what to say and hang up without leaving a message.

Instead I call his office. His secretary's chirpy voice hurts my ears. "He's out until Monday." And so is Detective James, she adds when I ask for her.

Putting my head in my hands, I lower it towards my desk, as my desperation intensifies. A breakthrough could mean anything but it can't be good. They must be getting closer to finding me. Somehow they must have come across evidence leading back to me.

How am I going to wait until Monday to find out what they have about me, what the development is?

There is only one thing I can do. I can spend time with my family. I need to stop wasting precious moments in a dark office and instead rush home. I can try to get there in time to connect with the children, tuck them into bed, tell them how much I love them. And then I can try to patch things up with my husband, get him to forgive me, try to save our marriage, before it's too late.

Chapter 41

My head is pounding, my eyes bleary by the time I pull into the garage. Miles' car is already there. I'm surprised. Even though we've barely spoken in the past days, he still tells me when he's leaving the hospital. Not today. I haven't heard from him for hours, thought he must still be in surgery. He's in the living room, sitting on the sofa. But for once he doesn't have a book or a journal in his hand. He's staring straight ahead, not even turning when I walk into the room until I call his name.

"Where are the kids?" I ask, looking at my watch, confirming that it's still before their bedtime.

He turns his head to face me slowly, as if the motion requires a lot of effort. "They're asleep."

"Already?" I cannot keep the disappointment from my voice. "I wanted to say goodnight. Maybe they're still awake." I start walking away, wanting to rush upstairs on the off chance Miles is mistaken. But he calls after me.

"Elizabeth, come over here please." His voice is stern, a sharp edge to it. "We need to talk."

Not tonight, I think. I feel an enormous urge to run away, as far from here as possible, to avoid the confrontation. Tell him that I need to take a shower, buy myself some time. Tell him about Detective Brown's message. But I know deep in my heart that it would only postpone the inevitable. I need to get this over with now.

So I turn around and walk towards my husband. Putting my bags down, I take a seat next to him. He shuffles backwards, away from me, and it feels like a dagger to my heart.

Miles keeps me waiting. He stares ahead, then holds his head in his hands, wrestling with the thoughts inside. Eventually he speaks. "I'm sorry Liz, but I cannot keep your secret. It's too much for me. It's crushing me. It's all I can think about. I'm terrified that at any moment you're going to be found out. I can't concentrate on anything else. I can't cope in the operating theatre."

Warmth moves up my body, inching its way to my head. The room spins around me. I feel the air knocked out of me and have to steady myself against the back of the sofa to stop myself from slumping forward. Of course he couldn't do that for me. I knew another person couldn't. And now I have so much to lose.

For days I'd known that I would have to confess. That this eventuality was unavoidable. But its reality now stops me in my tracks. Perhaps it's the wrong move. I want to argue, beg him not to make me do this, force him to understand that there's another way. That just like I've managed to live with this secret for all those years, so will he. We can support one another, talk to each other. Finally glancing up, I'm ready to put my thoughts into words but the stony look on his face stops me. His usually soft eyes are cold, devoid of emotion.

"Miles, the children…" I start.

"No," he interrupts, holding his open palm in front of me, inches from my face. "You're not going to use the children as an excuse. The children have already been affected. Your constant nightmares, your jumpiness, your fear of a simple colour. The children will be worse off if you're found out, dragged out in handcuffs in the middle of the night. What will all this teach them about facing up to their mistakes, about consequences, about truth? We cannot live our lives waiting for you to be found out, especially if there's someone out there who knows what you've done, who's been threatening you."

"We could leave the country, move somewhere far, try to put all this behind us."

But Miles shakes his head. "Our lives are here. This is the place the children know. We're not taking them away from everything for a gamble."

Any energy I had feels like it has been sucked right out of me and I have to struggle to stop my body from going limp. Hanging my head I stare down at my hands, twisting them in my lap, my fingers looping around each other. There's no point telling him about Detective Brown's call. It would only re-affirm his belief that I need to turn myself in. My biggest nightmare is happening right now. And this time I know I cannot wake up.

My mind is whirring, questions booming inside my head, getting louder and louder. Will our marriage survive or will Miles leave me? What will happen to my children? Will I even be allowed to see them? Do I want them to come visit me in prison? The image of Julian and Leah seeing me behind bars is unbearable and tears spring to my eyes. They are so young and I'm making them go through something no child should ever experience. What sort of mother am I? I abandoned one child and am turning the lives of my other two upside down.

It's as if Miles reads my mind. He reaches out and covers my hands with his. It's the first time he has willingly touched me in days and I allow myself to savour the moment. "I will do whatever I can to support you," he says. "But you need to come clean." His voice is barely a whisper, his eyes downcast. "Otherwise I'm going to have to do it myself."

"Please Miles, let's not take any hasty decisions."

He moves his hand away. "This wasn't a hasty decision. I've given this a lot of thought and it's the best for our family. For our children."

"What? Me going to prison?"

"Hopefully it won't come to that." He stands up and starts walking out of the room, before turning back. "But you're going to have to face the consequences of your actions. All of us will have to."

For long minutes after he leaves I am rooted to the spot, unable to move. I have to force myself to stand up and drag myself upstairs. Lying in the empty bed for hours, staring at the ceiling, sleep evades me completely. For years I have felt the pressure of fear at times almost suffocate me. But I've always held strong, refusing to break down, trusting my methods, and the more I put into the life I'd built, the harder I worked to stop it from crumbling if I let the truth slip.

Even though deep down I always knew my past would one day catch up with me, I feel completely unprepared. My priority has been to keep the truth hidden and I did nothing to prepare myself for the opposite. This shift knocks the breath out of me as I feel the whole world come crashing around me.

But now that the decision has been taken out of my hands, there's a part of me that yearns for release. Finally I'm going to be able to lift the burden off my shoulders. I will no longer need to be constantly looking behind me, terrified of being discovered.

But the thought of Maya finding out, her reaction when she realises that the person she's been looking for has been right down the road, terrifies me. How could she not hate me for not telling her, and detest the deceitful way I've been so close to her? She might see me as the monster who killed her father.

My thoughts turn to Ellen, the anguish she is going through, and the anger I know she'll feel if I come forward. Shaking my head I try to rid myself of that image, force myself to get some sleep. But for hours I lie on my back thinking the same thought about how my life has been turned upside down simply because I made the mistake of getting into John Larkin's car.

Miles has agreed to give me until Monday to put the wheels in motion. By then I will know what the detectives have found out. I might not even need to confess. I have one last weekend. And then the life I've worked so hard to build could be over.

Chapter 42

"Ellen?" I say, looking out onto the dark entryway. It's late in the evening on Saturday. "How are you? Come on in."

Opening the door wide, I wait for her to enter, but she remains rooted to the spot and I notice her face is hard with anger.

"How could you do this to me?" Her words dig into me.

The hot flush of guilt spreads through my body, starting from my feet and travelling upwards, until it reaches my face. Multiple scenarios rush through my head, heightening my fear. The detectives must have called her, told her about my connection to Maya. That has to be it. Or she finally realised I was the girl at the hospital. "Why don't you come in so we can talk?"

She starts shaking her head. The front light goes on at the house next door and Ellen glances towards it. We hear voices coming from that direction. Ellen takes a step towards me and I move back, making space for her. "Let's go into the study," I say, leading the way.

Closing the door behind us, I look at Ellen. There's a fury in her eyes that I've never seen before.

Her jaw is clenched, her lips set in a thin line. For long moments she's immobile, staring at me with contempt.

"Ellen, what happened?" I ask, my voice barely audible over the rhythmic thumping in my ears.

"This is what happened," she snaps, thrusting a sheaf of papers in my hand. I don't need to look to know it's the report on Nora Larkin.

"I don't understand. We already discussed this. What's wrong now?"

"I found this in Maya's bedroom," she hurls at me. "How could you give it to her? How could you go behind our back and tell her about that woman?"

It doesn't make sense. Maya left the copy I showed her in my office. I'd made sure she didn't take it home with her, wanting to avoid this exact confrontation. "Ellen, I didn't give her this."

"Then how come she has it?" Ellen's eyes are blazing as she stares at me.

"I don't know, did she tell you I gave it to her?"

"No, of course she didn't. She'd never tell on you. She treats you like an idol. Especially since you took her to the hair salon," she spits out.

"Maybe she found your copy?" I suggest.

"Don't try to blame me! I checked and my copy is in the safe."

"Ellen, I didn't give her this," I repeat. And then I am overcome by anger. I should be spending time with my family, playing with the children before they go to bed and not having this pointless discussion. "Some trust would be nice after all I'm doing for you," I lash out.

"You're not doing us any favours. We're paying a lot of money for your services and then you go behind our backs and give Maya this."

"I did not give this to her!" The lie sounds hollow to my ears, despite trying to convince myself it's the truth, that I didn't give Maya the report, only allowed her to see it.

She snatches the document from my hands in uncharacteristic aggression. "Tom warned me about you," she spits at me. "From the beginning he said there was something wrong with you. That you were too cold, always in control, like you were hiding something. But I wanted to give you the benefit of the doubt, be your friend. I liked you. I allowed my daughter to spend time at your house, take care of your children. And instead of gratitude I get this." She hits the document with the back of her other hand. "You went behind my back and did the one thing I specifically told you not to."

Before I can respond, she pivots around. As she storms out of the office, her flowing cardigan catches a thick glass vase sitting on one of the shelves. It topples precariously on its side, wobbling for a split second, before starting its descent to the ground. The sound of glass hitting the hardwood floors and breaking shatters through the silence.

For a moment I find myself transported back in time, to that night, the moment when he dropped the beer bottle, the noise piercing through my hope of getting away. That was the instant when my fate was sealed, when my opportunity to escape was lost. I have often wondered how different my life would have been had I managed to get away, had he not woken up. I would not be here right now, fighting with someone I had long hoped could be a real friend.

Shivers go down my spine, the hairs on the back of my neck spring upwards as the shards of glass scatter and bounce upwards before settling in a messy circle around the point of impact. I slam my hand over my mouth to stop myself from screaming.

Ellen stares at me and for a moment I think a softer look crosses her face. But after a fleeting second her icy glare returns. "I'll send you a cheque for this," she says, motioning to the broken glass. Then she turns around again and marches out of the room.

The front door slams shut. My legs are weak. I'm still struggling to catch up with what has happened. How did Maya get a copy of the report? It was on my desk before she left. How could she betray me after everything I said? What was I thinking to go behind Ellen's back, and get this so wrong?

The sound of the TV interrupts my thoughts. But I don't go back into the living room. My suspicion aroused, I boot up my laptop and look through my sent emails. There's nothing strange. Then I go through my deleted emails. And there it is. An email sent from my computer to Maya's address, the report on Nora Larkin attached.

"Fuck." Her deception stings. Clenching my fists, I bite them to keep myself from letting out the scream of frustration that's building in my throat.

Chapter 43

My fingers are tight around the phone, my knuckles white as I wait for Detective Brown to get on the line. Traffic whizzes by, its sound muffled by the closed windows of my car. As soon as my phone rang I had pulled up on the side of the road, suspecting it might be him.

A couple of minutes have passed. Classical music comes from the other side of the line, its intended calming effect completely lost on me. Finally the line crackles and Detective Brown's booming voice comes on. "Eliz... Mrs Perkins, thank you for holding on."

"Ye..." The lump in my throat gets thicker and I have to stop and clear my throat before continuing. "Your message said there was a breakthrough."

"Yes, we finally might have got lucky. I wanted to let you know so you can speak to Mr and Mrs McBride."

He pauses and I will him to continue but don't dare say anything, worried that he'll hear the fear in my voice, confirm any suspicions he might have.

"John Larkin has a cousin that he was close to. Terence Smith." The pounding in my heart intensifies as the detective continues. "He's in prison, has been in and out for many years. Quite the trouble maker…"

His voice trails off and I hear someone talking to him. Come on, come on, I urge silently.

"So, as I was saying, we went to speak to this man, to try to determine whether he knew anything that could lead us to Maya's mother. He said…"

The booming horn of a passing truck blocks out his voice. "Sorry, can you repeat?"

"He said he knows the name of the killer, has known all along, and will give us her name in exchange for immediate parole."

No, no, no! This is it then. The minute Terry gives them my name I'm done. Blood rushes to my head and I start feeling faint. Despite Miles' insistence that I confess, a part of me was still hoping I could keep my secret, despite the toll it's been taking on me and my family.

"Mrs Perkins, are you still there?"

"Ye…s, yes." My voice croaks. "So, you think he really knows who it is?"

"We'll have to wait and see. But this is the closest we've ever come to getting a name."

"And you think you can trust him? That he's not lying, throwing a name out there to get out of prison early?"

"That's a logical fear, but if DNA tests prove that she's connected to Maya we'll know we're on the right track."

Closing my eyes tightly, I try to compose myself, afraid that I'm going to break down, make a sound that will raise suspicions. "When do you expect him to give you the name?"

"We've started discussions with the parole board to see if this is doable and are waiting for an answer."

"Thank you for letting me know," I say. And then quickly I add: "I'll tell Mr and Mrs McBride."

For a few minutes after we hang up I sit in the car, staring right ahead, not yet ready to pull back into the busy road, scared that I might injure myself or someone else. My time is running out. If I'm going to turn myself in I have to do it quickly, before Terry gives them my name. There is no time to waste, no point in trying to dissuade Miles. He won't change his mind anyway, especially if he finds out about this latest development.

*

Luigi sits across from me, rubbing his stubble, staring right at my face. I walked into his office as soon as I got to work and confessed the whole story before I could change my mind. He hasn't said anything. It's the first time I'm seeing him completely lost for words. Finally, he takes a deep breath and exhales very slowly.

"You need to resign with immediate effect. You cannot have any link with the firm. I will buy you out."

"Ok." It pains me that he doesn't ask how I am doing, but goes straight into business mode. "Will you represent me?" I have nothing else to lose by asking him, and cannot imagine going to anyone else. The smaller we keep the circle, the better. And time is of the essence now that Terry is ready to give my name.

"I need to think about this," he says.

As I walk back to my office, I feel utterly alone, the weight on my shoulders dragging me down. The thought of losing the job that I love hits me like a blow in the stomach, knocking the breath out of me. I close the door behind me and lean against it, standing there for long minutes, wondering how I allowed my life to get to this point.

Chapter 44

Once things are set into motion, they move quickly. Two days after I speak to Luigi I'm signing the paperwork terminating my link to the firm I helped build up.

My fingers shake as I turn the pages and the pen feels heavy in my hand as I initial the thick contract. With every millimetre that the pen moves, the horror of what's happening becomes even more real. My mind goes back to our first day in business. We'd sat at Luigi's kitchen table brainstorming client acquisition strategies. This is a mistake, I had thought. I should never have given up a secure job for such a gamble. But over the years, with a lot of hard work and determination, we had managed to create a successful and well-respected firm.

Now I was giving up all claim to it. My name would no longer be associated with the firm. And chances that I will ever find another legal job are slim to nil.

For the past two days I've worked to tie loose ends, make sure that my notes on each case are clear for whoever will be taking over from me. With Luigi's blessing I called all my clients to let them know I would be moving away, citing personal reasons and refusing to give any further information.

"Are you ok?" Luigi asks, playing with the shiny square cufflink on his left cuff, twisting it round and round.

For a second I want to tell him that I'm not, that I'm falling apart, that I'm scared. But instead I just nod.

"Do you want a drink?" he asks. We're on our own in the boardroom, a pile of signed documents in front of us. Looking around at the scantily decorated room, I remember the day we moved into this building two years ago, when things started really picking up. We'd had a small party in the evening, once the removal crew had left and everything had been put in its right place. Everyone had gone home and Luigi and I sat on the large leather swivel chairs, the table scattered with paper plates and cups and remnants of food. We looked out of the window at the London skyline, the tall buildings glistening in the weak sunlight, and talked about the future.

"Sure." I'm not ready to leave the office yet. This morning was the last time I entered the building as part owner of the firm. Next time I set foot into the suite of offices it will be as a client. Luigi has agreed to represent me and we've been talking over the intricacies of my admission, how we're going to minimize damage. But despite our long conversations, we both know that this is going to be tough. At best my actions will be deemed as necessary to defend myself, but there is a cloud of doubt surrounding my years-long cover up of John Larkin's death.

Luigi hands me a glass of whisky and I take a small sip, wincing as the amber liquid burns a path down my throat. "I've secured an appointment with Detective Brown for Friday."

"Thank you. I'll speak to Maya beforehand."

"Is that wise?" Luigi asks. "Why don't you wait until we speak to the police? Avoid her telling anyone."

There's worry in his eyes, his usual carefree face creased into a frown. "I'm leaving it until the last minute, so that she won't have much time to let the secret slip, but I want her to hear it directly from me." What if I get arrested, taken straight to a lock-up while detectives show up at the McBrides' house to share the new discovery? No, I cannot take that chance. I need to look her in the eyes as I tell her who I really am.

"I have to do this," I insist.

"Ok, but the more people who know, the less able you'll be to change your mind if you decide to."

"It's too late for that," I say so softly that I wonder if he heard me. Then, after a few seconds I add: "What do you think will happen?"

Luigi rubs his stubble, his thumb and forefinger drawing circles on each side of his mouth. "We'll obviously try to convince them not to prosecute you, insist that this was pure self defence. But we won't be successful. You've tampered with evidence and they won't take kindly to that. Also, anything you said while representing the McBrides will be used to question your character. So if you ever said anything about finding Maya's mother, which I'm sure you did, while knowing it was you... Well, every small comment will probably be used against you."

Staring down at my glass, I swirl the amber liquid round and round, trying to remember everything I've said about the case, how I can explain my actions.

"Liz," Luigi says after a while. "I'm talking as your friend here. Are you sure you want to go ahead with this? You could wait it out, see what the detectives find. Perhaps they won't track you down. I can speak to Miles, tell him that this is a risky move, explain the repercussions. I'm sure he'll understand, especially once the shock wears off."

He's giving me a lifeline, a way out. He wants to help me stay safe, some part of him still believes in me. But my secret is out. Two more people know. And with Terry negotiating a deal, aside from whoever else he might have told, the danger of being found out creeps higher every day. I cannot live the rest of my life in fear. Frankly, I'm surprised I've made it this far.

And there's a part of me that cannot be responsible for Terry hurting anyone else. I need to tell the police about that call, his potential involvement. For years the thought of a predator still out there haunted me and I tried to push it to the back of my mind. But I no longer can. I need to do the right thing. What if he came after my children? Or Maya.

"No," I say, shaking my head. "This is for the best. I need to face the consequences."

*

The sound of the children playing with Miles wafts through the house. He's taken the day off to spend with us. Leah's belly laugh and Julian's infectious giggle make me smile. My eyes burn as I think about not seeing them grow up, being taken away from their lives. Tomorrow's appointment with the detectives fills me with dread.

But I do not have the luxury of breaking down. There is too much to do. Closing the door of the study, I take a deep breath. Then another. And another. I can do this. I have to do this.

Clicking a few keys on my phone to block my number, I quickly dial Maya. "Hello?"

The sound of her voice almost makes me choke up, even though I'm still shocked at her stealing the investigator's report.

"Maya, this is Elizabeth."

The sound of a door closing comes from the other end of the line, then silence. "Maya, are you there?"

"Yes, yes. Hello Mrs P." She sounds surprised and cautious.

"There is something I need to tell you about your biological mother." I quickly get to the point, not wanting her to hang up. "Do you have some time this afternoon?"

There's a pause and I wonder whether she thinks I'm trying to bait her, whether I just want to tell her off for taking the report. "Ok," she finally says, and I can hear the excitement and apprehension in her voice. "I can be there in two hours."

Looking at my watch, I walk back into the living room. Miles is on the ground tickling Leah, who is laughing so much I worry that she's going to forget to breathe. Julian is sitting on the floor, his back against the sofa, reading. I lower myself next to my son and put my arm around him. He doesn't take his eyes off the page but leans against me and I savour the feeling of his warm body against mine.

The house is otherwise silent as I walk through the hallway to answer the door two hours later. The children are reluctantly taking an afternoon nap.

"But Mum I'm not tired," Julian had complained over and over. I was insistent. I needed no distractions and wanted Miles to be with me when I talked to Maya. "Are you sure?" my husband had asked. "Yes," I'd responded. I needed someone to act as a witness in case this exchange was brought up in court and it did not feel right to ask Luigi.

"Come on in," I tell her, looking nervously towards the McBrides' house, hoping that Ellen won't see her walk in and storm over. The thought of Ellen finding out sends chills down my spine. She's going to be furious. She'd already made it very clear that she didn't want Maya to have anything to do with our family any longer. And that's before she knows who I really am.

"Sit down," I tell Maya when she follows me into the living room, motioning to the sofa and sitting down next to her. Miles comes in from the kitchen and sits on the armchair, right across from me.

Maya looks from me to him. "Look, I'm sorry. I know I shouldn't have emailed the report, but I wanted to have a copy, to be able to read it again."

Raising my hand, I stop her. Not that I'm not still mad at her, hurt by her actions. But it no longer seems important.

"Maya, there is something that I need to tell you, that I should have told you a long time ago." Swallowing the lump in my throat that is starting to make me hoarse, I look at Miles for reassurance and he smiles weakly. "When I was at university I did something stupid. I accepted a ride from a stranger. He drugged me and took me to a deserted room."

Her eyes open wide and I can see that she is putting the pieces of the jigsaw puzzle together. I need to hurry, continue talking, tell her everything before she figures it all out. I want her to hear it from me.

"He assaulted me. And he was attacking me a second time when I hit him with a piece of glass I found on the ground. I hit him in the neck, meaning to defend myself, and he died."

Maya gasps and continues to stare at me, her green eyes blazing with different emotions. Fear, surprise, curiosity.

"I was scared that nobody would believe he had attacked me, that they would blame me. So I ran away and never told anyone about that night."

Pausing, I give Maya some time to digest the information. "But a few weeks later I found out I was pregnant. I decided to give up the baby for adoption."

There's a knot in my throat and my vision is blurry from the tears that are forming in my eyes. Blinking hard, I clear my throat.

"Maya, that baby was you."

She sits still, her eyes never leaving mine, her hands clenched in her lap, the knuckles white. "Are you ok, Maya?" Miles asks and she tears her eyes away to look in his direction, her head still.

"Why?" she finally asks. "Why did you give me up? Was it your decision or did someone make you?"

A tear springs free and starts making its descent down my cheek. "I was scared, didn't think I would be able to take care of a baby. I thought you'd be better off being brought up by more responsible parents. Someone who didn't have such a skeleton in their closet."

"How did you find me?"

Remembering Luigi's warnings, I wonder whether I should answer her questions. But there's no going back now and I need to continue telling Maya the truth. "I saw your mother at the hospital, just after you were born. I knew she was the one adopting you. She dropped her driver's licence and I picked it up."

A new emotion flickers across her eyes and I realise that it's fear. She looks at me as if she's seeing me for the first time. Then she turns her face towards Miles. "Elizabeth wanted to make sure that you were safe, that you were well cared for, that you had a good life. She never forgot you. That's why we moved here."

Maya opens her mouth as if she's going to say something but closes it again. Her throat moves as she swallows. She brings her left hand to her face and tucks her flaming red hair behind her ear, then rubs her nose.

"Maya, are you ok?" I ask, reaching out to touch her arm.

She jerks back. "Don't touch me!"

I turn towards Miles and he gives me a watery smile.

"I'm sorry. I know this must be a shock to you," I tell her.

"I… I just don't understand. I've known you for all these years, even told you I wanted to find my birth mother, came to you for help. And you didn't think you should tell me it was you? How could you?"

"I'm sorry," I repeat, unsure what else I can say.

"Does Mum know?" Her concern for Ellen hurts me, and I hate myself for that.

"Not yet."

The seconds tick by as we sit in the living room, none of us talking, as the shock reverberates between us. I will Maya to understand my actions, to forgive me, to accept that I did this because I love her.

Finally Miles breaks the silence. "Maya, Elizabeth is going to speak to the police tomorrow. It's important that you keep this information to yourself until then. Can we trust you?"

She glances at him and then looks back at me. "Will you be arrested?"

The fear of the unknown shines in her eyes and I look away, down at my hands. "I don't know," I say softly. "Probably."

"Will you be put in jail?"

Lifting my shoulders in a shrug, I shake my head slowly from side to side. "Maybe. There are a lot of questions. It really depends on the judge and how sympathetic he or she is, whether they believe I was defending myself."

"But isn't that obvious?"

"No, unfortunately it isn't. See, had I spoken up when it happened, allowed the police to find the evidence, then it might have been a different story. But I was scared. I acted rashly. So, I don't know what will happen now."

She nods and I wonder whether she really understands. Whether all this is too much for a teenager to take in.

"I have to go," she says after a short while. She stands up, straightening her jeans-clad legs and pulling down her shirt. "Mum doesn't know I came here."

As I follow her to the door I am struck by the thought that this might be the very last time I see Maya. My body starts to shake, my arms aching to hug her, hold her close to me, bury my face in her hair, kiss her sweet face. But I don't have the energy for a rejection.

Suddenly she turns around and looks at me. "Was that why you went to the US? So that nobody would know about me?"

I simply nod, not knowing what else to say.

She takes a long look at me. "The red hair. Guess I got it from you."

"I'm sorry," I say, hoping to lighten the mood a little. "You have a lot to blame me for."

"I'll learn to live with it," she says. "See you around."

Standing in the doorway, I look at Maya walking down the street towards her house. Relief is mixed with fear. She knows. I've been as honest as I could. Now it's up to her to make sense of what I've told her.

Chapter 45

By the time dawn starts breaking the next day, my head feels ragged with going over the nightmare of the past, and the unknown ahead of me. I feel more alone than I have ever done, locked in the trap I've created for myself.

Unable to spend any more time in bed, I get up, select the dullest, most professional clothes I own, and lock myself in the bathroom.

Miles is waking up when I'm finally dressed and able to face the outside world. "How are you feeling?" he asks.

"Sick, terrified,"

"Liz, this will be ok. You'll feel relieved not to constantly have to look over your shoulder. To know the truth is out. The law should protect you."

He must be joking, I think. Does he really believe that I'm not going to have to pay a price for my encounter with John Larkin? This is a mistake. I want to tell him that, beg him to change his mind, try to explain how keeping this secret is the only option if we still want to have a life together. But it's already too late. Other people know. It's no longer a secret.

One by one I wake up Julian and Leah and help them get dressed. Leah's favourite pink cardigan is starting to look tight and Julian's trousers will soon be too short. There's a lump in my throat as I wonder who will notice that they need new clothes if I'm not around. I might have to miss seeing them grow up. Helping them with their homework. Listening to their fears. I'm failing them as a mother. Just like I failed Maya when I gave her up.

Miles comes downstairs and pours himself coffee and gulps it down. "Are you sure you don't want me to come with you?" he asks. "I can meet you after I drop the children at school." I shake my head.

"Liz." He stops, looks down into his mug, stirring his coffee so furiously that some spills over the side, onto the pristine countertop. He looks back at me. "I'm so angry at you. For not telling me, for what this might mean to our family."

Despair engulfs me. I knew he would leave me, walk away from our marriage, probably take the children. It won't be difficult, especially if I'm in jail. But I didn't think he would be so cruel as to tell me now, just before I walk into a police station to confess what happened so many years ago.

Clenching my hands into tight fists I look up at him. Make it quick, I think.

"I've been thinking about our marriage. What all this means for our future. Whether there even is a future for us."

Again he pauses and I want to scream. To beg him to continue, not to keep me waiting. For this to be over.

"It's too hard for me. I don't feel like I know who you are any more. All my images of you have been destroyed."

There is sadness in his eyes as he looks at me. Tears spring to mine as I wait for him to continue.

"But I love you. That's the bottom line. I always have. And I want to make our life together work. We have a family and that's the most important thing to me. If you go to jail we will all be waiting for you."

My bottom lip trembles uncontrollably. Tears spill out of my eyes before I can stop them. "Thank you," I manage to say.

Miles puts his arms around me and holds me close. I want to remain in this embrace forever, allow him to make me feel safe. But all too soon the moment is over. "I have to go. Call me as soon as you leave the police station," he says. "We have to go," he calls to the children, who are in the living room watching television.

"Too tight," Julian says, wriggling out of my embrace as I hold him for what I fear might be the last time. Letting him go, I kiss his forehead. "I love you so much," I whisper.

Turning to Leah, I take her small hands in mine and look into her big eyes. She smiles and touches her forehead to mine. Taking her in my arms, I bury my face in her soft hair, not wanting her to see me crying. "I love you, baby girl," I say. "Have a good day at school."

Alone in the kitchen, I put the dirty bowls and cups in the dishwasher. Taking one last look around, I square my shoulders, pick up my bag, and walk away. It's time to face the truth.

I walk to the tube station lost in thought. With no job there was no reason to drive into the city. The Tube is crowded but even surrounded by people I feel wholly alone. It's a short ride and before I know it I'm sitting in a cafeteria next to the police station, warming my freezing hands around a steaming cup of coffee, waiting for Luigi. Every sound startles me, every movement makes me whip my head round.

Luigi walks in when I'm on my third cup of coffee. My hands are shaking as I lift the cup to my lips to take the last few sips. I tell myself it's the caffeine and not the utter fear that's chilling my bones. He stands across from me. "Are you ready?"

No, I want to say. I'm never going to be ready for this. It's a mistake. I should run away as far from here as I can. But I know I cannot. This is it. I'm facing my fate. I'm doing what needs to be done for the sake of justice, and everyone who I love.

"As ready as I'll ever be," I respond, standing up and straightening my dress. I pick up my bag and follow Luigi to the door.

Chapter 46

The courtroom is cold, just like it always is. Shivering, I pull my jacket tighter around me and cross my arms, hoping to warm myself. It doesn't do much and I wish I'd worn something warmer. Perhaps even remembered to get a scarf.

Luigi and Doug, my other representative, are talking in hushed voices. Straining, I try to hear what they're saying but quickly give up. Instead, I close myself off in my imaginary world, trying hard to think of something else.

Detective Brown is sitting on the other side of the courtroom. I remember how his eyes had opened in shock when, eight months ago, Luigi told him who I was. He struggled to maintain a poker face, mask his surprised expression. He asked for the full details and Luigi gave him the story the way we'd agreed to tell it. He'd rubbed his temple and exhaled sharply. Then he cleared his throat. Once. Twice. He sounded almost apologetic as he led me to another room to take an official statement.

"We will investigate," he said when I told him about the phone call to someone called 'Terry' and my belief that he had been sending me the threatening letters.

Three days later I was officially charged with manslaughter and tampering of evidence. For days I barely left the house, and then only to pick up the children from school and go to Luigi's office, the office that had been mine, the company that I'd helped build. It was surreal to walk inside as a client, knowing that my fate rested entirely on the ability of the people who worked there.

Worry was my constant companion. I worried about my future, what would happen to me. How all this would impact the children. Whether they would eventually understand or if they would hate me for what I'd done. I worried about Miles, how he would be able to hold his head up at work as our life was being dissected in court. I worried about my parents and how the truth was going to shatter their image of their only daughter.

I worried about how Maya was doing. I had seen her once since I told her the truth. Coming back from the city, I had stopped the car to pick up the newspaper from the front garden. She walked out of her house and stared right at me. I lifted my arm to try a wave. But she looked down and walked away. I wondered whether she had told her mother. I had tried to talk to Ellen but she refused to see me. "Stay out of my life," she'd said when I called her. "And don't you dare come close to my daughter."

For a while I even worried about Mrs Larkin, and what she would do when she found out. But she surprised me. She called me a few days after I turned myself in. "I'd like to see you," she'd said. Fear crept up my body as I wondered what she was going to do, whether she had the strength to hurt me. But although I knew that I should refer her to Luigi, ask him to handle the situation, I agreed to meet her at a cafeteria in the city. I should be safe surrounded by people.

"What happened that night?" she asked me as soon as I walked in to find her already sitting in a booth.

I started telling her the story, everything that I remembered. "I'm sorry," I'd said. "I didn't mean to kill him. I just wanted him to stop."

"Did he suffer?" she asked.

"I don't know. I don't think so. It happened really quickly. By the time I ran out to get help he was gone."

"I didn't know he was doing that," she said, her eyes glistening with tears. "He was such a good boy." There was resignation in her voice and I thought that she had finally come to terms with who her son really was.

Shuddering again in the chilly courtroom, I wrap my arms more tightly around my body. This is going to be a long day. I wonder how long the trial is going to take, how many days I will spend sitting on this hard chair until I find out my fate.

The courtroom is filling up. My parents are here, having driven in last night. They'd offered to stay home with the children, but Miles wanted to be there himself. Although I miss having my husband here to support me, I wanted it to be him staying with the kids. We'd kept them out of school to make sure they didn't hear anything we were not ready to tell them. We both know that we cannot protect them forever but at least they can hear the information from us. Or from Miles if I get sent to prison.

Looking back I catch Mum's eyes. Her face is stony with fear. I give her a watery smile. Further back sits Chloe, nervously twirling her long hair around her fingers, her eyes flitting this way and that. It must be hard for her being back in a court room. I catch her eyes and smile, trying to reassure her, even though it's me needing comfort. But she's been through so much. The stress of the trial weighed heavily on her and led to substantial pregnancy complications. Thankfully, she recovered and her son, Samuel, was born healthy. With time on my hands, I had taken her under my wing, helping her apply for and secure social housing, allowing her to move away from the children's home she hated so much. We've remained in touch and I love hearing from her, seeing how far she's come, working hard and juggling school and a part time job, as one of Luigi's assistants, with caring for a new baby.

I'm turning back around when I see her. She is standing tall, her chin up, looking so young yet so in control. She looks around the courtroom, taking it all in. She looks right at me and her green eyes glisten as they lock on mine for a few seconds. Then she breaks the connection and looks towards the other side of the room where John Larkin's few family and friends, including his mother, are sitting behind the prosecution team. She smiles at Mrs Larkin, and the old lady shuffles on the bench, making space for her.

She takes a step forward, her black dress swishing around her legs. She stops and brushes off an imaginary speck of lint off her black shirt, a habit she surely got from Ellen. She takes another look around and runs her fingers through her red and golden hair.

I find myself holding my breath. I cannot stand this, cannot take her turning her back on me, taking his side. I know I don't deserve her understanding but I still crave it.

Every moment seems like an eternity. She smiles at Mrs Larkin as she walks towards her. My heart breaks.

And then she looks at me again, before taking a step in my direction and sitting down next to Mum. My heart leaps with joy. For a second I forget the ordeal that awaits me. It doesn't matter right now. What matters is that Maya is on my side.

Epilogue

Tightening the belt around my waist, I hope that the gathering at the back of my trousers will not show under the jacket. Turning around, I glance at the heap of clothes piled on the bed, a sea of black and grey drowning out the cheery colours of the flowered quilt cover.

Pursing my lips, I take another look in the full-length mirror, examining my reflection. My red hair is tied back in a neat bun at the nape of my neck, my makeup so subtle that it is barely visible. From the neck up I look like my old self, the person who showed up at the office every morning groomed to perfection. But my heart sinks as I look at the rest of my body. The white blouse is billowing around my willowy frame, looking the full two sizes too big that it is. My formerly tailored trousers are bunching up at the front, the fabric draping over my legs like badly hung curtains.

Only a couple of years ago losing a few pounds would have been cause for celebration. I would have jumped at the opportunity to go on a shopping spree, replace my wardrobe, show up at work in new outfits, perhaps have my favourite items professionally taken in.

But my life is different now. The suits and tailored dresses that I used to live in have been relegated to the back of my wardrobe. There's no reason to get dressed up to pick up the children from school or dash to the supermarket. Instead my current uniform has become yoga pants and baggy shirts. No wonder I had not realised just how much weight I'd lost.

My phone beeps and I pick it up, squinting around the diagonal crack on the screen to read the text message from the familiar number:

On the way

it says. A smile creeps to my face and I take a deep breath as I put on my jacket. It hangs loosely around my chest and I quickly pull a scarf and tie it around my neck in an attempt to hide the bad fit before heading off without another glance at the mirror.

On my way to the kitchen I pause for a moment outside the bedroom Julian and Leah now share, peeking inside at the toys still scattered on the floor, the colourful clothes spilling from the drawers. I'll deal with them later, I think as I close the door behind me.

Placing my bag on the small table, I busy myself clearing the kitchen, putting away bowls and mugs, wiping the countertop. There's a red circular stain from the strawberry jam crumpet that Leah was eating and I scrub at it absentmindedly before straightening the fruit-shaped magnets holding the children's paintings on the fridge.

My thoughts wander to the phone call of two days ago. Maya had sounded hysterical. "She's gone," she'd told me, her voice breaking into sobs. "Who?" I'd asked, even though I suspected the answer. For weeks her health had been deteriorating and I knew it wouldn't be long before she lost her battle to stay alive. But Nora Larkin had surprised us all. She wouldn't give up, and even the doctors were baffled every time she recovered. It looked like she was determined to make up for lost years and spend as much time as possible with her granddaughter.

It was not the first time Nora Larkin had surprised me. I was in Luigi's office just after the verdict came in. My heart was still pounding in my chest, my breathing coming in rapid gasps. Although the jury had decided I had used reasonable force to defend myself, I'd been found guilty of tampering with evidence and hindering a criminal investigation. I was going to have to pay a price for what I'd done all those years before. Luigi excused himself to take a phone call. "It's going to be ok," Miles had said, putting his arm around my shoulder.

Luigi's eyebrows were knitted in a frown when he walked back into the room. "Liz," he called from the doorway, nodding at me to join him. I followed him to an empty office and watched as he closed the door. "What happened?" I asked, alarm increasing by the second.

"How well do you know Nora Larkin?" he'd asked.

"I don't."

"She wants to give a character reference on your behalf," he said.

The gasp escaped before I could control it. "What did she say?" I asked after a moment.

"Not much." Luigi gave an exaggerated shrug. "Just that she wanted to appeal to the judge to be lenient."

"Uhm... I don't understand," I start. "I... I... killed her son. Why would she do that?"

Luigi shook his head.

"Could she be setting me up? Use this as an opportunity to make a statement," I ask, my mind whirring so fast that the pain in my head is intensifying.

"That's a possibility. We need to find out. Frankly though, you need all the help you can get."

Luigi's words made me wince, the reality of my situation reverberating in my head. "Should I speak to her?"

For a few moments Luigi didn't respond. He stared right at me, nodding his head in minuscule forward and backwards movements. He exhaled deeply. "No. We cannot appear to be trying to influence her. You need to stay out of it. Don't contact her."

"But…" I start.

"Do you hear me? Don't contact her. I will deal with this."

Later that week we were sitting in the courtroom waiting for the judge to come in and hand out his sentence. After two long conversations with Mrs Larkin, Luigi had recommended letting her speak. Fear at what she would say mingled with curiosity. Why would she want to do this for me?

Her hands trembled around a crumpled piece of paper as she stood up. Her mouth opened but no words came out. She cleared her throat, once, twice. "My son, John, was wonderful. Kind, helpful, friendly…" As her voice broke into a sob I turned towards Luigi, panic bubbling in my chest. This was going to do more harm than good.

"At least that's what I thought. I never knew what he was doing to these girls, what he did to Mrs Perkins. Had I known I would have stopped him. But I didn't realise that he was hiding a horrid secret. Mrs Perkins robbed me of my son. But her action stopped him from hurting others. She shouldn't be punished too harshly. Thank you."

There was a gasp in the courtroom as she sat back down. "Order," the judge snapped. Then he turned towards me. Luigi stood up and I followed.

"Mrs Perkins, I have reviewed your case carefully. Although I am convinced that fear drove your decision to flee, the way you meticulously cleaned the crime scene to avoid being caught shows presence of mind. You knowingly took action to avoid being caught. It also astounds me that despite suspecting that Mr Larkin had an accomplice, you never came forward in a bid to protect others from being attacked. And finally, you lied to the police who were searching for you after Maya McBride's DNA surfaced.

However, I need to balance your actions with the contribution you have given to society, your tireless work with victims of abuse. You have tried hard to redeem yourself. With this in mind I sentence you to two years in prison, suspended to five years and two hundred hours of community service."

The sound of the gavel hitting the bench made me jump. For a second I'd thought I was dreaming. Could I have possibly avoided jail? Looking behind me I caught Miles' eyes. He was smiling. "You're coming home," he said, leaning over to hug me.

Breaking away from Miles' embrace, I looked around me. I scanned the room, looking for her. But she was nowhere to be seen.

Hours later I parked the car in front of the small house with peeling yellow paint. Taking a deep breath, I got out of the car, rushing to the door before I had time to change my mind. My hands trembled as I rang the bell and for a moment I wanted to run away. But then she opened the door.

"What are you doing here?" Mrs Larkin asked.

"Why did you do it? Why would you try to defend me? I killed your son. I kept your granddaughter away from you."

She took a step back. "Do you want to come in?"

Panic started building inside me. "No, no," I shook my head so vigorously that my hair slapped me across the face.

She stared at me and her eyes started to soften. "He was my son. It was my job to make sure he didn't do any harm. It was my job to protect you and the others. From him. From Terry. I didn't know he had been threatening you for all these years."

At least Terry was being charged for his involvement in the death of the other girls. After analysing the letters that had been sent to me over the years, the detectives had confirmed he was behind them. He had even got his mother to send some of the letters, although she still claimed that she didn't know what they meant.

"I'm sorry." Mrs Larkin's broken voice interrupted my thoughts. Tears started springing in my eyes and I turned back before they could spill onto my cheeks, driving away although I could barely see.

A few days later I called Mrs Larkin to apologise. And somehow we started talking often, until we decided to meet for coffee. It became a frequent ritual. She'd talk about her son and I'd tell her about the job applications that I'd sent, the hours I'd spent making phone calls that would never be returned, the despair that I would never be able to work again. She was the one who held my hand as I cried when our house, which I had fought for so long to buy, was put on the market. Miles had made it perfectly clear that he didn't want to live there any longer. *The future of our marriage depends on it*, he'd said when he saw my resistance. In the end, I had no choice but to let go, give up on the house where my children learned to walk, uttered their first words, their first home. And most of all the house down the road from Maya. *It's too soon*, I'd told Miles when we received a full-price offer less than a week after we put it on the market. *Perhaps we priced it too low. We could re-list it at a higher price.* But I was clutching at straws. Miles' stern look was the reality check that I needed. That life was over. We signed the paperwork and within a month had moved to the rented flat.

The doorbell rings and I look at my reflection in the glass microwave door, tucking a tendril of red hair that escaped the confines of my bun back in place. "I'm a little early," she says when I open the door. "Hope you don't mind."

"Of course not," I quickly respond, opening the door wide and summoning her in. "Would you like a coffee?"

"Sure." She follows me, the clicking sound of our heels piercing through the silence. I busy myself filling the kettle and fetching cups while waiting for the water to boil, snatching glances at her. Her black knee-length dress hugs her lean body. Her legs are sheathed in opaque tights. The square-toe shoes look new. She puts her bag on the table and I catch a glimpse of her neatly trimmed nails, painted a pale pink. She no longer bites them, I think. Her hair is shorter than the last time I saw her, with a wispy fringe framing her face, making her green eyes pop out.

"How've you been Maya? It's been a while." My voice sounds a little shaky and I look away, afraid of being carried away by emotion.

"Good, busy. A levels are tough." She pauses for a second. "What about you? Any job leads?"

"No, still looking." I force a smile, my cheeks hurting from the effort. But I cannot show her how disappointed I am, how deflated I'm getting. For the first weeks after the trial I'd crammed my schedule, working hard to finish my community service. And then it was over and I was suddenly all alone at home for most of the day. Calls to former colleagues were not returned. Emails went unanswered. Regret emails started flowing in for every job I'd applied to. A year on and I still had no leads. Plans to purchase another house were put on hold and the small flat that was meant to be temporary accommodation started looking like a long-term solution.

The call had come on a day when I was feeling at my lowest. I had been turned down for a voluntary position at a women's shelter, giving legal advice to residents. Although my licence was only suspended for six months, the fear that I might never be able to practice law again was becoming more and more real. When I looked at the name flashing on my screen I could barely believe it. My brain must be playing tricks. But when I answered it was her. Maya. She wanted to see me.

"We should probably go Mrs P," she says now.

"Yes, yes," I respond.

My mind goes back to a conversation we had when we first started meeting. "What should I call you?" she'd asked.

My heart had started beating faster and faster. "Whatever you want," I'd said.

"I cannot call you 'mum'."

There was a tightening in my chest. "No, of course not," I said quickly, looking away, not wanting her to see my disappointment.

"Does anyone else call you 'Mrs P'?"

"No, just you."

"Ok, then that's what I'll continue calling you. It will be our thing."

We bundle in my car. "Don't forget to put on your seatbelt," I tell her, leaning over to make sure she's safely buckled. She laughs and the sound fills the small space. And I cannot help but smile. My life is not perfect. There's a lot I would like to change. Many improvements that could be made. But finally I have a relationship with my daughter. And that's all that matters.

We hope you enjoyed this book.

Cynthia Clark's next book is coming in winter 2018

More addictive fiction from Aria:

 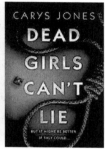 

Find out more
http://headofzeus.com/books/isbn/9781786699633

Find out more
http://headofzeus.com/books/isbn/9781786692504

Find out more
http://headofzeus.com/books/isbn/9781786699015

Acknowledgements

There are several people without whom this book would still be a figment of the imagination. Heartfelt thanks go to Laetitia Rutherford, my agent, who saw the potential in the first draft of If You Only Knew and whose guidance was instrumental in turning that early version into the story of today. I am so grateful to Sarah Ritherdon, my editor, for her support and enthusiasm and her gentle direction. And to Mark Baynham for his patience and determination to get a decent photo of me.

My mum will never read this, but it is thanks to her and Dad that I love immersing myself in stories from near and far. They filled our home with books, left them within reach of a toddler, and always encouraged me to pick one up and leaf through the pages, even before I could read.

The bulk of work on *If You Only Knew* took place while I was expecting my twins. Every kick, every move, every hiccup kept me going. Ella Wren and Raina Neave you were my inspiration even before you were born.

I am so grateful to my in-laws, Jack and Louise, for taking care of the girls for several hours every day of their last trip to London while I made the final tweaks.

And lastly, but mostly, the biggest thank you goes to Justin, my husband. *If You Only Knew* isn't dedicated to him by accident or because it was the appropriate thing to do. He has always been my biggest supporter, the one who pushed me to follow my dreams, who listened to me ramble on about the characters as if they were our closest friends. Thank you for always being there.

About Cynthia Clark

CYNTHIA CLARK was born and brought up in Malta, where she graduated in Communications and went to work for a daily newspaper. She has since lived in the US, where she worked as a writer in online business journals. She and her husband now live in London with their twin daughters.

Become an Aria Addict

Aria is the new digital-first fiction imprint from Head of Zeus.

It's Aria's ambition to discover and publish tomorrow's superstars, targeting fiction addicts and readers keen to discover new and exciting authors.

Aria will publish a variety of genres under the commercial fiction umbrella such as women's fiction, crime, thrillers, historical fiction, saga and erotica.

So, whether you're a budding writer looking for a publisher or an avid reader looking for something to escape with – Aria will have something for you.

Get in touch: aria@headofzeus.com

Become an Aria Addict
http://ariafiction.com/newsletter/subscribe

Find us on Twitter
https://twitter.com/Aria_Fiction

Find us on Facebook
http://www.facebook.com/ariafiction

Find us on BookGrail
http://www.bookgrail.com/store/aria/

Addictive Fiction

First published in the UK in 2017 by Aria, an imprint
of Head of Zeus Ltd

9 7 5 3 1 2 4 6 8

A CIP catalogue record for this book is available
from the British Library.

ISBN (E) 9781786699657

Aria
c/o Head of Zeus
First Floor East
5–8 Hardwick Street
London EC1R 4RG

www.ariafiction.com

19953263R00272

Printed in Poland
by Amazon Fulfillment
Poland Sp. z o.o., Wrocław